# A HELL FAR FROM HOME

The vast square was a field of carnage. Hundreds of torn bodies littered the pavement. Shouting and gunfire echoed up from further on, down by the docks. Andrew Keane hesitated, then raced for the palace steps.

"Skirmish line across the square," he shouted as he ran. "Take the Senate building on the far side. Thirty-Fifth Maine to me!"

The men fanned out, a knot of blue clad soldiers spreading out around Andrew.

"Merciful God," he whispered as he climbed the steps and surveyed the hellish scene before him. Then he shouted the rally cry again, "Thirty-Fifth Maine!"

*But they were fearfully far from Maine now . . . in a swirling blood-bath of a battle these Civil War soldiers had not been trained to fight . . . and that in this world of savage surprises they had to find a way to win. . . .*

# WORLDS AT WAR

- ☐ **THE LOST REGIMENT #1: RALLY CRY by William Forstchen.** Storm-swept through a space-time warp, they were catapulted through Civil War America into a future world of horrifying conflict, where no human was free. (450078—$4.95)

- ☐ **THE LOST REGIMENT #2: THE UNION FOREVER by William R. Forstchen.** In this powerful military adventure, soldiers from the past are time-space-warped to a warring world of aliens. "Some of the best adventure writing in years!"—*Science Fiction Chronicle* (450604—$4.95)

- ☐ **DAWN'S UNCERTAIN LIGHT by Neal Barrett Jr.** In a devestated, post-holocaust future filled with Wild West savagery, civil war, and irradiated mutant humans, orphan Howie Ryder grows up fast while searching to rescue his sister from an inhuman doom inflicted by a government gone awry. (160746—$3.95)

- ☐ **JADE DARCY AND THE AFFAIR OF HONOR by Stephen Goldin and Mary Mason.** Book one in *The Rehumanization of Jade Darcy.* Darcy was rough, tough, computer-enhanced—and the only human mercenary among myriad alien races on the brink of battle. She sought to escape from her human past on a suicide assignment against the most violent alien conquerors space had ever known. (156137—$3.50)

- ☐ **STARCRUISER SHENANDOAH: SQUADRON ALERT by Roland J. Green.** The United Federation of Starworlds and its most powerful enemy, the Freeworld States Alliance, must prepare for a war they hoped would never start. (161564—$3.95)

Prices slightly higher in Canada.

---

Buy them at your local bookstore or use this convenient coupon for ordering.

**NEW AMERICAN LIBRARY**
**P.O. Box 999, Bergenfield, New Jersey 07621**

Please send me the books I have checked above. I am enclosing $_____ (please add $1.00 to this order to cover postage and handling). Send check or money order—no cash or C.O.D.'s. Prices and numbers are subject to change without notice.

Name_____

Address_____

City _____ State _____ Zip Code _____

Allow 4-6 weeks for delivery.
This offer, prices and numbers are subject to change without notice.

# THE LOST REGIMENT #2

# UNION FOREVER

## BY
# WILLIAM R. FORSTCHEN

A ROC BOOK

ROC
Published by the Penguin Group
Penguin Books USA Inc., 375 Hudson Street,
New York, New York 10014, U.S.A.
Penguin Books Ltd, 27 Wrights Lane, London W8 5TZ, England
Penguin Books Australia Ltd, Ringwood, Victoria, Australia
Penguin Books Canada Ltd, 2801 John Street,
Markham, Ontario, Canada L3R 1B4
Penguin Books (N.Z.) Ltd, 182-190 Wairau Road, Auckland 10,
New Zealand

Penguin Books Ltd, Registered Offices:
Harmondsworth, Middlesex, England

First published by Roc, an imprint of New American Library,
a division of Penguin Books USA Inc.

First Printing, February, 1991
10  9  8  7  6  5  4  3  2  1

ROC IS A TRADEMARK OF NEW AMERICAN LIBRARY,
A DIVISION OF PENGUIN BOOKS USA INC.

Printed in the United States of America

For Dr. Gunther Rothenberg and
Dr. Vernard Foley, professors of history,
mentors, and friends.

# Prologue

"Now! Close the horns!"

With a triumphant shout, Jubadi Qar Qarth, leader of the Merki horde, rose in his stirrups, clenched fist raised to the everlasting sky of heaven.

Blood-red signal pennants snapped into the air around him, held aloft by the standard-bearers, showing brightly in the early-morning light. Looking east against the first light of dawn, he saw a red standard rise up out of the high grass, and beyond that, along a distant ridge, another scarlet square, and then yet one more, a tiny pennant, lost against the vastness of the endless steppe. Westward his gaze turned, and there upon a distant slope were yet more flags, the only splash of color to contrast with the endless sea of green.

"Everyone back, keep moving!" Jubadi roared, and with a vicious swipe of spurs he urged his mount forward, his staff falling in around him.

A hissing roar filled the heavens, and a shadow raced across the steppe, darkening the sky. Jubadi swung low, keeping his one leg in the saddle, dropping down against the animal's flank even as he turned his mount about, letting its body act as a shield from the feathered death racing down out of the morning sky. The horse reared, screaming in pain. With a wild kick Jubadi pulled himself back up and spurred his mount onward, covered now with the blood spraying out from the horse's neck.

"My Qarth!"

Jubadi looked over his shoulder. It was Hulagar, shield-bearer and blood guard to the ruler of the Merki horde. Jubadi could see the fear in his companion's eyes.

"It is nothing," Jubadi shouted, laughing with battle rage even as he spurred his dying mount onward. Pulling out his war bow from its scabbard, Jubadi feathered a shaft. Turning in his saddle, he looked back over his shoulder. The hill behind him was bare, yet the thunder was near, very near, filling the world with its power. His staff closed in around him, leaving the dozen who had fallen under the last volley. Jubadi saw a tall graying form struggle out from beneath his dead mount and with a flourish pull out his two-handed sword and raise it to the heavens. The ululating cry of the lone Merki echoed even above the death coming down upon them. Jubadi smiled.

Vorg would not feast with him tonight; it was his moment of death. But he would die with sword in hand, killing his enemy. His cousin would die well. Already the ancestors would be gathering above him, calling out encouragement to his ka, his warrior spirit, about to embark upon its final ride.

They appeared at last, and his heart thrilled with the sight even as he drove onward, running from the death that reached out with feathered hands. The leading line of the Bantag Umen, warriors of the southern horde, cleared the ridge. A shower of arrows slammed into Vorg, who staggered and went to his knees. With a last wild cry he rose up, swinging his sword low, bringing down a horse and rider, and then he was gone beneath the crush.

A cry of approval rose up from the fleeing Merki, urging Vorg to the everlasting sky. His song would be sung by the chanters of how alone he had faced ten thousand, singing his death song. Fate had been kind.

Jubadi, raising his bow up, slammed out an arrow into the Bantag lines. Feathered death winged back, lifting a standard-bearer out of his saddle, red signal flag dropping. Hulagar swung in by his Qarth, holding his shield aloft, placing his body between the enemy and his ruler. Onward they drove, down into the grassy swale of high spring grass, and plunged onward up toward the next ridge a hundred yards away.

"Now, they should strike now," Hulagar roared, looking to the grassy ridge before them, motioning to the standard-bearer by his side, who trailed a yellow pennant low to the ground.

"Not yet!" Jubadi screamed.

"Damn you, now! Their next volley will kill all of us!" Hulagar bellowed. Tossing aside his shield, he swung in by the standard-bearer, reached out, pulled the banner away, and snapped it upright.

A dozen yellow standards rose up out of the high grass along a front of half a mile. The crystalline blue sky turned as dark as night as ten thousand arrows leaped into the air from behind the next ridge. The storm rushed ever higher and seemed to hang directly overhead for what appeared to be an eternity. A wild scream of fear and shock cut across the Bantag advance, who but moments before believed they were closing for the kill.

Jubadi and his staff swung down on their mounts, knowing that some of the shafts would fall short. The rain of death swept over them, the steel-tipped shafts striking Bantag flesh, horses, armor with a thunder like iron hail.

Jubadi reined in his trembling mount and rose up in his stirrups, holding his bow aloft, shouting with a fierce all-consuming joy. From over the crest the first wave of the Vushka Hush, the elite umen of the Merki horde, came storming down, bows drawn, slamming out another volley into the mad confusion of the enemy ranks.

"Merki!" the scream arose from ten thousand throats. The lead ranks of the Bantag charge reined in, slashing out with a volley that dropped dozens of the advancing Merki even as the storm of arrows continued to fall around them.

The first wave charged past Jubadi, who, roaring with triumph, turned his tortured mount to go back into the charge.

"My Qarth!" Hulagar cut before Jubadi, grabbing hold of his horse's reins.

"In, in and after them!" Jubadi screamed.

"My Qarth, your place now is to command, and let the others lead!" Hulagar shouted. "Your mount is finished!"

As if emerging from a dream, Jubadi looked at Hulagar, and could see the concern in the shield-bearer's eyes.

Without a moment's pause, Jubadi regained control, shifting away from his lust, his fierce joy of battle shock. He was again Qar Qarth. Hulagar nodded with approval. As shield-bearer it was his appointed task to be the balance to the Qar Qarth's ka, his warrior spirit.

Jubadi swung his mount about and continued up the hill even as the storm of the Merki horde thundered forward into the heart of the battle. Gaining the ridge, Jubadi turned to look southward, and there before him the battle was laid out, coming to fruition even as he had planned it.

He had been the bait, a trap within a trap. The Bantag horde had come yet again, crossing to the preserve of the Merki horde, demanding of him the grazing, the lands, and the cattle that were his. So it had been across half a circling, ten years, vicious cruel years of deprivation. This time there had been a parley, under the protection of blood oath. But a Bantag oath, as it was said, was as permanent as words whispered in the wind.

That was how they had killed his grandsire three circlings ago, under the guise of such an oath, and the story was remembered. They would lure him into a parley and then strike down the Qar Qarth of the Merki horde as he returned to his people.

Jubadi laughed grimly as he watched the results. This time he was ready. He had left the parley and ridden out of the encampment at a gallop. The moment he had cleared the four marking posts of the neutral ground, the pursuit had started. They had chased him for two days, across a hundred miles, with ten thousand, the elite umen of the Bantag. They had chased him straight into this trap.

"The horns close," Hulagar said, pointing to the east and west.

From out of the folds of the rolling steppe Jubadi could see the two halves of the Vushka Hush, his elite umen, riding forward with red standards marking the advance, the Targa Vu, the ten thousand of the horsehead clan swinging out beyond the flanks already turning inward to close the trap. Each wing was a league or more away, cutting in behind the enemy, closing all hope of retreat.

"It is good, my Qar Qarth, it is as you said it would be," Hulagar said approvingly, while the roaring crash of the slaughter echoed across the hills.

From across the ridge came half a dozen warriors, and Jubadi gave a wolflike grin of acknowledgment as Vuka, his firstborn, reined in his mount.

"Magnificent slaughter!" Vuka called. "That will keep those bastards away from our lands."

With a cold eye Jubadi looked back at the battle, which already was driven beyond the ridge where he had paused but moments before.

"The Bantag are beyond counting," Hulagar said coldly. "Their warriors are as numberless as the stars."

Vuka did not reply.

"In the end our pastures must still be changed," Jubadi snapped. "All we can do is slow them for now."

"After this victory?" Vuka shouted, the impetuousness of his angry youth showing through, something which left Jubadi with a cold sense of rage. Someday he would be the Qar Qarth—he must learn to see the truth when it was before him.

"Yes, after this skirmish!" Jubadi growled. "It is merely an entertainment, an opening."

Vuka looked at him coldly, as if his words were meant to shatter the joy of this moment.

"While we were away, did the reports come back?" Hulagar asked quietly, as if they were talking by the evening fire, rather than on a field of deadly strife.

"Yesterday," Vuka replied sharply, bridling with impatience.

"And?"

"It is true, the cattle have driven them. Our spies looked down upon the city and saw the wreckage of the battle. The reports of the strange weapons that can kill from afar are definitely true. Already the cattle are starting to rebuild their walls, and they were seen practicing with their weapons. Other scouts circled in close to the remnants of the Tugars. We counted but thirty thousand of their warriors left. It is reported that the next city of cattle eastward will fight as well. It is even said that the Tugars will beg for food in return for some mystery of healing craft that will end the sickness striking the northlands cattle. Such things almost cannot be believed."

"They lost over seventeen umens, maybe twenty!" Jubadi gasped.

"Believe it," Hulagar whispered, "for if it happened, then it must be believed. The cattle have new weapons, they have learned to fight."

"Cattle that kill those of the people of the horde—it is

disgusting to contemplate," Vuka snapped, his face wrinkled with disdain.

"Disgusting or not, it must be faced," Jubadi retorted.

Jubadi looked over at Hulagar, who smiled softly and nodded.

"And the ship that vomits smoke and moves without sails?" Hulagar asked.

"Even now he harries the Carthas of our domains. He has not returned to the fold."

"Good, very good," Jubadi said with a smile.

"Cattle driving those of the Chosen Race," Hulagar whispered. "It has never been done."

"After all, they were only Tugars," Vuga sneered.

"They were of the Chosen Race, even if they were our enemies," Jubadi snarled in reply. "Remember that—they were of the Chosen, damn you. They have failed, and it must be our problem if the old ways are to survive."

Embarrassed by his father's rage, Vuka fell silent, looking sullenly at his staff, who lowered their heads so as not to see the shame of their leader.

A triumphal shout rose above the thunder of battle, and turning, Jubadi could see where the cattle-skull standard of the Bantag Umen was now caught in the middle of the crush. It wavered for a moment and then went down.

Vuka, like a fox scenting blood, looked back to his father.

"Go on, boy," Jubadi said, a smile crossing his features. "There's blood to be taken."

With a wild shout, Vuka unsheathed his scimitar and, standing high in the stirrups, charged down the hill, his young staff following in his wake.

"Tamuka!" Hulagar shouted.

A towering form nearly ten feet in height turned in his saddle and looked back at Hulagar. The shield-bearer of the Zan Oarth Vuka held up the heavy brass aegis of his office, nodded a salute, and then continued on, pressing in by his charge's side.

"He'll have his realm, when the time comes," Jubadi said evenly, a note of fatherly pride showing as he watched his son charging into the fray.

Jubadi looked over at Hulagar, who was silently watching as Vuka disappeared into the fray, and nodded as if to himself.

"Then the rumors are true," Jubadi continued. "We might

turn this to our salvation. The plan might come to pass after all."

"Shall the next messengers be sent?" Hulagar asked, the relief in his voice evident.

"Let it be done. Send them out tonight. We must move quickly."

Jubadi turned to look back at the battle. The wings of the Vushka and Targa regiments closed inexorably around the Bantag, vast sheets of arrows darkening the sky. The steppes echoed with the shrieks of the triumphant, the wounded, and the damned.

"It is almost beyond belief that the rumors of the Tugar fall were true," Hulagar said, bringing his mount up to Jubadi's side.

Jubadi looked up and smiled.

"Against cattle, it is disgusting."

"Well, the boy was right," Hulagar ventured. "They were only Tugars."

"Remember they beat us at Orki," Jubadi said evenly.

"I have not forgotten, my Qarth," Hulagar replied, the slightest edge of anger in his voice. "Remember I lost my father there as well."

Jubadi nodded, taking no offense, for after all, Hulagar was shield-bearer, the only one among all the warriors of the Merki horde who carried the right to speak to the Qar Qarth without fear. He was the other half of the ruling spirit, the one trained to advise, to guide, to provide the brake upon the ever-burning spirit of his Qarth's warrior ka.

"As I wished to point out," Hulagar said quietly, "the Tugars have not fought against any of the Chosen Race since Orki. We can only hope that their edge has grown dull. When they mysteriously moved two years ahead of our march, I feared at first they were plotting to cut into our territories. At least now we know different. They have been removed.

"They had grown weak from not fighting. It is only through blooding that a people are strong. When we ride against those cattle they will know terror."

He looked over at Hulagar and smiled.

"But we will not make the same mistakes as our northern brothers did. Their fall might save us yet. We have a year, perhaps two at most. We will use them wisely. First we learn how they lost. We will weaken them for the harvest before we bring them to our tables."

"I still don't like the idea of arming cattle to fight cattle," Hulagar ventured.

"Better that a cattle dies than a Merki," Jubadi replied. "Our numbers are stretched beyond the breaking point. The Bantag harry our southern flank without letup. We will let the cattle fight for us against those in the north and bring these new cattle under our control. We will observe, we will learn, and then we will take all that we have acquired and turn it against the Bantag. We will have two great advantages the Tugars did not—we will understand first how these ways of fighting are done, and we will have such weapons ourselves."

"Remember, though," Hulagar interjected, "the cattle have tasted of our blood. They have sown the fields before their city with the bones of the Chosen Race. If we give such weapons to our own cattle, the gift might one day come back to haunt us all."

"You have heard the reports that have come back," Jubadi replied. "Only the cattle know how to make such things. We must find a means to have our cattle make these weapons as well, to fight our battle in the north while we hold in the south. When the time is right, then we will garner all these weapons, these mysterious buildings they are made in, to our own hands and slaughter the lot of them. I will offer an exemption to the Carthas from the feasting pits, if they lay open the way to defeat these Rus, these Yankees, whatever it is they call themselves. That should give them a reason to do my wishes. What comes later is of no concern to them now."

"My Qar Qarth," Hulagar said formally, "we have debated this before. I obediently yield to your decisions, for I am but a shield-bearer and the things of war are beyond me. But consider my voice as a warning nonetheless. These things might very well be our salvation against the Bantag, but nevertheless I fear them."

"We are between two fires," Jubadi whispered. "One will burn us, is burning us. But the other will warm us and give us strength. Then we will crush the cattle and have both the Tugar realm and our own. Let the Bantag take what is left. We can turn these new things to our advantage.

"We must keep our wits about us, Hulagar," Jubadi said

evenly, a smile crossing his features. "Send out the envoys tonight."

"To the Rus as we first considered?"

"That is useless. They are victorious and will fight us as they fought the Tugars. It would serve as warning to them as well. We must assume they will watch us, and are preparing, but they will never know our true intent until it is too late. We must abandon that idea. But to the others, yes."

"As you command, my Qar Qarth," Hulagar whispered.

Jubadi fell silent and looked back to the battle, which was now shifting southward, the slaughter pen closing in tighter and tighter. Thousands of forms littered the steppes, and already the bringers of death strode from warrior to warrior, cutting the throats of all those who could not rise.

The songs of battle would rise high tonight, giving strength to the sires of the Merki horde who rode upon the endless steppe of the everlasting sky. Around the fire of the stars that shone in the great wheel of the nighttime new warriors would gather in the twilight. His thoughts drifted to Vorg, companion of childhood, cousin by birth, brother by the ritual of blooding.

It was a good death, Jubadi thought. There was nothing more in the end but the hope for a warrior's death, sword or bow in hand. All else was meaningless.

A shudder ran through his horse, and Jubadi could feel the animal sinking to its knees.

Leaping clear of the stirrups, Jubadi alighted on the ground and looked down at the horse that had served him for half a circling, ten years of riding that had taken them halfway around the world.

Drawing his scimitar, Jubadi leaned over and with a backhanded slash cut the horse's throat. With sad pleading eyes the beast looked up at him, and then ever so slowly laid his head back and then was still.

Bending over, Jubadi wiped the blade on the ground and sheathed it. Without a backward glance he turned and walked away.

"Cartha ram ships in sight, admiral."

"Clear for action," Cromwell roared, a cold grin of satisfaction lighting his coarse puffy features.

Hands clasped behind his back, Tobias Cromwell of the *Ogunquit*, former captain in the United States Navy, turned about and cast his gaze astern across the narrows that divided the Inland Sea into its northern and southern half.

How long has it been now? he wondered to himself. They had cleared the headwaters of the Chesapeake on the evening of January 2, 1865, bound for an amphibious operation off North Carolina. And then the storm, the gate of light as they called it here, had dragged him, his ship, and all aboard through to this nightmare world. Two years at least, he thought dryly.

There had been the boyars of Rus, and then the overthrow of them by that arrogant Colonel Keane.

"Damn him forever," Tobias growled, and his ensign turned about as if an order had been given. Tobias shook his head and turned away.

If only Keane had played along with the boyars. They could have ridden out the Tugar occupation—hell, some of the men might have been taken, but certainly the officers would have been saved. But he had to go ahead and fight not just the boyars, but the Tugars as well.

The memory of that last night of battle sent a cold chill running through him. He had done the only logical thing—no, the only sane thing in an insane world. He had gotten the hell out of the city of Suzdal and fled south with his ship. The battle was lost; that was obvious to any man of intelligence.

And how the hell was he to know that those bastards would beat the Tugars after all? Of course, there was no going back. Keane would have him shot as a deserter, and besides that, he had had it with Keane, his damn Maine regiment, the whole lot of them. He could imagine the dark laughter, the taunting eyes gazing at him as he was led to the wall.

"The hell with all of them," he whispered.

It must be four months back now, maybe more; he'd lost count of the days a long time ago. After all, what did it matter anymore?

The first couple of months had been the worst, raiding the Cartha shipping, after those arrogant dogs refused him safe haven. It'd been a living, but getting enough wood to feed the boilers below deck was a constant worry. All the lumber was up north, or along the eastern shore, which was heavily patrolled by Cartha ships. The only alternative was to run through the narrows before Cartha and venture into the unknown waters of the steamy southern ocean in search of a safe haven to refit.

The great ocean had broadened out, running easterly and south, and he had followed its course. The eastern shores and islands were covered with high towering forests teaming with life—life that unlike that of the northern regions had a strange exotic bend to it, with strange winged creatures half the size of a house. There at last was a place to refit, but it was a region that filled him with a certain premonition of dread. Half a dozen crew members were lost to forest animals unlike anything he had ever seen upon earth, cats with great tusks, bearlike creatures with yellow fur and the size of a small elephant, and the great birds which could sweep a man off a beach and disappear into their high mountain aeries.

There were signs of something else as well, footprints in the sand neither human nor Tugar, snares in the forest that decapitated a crew member before his eyes, missing watchmen, the only thing to be found in the morning a bloody track into the hills.

They had pushed on southward, finding in an empty stretch of the southern sea a broad open island of high cloud-capped hills. Rounding into a narrow bay, they had anchored for the night, hoping like castaways that perhaps here would be a safe place to secure as a base. It was a place of broad shimmering beaches and trees that soared hundreds of feet into the heavens.

In the morning he had awaked to the sight of two ships riding at the mouth of the channel, their high sterns and great spread of square-rigged sails the mark of ships he had seen only in pictures—galleons lost like the *Ogunquit* upon a strange and distant sea.

Amazingly they had greeted him with a ragged broadside, across his bow. A little display of steam power had been enough to force the stunned pirates into negotiation, for both could see an advantage—together they could take Cartha for their own.

The story had been a remarkable one. The thousand-odd men and women were descendants of four pirate ships that had been swept through in the late sixteenth century, most likely near the same spot where the *Ogunquit* had been caught. Their one encounter with the Tugars had cost them two of their craft and struck such terror in them that they had hidden ever since, surviving on the islands and indulging in occasional raids against human cities far to the south and east. Most remarkable of all, they had preserved the art of gunpowder and gun casting.

Tobias found them to be a degenerate lot, wallowing in licentious behavior and given to drunken debauchery. But they could fight, and had rallied to his dream of seizing the Cartha realm for their own.

"Admiral, the Cartha fleet's retreating," the forward lookout cried. "They're striking their colors!"

"What the hell!" Tobias shouted, swinging his glass forward. The threescore ram ships which had sallied out of the harbor to meet them were swinging about, their purple standards fluttering down from their masts. A single ship of the fleet continued onward, its oars flashing like jewels in the sun.

Grabbing a speaking trumpet, Tobias swung around toward his ally's flagship.

"Jamie, they're striking colors. Don't fire unless I command."

"So the dogs haven't got the belly for a fight," the pirate captain laughed.

The *Golden Scourge* dropped off the wind to swing in close by the *Ogunquit*. The vessel was making good headway, running now on a broad reach. The galleon handled lively, its bluff bow plowing up two curving furrows of foamy white sea, its gunports open, revealing the muzzles of half a dozen guns.

Swinging up into the rigging, Tobias could see Jamie, dressed in ragged breeches and a faded linen shirt, leaning over the side to look forward.

"Filthy buggers. At least they could have shown us some fun first."

The disappointment on Jamie's scarred and twisted face was obvious. The man had a thin and desiccated look, as if the long years in the tropics forever staring at the glare of the great red sun had dried out his body and soul.

Tobias watched him carefully. He knew the man was untrustworthy. None of them, for that matter, could be trusted; given the slightest opportunity they'd seize the *Ogunquit* and throw him overboard. Tobias looked around at his crew and could see their nervous stares at the two pirate ships. Hell, they'd been nervous for months, and he half suspected that if Jamie didn't kill him, they most likely would if they felt there was any chance of making for home. He had to find a home port and damn fast if he had any hope of surviving much longer.

"Let's hear what they've got to say," Tobias said evenly.

"I'd rather pillage the bastards—burn the city to the ground and be done with it."

"Eight ships and a thousand men against a city-state of maybe a quarter of a million? You must be mad."

Jamie snorted with disdain.

"With your guns and that steam devil below deck anything could be ours. The legends of the ancestors speak of a don devil who slew a million heathen bastards on the old sea."

As near as Tobias could figure out, Jamie's band were descendants of English and French pirates who had raided a Spanish treasure fleet toward the close of the sixteenth century and then were pulled into the tunnel. How they had kept the *Golden Scourge* afloat across the centuries was beyond him. At least there were no shipworms in this sea, and as near as he could guess they had replaced her piece by piece as the years passed, and built five more like her down through the years.

"She's heaving to," Tobias announced, pointing back to the Cartha ship, which now lay a hundred yards ahead.

"All engines stop."

The pounding shudder which had been running through the *Ogunquit* eased off. Overhead a pluming vent of steam escaped, and Tobias smiled as Jamie looked over at him with a fearful gaze. For good measure Tobias walked over to the pilot house and pulled the whistle down. Its high-pitched shriek echoed across the rolling sea.

Raising his glass, Tobias scanned the Cartha ship, which bobbed clumsily on the waves. The rowers leaned over their oars, obviously exhausted.

Barking out sharp commands, Tobias guided the *Ogunquit* about to the ram's windward side. Lines snaked across between the two vessels. The *Golden Scourge* swung about on the leeward side, turning into the wind, and a longboat was lowered away. Scrambling over the side, Jamie and a boarding crew set out.

"Gunners stand ready," Tobias cried. "On my command only, open fire."

Raising himself up ramrod-straight, Tobias strolled over

to the railing and looked down on the ship bobbing along-side. A dozen Carthas stood upon the stern of their vessel dressed in ceremonial capes of purple, their bronzed faces, wreathed in jet-black beards, turned upward. They looked at Tobias with a cold defiance. At their feet were several iron chests.

There was a wild shout of delight as Jamie scrambled up on the deck followed by his men with cutlasses drawn.

"No violence!" Tobias shouted. "Let's hear what they have to say."

Jamie laughed with an open insolence as he strode up to the Carthas and then with the point of his sword flicked a chest open.

"Bugger me blind, it's gold," Jamie hissed, and falling on his knees he scooped his hands into the chest, raised them up, and roared with delight as a showering cascade of coins rained down on the deck.

Shouting in their high guttural tongue, the Carthas ignored Jamie and gestured for Tobias to come aboard. Inside he felt the fear rising again. It could be a trap to kill him. After all, what was a Cartha ship and its crew compared to himself?

"The devils want you to come aboard," Jamie announced, looking over at Tobias with a grin.

"The hell with 'em," Tobias said haughtily. "If they want to talk, let them come aboard my ship. Tell them that."

Tobias looked over at Jamie and could see that the free-booter was sneering inside at his discomfort.

Laughing, Jamie nodded to one of his crew, who stepped forward and spoke to the Cartha. The Cartha ignored Jamie and, speaking rapidly, pointed back to Tobias.

"Come on, my lord admiral, there's gold to be had."

Tobias hesitated, and Jamie looked back at him.

"Barca here told the scum if they try anything my men will carve their eyes out and cram 'em down their throats. He said they want you to come aboard. But if you're afraid . . ."

"If you want, I'll go."

Tobias turned to see Jim Hinsen, the one deserter from the 35th Maine, standing alongside the railing, looking down greedily at the gold.

He still could not decide if bringing this man along had been the wisest of decisions. Hinsen was a sycophant, slavishly obeying Tobias's slightest wish. Yet the man always seemed to be somehow on the prowl for something more. As long as it was power under Tobias's own shadow, it could be accepted, but he could not shake the suspicion that Hinsen was learning far too much about the *Ogunquit* and the mysteries of her running, which he had deliberately kept secret.

Tobias looked down at his men lining the deck. Already Jamie was winning more than one over with his swaggering way. Breathing a silent curse, Tobias climbed over the rail. Waiting for the ram to ride up on a wave, he leaped across, nearly falling back over the side of the Cartha ship before several rowers reached out and pulled him aboard.

A Cartha delegate stepped forward and gestured toward a closed hatchway, speaking rapidly.

Tobias looked over at Jamie Fitzhugh, who smiled at him with a toothless grin.

"The bugger wants you to go in. He wants to show you something."

Tobias felt a cold chill.

"Like hell."

"My sentiments exactly. If they got something, let 'em bring it topside," Jamie growled and then snapped off a quick reply.

The delegate shrugged, then went over to the hatch and pulled it open.

Nervous, Tobias looked up at his men lining the deck.

"Train your muskets on that hatch!" Tobias shouted as he drew his revolver.

The delegates backed away from the hatch as a shadowy form filled the darkness. As one the delegates went to their knees.

Tobias drew in his breath with a hiss.

The form bent low, its spiked helmet emerging, and then reared up to its full eight feet of height.

"A Tugar!" Tobias hissed. With shaking hand he cocked his revolver and brought it up. Jamie, his features pale, scrambled backward, dropping the gold in his fist so that the coins rattled across the deck, some of them rolling unnoticed into the sea.

The towering form gazed upon Tobias, its yellowed teeth bared in an evil grin, its cloak of human hide swirling about in the rising wind, fluttering and shifting. Coal-black eyes looked down on Tobias with a hawklike gaze, cold, dispassionate, haughty.

"You are the renegade Yankee Tobias?"

Stunned, Tobias could not reply.

"A Tugar," Tobias whispered unbelievingly.

"Merki! The Tugars are but weaklings fit themselves for the pit. I am the Namer of Time of the Merki horde, sent to seek you."

Incredulous, Tobias started to back up, the revolver shaking in his hand. Jamie, crouching low, brought his cutlass up, and the Namer, grinning, started to laugh.

"Call back your dog, Cromwell," the Namer hissed in Rus. "It is time that we talk."

"With a Tugar?" Tobias whispered. "Like hell."

"Merki!" the Namer snarled, and then his features softened.

"Hear this, Cromwell of the ship that sails without sails. For it is commanded by my Qar Qarth that I seek you out. To seek you even upon this sea. Hear now the words of Jubadi Qar Qarth, ruler of the great middle steppe, for it is his command that I offer unto you an arrangement of understanding."

"An arrangement?"

"Call it an alliance," the Namer replied, a grin lighting his features.

"Against whom?" Tobias replied, the confidence returning to his voice.

"For it is my Qar Qarth's wish that you be an ally with him. We have granted exemption from the pits to you, all who follow you, and to the Cartha. Already we have prepared a place for you in their city. Teach us and the Cartha your ways of war, Tobias Cromwell, and we will raise you and your followers above all other humans. Serve us and it will come to pass that in the name of the Merki you will be the ruler of the realm known as Rus."

Stunned, Admiral Tobias Cromwell slowly lowered his revolver and smiled.

# Chapter One

Stepping down from the train, Colonel Andrew Lawrence Keane looked about with an approving smile.

"We've come a long way, colonel."

Andrew looked over his shoulder and grinned at Hans Schuder, his old sergeant major with the 35th Maine and commander of the armies of the Republic of Rus.

"That we have, Hans, that we indeed have."

Just how far have we come? he wondered.

He found that his thoughts turned back to earth less frequently of late. If given the choice now of returning, he knew what the answer would be for himself, and that thought brought him a deep sense of satisfaction. It had been nearly a year and a half since victory over the Tugars—and what a world of change they had wrought since then! And thank God above all else there had been peace, the first he had really known in over five years.

Stepping back from the train, Andrew shaded his eyes from the red glare of the sun and looked back westward. Though he had never been out west, he imagined that this must be how it looked. The prairie grass was nearly waist-high, shifting and flowing like waves upon the sea as the warm summer breeze flowed across the endless steppe.

The air was awash with the scent of wildflowers, which dotted the rolling hills with exuberant splashes of lavender, yellow, and brilliant reds. The warm breeze rippling past him was so fresh and pure that he felt that if there had ever been a Garden of Eden, this is what it must have been like.

17

Turning to look northward, he could see the rising fir-clad hills a dozen miles away, the southern edge of the great woods which he imagined must march off for thousands of miles to a mysterious land he knew he would never see. Chuck Ferguson, his ever-inventive engineer, had calculated several months back that the world they were on was nearly the same size as earth, some twenty-two thousand miles around. It had been an ingenious experiment. Using one of the new accurate clocks that they had recently started to turn out, he had measured the position of the noonday sun back in Suzdal, and with another clock set to the first one his assistant had measured the angle at precisely the same time here nearly five hundred miles east. Ferguson claimed he had learned the trick from an account of Eratosthenes, an ancient Greek who had done the same thing two thousand years ago.

But there was still the world straight ahead, and someday, maybe twenty years hence, the train line they were building would completely encircle the world. Andrew looked appraisingly at the steam engine *Malady* before him. It was named after yet another hero of the Tugar war. No finer tribute, he thought wistfully, looking at the Medal of Honor painted beneath the dead engineer's name.

If only Malady were here to appreciate all of this, Andrew thought wistfully. Malady and the two hundred other boys from the 35th Maine and 44th New York battery, and after all, most of them had only been boys, who had given their lives in the war to make Rus free from the Tugar scourge.

The engine was the best one built so far, on the larger three-and-a-half-foot gauge which they had decided would be the standard size for the rail line until the current frenzy of emergency development had passed. It was still smaller than the wider gauges back on earth, but there had to be a trade-off, given the limited resources available as of yet, and the need to have a lighter rail to conserve on iron.

How many tens of thousands of tons have we gone through so far on this insanely wonderful project? he wondered as he looked back westward to where the rails finally vanished on the far horizon. He knew if he shot the question to John Mina, his chief of industry, the man could give him the figures to the nearest pound. Smiling, he looked up to see Mina stepping down from the train. The stress of the war was long gone, and the colonel, being recently married to a cousin of Kal's, was already showing some additional weight from his wife's typical Rus cooking.

The car Mina was stepping down from reflected the usual superb woodworking skills of the Rus, unlike the slapdash flatcars and hoppers of military necessity. With the Suzdalian penchant for woodcarving not a single square inch of the car was left plain. This particular one was adorned with a panoramic scene of the Great Tugar War, as it was now called, showing the famed charge of the 35th Maine across the great square in the center of Suzdal at the climax of the battle. Andrew looked at the car with a touch of embarrassment, for at the head of the charge was a perfect likeness of himself, left sleeve empty, sword raised in right hand, the American flag behind him. Tugars, eyes wide with terror, were fleeing from his wrath; his own visage was grim, commanding. Is that how I looked? he wondered, for all he could recall of it now was the terrible sense of doom, and fear that all was lost.

It seemed like a different world, now that the constant nightmare dread no longer hung over him like a veil. A smile creased Andrew's features as he stepped back from the car and looked up.

Atop the car, at the front end, were four carved and painted figures, three of them Union soldiers, one holding the American flag, the other two the standards of the 35th Maine Volunteer Infantry and the 44th New York Light Artillery, while the fourth figure in the middle of the group, depicted in the plain white tunic and crosshatched leggings of Rus infantry, held aloft the flag of the Rus Republic, a blue standard with a circle of ten white stars in the middle representing the ten cities of the Rus.

The other cars of the train showed various Rus regiments in action, the doomed stand of the 5th Suzdal and the fourth Novrod battery at the pass, the 1st Suzdal holding the ford, or the gallant action of the 17th Suzdal holding the southeast bastion to the last man. The next-to-the-last car on the train was one of his favorites, showing Vincent Hawthorne, crashed balloon behind him, blowing up the Vina Dam, the action which had saved all of them when the flood wiped out the Tugar host.

The very last car was adorned with a scene that reminded Andrew of Stuart's famous painting of the signing of the Declaration of Independence, the carving depicting the formal signing of the Constitution of the Republic of Rus. The car was now the presidential carriage, and Andrew looked back at it and smiled, wondering how its most illustrious passenger was faring after the bouncing, swaying ride.

"Five hundred and eleven miles down, only twenty-one thousand and a half to go," Hans said, as if to himself, as he came up alongside Andrew.

"The first five hundred are more than enough for me, sergeant."

Andrew looked up to see Emil Weiss, the regimental surgeon, stepping down from the train, dusting himself off, with General Pat O'Donald, artillery commander of the old 44th New York, at his side. O'Donald, his red-bearded face aglow, staggered slightly, and it was obvious it was not from the effect of the swaying train ride.

"Our dear president sure has a bug under him about this Manifest Destiny and transcontinental rail project," Emil said with a laugh. "That's all he wanted to talk about for most of the day."

"How is our dear president?" Andrew said shaking his head.

"Just carsick, as usual. Give him a couple of minutes more and he should be ready."

"It was a bit rough at that," Hans mumbled, and looking over, Andrew could see that the sergeant was still a bit green around the gills, as he knew he was as well.

Ferguson had been at the throttle since they had pulled out of Suzdal the night before, and he had kept the engine wide open, pulling along at a good forty miles an hour, stopping only for water and wood. Though the new passenger cars had springs, the ride had been a jostling, bouncing affair. Andrew stepped back from the train as a vent of steam hissed out and looked at it appraisingly.

In the spring after the war, the new Senate had voted to approve the transcontinental rail project, something which all the men associated with the iron mill had lobbied hard for. Reconstruction after the devastation of the Tugar war had, of course, come first, and it hadn't been till early summer that the mills, wiped out when the dam was blown, had been replaced and expanded so that a surplus of metal could be allocated beyond the needs of replacing lost tools, military equipment, and farm machinery.

There had been a nearly overwhelming amount of work associated with rebuilding Suzdal and the entire realm of the

Rus, along with the ordering of a new republic. But Andrew could see that the rail line had helped to create a dream of exploration, trade, and expansion. Every society needed a frontier, Andrew realized, and though the rail line was consuming the labor of tens of thousands, the long-term benefits would be incalculable.

Besides that, there was above all else the military necessity as well. The population of Rus had been cut in half by the war and smallpox. If the southern hordes should ever turn their attention northward, alliances would be essential for survival.

"Colonel Keane, I wish to report that all is in order, sir."

Smiling, Andrew turned about to face Vincent Hawthorne, now a general in command of a brigade and also ambassador to their new ally.

The slight youngster—and Keane still could not help but see him that way—stood rigidly at attention, dressed in a plain white belted tunic, adorned with the shoulder stars of a Suzdalian general, his staff drawn up stiffly behind him. As one, Vincent and his staff saluted.

Andrew, drawing himself to attention, saluted in reply.

"Stand at ease, general," and he warmly grabbed Vincent's hand.

Not even twenty-one, Andrew thought, and already a holder of the Suzdalian Medal of Honor for saving all their hides by blowing the dam in the final battle of the war. He could see by gazing into the young man's eyes that the anguish had softened somewhat of late. His Quaker upbringing had created a terrible inner struggle over the slaughter he had wrought. There had been a period of several months when he had feared that Vincent would drift away into some inner darkness. Perhaps it was the birth of the twins that had finally pulled him back, giving to him a sense that without his sacrifice the new life he had helped to create would have never been born.

It was strange, Andrew realized, but that inner anguish was leaving him as well. Three years of war against the Confederacy at home and then another hard brutal war here on Valdennia had driven him near to the edge as well. There were still nights when the demon would return. It was no longer about his brother Johnnie—no, that had been laid to rest at last. Now it was that terrible moment when the Tugars were swarming over the wall, and the city was in flames, the moment when he knew that they would lose and worse yet, that Kathleen would be lost as well at the very moment when their love was finally realized. It was still there, but the year and a half of peace had finally started to heal his soul at last.

"Your wife, sir, is she well?" Vincent asked eagerly, and a round of chuckles rose up from the group. Nervously, Andrew looked about.

"I think the father-to-be is having a more difficult time than the mother," Emil growled.

"It's nothing, sir," Vincent replied. "You'll get used to it. The first one's always the toughest."

"Ah, the veteran speaks," O'Donald retorted with a grin. "Good God, son, can't you give your poor wife a rest? Twins, no less, the second time around."

Vincent visibly blushed.

"Kathleen's fine, Vincent, and asked for you. Your Tanya is taking good care of her. She sends her love as well and wanted me to tell you that young Andrew keeps asking for you."

Vincent looked about proudly at the mention of his son.

"Everything in order, Vincent?"

The delegation is ready, sir."

"Well, all we need is our president and we can get this show on the road," O'Donald growled. "Just where the hell is that man, anyhow?"

"Remember he is our president," Andrew replied evenly, with the slightest tone of reproach in his voice.

"President, is it, and a good thrashing it was I gave 'im one night, just before the war, and now himself that I gave the black eye to is the chief."

Startled, Andrew looked over at his slightly drunk artilleryman.

"Ah, it was nothing," O'Donald said. "Just a little argument about a gambling debt."

"And if I heard it correctly," Emil interjected, "you came out of it with a lump on your head the size of an apple."

O'Donald rubbed his scalp and smiled.

"Hit me from behind, he did, with a chair leg."

"Like hell I did—it was my good drinking mug, and your thick skull broke it!"

"Gentlemen, attention!" Andrew growled.

Looking up at the train, Andrew snapped off a salute.

Kalencka, President Kal as everyone called him with affection, stood on the car platform looking down at them with an open grin, though it was evident that he was still a bit unsteady from the long train ride.

Andrew had difficulty restraining a smile at Kal's appearance. The near-mythical standing of Abraham Lincoln with the men from the Union Army had been conveyed to the Rus with endless anecdotes about the beloved president's wisdom, compassion, and style that bespoke an understanding of the common people from which he came. Kal stood before the group sporting the famed chin whiskers of Lincoln, cut back from the traditional flowing beard of the Rus. He had even adopted the rumpled black coat, pants, white shirt, and stovepipe hat, which Andrew suspected would forever be fixed now in the minds of the Rus as the proper uniform of a president. It was a somewhat ludicrous sight on Kal's rotund five-and-a-half-foot form, yet Andrew could not help but feel that if the real Abe should somehow ever cross to this strange world, he and Kal would easily sit down together and trade witticisms far into the night.

Andrew found his thoughts drifting to the day Lincoln had stood by his hospital bed and chatted so pleasantly, and with such heartfelt concern, after presenting him with the Medal of Honor for his action at Gettysburg. Absentmindedly, Andrew touched his empty left sleeve, the ever-present reminder of that day at Gettysburg, as he looked up at Kal, whose own right sleeve was empty as well.

The impression of Lincoln had settled on Kal during the presidential campaign against Andrew the previous summer. Andrew knew the race was a foregone conclusion; he had run upon the insistence of his men, but realized from the beginning that he did not stand a ghost of a chance against the favorite-son candidate of Suzdal. If anything, his effort was more a civics lesson in the multiparty system for the newly freed Rus than any serious bid for a job he did not want to have. He had even cherished a hope, a foolish one he knew, that he could retire and perhaps take the position of president of the small college the men had set up to teach engineering, agriculture, medicine, and metallurgy. Kal had insisted that he serve as vice-president and also wear the hat of secretary of war. The cabinet had been filled out with several other Maine men—Bill Webster, the banker, was in charge of the treasury, Emil directed the department of medicine and public health, Bob Fletcher, who had built the first grain mill, was now in charge of agriculture, and Mina held the post of secretary of industry.

"Stand at ease, my friends," Kal whispered self-consciously as he stepped from the train. "You know I can't stand all this foolish ceremony."

Even as he spoke, the assembled band raggedly started into a dissonant version of "Hail to the Chief," yet another import from the world left behind. The 5th Suzdal, Hawthorne's Guards, as they were now affectionately known in spite of all his protests, arrayed in double rank behind Vincent, snapped to attention with the first note, their tattered battle standard dipping to the ground, while the new emblem of the Republic of Rus was held straight aloft.

"We must impress the others, Mr. President," Andrew whispered, leaning over to speak to Kal as he stepped off the train. "They put a lot of stock in such things."

Kal nodded and stood self-consciously as the last notes of the piece drifted away. He was about to step forward when the band struck up "The Battle Hymn of the Republic," and with a bit of a self-conscious grin he came back to attention for the new national anthem.

The music finished, Kal relaxed and, extending his left hand, stepped forward to embrace Vincent, kissing him loudly on either cheek. Vincent, unable to relax, accepted the embrace woodenly.

"Come now, can't my own son-in-law give his father an embrace?"

"Father," Vincent whispered, "this is a diplomatic ceremony."

"I know, I know, and the mouse must look like a lion," Kal replied with a chuckle,

"Mr. President, the boy's right, you know," Andrew whispered. "Our friends on the other side are somewhat more stoic than we are."

"All right, then," Kal said, his features fixed with mock seriousness, "let's get started then."

Vincent stepped back and with a flourish pulled out his sword.

"Regiment, present arms."

As one the battle-hardened troops snapped their muskets up.

"This way, Mr. President," Vincent announced, and he started to walk down the hundred-yard front of line, with his father-in-law by his side, while Andrew and the rest of the delegation fell in behind him.

Kal scanned the regiment and nodded, the men in the ranks grinning back at him.

"Ah, Alexi Andreovich, your wife sends her greetings," Kal called out, stopping before a gray-bearded soldier.

"Did she?" Alexi asked incredulously, and a chuckle came up from the ranks. Vincent, standing behind Kal, gave a look of cold anger, and the laughter instantly died.

"She made me promise to tell you you're forgiven, but if she ever sees you with Tetyana again, she'll cut both your hearts out."

The men broke into laughter, unable to contain themselves.

Kal drew closer and in a fatherly manner put his hand on Alexi's shoulder.

"She's a good wife and mother to your children, Alexi," Kal whispered. "You and I both know that. By rights she should lock her door to you forever. When you get home, confess your sins to Father Casmar, make peace with her, and then light a candle to Kesus for forgiveness. Promise me that, my old friend—I want to see peace in your family."

Alexi reddened, dropping his head in shame.

"That's a good fellow. I didn't want to embarrass you here, but you needed to learn this. Forgive me that."

"There is nothing to forgive," Alexi whispered.

"Good then," Kal said gently, drawing back, as the men who had heard the exchange nodded to each other with approval and affection for their old friend who had not become like a haughty boyar.

Andrew smiled inwardly. It might not have fit the occasion, but it was by such things that Kal kept his touch with the people he now served.

"Shall we continue?" Vincent asked stiffly.

"Of course, son, we mustn't keep them waiting."

Kal continued down the regimental line, past the still-steaming engine. Fifty yards ahead of the engine the track came to a stop, the eastern edge of the MFL&S railroad, the end of the line marked by the flag of Rus. Just on the other side the roadbed continued, crossing a high trestle bridge five hundred feet long across the Sangros River, which marked the western edge of cultivated land under the Roum. Looking across the river, Andrew could see the low walls of the border town and the irrigated fields beyond, cut by the twin lines of the paved Appia Way and the roadbed of the railroad beside it, cutting through the low rolling hills on a southeasterly line to the capital city seventy miles away.

The area on the west side of the river was covered with the vast array of equipment marking the rail head of an advancing line—piles of fresh-cut stringers and bridging timbers still oozing tar, stacks of gleaming rails three days old out of the foundry back in Rus, barrels of spikes, footers to secure the rails, sidings filled with dormitory and kitchen cars, crane cars, flatcars, and even one of the new steam land locomotives used for moving earth. Swarming over the cars, jostling for the best view of the ceremony, were the three thousand men of the road gang, happy for this brief respite from the back-breaking round-the-clock schedule.

Coming up to the end of the track, the group came to a halt before the flag of Rus. A small pavilion was laid out before the colors, a simple rough-hewn table in the middle, and behind it there was another standard, this one a silver pole surmounted by a golden eagle with wings extended.

From across the bridge a flourish of drums sounded, counterpointed by a high clarion cry of trumpets.

With steady measured step, a column of men started across the bridge and Andrew felt a cold thrill at the sight of them, as if he had somehow crossed through time to gaze at another age.

The first consul of Roum marched at the head of the column, his silver breastplate shining in the morning sun, his purple cape fluttering in the breeze. Behind him came two dozen toga-clad men bearing the traditional bundles of fasces, the mark of the consul's rank.

"It looks straight out of the history books," Emil whispered in fascination.

"Got here the same as we did," Andrew replied, "only two thousand years earlier. They kept the same traditions and customs as well."

"Castrated by the Tugars, nevertheless," O'Donald growled.

"They'll learn," Kal said evenly, looking back at O'Donald. "Remember they fought the remnant of the Tugar horde that drifted this way, and held them back."

"And they still have slaves. That Marcus fellow ain't none too pleased with our talk about freedom. They got the same system the Rus did when we first got here."

"Give 'em time," Andrew said evenly. "Marcus wants trade and an alliance. We can show them a better way." The tone of his voice indicated that the debate was ended.

"It still sticks in my throat," O'Donald snapped in reply, unable to contain himself.

"They need us as much as we might need them," Kal said, looking back at O'Donald. "We still don't know where the Tugars drifted off to, and there are still the other hordes to the south. Our people need allies if we are to survive in this world."

Unable to respond to a logical military answer, O'Donald fell quiet.

The leader of the Roum strode forward, his sharply chiseled features set with an even expression. His eyes were deep-set, nearly hidden by a dark jutting brow and sharp aquiline nose. His bearing was erect, an outward expression of the rigid self-control and regal bearing of a man used to absolute obedience from all who served him. The only mark of emotion was in his gray hawklike eyes, which betrayed open curiosity at Kal's strange garb and appearance.

Behind Marcus the cohort of troops advanced at a steady rhythmic pace, a near mirror image of the 5th Suzdal, which fell in behind Kal in a regimental front by companies.

"Good-looking troops he's got," O'Donald said appraisingly. "I'll give the devil that at least."

"Roman tradition," Andrew replied, trying to contain his inner delight at this formation, which seemed to appear ghostlike out of the lost realm of history. The men were dressed in heavy leather tunics fronted with iron plate, their bronze helmets shining blood-red in the morning sun. Centurions, dressed in red cloaks, marked the pace, barking out commands, knowing they were on parade and ready to show the pride of the Roum off for the strangers who had come out of the west.

The drum cadence ruffled, and as if guided by a single hand the formation stopped before the standards. Behind Andrew, shouted commands echoed down the Suzdalian formation, which now as if in rivalry came to a halt and as one presented muskets in salute.

Vincent with sword drawn looked back at Kal, motioning for him to stay in place. He stepped forward and approached Marcus. Bringing his sword up, he saluted.

"Marcus Licinius Graca, it is my honor to present to you

President Kalencka of the Republic of Rus," he said in Latin.

Andrew smiled at Vincent's fair grasp of Latin, learned at his Quaker school and honed to the needs of his new job. It was one of the reasons he had been appointed ambassador, since besides Andrew and Emil there were only half a dozen other men in the regiment who knew the language at all. The Latin spoken by the Roum was, of course, not the standard textbook version learned out of Caesar's *Gallic Wars*, it was a far more vulgar form, but across two thousand years the language had changed surprisingly little except for the smattering of Tugar words which seemed to be common to all who lived under the horde.

He had sent the boy out here to provide military command for the work crew, which was also a fully armed brigade ready to fight at a moment's notice. But beyond all those other qualifications, Andrew realized that Vincent was imbued with the highest ideals of the republic, a fact which he wanted Marcus exposed to from one who held little if any guile in his soul. Perhaps guilelessness was not the best trait for an ambassador to have, but it was a risk worth taking in this delicate opening stage of development for Rus's first alliance.

Marcus, his features cold and fixed, eyed Kal appraisingly. The two were a marked contrast in rulers. Kal, obviously of peasant stock, his rotund form draped in a rumpled black suit and topped with the slightly ludicrous stovepipe hat, smiled openly at the Roum patrician, who stood before them like a statue come to life from a distant legendary age.

The two stood in silence for a moment until Kal, breaking the ice, stepped forward, extending his left hand.

Marcus looked at the empty sleeve, and his features lightened even as he took Kal's hand.

In Latin, he said, "Your arm—no one ever told me. It is gone, like Keane's," and as he spoke he looked over at Andrew and smiled.

Andrew and Marcus had met on several occasions, when negotiations for trade and military alliance between the two peoples had first started. Between them a friendship had started to form, the bond of two men who knew command.

"President Kalencka lost his arm defending Suzdal against the Tugars," Andrew interjected.

"Then he is a warrior like you," Marcus replied approvingly, looking at Kal with respect.

"Nothing like being a war hero to impress the people," Kal said openly, sensing the nature of the exchange between Marcus and Andrew.

"It helps," Andrew responded.

"Well, let's get on to the signing then," Kal interjected and with a smile motioned to the table set up on the roadbed.

The diminutive president and the consul walked over to the table, covered with purple cloth upon which were spread two documents, one in the Cyrillic script of the Rus, the other in Latin.

Marcus, taking a proffered quill from Vincent, signed his name across the bottom of each, and then Kal, a bit self-consciously, simply drew his mark, a stylized mouse, an action Marcus watched with interest.

"You cannot write?" Marcus asked, again in Latin.

Again Kal, sensing the meaning of the Latin, looked up at the consul.

"I was merely a peasant before the coming of the Yankees. But they made me, made all of us, men who are free, equal, and no longer cattle of the Tugars. I am learning to write, but I still prefer the mark of my nickname—the Mouse."

Andrew quickly translated. It was not the most diplomatic of replies, Andrew instantly realized. The Roum had successfully repulsed the tattered remnants of the Tugars without benefit of the social revolution the Rus had undergone first. Marcus, as a member of the ruling caste, though joyful at the overthrow of his old overlords, was evidently not pleased at what the broader social implications the Republic of Rus represented. It was an issue which Andrew had been forced to negotiate with finesse. The treaty just signed, he had to remember, was an agreement between two independent peoples, for mutual protection, the opening of free trade, and transit rights for the railroad to continue eastward. The agreement had been reached in a letter of protocol a year ago, but this day, when the first length of iron would be laid in Roum territory, was a fitting time to bring the leaders of both countries together for a more formal signing. Andrew repeatedly had to emphasize to Marcus that it was not the harbinger of an ongoing revolution, which some of the more radical elements in the Rus Republican Party advocated in their call for a program of Manifest

Destiny. His concern was that Kal himself advocated such an ideal. In his heart he knew that Marcus realized that this over time would be a threat as perilous as the Tugars.

"If you lost your arm in fighting the Tugars, you are surely the equal of anyone," Marcus finally replied, looking down at Kal and smiling, and Andrew winced inwardly at the subtle implication.

Kal winked knowingly at Andrew as he translated, and not taking offense, he again offered his hand to Marcus, who, finally smiling at last, grasped it with both of his own and then held it aloft.

A wild shout went up from the Roum soldiers drawn up behind him.

"Run up those rails," Kal shouted, looking over at the work gang, who stood to one side, waiting expectantly.

With practiced skill a work team brought up four sections of rail and slapped them down on their stringers. Hammers rang out as spikes were driven into place. The first set of rails crossed onto the bridge, with two more laid out in front. A heavy two-handed sledge was brought to Kal, who awkwardly grabbed hold.

Following one of the workers' lead, Marcus stepped over to the track, where a spike was already set. With a powerful swing, Marcus brought the hammer up and slammed it down, driving the spike in nearly to its head with a single blow. An appreciative shout went up from the road crew. Kal, stepping up to Marcus's side, lifted his own hammer up, and an expectant hush came over the Rus workers. The hammer arced down, striking hard on the spike head, driving it the rest of the way in, and a wild flurry of shouts rose up.

"Regiment poise muskets!" Vincent shouted, and as one the five hundred men raised their pieces heavenward.

"Take aim!"

"Fire!"

A perfectly timed volley snapped out, counterpointed by the blast of a dozen four-pounders from two Rus batteries fired in unison, while Ferguson cut loose with the *Malady*'s shrill whistle. The Roum cohort broke ranks at the volley, the men drawing back, shouting with fear. Marcus, who Andrew had made sure had seen such a demonstration before, barely flinched, but the touch of fear was still evident. Thinking quickly, Andrew stepped forward and with a flourish unholstered his revolver, pointed it skyward, and handed it to Marcus.

The consul grasped the weapon and then, turning to face his command, fired off six shots into the air, and at the sight of their commander, the cohort first fell silent and then, cheering, broke ranks and rushed forward to surround their leader, while the Suzdalian regiment, breaking ranks as well, surged in.

"Good hammer swing, Kal," O'Donald shouted, pushing through the crowd.

"Been practicing for weeks," Kal replied, obviously pleased with himself, as the men from both sides intermingled, the railroad work gang surging in to join the celebration.

"This party's going to ruin the work schedule for the rest of the day," Vincent ventured glumly as he sheathed his sword and came up by his father-in-law's side.

"Relax, son," O'Donald shouted, trying to be heard above the roaring crowd. "The boys need a day off."

"That Roum wine of theirs is near as bad as your damnable vodka. The men will be useless tomorrow."

"Ah, still trying to be a temperance man, I see," O'Donald laughed. "And you the best killer and swearer of the lot."

Vincent looked at O'Donald coldly.

"It's all right, laddie, some of it you couldn't help. But don't worry about the boys—they'll be back on the line tomorrow."

"I was hoping to be into Hispania by this evening," Vincent said glumly. "Ferguson's got a little surprise cooked up for us."

Ferguson, the young engineering student who was the driving force behind so many of the technological innovations that had saved Rus, pushed his way through the crowd.

"Don't worry, sir, I had some of it brought here," Ferguson ventured, stepping forward, and with a smile he nodded to Marcus. The consul and the engineer stepped off to one side, chatting amiably in Latin, the consul obviously friendly to the young soldier, who must appear to the Roum to have the mind and spirit of a magician.

Marcus beckoned to one of his officers, who approached the table nervously, gingerly carrying a wooden board upon which rested a hammer and a small pile of white crystals.

The officer placed it on the table where the treaty had just been signed and drew back hastily.

"All right, Ferguson, what've you been up to?" Andrew asked, knowing that another surprise was about to be sprung on all of them.

Ferguson, smiling as if he held a great secret, walked up to the table and took up the mallet.

"Just watch this!"

With a sharp quick movement, he snapped the hammer down onto the pile of crystals. A snap of light shot out with an explosive crack. With a yelp, Ferguson jumped back, madly patting at the smoldering flame which had ignited his jacket sleeve.

"Percussion explosives!" O'Donald roared with delight, rushing forward to help Ferguson put out the fire. "By God, we can finally put friction primers on our field pieces."

"And get rid of those damn flintlocks for percussion caps on the muskets," Hans growled.

Ferguson looked back at Andrew with obvious pleasure, just waiting for the questions.

"All right," Andrew finally ventured, "just how the hell did you come up with this one?"

"It's Marcus's silver mine above their town of Hispania," Ferguson replied. "Something in the back of my mind kept playing on how the old Romans, with their silver mines in Spain, also got quicksilver, mercury, from the same place.

"Well, that started me to thinking some more. So last time I was up here I spent a couple of days experimenting—that's how me and Marcus—excuse me, the consul and I—got to know each other," and as he spoke he looked over at Marcus, who smiled in agreement.

"He is a wizard," Marcus said in Latin with an evident note of respect.

"I didn't want to get anyone's hope up, so I kept it quiet. I knew our musket caps were made of fulminate of mercury—it's just getting the fulminate part down so the stuff would explode when hit.

"Anyhow, I finally got it figured out. I think, sir, we could arrange a little trade agreement on their mercury and in short order we can reconvert all our shoulder weapons."

"Well, thank heavens the Roum have copper and tin—you'll be able to make caps for the muskets," Hans stated, full of enthusiasm. "The supply of caps left for our own Springfields and revolvers was damn near depleted as is."

"And metal for bronze guns," O'Donald said glowingly.

"Damn me, I always did prefer good bronze Napoleons to iron guns."

The mention of copper pulled Andrew's thoughts back from the delight of those around him. In the spring after the war trade ships had ventured out to make the first run down to Cartha, and they had not returned.

Throughout the summer, more ships had ventured forth, until finally in late autumn, one had returned, badly damaged, with word that they had been attacked by Cartha ram ships.

So apparently the sea power to the south had adopted a belligerent stance. He could see the logic to it. The southern horde would be approaching that city this coming fall, if reports were correct, and undoubtedly they had been ordered to cut all contact with the renegade Rus to the north.

That had been his one overriding concern. The Tugars, he felt, would not be back—they had tried to attack the Roum and were driven off, and all contact had been lost with them. But the southern horde, moving across the steppe over seven hundred miles to the south, was a potential threat if they should ever decide to turn north. The defensive lines he was laying out a hundred miles southwest of Roum would be ready by then, but without Roum manpower as a backup if the Merki horde should turn north, he knew the situation would be desperate.

But there had been something else to the tale the survivors of the Cartha attack brought back that was far more disturbing. They claimed to have seen, as darkness had fallen, a large three-masted ship on the horizon, trailing smoke. The *Ogunquit.*

Nothing had been heard of Tobias since his defection. Andrew had half hoped that the recalcitrant captain would return. There'd be a chewing-out to be sure, but in all honesty he couldn't blame him for running; the battle was lost, and aboard ship he had a means of escape.

That was the other thought that had bothered him ever since. If Tobias had not returned, then what exactly was he up to?

"Some wine?" Marcus asked in Latin, coming up beside Andrew and holding out a silver goblet.

Andrew took the drink and tried to force a smile.

# Chapter Two

The humiliation burned into his soul, tearing his heart, which he felt could not bear yet another pain. Muzta Qar Qarth, leader of the Tugar horde, stood alone upon the bow of the ship crossing the narrows of the inland sea.

Qar Qarth, he thought coldly, leader of a horde that is no more. Once his warriors were as numberless as the stars in the heavens, as powerful as the wind that flashed with the light of the everlasting fire of heaven, as terrifying in battle as Bugglaah, Goddess of Death, who did his bidding and slaughtered all who opposed him.

And now they were gone, the power, the majesty, of the Tugar horde, reduced to a starving, tattered remnant; reduced by cattle.

He turned to look back at the Merki escort who stood at the stern of the ship. The Horde of the Red Sun, across the endless generations the hated foe whom his father before him had bested at Orki, with Qubata at his side.

"My old friend Qubata, would you have counseled me to this path?" Muzta whispered.

"My lord, did you say something?"

Muzta looked over at the arrogant young Merki who came up to stand behind him.

With a growl, Muzta shook his head.

Others had noticed it, this talking to Qubata, as if his old graying friend still rode by his side. In a way he did, Muzta thought, letting the faintest of smiles crease his features. What would Qubata now counsel in this final humiliation?

34

He would tell him to do this, for there was no other path to survival for now.

After the debacle before Rus, the fewer than thirty thousand warriors who had survived, with the vast numbers of women and children, who had providentially been out of the path of the flood, had moved east and south. He had agreed to let the healers of cattle, given by the Yankee Keane, to go beyond him, to stop the spread of the pox. But for the Tugars, starvation had dogged their tracks. Humiliation had been compounded when the Roum, having learned of the success of the Rus, blocked his advance beyond the realm's outlying villages, refusing even to barter for food. To continue on would be senseless; the taking of every people, the Roum, the Kan and Kathi, and the races beyond, would wear his people away to nothing. For the wanderers had gone ahead of them, spreading the word about the world how cattle had fought and won.

His only hope was to somehow find safe haven, to find a place where the children of the horde could come of age, to fill out again the empty ranks, to give unto his one surviving son a people who might one day be masters again.

And then had come the envoys of the Merki horde, appearing before him like gloating vultures. Telling him to appear at the cattle city of Cartha under the protection of blood bond to appear before Jubadi Qar Qarth. If he refused, his people would be annihilated. His followers were now a thousand miles away, encamped in a circle of high hills, living off their own horseflesh and cattle they could catch unaware, awaiting the return of their Qar Qarth with word either of haven or of death.

The boat continued to rock beneath his feet, and he felt a strange turning of his stomach. He had always hated water. The Tugars' march had carried them around the great waters, unlike the march of the southern hordes, who were forced at several points, such as this one, to rely on cattle to ferry them across.

It was the first time he had ever laid eyes upon the Cartha realm, and he could not conceal his admiration for the power of these cattle, their vast city making the Rus and the other realms of the Tugar march look small and weak by comparison.

The city was laid out along the banks of the sea for several miles, the limestone walls and vast towering temples shining with a red brilliance by the light of the midmorning sun. Beyond the city he could see endless terraced fields, the hundreds of great water wheels that raised up the water from the sea forever turning by the strength of the tens of thousands who manned them.

Around him a hundred ships rode low in the water, the rowers keeping a steady rhythmic beat, the oars dipping and lowering, the blades dripping with red crystalline light. Looking over his shoulder, Muzta could see the bent backs of the rowers in his own ship glistening with sweat, their muscles rippling. The sight of them made his stomach growl with hunger.

"How many cattle in this realm?" he asked quietly.

"Of the Carthas it is believed there are over four million," the Merki guide said evenly, a note of pride in his voice. "How many were there of the Rus?"

Muzta looked at the warrior, who smiled evilly. Muzta turned away without comment.

The throaty roar of a hundred nargas rent the air. Roused from his thoughts, Muzta looked to the shore as they passed between twin moles that marked the outer harbor of the city. As they entered the center of the bay he saw a channel turning off to the right and disappear, a line of smoke plumes rising up beyond where the channel turned. Directly ahead, a thousand of the Vushka Hush, the elite umen of the Merki horde, were arrayed along the walls of the harbor, battle pennants snapping.

He felt cold inside, naked as he gazed upon their horsetail standards. They were here early, at least six months early, and it made him wonder if somehow the Bantag had been turned back and Jubadi now had strength to spare, to rush forward into this city. The small hope he held that perhaps the Carthas would rise up and give unto the Merki what he had received finally vanished. It was right to come here, he finally had to admit. For over a year he had evaded the searching probes of Jubadi; now there would be no stopping him.

If I but still had such power, he thought sadly and then blocked the thoughts away.

The steady beat of the rowers ceased. Commands in the high guttural tongue of the Cartha cattle echoed across the water as the ship cut in through the inner mole. In the vast inner circle rode yet another hundred ships, and even to someone untutored in the ways of the sea, Muzta could see that the vessels were freshly made, while up on the shore gangs of laborers worked on yet more ram ships.

Curious, he looked about, but would not degrade himself further by asking yet another question. The purpose of the vessels was obvious, but against whom would they be used?

The gates of the city were flung open, and as the ship drifted into its slip a thunder of drums rolled and a column of warriors rode out.

Muzta gazed at them in silence with practiced eye, measuring their strength, sensing their power and arrogance.

The ship tied off, Muzta leaped onto the dock, and watched in silence as a mount was led up to him. Climbing into the saddle, he suddenly found that he felt better, as if the horse between his legs somehow returned his strength. Absently he leaned over and patted the mount as he watched more and yet more warriors pour out of the gateway, lining the dockside with their commanding presence.

"The Vushka Hush, hunting eagles of my lord Jubadi," the Merki officer announced with a growl of satisfaction, swinging his mount up alongside Muzta.

"I know," Muzta snapped, "for I saw their standard-bearer struck down by the great Qubata at the battle of Orki."

"And where is your Qubata, your Orkians, your score of umens now?" the Merki snarled back in reply. "What did the Yankees do to their bodies?" The Merki laughed, his features contorted with disdain.

Mutza felt his heart trembling with rage. If he was being brought here for the purpose of humiliation he might as well end this farce now.

"I am still Qar Qarth of my people," Muzta roared, turning in his saddle, his sword snapping from its sheath.

The Merki warrior gazed at him with open hatred.

"You were respectful enough when you came into my tent, offering this parley," Muzta shouted. "And now that I have come with you under the blood pledge of your Qar Qarth for my safety, now you hide beneath the swords of your warriors, and taunt me."

The officer with cruel kicks spurred his mount around, drawing his blade.

"Tugar, the cattle eat the flesh of your warriors. You are beneath my contempt. I soil my steel by drawing your blood."

"Nartan, drop your blade!"

Stunned, the Merki warrior looked away from Muzta, who now stood in his stirrups ready to strike. Muzta, hesitating, followed the Merki's gaze.

Standing before the entry to the gate was a lone warrior, short in stature, his head barely reaching the shoulders of his nine-foot-high guards. His long arms rippled with power; his black shaggy hair glistened with a fresh coating of boiled cattle fat. Muzta knew without asking that before him was Jubadi Qar Qarth, master of the Merki hordes.

Nartan, as if stricken, let the blade fall from his grasp, and it clattered on the stone dock, the high metallic ring the only sound to break the expectant hush that had fallen at the sight of the confrontation.

"Pick up your blade and come forward to me," Jubadi roared.

The warrior leaped from his saddle, scooped up his sword, and strode down the length of the dock, head high with defiance.

"My orders were," Jubadi said coldly, "to bring unto me Muzta, Qar Qarth of the Tugar horde, without insult or injury. I expected it done in a third of the year. You have taken four times as long. Beneath the very shadow of my tent, which I had pledged to him as a place of safety, you have seen fit to bring insult to him and to me."

Nartan stood silent.

"Kill yourself," Jubadi said coldly.

Nartan turned away and looked back at Muzta, icy hatred flashing in his eyes.

Kneeling, he braced the pommel of his sword on the ground, poising the point directly under his ribs.

"Tugar, watch how Merki obey and die," Nartan hissed, and without the briefest of hesitations he threw himself forward. Muzta, sword still in hand, watched, hiding his admiration, as the Merki continued to bear down, the gore-tipped blade punching through the back of his leather armor.

No cry escaped his lips, as farther and farther the blade slid in. A convulsive tremor coursed through the Merki's body as a great gout of frothy blood cascaded from his mouth. Ever so slowly his knees started to tremble as the blade continued to drive through. Without a sound the body slid forward, slamming into the sword's handguard. The warrior was dead before his anguish-contorted face touched the ground.

Without a glance to the still-trembling body before him, Jubadi rode past, coming up to the side of Muzta's mount.

"Debt is paid for the insult," Jubadi said evenly.

Muzta looked over at one whom he had once faced as an equal on the field of battle and now appeared before as a pauper.

Without comment, Muzta leaned over, touching the tip of his blade into the pool of blood coursing out from under Nartan's body. He ran the flat of the blade across his horsehide boots and then sheathed his sword.

"Though it has already been said," Jubadi announced with a high clear voice, "I ask you, Muzta Qar Qarth of the Tugar horde, to accept my blood pledge while you repose in my tent. Within the limitless domain of the Merki horde no harm will come unto you."

"I come not with intent of death to you or to your people, as long as I tread beneath your pledge," Muzta announced, bristling inwardly at Jubadi's use of the word "limitless" in describing the Merki realms.

This was the first time he had ever set eyes upon the one who until a year and a half ago he would have called his equal in power. Jubadi was shorter than he, but he could sense at a glance that in a one-to-one match Jubadi might very well best him, so powerful were his arms. There was a sharp virility, a coiled strength that Muzta found to be unsettling. Muzta knew that his own experiences of the last year had changed him beyond measure as he looked from Jubadi's powerful arms to his own, which were now matted with graying hair. He looked back up into Jubadi's eyes and could sense the slightest of derisive thoughts, as if his rival could not take him all that seriously.

Let him think it, Muzta cursed inwardly. If it were he that had come by my command I would feel the same. And in that realization Muzta for the first time felt the first calming, the understanding of a potential not yet even formed in his mind.

Jubadi returned Muzta's gaze without comment. So this is the fool, he thought quietly. How one of the Chosen Race could have allowed such a disaster to befall him was beyond comprehension. For the briefest of moments he wished he could spit in Muzta's face for all that had happened. Yet without what had happened, Jubadi realized, the hope for the Merki to survive the advances of the Bantag horde would be nonexistent. The thinnest of smiles creased Jubadi's features.

Jubadi turned his mount and started back to the gate, Muzta falling in beside him. Pausing between the two ceremonial fires that flanked the entryway into Cartha, the two leaned over in their saddles, bowing first to the east, the place of the never-ending ride, the direction that while living all of the Tugar, the Merki, and the far southern hordes of Bantag and Tamak rode. Turning, they bowed westward, to the direction of rest, the ending of day and of time, the pathway to the stars. Muzta silently prayed that even now, Qubata and all those who had fallen were riding that endless steppe of night, looking down upon him, whispering to him as he dream-walked the eternal realms.

Crossing under the gate into the city, Muzta relaxed in the momentary coolness. These southern realms were too damn hot, and though the occasion demanded it, he wished he could have avoided wearing the heavy ceremonial armor, cattle-hide cape, and heavy war helmet adorned with four cattle skulls. The brief moment of coolness passed as they rode on into the city of cattle.

The stench of it was so overpowering that Muzta struggled to keep from gagging. How cattle could live in such places had always been a mystery to him. They seemed to prefer living in their own stink rather than in the freshness of the open steppe.

"How they can stand this smell is beyond me," Jubadi growled, wrinkling his nose with disdain.

"They are cattle—they know no better," Muzta replied.

As he looked about he saw no cattle present, and it stirred a thought.

"You are here earlier than expected," Muzta ventured. "Were these cattle ready to receive you?"

Jubadi smiled.

"They were ready, though I am here only with one umen of my guard. The rest of my horde still marches seven months away."

He paused for a moment.

"They knew as well what had been done up north."

Muzta had secretly hoped that the Carthas would rise against Jubadi, weakening him as he had been weakened. Could it be that Jubadi had hurried here to prevent such an action?

"I have granted all of them exemption, except for the moon feast," Jubadi said evenly.

Stunned, Muzta turned to look at his companion.

"How will you survive?"

"Better to tighten the belt than to see your host as corpses," Jubadi said coldly. "We eat horseflesh, I send raiding parties ahead of the Bantag advance to harvest cattle, but for the Carthas there is exemption."

So there is something behind all of this, far more than I thought, Muzta mused. He knew that Jubadi would reveal the reasons soon enough, so he hid his curiosity behind a mask of indifference.

Muzta looked to either side of the street, which was lined with the warriors of the Vushka standing shoulder to shoulder with double-handed swords before them, points resting on the ground, hands resting upon the pommels. Muzta looked at them appraisingly. They were good, battle-hardened, tough, many showing scars on limbs and face.

"I hear your war with the Bantag goes poorly," Muzta ventured.

"You hear correctly," Jubadi retorted, his voice edged with bitterness.

"Such frankness surprises me," Muzta replied with a cold laugh.

"It is a time for frankness between Merki and Tugar if we are to survive."

So that's his game, Muzta thought, feeling the inner tension draining away at last. He needs me for something.

Muzta settled back, waiting for more, feeling that he was gaining control of this situation, but Jubadi was silent as they rode on through the city. Passing into the central square of the city, Muzta looked around with open wonder at the wealth of these cattle. All the buildings were of carved stone, temples rising to the sky, fires burning atop them with a strange oily smoke. From the high parapets of a vast columned edifice he could see anxious cattle faces peering out, but the square was empty, except for the endless ranks of the Vushka. Cutting across the square, the two turned to ride northward, following the lane marked by the ranks of the guard.

Panting for breath beneath the scorching heat, Muzta endured the ride in silence, as Jubadi led the way through narrow alleyways back again down toward the ocean.

Muzta looked around, realizing that there was much new construction in this area, long shed structures of rough-cut stone and timber. From within came the sounds of incessant hammering. With a hissing roar a vast thundering column of sparks soared up out of an open-roofed building, and Muzta nervously reined his mount in. A heavy fetid smoke poured out of the building, and Muzta felt the hairs on the nape of his neck stand out.

Jubadi laughed darkly.

"Just a bit farther," he said.

Spurring his mount forward, Jubadi cantered down the length of the alleyway and disappeared around a bend in the road. Muzta could feel the sarcastic gaze of the Vushka warriors who still lined the road, and with a muffled curse he spurred his mount forward. Turning the bend in the road, he pulled his mount up beneath the gate out of the city and gasped out a startled cry.

The great ship of the Yankees rested in the dockyard before him.

Jubadi looked over as his companion leaned back and barked out a laugh.

"You want to ask how, but your pride prevents you," Jubadi roared.

Wordlessly Muzta slowly rode forward, guiding his nervous horse up onto the dockside. The ship looked different, lower in the water, its masts gone, but it was the damnable Yankee ship nevertheless. He was certain of it.

Drawing closer, he eyed the vessel carefully, comparing what he now saw to the memory of the year before.

The wooden sides of the ship had disappeared. In their place were black sheets of metal, skirting the sloping sides of the vessel from one end to the other. Small doors had been cut through the metal, and out of each opening a dark angry snout protruded—thundermakers of the Yankee warriors. But these were thundermakers beyond anything he had ever seen before. The opening in them was so big he could have slid his balled fist into it.

He did not know whether to curse or laugh with joy at the sight of this weapon in Merki hands.

"Muzta Qar Qarth, may I present the warrior of this ship," Jubadi announced, "and Hamilcar, ruler of the Carthas."

Muzta turned in his saddle and looked down at the two cattle who, coming out of an opening in the side of the ship, stepped up to stand by Jubadi's side.

The one man was not Keane, Muzta realized at a glance, and he felt a tug of regret. Keane was one he still wished to see again, though of late he found he could not decide what his reaction would be at that confrontation.

This one was shorter, fat almost, with a florid face running with sweat. The uniform was different as well. It was the same blue as the Yankees wore, but longer in cut, reaching to the man's knees and adorned with golden lace and twin rows of buttons.

The Cartha towered above the Yankee, his dark beard and hair oiled, his bare chest a mat of hair, almost like a Tugar's. Muzta could see the veiled caution in the eyes of the Cartha, but the Yankee seemed to have a smirking air of triumph.

"We have met before in battle," Tobias said, his words stumbling over the guttural intonations of the Merki tongue. The dialect was similar to Tugar, but to Muzta it sounded even stranger coming from the throat of a Yankee.

"Your ship looks different now," Muzta replied sharply.

"Now it is a true vessel of war," Tobias responded proudly.

"Show him how you did this," Jubadi ordered

Tobias led the way, pointing for Muzta to follow him down the dockside. Falling in behind the two cattle, Muzta looked over at Jubadi, who smiled openly.

"Surprised?"

"I would lie if I said otherwise," Muzta growled.

Doubling back up the path which led down to the northern harbor, Muzta rode in silence. The path they had followed through the city had been cleared of all cattle, but he could sense that just on the other side the buildings were a hive of activity. Cattle voices were shouting, strange hammering sounds echoed, sparks soared up out of buildings, and above the rooflines of the vast sheds he could see the tops of great wooden wheels turning.

Tobias and Hamilcar stopped before an arched doorway and beckoned for the two Qar Qarths to dismount. Muzta came down off his mount and drew up before the Yankee cattle, who looked up at him with that infuriating air of disdain.

The doorway swung open, and Muzta gasped for breath with the rush of scorching heat that flooded out to greet him. He felt a knot of fear but held it in check as he bent low and walked into the hellish scene before him.

The far side of the vast cavern was dominated by a high brick structure that filled one entire wall. The shed roof was open around it. A glaring red heat like the eye of the sun shimmered in the center of the wall.

"Our iron kiln," Tobias announced. "We're getting three tons a day out of it.

"Straight ahead is the furnace where we convert the pig iron into cast," and he pointed to where dozens of cattle, naked except for sweat-drenched loincloths, labored over a vast shimmering pit, stirring the molten metal with long metal rods.

"It is a Yankee building for the making of metal," Muzta whispered out loud.

Tobias looked back at him and smiled.

"His men made it for me," Jubadi announced proudly.

A thundering boom started to echo down the vast shed with a rumble like a thousand war drums, and Muzta looked around nervously.

"The tilt hammers," Tobias announced, and he continued down the vast length of the shed and stopped before a series of man-size hammers that slowly rose up and then dropped down, striking sheets of hot metal, sending out vast showers of red-hot sparks. Crews of Cartha laborers moved the metal with heavy tongs. As the group watched, a gang of workers lifted one sheet off, carried it over to a blazing kiln, and slid the metal inside, while another crew took a red-hot sheet and maneuvered it between two stone rollers. As if moved by unseen hands, the rollers started to turn. The red-hot iron passed between the rollers, flattening out into a long sheet. Tobias led the group around to the other side, where another team of workers stood ready, pulling the sheet over to a long table, where they started to trim the edges, squaring it off, while others, with heavy hammers and spikes, proceeded to punch holes around the sides of the glowing sheet.

"One-inch armor plating for the *Ogunquit*, and the other gunships," Tobias announced proudly.

"It is hellish, this Yankee creation," Muzta whispered, unable now to hide the fear.

"I thought the same," Jubadi replied, looking over at Muzta. "Yet it is now a hell I control."

Tobias turned away from the rollers and continued on to where a vast bed of sand was laid out on the floor. To one side a tower of dried clay rose up higher than Muzta could reach, its sides as thick as the body of a horse. Above the clay tower a dozen Cartha laborers stood on a platform maneuvering a heavy dark ladle into place. The ladle tipped over, and out poured a river of molten iron.

Muzta looked over at Tobias with an inquisitive gaze.

"Show him the result of this," Jubadi announced, and pointed to an open door flanked by half a dozen guards of the Vushka.

Grateful to be escaping the scorching heat, Muzta went through the doorway, gasping for breath. The noonday heat of Cartha now seemed cool by comparison.

He paused for a moment in wonder as he turned and looked at the long line of wooden wheels, each nearly twenty feet high, that lined the side of building. Inside each of the wheels, dozens of naked cattle walked endlessly, as if they were trying to climb the inside of the wheel, which kept turning, defeating them in their purpose. For a moment Muzta looked at the strange procession as if the men were mad. Why would anyone walk inside a wheel?

"We use manpower to turn the wheels that power our machinery," Tobias said. "We've got two thousand of them at this day and night. Eventually I'll get steam to do it for us."

Muzta still did not understand, but he hid his confusion and turned away.

Walking down the length of the building, Muzta tried to block out the sour stench of the laboring cattle. The smell and desiccated look of his old food made his stomach want to rebel.

The courtyard outside the factory was aswarm with workers. A high earthen ramp led up one side of the building. An endless procession of laborers walked up the ramp with woven baskets on their shoulders. As each reached the top he handed the basket to another who emptied the contents into a smoking hole, which Muzta reasoned must be the top of the furnace out of which the iron came from.

"We have to ship in the charcoal from the southern forests, the ore from nearly a hundred miles away. I've got at least five thousand men working on this," and Tobias's voice was filled with pride.

Muzta looked around appraisingly. There was a lot here that was missing from the old Yankee factories which he had surveyed after they surrounded Rus. Somehow the Rus works seemed more mysterious. There were no strips of iron laid on the ground here with the fire-breathing machines, the great water wheels were driven instead by sweating cattle, yet there was power here nevertheless.

"You are making thundermakers," Muzta announced, knowing he'd be a fool not to see the obvious.

Jubadi laughed.

"Let's go back to your ship, Tobias."

As they made their way back down to the dock, Muzta kept silent, cursing himself inwardly. If he had but known the true power of the Yankee weapons he would have done such as this. But damn them, all the Merki now had the advantage from his mistakes.

Reaching the ship, Tobias strode up the gangplank. A strange shrieking rent the air, and Muzta looked around suspiciously as he stepped aboard and saw the blue-clad cattle standing rigid before him, one with a curious pipe to his lips. Tobias saluted the red-and-white striped flag with a blue square filled with stars floating on a pole above the stern. But Muzta barely noticed that.

His eyes looked greedily at the long line of thundermakers lining the deck. Behind each of the weapons stood four cattle.

"Six-pound iron field pieces," Tobias announced. "Freshly made here by the Carthas," and he looked over at Hamilcar, who had been silent throughout the tour but now let a look of pride light his features.

"My Qarths," Hamilcar announced, pointing over the side of the ship. A small battered craft was anchored in the middle of the northern harbor, a hundred yards away.

A thunderous crack echoed down the ship. All the old horrors came rushing back, and Muzta recoiled with barely concealed terror, thankful for the cloud of sulfurous smoke that enveloped him to hide the fear in his eyes. As the smoke cleared he saw a geyser of spray kicking up around the vessel, showers of splinters boiling up into the air.

The smoke blew away, and the Cartha cattle around him cheered lustily. The small boat bobbed and swayed in the foaming water, and ever so slowly started to settle.

Muzta started to turn away.

"We are not done yet," Jubadi said calmly, nodding to Tobias. The Yankee nodded, and leaning over an open hatchway he waved his hand.

"Number one fire!" Tobias roared.

Stunned, Muzta grabbed hold of the ship's railing as the entire vessel seemed to surge as if a giant had struck it with a hammer. A fountain of smoke cascaded out from beneath his feet, illuminated by a slash of fire. An instant later the target ship seemed to lift into the air, its back broken.

"Numbers two and three fire!"

Two more shots screamed downrange. One of them smashed through the vessel's stern, ripping it clean off in a shower of splinters. Muzta could see the other shot continue on, striking the water once and then again several hundred yards away, the ocean erupting from the impact, and then it disappeared from view.

"Such power," Jubadi whispered.

"The guns are the most powerful in the world, my lord," Tobias announced proudly. "Fifty-pounders. The four-pounders the Tugars faced are as nothing compared to what I have created."

"How many so far?" Jubadi asked.

"Fifteen, my lord. We'll have thirty by the time we sail. Along with two that can shoot a hundred-pound ball."

"What have you done to this ship?" Muzta asked, unable to hide his curiosity.

"We cut off the entire top deck and dropped the masts," Tobias said proudly, as if lecturing a group of admirers. "Beneath your feet is a gun deck running a hundred and thirty feet in length, sheathed with two inches of iron, backed by nearly two feet of wood. The ship will mount five guns on each broadside and one heavy gun forward and another aft. The sides, as you can see, are sloped to cause shot to rebound away, and up forward is a metal ram."

"Tell him of the other ships," Jubadi said proudly.

"I'm building eighteen gunboats. Each one will carry a single fifty-pound piece inside an armored housing, and there will be two boats that can carry heavy mortars."

"Mortars?" Muzta asked. It was hard enough to understand the Yankee's terrible accent; the strange words he said made it nearly impossible.

"Short fat cannons that will hurl hundred-pound balls filled with exploding powder up to four miles. We have a way to make exploding shells, like the ones you saw used by the guns the Yankees brought with them."

"The powder?" Muzta asked.

"The Yankees had traded some of it to us before the war started," Hamilcar announced. "We bribed a Suzdalian merchant to reveal the secret to us and were already making it before the Namer of Time had even come."

Muzta looked over at Jubadi and allowed the slightest of smiles to cross his features. So the Carthas were thinking of fighting you as well, he thought with a certain satisfaction. Too bad they didn't have enough courage to do it.

"You have served me well," Jubadi said quietly. "All of you may go now. I want this ship to myself."

Tobias looked at the two for a moment, and Muzta could sense the slightest edge of resentment in this one. Hamilcar stood in silence and with a bow turned away, Tobias following in his wake. From below deck a swarm of Cartha gunners came up, looking at Jubadi and Muzta with outright awe as they filed off the vessel.

"You are too stiff-necked," Hamilcar whispered as he and Tobias alighted on the dock.

"Without us, the bastards would have none of this," Tobias hissed softly. "They should realize that."

"They know that. And I know that the Merki are not as foolish as the Tugars. They placed their best umen here to ensure we would not arm against them. We must play their game, and above all else not arouse their ire. Learn that, Tobias, if you wish to survive, for if you should turn them against us I'll kill you myself."

"I am under his protection," Tobias snapped.

"They will not be here forever," Hamilcar retorted as he stalked away.

"What the hell was that about?"

Tobias turned and smiled as Jim Hinsen, with Jamie swaggering by his side, came up to stand beside him.

Tobias looked over at the young infantryman, the only member of the 35th who had joined him when he fled Rus. The boy had proved himself well enough. The information he had gleaned about manufacturing of powder and guns had been invaluable. Tobias sensed from the beginning that this one had the instincts of a cat and would always land on his feet, no matter what the situation.

"That Hamilcar is running too scared of Jubadi, that's all," Tobias snorted.

"I still wouldn't cross either him or the Merki," Hinsen said.

"With the *Ogunquit* fully armed, I'll play their game," Tobias replied, "I'll play it just as he wants it, but don't forget we have our own plans as well."

Tobias looked back to the deck where Jubadi and Muzta stood alone.

"I still don't trust the bastards," Tobias whispered.

"You shouldn't trust anyone," Jamie replied, the thinnest of smiles crossing his features. "Especially them man-eating devils. Come along—I've got a powerful thirst, and by God's hairy ass a need to sheathe myself as well."

Tobias looked over disdainfully at the pirate and walked away, Hinsen and Jamie following in his wake and laughing softly over some private joke.

He wanted to look back, to rebuke them, for he could sense they were laughing at him, but said nothing as he stalked away.

Muzta watched in silence as the cattle turned away from the dock and disappeared up the alleyway that led back to the foundry.

"Do you really trust them?" Muzta asked as if to himself.

Jubadi laughed darkly. "About as much as I trust you," he said evenly.

Muzta did not reply. The reason why he had been summoned to this parley would now be revealed, but he wished not to divulge that he was in a hurry.

Turning away from Jubadi, he strode down the length of the ship, which was cut flat from bow to stern except for a single funnel for the steam engine, a small open pilot house, and half a dozen horn-shaped vents which forced air below. The deck was covered with iron plates like the one he had seen being forged in the mill. That in itself was a mystery. By what witchery could these Yankee cattle make a thing of iron float on water? The thundermakers along the deck were larger than the ones he remembered from the Yankees, and looking at them closely he saw that the metal-working was cruder, the barrels were rough-shaped, thicker. Going up to the edge of the railing, he looked over the side of the ship, which sloped outward as it reached the water. The sides were shrouded with the iron plates as well, and he realized at once that this vessel had been rebuilt to go against the Yankees—what other purpose could it possibly serve?—and his pulse quickened.

Going over to a hatchway, he scrambled down below and

felt a cold surge of uneasiness. The gun deck was gloomy, lit
only by narrow shafts of sunlight coming down through the
occasional breaks of open grating above his head. The heat
was stifling, the stench of gunsmoke so heavy in the air he
thought he would choke. Panting, he gasped for breath, his
tongue lolling out in the boiling heat. The deck was made
for cattle, not Tugars. He wanted to get out from the killing
heat, but curiosity drove him into the darkness. Squatting
down on his haunches Muzta crawled forward. The thunder-
maker before him filled him with a near-reverent awe.

The barrel was of iron, and at a glance he estimated it
must weigh twenty, maybe even fifty times as much as the
thundermakers on deck. Round iron balls were lined up in a
rack along the bulkhead. Crawling over, he hefted one up,
and the muscles in his arm tightened.

"By Bugglaah," he whispered, "if such could have served
me."

His imagination raced. With such weapons as these he
could have smashed the Yankees down, rending their city to
splinters. The thought of Jubadi's now possessing such power
sickened him. He placed the cannonball back on the rack.
Settling back, he looked down the length of the gun deck,
his eyes growing accustomed to the gloom. There were ten
such guns down here. Up forward he saw one nearly twice
as big as the others, and he crawled up to the massive
weapon and sat down beside it, his heart pounding. Is this
what war has become? he wondered darkly. Buildings of
cattle turning out things that could strike down a man at ten
times the range of an arrow? It made him feel sick.

He sat in silence for long minutes, letting all that he had
seen be absorbed. There were paths within paths here, plans
weaving around yet other plans.

"So what would you now counsel, my good Qubata?"
Muzta whispered, and a sad smile crossed his features as the
first shadows of answers began at last to form.

Jubadi rose up with a languid air from where he had been
leaning against the ship's railing as Muzta reemerged upon
the deck. With a friendly gesture he beckoned for Muzta to
join him under an awning at the stern of the ship, where a
table had been set out. Taking off his helmet, Jubadi settled
down on a saddlelike chair. Reaching over the side of the
vessel, he pulled a line up, on the end of which dangled a
heavy sealed crock. Pulling the lid open, Jubadi poured out

a long draft of fermented horse milk into two cattle-skull goblets.

With a sigh of relief, Muzta took the goblet, nodding to the west as he poured out a small libation. Raising the skull up without any hint of ceremony, he drained the contents off in a single gulp, absorbing the cooling draft with relish. Without hesitating he took the heavy crock and poured another drink.

"How you people stand this heat is beyond me," Muzta growled as he drained off the second drink with almost as much dispatch as the first.

"How you stand your damned frozen north is a mystery to me as well. Anyhow, it is better than the Bantag realms."

"Ah yes, the Bantag," Muzta said, looking over at his host. "I think in the end all of this revolves around the Bantag."

"Our sires, our grandsires unto countless generations, have fought," Jubadi said, the faintest of smiles lighting his features as if recounting a treasured memory.

"As it has always been, for what is the source of pride, the reason for our existing, but to show the strength of our arms?"

"And that strength is gone, my old enemy," Jubadi replied.

Muzta started to bristle, but he sensed no taunting in Jubadi's voice.

"For how else could we prove our valor, our strength, our pride," Jubadi continued, "but by the crossing of swords, of Tugar against Merki, of Merki against Bantag? For are we not of the same race? Has it not always been such even in the days of our father gods who walked between the stars?"

Muzta nodded slowly in agreement. Across the circling of his youth, and after the last great war, had not the nightly fire been kindled and burned to the singsong chant of the legend keepers, recounting the tales of valor? Had he not dreamed in his youth that when he too should fly westward, when he reposed in the heavens of the endless steppe, he would hear at night the chants of his people below, singing yet new songs of his own valor when he had walked among them as their Qar Qarth?

"We could crush you now," Jubadi said, his voice distant and cold. "You are burdened down. For every warrior you have, there are twenty children to be fed. Even your women now ride as hunters. I can send forth my Vushka Hush to

ride like the wind. Your people could not hide forever—
within a year we would find you and slay all that remained.
I could send forth but two umens to range ahead, to sweep
north and east, and in the end we would catch you in our
net, for my warriors could cover in but a day what your
yurts could travel in four.

"I need but to reach out my hand and the memory of the
Tugar race will disappear forever. Your ancestors before
you, their spirits would then disappear, for no more would
the songs of their people rise up at night to give them
renewed strength. So that even in the endless steppe of the
western sky the name of the Tugars would be forgotten."

"Then why don't you?" Muzta growled. "Or do the Bantag
to the south press you too hard?"

Jubadi looked over at Muzta with surprise, and the Qar
Qarth of the Tugars smiled for the first time, knowing he
had caught his rival off guard.

"I know that you lost against them early last spring near
the crossing narrows of the salt sea far west of here and only
by a ruse did you destroy their elite umen and force but a
temporary withdrawal."

"Do the ears and eyes of Muzta have wings?" Jubadi
asked.

"Remember always the cattle known as Wanderers," Muzta
replied softly. "I have learned that they are more than just a
nuisance, like flies buzzing about our ears. The word of
what happens passes between their lips like the wind.

"Word of victory runs fast, but the news of defeat has
wings," Muzta went on evenly. "We have both had troub-
les, Jubadi Qar Qarth."

"But my inconvenience was at the hands of the Chosen
Race, not cattle," Jubadi snarled. "Remember, Muzta, you
can be smashed by my merest whim."

"Then do it!" Muzta roared, coming to his feet. "I choose
not to live by the mercy of a Merki. If it is the end of my
people, I will face it with sword in hand. If the ancestor
gods themselves will not help me, then they can burn in
torment as far as I am concerned."

Jubadi threw back his head and barked out a laugh.

"Brave words, when you know by my pledge I cannot
fight you now. Not until you have safely returned to your
people."

"If you have not decided to slay us, then there is a

reason," Muzta replied coldly. "Now speak it. I have ridden fifty days to stand thus before you. I have no desire to stay with you, your people, and these machines a moment longer than necessary."

"At least you are not broken," Jubadi replied.

Muzta stood expressionless. If only his hated foe truly knew, he thought inwardly. But moments before as he had watched the Merki envoy die, he had felt envy for him, an inward wish that the burden of his responsibility and the humiliation of having been defeated by cattle could finally be washed away. But then he feared to face his father beyond, for all would know that he, Muzta, had allowed the lowest of races to best him. Death would be no escape. The burden that awaited him there was a terror that haunted him. There would be no escape in this world or the next, and that drove within him a torment that racked his sleep with terror dreams of loathing.

"Why did you summon me here?" Muzta asked, coming at last to the heart of the matter.

It had been his hope that somehow the Merki horde would pass to the eastward without pursuing him, then after several years he could swing in behind them, perhaps to forage in their path, perhaps even to reach the Bantag horde. As sworn enemies of the Merki, perhaps the Bantag could reach an understanding with the Tugars. The chant singers told how twenty-two circlings before, the Bantag and Tugars had united in such a way and driven the Merki to near extinction, until at last the two had fallen out over the spoils, with Merki and Bantag uniting against the Tugars to drive them back into their northern realms.

It was obvious that Jubadi had brought him here to show that the Tugars were trapped, and now lived merely by his whim. With the dreaded Yankee weapons in their hands, all hope was forever gone.

Jubadi reached out to refill Muzta's cup, and with his own he beckoned toward the row of guns lining the deck of the *Ogunquit*.

"With a hundred of those small weapons, you could have smashed the Yankee cattle as they smashed you."

Muzta sensed a tone of sympathy in Jubadi's voice and looked back at him.

"Your foolish pride," Jubadi said evenly, almost with a tone of understanding.

"You were not there,"

"But I received my reports.".

Muzta gazed at his old rival sharply.

"Come now, we each have spies in the other's camp. We disdain them, we hate any that would betray his clan, but you use them too. One of them survived your debacle. You should have listened to your Qubata and not charged head-long, bleeding yourself white. These were not cattle you were fighting, these were men."

Muzta could not reply.

"And now I will give back to them a hundredfold what they have done to you," Jubadi snarled coldly. "You left me an ugly mess, Muzta. Think you that I could leave such as they to the north as we rode on eastward? When again we circled they would have armed all cattle, have made all of them into warriors. Remember we of the Chosen Race are few now. For every Merki there are a hundred times that number of cattle. Your Rus were but a minor herd compared to the Khita, the Constan, the Eptans. Think of them united against us. Have you not noticed that even as we devour their flesh, yet with every circling there are more of them, while our numbers stay the same?"

"It is obvious the pox did not come south."

"And you should have let it continue to spread!" Jubadi roared, his temper flaring out. "Instead you let the cattle healers move ahead of you. Think, damn you, if your Roum had been weakened you could have fed off them. But no, you could not see that! You let not just one thing spread before you but two, the end to the pox and the knowledge that we could be beaten."

"If the cattle died, then we would starve, all of us."

"Better to let them all die than to let them learn they could fight against us. This Yankee thinking is a threat far beyond our empty stomachs. With these," Jubadi shouted, pointing at the guns, "they will finish us, not just Tugars, not just Merki, all of us, and this will be a world of cattle."

Muzta lowered his head.

"Then the old ways are finished."

"Only for the moment," Jubadi replied sharply.

"Is that it, then, is that why you brought me here, to simply show me the thundermakers and thus demand my obeisance to you?"

Jubadi laughed softly. "You are impetuous, Qar Qarth of

the Tugar horde. I would have expected less talk and more silence from you."

Muzta bristled inwardly. He knew Jubadi to be right. But all that he had carried had made him more brittle of late. A Qar Qarth must be silent, must spend his words as sparingly as the strength of his warriors. Must hear much and say little. Inwardly he cursed.

"I wish to make you an offer," Jubadi said quietly.

Muzta laughed.

"Against the Bantag in exchange for the safety of my people," Muzta ventured. "Perhaps I should wait and see if Mangu Qar Qarth of the Bantag can make a better offer to me."

Muzta knew that his words held no weight, did not even begin to touch upon Jubadi's true intent. In his heart he realized that there was a chance in the offing for the Tugar horde after all. The Merki would not strike, at least not yet.

"Try it," Jubadi retorted sharply. "You would have to move your people more than two thousand miles to the south, across the narrows of the eastern sea, across the front of my realm. If you dared it, my umens would fall upon you and destroy you. Your agreement must be with me, Muzta of the Tugars, or not at all."

Muzta snarled darkly, outraged at the effrontery of Jubadi for not addressing him as Qar Qarth.

"I am offering the following," Jubadi retorted coldly. "The Bantag are but the threat of the moment, as has always been the nature of our wars."

"A war which I have already said you are losing," Muzta stabbed back.

Jubadi fell silent for a moment.

"I can still bring you down with me," he said coldly.

"You need me now, don't you, Jubadi of the Merki?" Muzta snapped.

Jubadi struggled to control his rage.

"You have fought with the Bantag for half a circling, and you are losing. This is no raid and counterraid, this is a war for survival. Something is driving them as well, making of this a war not just for sport or for some momentary advantage. They are pressing for some reason to the kill. We, the Tugar horde, gutted you at Orki. Now the Bantag are smelling blood and coming in to finish the kill we started."

"You do not understand," Jubadi roared, slamming the table with his fist.

"Oh, I do understand," Muzta growled in reply. "You will first use the cattle to fight the Yankee threat to the north, and at the same time learn their weapon skill. You will annihilate the Yankees using the Carthas. Then you will devour the Yankees and Carthas in turn, take the weapons that are needed, and turn them against the Bantag."

A thin smile creased Jubadi's features.

"So why tell me?" Muzta continued. "With that strength I don't see where Tugars fit into your plan."

"I pledge you freedom of your own realm, the great northern steppe, in return for your alliance now."

"And if I say no?"

Jubadi beckoned back to the factory.

"The power I am forging in there will be turned against you. Cattle have always made us what we desire, even our war bows. Let them now forge new weapons for a new task.

"They will forge five hundred of those thundermakers for me by the next spring," Jubadi announced proudly, beckoning back to the row of field pieces.

Stunned, Muzta looked at the guns with envy.

"And the powder?"

"More than I will ever need. Five hundred of those, and scores of the great guns you saw below the decks. That will be the new source of my power."

"The small weapons carried by men?"

"They are useless for my task," Jubadi replied. "Our great bows carry farther. Oh, we will make some for the cattle, to be sure, but not too many, for it will be easy for us to count, to control the great thundermakers, but the small ones are to be feared in the hands of cattle who serve us. That I shall not allow beyond a small force of several thousand.

"Those who make them, if they please us, we'll keep them; if not, we can still feast upon them later. You, on the other hand, you can starve or you can fight for me. There is no other choice."

Jubadi reached into a leather case resting against the side of the table and pulled out a map, which he unrolled across the table.

"You are a season's ride to the east and north of the Carthas," Jubadi started, pointing to an empty stretch of steppe astride what had been the old boundaries of their two realms.

"My horde is still a season away to the west, our southern flank protected for now by the great stretch of high mountains which here runs west to east. The Bantag keep pressing at the passes and are already racing eastward, attempting to outpace me, to cross the inland sea to the south and then swing north, hoping to block my passage across the narrows. They will be here in a year's time."

"And you will want me to hold this side of the narrows open when they do so. You don't have enough warriors otherwise."

"Not if I am to guard the passes, occupy Cartha, and swing north to finish the Yankee city and end their scourge."

"That is my territory," Muzta said, knowing that his words were hollow.

Jubadi looked over at him with a sarcastic smile.

"And besides," Muzta added quickly, "you can send twenty umen against them and still I would not give you an even chance of success. Do you think they have stopped building since last year? Already it is known they have built their fire that rides upon iron strips all the way to the Roum."

"Remember I am arming cattle to fight cattle," Jubadi replied.

A madness that will come back to haunt us all, Muzta thought coldly.

"Within the month we will move against the Yankees and their allies, and not one Merki will need to fight. We have established contacts within the cities of the Rus—there are some who even now do not know that in fact they are serving our plans. The Yankee Tobias is ambitious—he is like the cattle we have always used to rule cattle. Without his kind the world created by our grandsires could not exist. If he succeeds, we will reward him as we always have those who rule in our name."

"And do you really expect that after we allow cattle to use these new weapons they will quietly give them back to us? Jubadi, remove the blinders of a horse from your eyes. The old ways are gone forever—cattle have slain us, and it will not be forgotten so easily."

Muzta grimaced inwardly at his own words, but he knew them to be the truth.

"How else do you propose to destroy those who destroyed you, and now threaten all of the Chosen Race?"

Muzta was silent. He could see that inwardly Jubadi was right; flame must be used to burn out the flame.

Muzta looked back down the length of the ship.

"One of these will not defeat the Yankees." Muzta snapped. "Their army in the fastness of Suzdal will not be reduced by this iron ship. You could land ten umens of cattle against them, all armed, and still the Yankees and their Rus would defeat them. I should know that more than anyone else, Jubadi."

"There will be more, Tobias told you that. The Yankees have these things that Tobias told me of and you have seen, these fire breathers that move upon iron strips. But we will control the waters. Tobias has devised a plan to use that to our advantage to drag out the Yankees from behind their fortresses and defeat them, perhaps without our even having to fight a battle."

"So you are offering me terms, then," Muzta replied suddenly, driving the issue to the main point of his concern.

"There is no choice for you," Jubadi replied. "Join under my banner. If not, despite all that is happening I will hunt the rest of your people down. For you know that I will defeat the Yankees, and then in turn will throw down the Bantag. When that is done, Muzta, I will turn my attention to you. Protect my eastern flank, or die. When the campaign begins against the cattle, I will expect one umen of your warriors to ride to the north upon the other side of the sea, while your other two umens protect the southward marches ahead of me. In return your people may graze upon my eastern lands, may even harvest my cattle to the number of one in twenty."

Muzta smiled inwardly. He had gotten more than he had ever hoped for. Reaching over to the half-empty jar, he poured the remaining contents into his goblet and Jubadi's. Standing up, he held his goblet high, raising it ceremoniously to the four winds. Jubadi, with a fierce grin, stood and did the same. The two exchanged cups and then drained them.

The pact had been signed.

"I just wonder what Keane will do regarding all of this," Muzta said quietly as he sat back down.

"Keane?"

"Someone you will find to be rather interesting, my ally," Muzta said with a smile.

\* \* \*

"Sir, give my men three months and they can triple your iron production up to seven, maybe ten tons a day. Your big problem is fuel. Heavy stands of woods are nearly seventy miles from here, and we haven't found any good coal."

Vincent looked over at Marcus, who shook his head in confusion.

"Maybe the best bet, once the line gets here, is simply to bring the coke up from Suzdal. It'd cost a bit, but it'd still be cheaper to make the rails here, where you've got good ore, rather than haul them in five hundred miles as we're doing right now. Once we get rail production going here I'd be tempted to run a spur line north to the forests. We could use the lumber for building material and rail ties, as well as for fuel for the foundry and for our locomotives."

"And for us?" Marcus asked suspiciously.

"Well, figure out a trade for the rails and other material that'll be fair to both sides. By our treaty, the rail line we are running through your territory is the property of the Maine, Fort Lincoln and Suzdal Railroad Company."

"Of course," Marcus said dryly.

"Now, don't quote me on this, sir," Vincent said in a conspiratorial whisper, "but if you and your people should form your own railroad charter and run that spur line up to the woods yourself, you'd have a damn nice profit out of it in no time. It'd be cheaper for the company to buy the lumber supplies from you rather than ship it across five hundred–odd miles of track.

"I'd suggest hiring away some of the Suzdalian road crew bosses to lay it out for you. They could train your people, and with a couple of thousand laborers the line could be surveyed, graded, and laid out before winter. Besides, once you have the skills you'll want to run connecting lines to your other cities and villages as well. Our rail line is already surveyed to continue a straight run toward Khitai, twelve hundred miles to the east. It'll be a project of a couple of years at least, maybe more with some of those high hills. That's all we're legally entitled to run in your territory. Your company could run connecting service out to the rest of your realm—that's quite a few hundred miles of track, but it'll link your territory together. Hook those lines into the MFL&S and trade will increase like anything.

"You've got copper deposits and tin for bronze, zinc, some excellent wine, and exquisite glassworks, and that oil that you told me bubbles out of the ground near your city of Brindusia has some great potential. We've already tried it as a lubricant on the engines, and some of the boys are already boiling it into kerosene. There's going to be a big market for that.

"Your people are far better weavers than the Rus. I could bring up a couple of the boys from the 35th who worked in a linen mill and they could help design machines that would give you a real export market in that area."

Vincent didn't mention the cotton plantations owned by Marcus and the other patricians. That issue was already a sore point between Roum and the Union men, since it was far too similar to the system they had fought a war against back home. It had already been decided by Kal and the members of his industrial committee to withhold information about the cotton gin for now, for with a such a machine the profitability of cotton would skyrocket and make any attempt at social change that much the harder.

"You certainly have plans for me," Marcus said evenly.

Vincent, deciding to ignore the sarcasm in Marcus's voice, continued, "Sir, it's a world of trade we're building with this railroad. I want to make sure you have certain advantages, because if you don't there's more than one young capitalist back in Rus who will take it himself."

"Capitalist?"

Vincent had heard Andrew talk about the writings of Adam Smith, and wished that somehow a copy of the book had come through with them so that he could translate it for Marcus. There seemed to be just too many things to be done. Here he was a soldier, a political leader, an ambassador, and now an economics teacher.

"I'll try to explain that later, sir," Vincent said quietly, sensing he was getting too far ahead. "But remember, I didn't tell you any of this."

Vincent Hawthorne grimaced inwardly at what he had just done. If Ferguson, Mina, and the others ever heard that one of their own had suggested that the railroad's monopoly on construction be broken, there'd be hell to pay. As the first ambassador to the consul and Senate of Roum, he felt, however, that he was simply fulfilling his duty, at least the duty of a good Quaker ambassador who felt that the first formal allies of the Republic of Rus should not be exploited.

The railroad project had seized his old comrades and the

Rus with nothing short of a full-blown passion, which was already transforming all aspects of Rus life. The mandate of the railroad was to continue pushing eastward with the dream of uniting all the former subjects of the Tugar horde into one vast alliance for trade and mutual protection. There was even talk of running another line westward when there was finally a pool of additional workers after the southwest fortifications and the military rail line in that direction had been completed, even though scouting reports indicated that for over a thousand miles the region to the west was nearly a ghost land, so devastating had been the effects of the Tugars and smallpox. Without the railroad and telegraph lines, Rus and all the other peoples of the endless northern steppes would be forever isolated and subject to attack.

Marcus and the Roum had yet to grasp the full import of what this strange machine would do for them. The sooner the Roum started building their own lines, Vincent now realized, and the sooner they gained control of internal trade as a result, the better off they'd be, and the better allies they'd be as well in the long run. It was something he had yet to discuss with Keane, but he had a gut feeling the colonel would agree.

"So I have not heard you suggest that I should start building my own railroads and become what you call a capitalist," Marcus replied with a shrewd smile.

Vincent did not reply and turned away to look at the work going on in the foundry. The laborers continued their toil as if their consul and the Yankee did not even exist, for to stop work in their presence would have the worst possible consequences. Vincent was repulsed by what he saw. There was no mechanization to speak of; all labor, right down to the manning of the bellows, was done by slaves. A contract had been let out to Marcus, who of course owned the foundry in his capital city, to supply spikes and tools for the line. Using slave labor to supply the railroad Vincent found to be morally objectionable, but he had to agree with Andrew that the first step was to make them part of the system, and then to work on changing what their system was.

Marcus looked over at Vincent and could see the look of disdain on his young open features as he watched the sweat-soaked laborers manning the bellows.

Everything was going far too fast for his liking. When the first Wanderers had come nearly two years earlier than usual, he had feared the worst, that the Tugars would soon be at his gates yet again. He had remembered their last visit and had ever since lived in dread of the return.

But the news the wanderers carried had been beyond belief. He had spurned at first the offering of the protection from the disfiguring pox, but when it was obvious that an epidemic was starting he had allowed the healers who had arrived from the land of the Rus to attempt a cure. Within weeks they had brought the epidemic under control. He tried to block out the memory—if only they had arrived earlier, his only son and the wife whom he had loved for thirty years would still be alive.

That was the beginning. A contingent of two hundred Rus warriors had arrived, bringing with them several of the blue-clad men called Yankees, and with their aid the tattered remnants of the Tugars had been driven off when as one patricians, plebs, and slaves rose up and fought with fanatical fury for a dream of forever overthrowing their hated lords.

From that Marcus found as he rose out of the shadow of personal pain that he could dare to dream, that now he could live beyond the shadow of fear, and that as in the legends of old, he would as a true patrician rule, with no Tugars to dread.

"I've had reports about the conversations your soldiers who came with you have been engaging in about the city," Marcus said quietly, leading Vincent back out into the street and away from the din of the workshop.

Vincent grimaced inwardly. He had known this was coming. Since their arrival in Roum yesterday the city had been wild with celebration at the appearance of the 5th Suzdal and the 2nd and 3rd Novrod light batteries. He knew how his men, who but a few years before had been slaves under the boyars, would react to what they saw. The difficult times that Andrew had counseled him about were now here. He wished that somehow it was Andrew who would handle these problems and that when the train had left Hispania to return back to Suzdal he had been aboard. It had been nearly two months since he had last seen Tanya and the children, and the enforced absence, which would last at least another several months before the twins were old enough to travel safely, weighed heavily upon him.

"I would guess that it has something to do with our politics," Vincent said evenly, looking straight back at Marcus.

The consul smiled at the guileless approach of the young ambassador, a quality he found to be wonderfully refreshing.

"Our treaty agreement said that there would be open trade between us, consul. We both know that we need each other now."

"Oh, I fully agree with that," Marcus replied. "There is no telling who will come against us, Tugars or their rival hordes to the south. I want your weapons, and you need our metals."

"But you don't want what our men say about equality and freedom."

Marcus smiled and shook his head.

"Even though they don't speak our tongue, or my people your language, still their feelings are already understood concerning our way of living."

"You know how I understand your language?" Vincent replied.

"It does seem a bit strange."

"We, the Yankees, came through the gate of light, the same as your ancestors did over two thousand years ago. Marcus, back in our old world, your Roum became legendary for its form of government. That is what we Yankees modeled our own system on."

Vincent had let drop the later history of the Roman Empire completely. Though lying was still a sin to him, he saw no moral problem with simple avoidance, since the ancestors of these people had apparently crossed through sometime during the old Carthaginian wars. As near as he could figure out from their legends, they had been part of a Roman fleet in the First Punic War that had disappeared, and after arriving here they had been given this land and women from other tribes by the Tugars, who, as they had all others that had passed through the gate, allowed them to grow and then started to harvest their descendants for food. It explained as well the undying rivalry with the Carthas to the south, who had crossed from the old world to this in the same tunnel.

Before Muzta had released him he had explained these things, telling him how without any pattern it appeared as if humans from half a dozen points around the world would occasionally be swept up, disappearing forever from earth and arriving here. So it had been for the Roum and Carthas.

Unlike the Rus, neither had ever traded. The prevailing south and westerly winds had discouraged any maritime efforts on the part of the Roum, for they had to cross up the long narrow bay leading to the Inland Sea. The undying enmity between the two peoples had held as well, and thus the Roum had built only enough ships to protect the entryway into the bay and large vessels to move grain from outlying districts back to the city. As it was, a ship running down from Rus could make but one voyage in a season, so difficult was the return voyage against the wind. And galleys were just not practical as cargo ships. The Roum interaction with the Carthas was limited to occasional pirating and no more, when the Tugars or Merki were not around.

"When you speak to me of this old world of ours," Marcus finally ventured, interrupting Vincent's thought, "you are saying we've forgotten our old ways, is that it?"

Motioning for Vincent to join him, Marcus stepped into his chariot, and together they clattered down the dockside lane of the city. The waterfront area was bursting with activity. Until last fall the city of Roum had been cut from the bay, since the Tiber River, which flowed along the east side of town, dropped through a final series of rapids. All shipping had to be unloaded at Ostia five miles to the south and brought up by wagons. It was a system, he realized, that perfectly mimicked ancient Rome, built at a similar point to protect it from coastal pirates. Andrew had decided to allocate several tons of precious powder along with a couple of Ferguson's engineering assistants to cut a canal with a single lock to bypass the drop-off. It was a goodwill gesture that had delighted Marcus and was rapidly changing the commercial life of the town. It had made an enemy in the Senate as well, since the city of Ostia was owned by a Petronius Regulus, who had now made it a habit to denounce any help, even the weapons the Rus might offer.

Marcus nodded with approval as they cantered along the new wharfs going up, the docks already lined with ships. Reaching the base of the hill, he turned the chariot west and started the long climb up toward the forum.

For the moment Vincent forgot their debate as the two massive horses trotted along the cobblestone road past a columned temple and the communal baths.

His one and only experience there last night had shocked his Quaker sensibilities to the core. When first offered a bath he had rejoiced that at least the Roum, unlike his Rus friends, felt that regular bathing was a fundamental right that should be observed regularly.

But disrobing and lolling about with hundreds of naked men had left him uneasy. The worst shock, though, was when he saw several men in a darkened alcove engaging in activities that he did not even know existed until that moment.

For once he let his ambassadorial front drop. The matter was made worse when Marcus indicated that if he was interested Vincent would certainly be welcome to join the group. Such things simply didn't happen in God-fearing Maine!

From now on, local custom be damned, he'd bathe in private.

"You are still upset about the bath," Marcus ventured, looking over at Vincent, who was staring at the building as if he expected a horned satan to come leaping out of the door.

"It's your custom, but not mine," Vincent said coldly, leaving out the part about damnation he had sputtered out when he had stormed out of the room.

"The same stands in both directions," Marcus rejoined, as if he had won a telling point.

"Sir, your practices when you are alone should be no concern of mine."

"Even though you find them disgusting."

"I did not say that."

"But you're thinking it," Marcus replied with a laugh.

Vincent, feeling he was definitely losing this one, did not reply.

"Perhaps I am being a bit unfair," Marcus said after several moments of silence. "But what your men are spreading about in our taverns and in our public amusement houses is certainly my concern, and to my fellow patricians and our free class of merchants and skilled craftsmen it is equally disgusting to contemplate."

That was another thing that worried him, Vincent thought sharply. In his walks about the city since their arrival, he had seen a number of establishments that were obviously havens for soiled doves, and more than one of his men had quickly ducked the other way at his approach.

"These difficulties go both ways," Marcus continued. "When that train track of yours comes into the heart of my capital in another two months, thousands of your people and mine will make a journey that not a handful made in a year.

"Though I need what you have, I do not want what your people seem so eager to give."

"A free government and the end to slavery," Vincent replied. "Marcus, the world is different now. The Tugars wanted you to rule through slavery—they did the same with the Rus, and with all the peoples of this world. But they are gone, and freedom is pushing in."

"And if I walked into my Senate right now and told the patricians, the estate owners, that their slaves could now vote, could now work as they pleased, I would not walk out of there alive."

Would it be this way with every city they came to? Vincent thought. Before, in Rus, it had seemed so easy. The boyars wanted the Yankees dead. The rebellion had been forced on them when the peasants spontaneously rose up against their hated masters. Vincent could sense that hatred was here as well; already the slaves he passed, and the whole damn city seemed to be full of slaves, were looking upon him with outright awe. Could he be part of instigating a rebellion that would kill yet more? Would they have to fight a revolution in every city, to advance sword in hand in an unending series of wars? Thousands would die, and the thought made him sick; he had had enough of killing to last a lifetime. Perhaps this was why Andrew had appointed him ambassador and Kal had confirmed him when he had become president. As a Quaker he had to find a better way than the sword he had carried before.

"Then we are presenting you with an unsolvable problem," Vincent replied evenly, hanging on as Marcus maneuvered the chariot through a tangle of traffic which scattered in every direction at the approach of the first consul.

"It's your job to figure out that answer," Marcus said coldly as they burst out of the thoroughfare and into the open plaza of the forum. Vincent smiled in wonder at the sight. The buildings flanking the acre-size square were all of limestone. The forum was faced with fluted columns and surmounted by a dome atop which was the marble figure of Jove.

Marcus's palace across the square stood out brilliant white in the afternoon sun. The other sides of the square were faced by the smaller palaces of the twenty families that ruled the vast domain and nearly two million inhabitants of Roum. Unlike the Rus, the Roum had never fallen into an unending rivalry between boyars but had always stayed united under one consul, a position passed down unbroken from father to son for hundreds of years.

That alone had given Vincent pause in all his musings about the political job before him. At least among the boyars the rivalries had enabled the Yankees to survive at first and helped to set the seeds for the revolution. There were no such rivalries here to play on, nor was there a church; though at first the Rus church had been an enemy, it had now become a staunch ally of the republic. Beyond that the Roum simply outnumbered the Rus by more than three to one, since they had not suffered the ravages of the war.

If they should teach Roum how to arm and in the end it became a hostile power, the difficulties might be insurmountable. Vincent could sense they were in a delicate time, when the novelty of this new contact and the sense of freedom from the Tugars created an openness between the two countries. One wrong move could change all of that, setting a precedent that could doom forever the dream of unification and manifest destiny. There were seeds here for a serious problem in the future, offset for now by superior technology, but even that might be balanced out in time.

"I'm going in now to face my senators and listen to their ravings about your men inciting servile rebellion," Marcus said, in what to Vincent's surprise was an almost warm manner.

"Marcus, you've only seen the beginning of what free men can create," Vincent replied, taking hold of the consul's arm.

"Is that a threat?"

"No, sir, a promise of what Roum could be. Would you agree that slaves in general are a lazy, shiftless lot, ready to cheat, to steal, to do the least amount of work whenever possible?"

"Of course," Marcus laughed. "They are lower than scum and dumber than my horse."

Vincent winced inwardly, for the slaves who with wooden faces came forward to hold the chariot acted as if they had heard nothing.

"All of the Rus soldiers, you see, were slaves. The men building the railroad were slaves, our army that destroyed the Tugars were former slaves. Now you see the most industrious people on the face of this world. Every day in Rus, a free man, a former slave, mind you, looks at how something is done. He thinks of a better way of doing it, a new machine perhaps, and eagerly he sets out to improve something."

"Whatever for?" Marcus asked, unable to understand such thinking.

"Because he is a free man. If he makes something better he'll make money. Every time someone does that, it makes our people stronger, wealthier, all of us living better than before. Our government taxes little, it tries not to interfere in people's actions, for it knows that if it did that it would weaken itself as well. That is the secret of our strength, Marcus, and it could be the source of your strength as well. Think about that, Marcus. Your people could be that industrious."

Marcus paused for a moment and looked at Vincent as if he had spoken an impossibility.

"Your landholders could tax your people instead of taking from them. If people believed that they could work for what they owned, they'd produce three, four times as much, and you and your senators would not lose anything in the process.

"And if we allowed the mob to represent themselves their first act would be to drive us out," Marcus retorted.

"With our help you could draft laws that would allow your families certain rights to guarantee their wealth, in return for the freedom of everyone.

"As in your legendary Rome of the old world, or a country like our own called England, we could have two representative groups, one for the patricians and one for the common people. Both groups would have to agree upon a law before it could be passed. That would be fair to everybody. There could be two consuls as well, one from each group, who would act in agreement."

Vincent groaned inwardly at what he had just offered, a guarantee to a landed aristocracy to continue to exist. If Tom Jefferson were here, he thought sadly, the man would most likely tear him apart. Being an abolitionist was becoming far harder than he had ever imagined.

"We've got plenty of time to discuss this later," Marcus announced as the lictors, bearing their ceremonial bundles, came out of the Senate and lined the stairs for the consul. "For right now I've got more immediate concerns. We'll talk again tonight."

Turning away, Marcus started up the steps, then paused and looked back at Vincent.

"It's terribly hot out. Why don't you go to the baths?"

"I'd rather go to your palace," Vincent snapped back, unable to hide a tone of peevishness.

Laughing, Marcus continued on his way.

Shaking his head, Vincent jumped down from the chariot, and waving off the escort of a slave carrying an umbrella against the sun, he stalked across the square back toward his quarters in Marcus's palace.

Play the game out a card at a time, he thought. Let the aristocracy have their land. But it'll be industry that drives this economy in a couple of years. As the railroad pushes on eastward to the land of the Khitai, and Nippon beyond, Roum will be a major center for the new industries. The small group of plebs and eventually the freed slaves will flock to that, and they can build their power from there. Introducing farming machines will create a vast surplus of labor, the same as it has in Rus, freeing men to work in the new industries. The key trick is to let the nobles continue to view involvement with these new trades as beneath their dignity and they'll die on the vine like English nobility.

Relaxing a bit, Vincent started to smile. Suddenly he realized that there was a shadow around him, and looking to his side he saw that the slave had come up behind him still bearing the umbrella.

"Close that damn thing up," Vincent snapped, and the slave, obviously frightened, did as commanded.

Cursing again, he thought angrily. He had yet to shake that habit.

"What's your name?" Vincent asked, looking back at the slave.

"Julius, noble one," the slave stammered. "Household servant of my lord Marcus."

The man was nearly the same height as Vincent, something that made him feel comfortable, for nearly all of the Roum except for the patricians were of smaller stature and build than the Rus. Julius's hair was graying at the temples, and his face was tanned dark and craggy with lines. His arms were slender but knotted like stretched whipcord. Julius looked at him with awe, as if he were a god, and the gaze made Vincent uncomfortable.

"What do you know about me?" Vincent asked.

"That you are a Tugar-slayer, the new master of the Rus, most noble one."

Vincent leaned back and laughed, and Julius smiled nervously, obviously relieved that he had answered correctly.

"You have a family, Julius?"

"Yes, noble one. My wife, Calpurnia, and four children."

"I've just had twin girls," Vincent announced proudly, and reaching into his breast pocket he pulled out a miniature portrait of his family that Andrew had presented to him after the track-laying ceremony.

Julius looked at the portrait and smiled obediently.

"May the gods bless them and you," Julius said.

Vincent bristled inwardly. This man was so frightened of him that all he could do was grovel. Pulling out a handkerchief, he lifted his kepi and wiped the sweat from his brow, and then a thought formed.

Smiling, Vincent put his hand on Julius's shoulder.

"Come on, Julius, let's go back to the palace and we'll sit down and have a drink in my quarters."

"You'll have a drink of wine with me, noble one?" Julius asked, incredulous.

"Certainly. Why shouldn't I? You look like you could use one."

"I am your servant, to keep the sun from your brow and also to act as your bodyguard."

"Well, damn it all, man, where I come from that doesn't mean we can't have a good drink together. Tell me, does your Calpurnia cook a good meal?"

"The finest, noble sir. She works in the kitchen of my lord."

"Well, let's get a bit drunk, then see if we can persuade her to cook dinner for me and we'll sit down in the kitchen and eat it."

Julius looked at him in disbelief. "But noble sir, you are a guest of the noble Marcus—you should eat at his table, not in the quarters of slaves."

"Don't worry about that," Vincent replied, trying to keep

the exasperation out of his voice. Forcing a smile, he put his hand on Julius's shoulder.

Vincent noticed the beginning of a genuine smile lighting Julius's features.

He tried to argue with himself that this was after all an excellent means of finding out more about how the common people viewed the arrival of the Rus. But inwardly he knew he was failing again. He could stop the cursing someday, but damnit, ever since a round of evenings with Pat O'Donald, wine did have a certain appeal. The thought of his parents, let alone his church elders, seeing him breaking yet again the Temperance Pledge was enough to give him a wonderful sense of guilt. He could just imagine Elder Gates coming in and with a shout of outrage attempting to drag him out by his ear.

"Why are you laughing, noble sir?" Julius asked, unable to hide his curiosity.

"There's no way I could possibly explain it," Vincent said with a smile.

Reaching the steps of the palace, Vincent strode up the white limestone stairs. Pausing at the top, he looked back across the sunbaked square. It was nearly noon. A lazy sense of relaxation seemed to float in the air, the merchant stalls were closed, windows were shuttered to keep out the heat, and all, except for the ever-toiling slaves, had disappeared into their courtyards or baths until the coolness of late afternoon settled in.

Rubbing his hand against the back of his collar, he felt as if he were drenched clean through with sweat. Wrinkling his nose, he knew that there was a decidedly unpleasant odor around him.

"Julius."

"Yes, noble sir?"

"Before that drink and a meal, could I trouble you to arrange a bath, and maybe have my uniform cleaned?"

"Of course, noble sir," Julius snapped, and closing his umbrella he motioned for Vincent to follow him through the main doors into Marcus's palace.

The heavy bronze doors appeared to swing open as if by their own power as he approached, and the effect gave him a bit of a pleasant chill, even though he knew that two servants stood behind the barrier at all times, their sole job to open and close the doors. It was a terrible waste of labor, he felt.

Julius raced ahead and spoke quickly to the majordomo, who scurried off. The arched corridor into the courtyard was deliciously cool, and he took off his kepi and unbuttoned his collar.

Stepping into the inner courtyard, Vincent looked around at the opulent splendor. The garden was a good thirty yards square, filled with fragrant splashes of flowers, trees burdened with a delectable fruit, pinkish in hue and unique it seemed to this world. A light misty spray floated down over the garden, and walking into the courtyard he looked up at this unique marvel. A latticework of pipes filled the open space above the second floor. He knew that down in the basement a gang of slaves labored over pumps, forcing water through the pipes under pressure to jet out of thousands of tiny holes in a light spray to cool the air. Even as he enjoyed the effect he felt a touch of guilt knowing that men slaved to give him this momentary pleasure.

The noonday sun was blocked out by a vast awning raised up on poles like a giant sail reaching across the broad open space, the light filtering through, giving a soft diffused glow. The colonnaded walkways of the second floor were a perfect match of symmetry of marble and darkly polished wooden rails. All of this vast palace for but one man, he thought sadly. He could sense the emptiness of the house, the emptiness inside of Marcus, though more than a hundred labored here to fulfill his every wish.

Bowing low, the majordomo reappeared and whispered to Julius, who had stood respectfully to one side.

"Your bath is ready, noble sir," Julius announced. "I will go to the kitchen to see to your meal personally."

"You're joining me for it, of course, and the drinks as well?" Vincent asked.

The majordomo looked up in shock.

"If you so wish it, noble sir."

"Of course I do," Vincent said, trying to keep his temper in check, "and Julius, my name is Vincent, not noble sir."

Flustered, Julius bowed low and scurried away.

"This way, noble sir," the majordomo whispered.

Vincent was tempted to explain the rules of how to be addressed to this man as well, but gave it up with a sigh.

Going out the east side of the courtyard, Vincent followed the majordomo down an open corridor paved with an intricate display of colored tiles depicting what he thought might be a scene from the myth of Prometheus. Perhaps we are the new Prometheus, he thought with a smile.

The servant opened the door before him, and Vincent stepped into a small chamber, dimly lit by a single window, covered with a heavy pane of amber glass. A small pool was in the middle of the room. The tiles on the floor and walls showed scenes of fish and undersea creatures.

"Your clothes, sir," the majordomo asked.

Feeling a bit self-conscious, Vincent disrobed, the servant helping him to pull off his boots, which he felt was a major source of embarrassment, the heavy wool socks giving off a decidedly gamey aroma. He hesitated as he got down to underwear, but the servant stood before him hand outstretched.

Dropping his eyes, Vincent pulled the garment off and handed it over.

"Fresh breeches and a shirt of silk in the style of your people await you over there, my lord," the servant announced, pointing to the change of clothes.

"Those aren't mine," Vincent replied lamely.

"They were cut to your size and sewn for you this morning, my lord, at the express orders of my master. You'll find them to be more comfortable for occasions when you do not need your uniform."

Vincent looked over at them and felt himself give way to the temptation. He had worn his officer's uniforms, made for him by Tanya, for months on end. It would be pleasant to get out of the heavy wool for a change.

The majordomo bowed and withdrew, and Vincent slipped into the cool bath with a sigh. He floated languidly for several minutes. Hell, back home the winter bath had been in a narrow tin tub set next to the kitchen stove, usually with a cold chill blowing in under the door. This was like paradise. Stretching out in the pool, he dipped under the water and came back up.

"May I scrub your back for you?"

With a start he looked over his shoulder and saw a slim, tall girl with long black hair standing behind him. Her almond-colored eyes looked at him with open amusement. Her lips were parted in a sensual smile, accentuated by the deep-set dimples in her ivory cheeks.

Stunned, Vincent could not help but stare at her for several seconds before his senses returned.

"Get out of here, woman!"

A flash of disappointment crossed her features.

"You are not angry with me?" she whispered.

"No, damnit, but please leave."

"This is my job," she whispered softly. "If you are unhappy with what I do and send me away, Antonius will beat
me."

"Antonius?"

"The head servant. He ordered me to attend to you."

"I'm a married man," Vincent gasped.

The girl laughed.

"I'll not violate you, if that is your concern," she said,
"Just look straight ahead and let me wash your back. I'll use
a brush and not even touch you. It will feel wonderful. Have
you ever had it done before?"

"Actually, no," he whispered. The thought was certainly
appealing, he tried to reason. Tanya, like most of the Rus,
certainly did not take bathing as something that was al-
together necessary, and having his back scrubbed was a
temptation hard to resist.

"Nothing else, just my back," Vincent whispered, feeling
guilty about it but reasoning that it would not harm his
immortal soul or violate his Christian character in any serious way.

"Then sit up and move forward," the girl said with a
laugh.

Moving to the edge of the pool, he sat on a narrow stone
bench and leaned over to cover himself. There was a splash
of water behind him, and he held his breath as a gentle
sponge ran up and down his back. The motion of the sponge
was replaced by a soft bristled brush, and he sighed with
contentment as the girl worked it up over his shoulders and
across his neck. For long minutes she continued to scrub
him, and he felt as if the dirt of years were being pulled up
out of his pores. His body tingled with this wonderful new
sensation.

He barely noticed it when her hands began working the
kinks out of his neck and shoulders, and then scrubbing his
hair, the soapy water running down around him. All the
time she kept up a light prattle of talk that he barely paid
attention to as he felt as if he would gradually melt away.

"Shall I do the rest of you?" she whispered.

"Huh?" He roused himself out of the drifting sensation
that had enveloped him.

"The rest of you, noble sir," and he suddenly realized that there was a wonderful scent around him, with long strands of wet dark hair cascading down around his shoulders.

Startled, he turned to look back.

She was kneeling behind him, her full naked breasts dancing before his eyes, the dark red nipples taut with excitement.

"My God in heaven," Vincent gasped, even as she nimbly moved forward, pressing his head into the soft ivory mounds.

He could feel a sudden surge of excitement grow inside him. It had been months since he had been with Tanya, and the inner tension was a near-constant torment. For a brief second he was tempted to let go, to press his arms around her and pull her into the pool.

And I'll betray her and burn in my own torment.

"I'm a happily married man," Vincent gasped, pulling back.

"So, all men have their consorts," the girl giggled.

"Not this one!" Vincent shouted, pulling back.

The girl looked at him in confusion.

Like Venus rising out of the ocean, she stood up, exposing her full charms.

"Don't you find me desirable?"

"I certainly do," he gasped, unable to lie.

She looked down into the water, and her eyes came up again to lock on his.

"I thought for a second maybe you preferred men, but I can see that I am exciting you."

Horrified, Vincent realized just how exposed he was as well, and he quickly backed out of the pool and grabbed a towel to wrap tightly around his waist.

"Look, I think you're beautiful. It's just that where I come from a man makes a vow to one woman and keeps it. If a man or woman breaks that vow it's terribly wrong."

She looked at him intently.

"Are you serious?"

"I love my wife. If I did something like this it'd break her heart and mine as well. I couldn't live with the shame of it."

He had learned how to drink, to swear, and to kill, and at the moment he felt a terrible tormenting drive to lie with this woman and the hell with what was left of his ethics. He kept trying to force up the image of Tanya in his mind, the look in her eyes if she ever found out. She trusted him more than anyone in the world. He could not break that trust.

"Please," Vincent whispered, "the temptation of you is driving me crazy."

The girl nodded and stepped out of the pool. She quickly slipped back into her robe, which clung provocatively to her wet body.

"Actually, noble sir, I think there's something wonderfully nice about your saying no like this," and with a graceful bow she left the room.

"Merciful God," Vincent gasped. He dropped the towel and leaped back into the pool, the cool water helping him to calm back down. He knew the damn girl was now going to haunt him.

"Tanya, I wish the hell you'd get here," he snapped, and climbing out of the water he toweled off and put on the new clothes.

They felt wonderfully soft, almost as if he were wearing nothing at all. He slipped on the sandals, which were a curious sensation, and left the room. Going back down the corridor, he turned for the kitchen area in the back of the palace, lured by the wonderful scents.

Opening the doors, he strode in. The servants looked up in startled surprise.

"Over here, noble sir," Julius said, proudly pointing to a set table.

"It's Vincent."

"Ah yes, noble Vincent," the servant said.

Giving up, Vincent settled into the chair and poured his own wine before Julius had the chance. In the far corners the other servants looked over at this strange spectacle and whispered to themselves.

Raising his goblet, he looked over at Julius, who nervously returned the gesture.

"To the friendship between the common people of Rus and Roum," Vincent said loudly.

Julius, smiling openly, nodded in reply, and the two drained their cups.

He looked at the repast spread out before him. There were several dishes of baked fish, and another of thin strips of meat smothered in mushrooms.

"It all looks delightful."

"Go ahead and start, noble Vincent."

"Not until your wife joins us."

Julius looked at him curiously.

"Come on now, fetch her over here and then we can start."

Julius motioned to a heavyset woman standing nervously by an open oven. Cautiously, she approached the table.

"My name is Vincent Hawthorne. What's yours?"

"Calpurnia, noble sir," she whispered.

"Where I come from, a man and his wife eat together, especially when they have company. Please sit down and join us."

He could see that she was almost shaking as she sat down on the opposite bench and looked back at her friends.

"How was your bath, noble Vincent?" Julius asked with a smile.

"Ah, different," Vincent replied woodenly.

Julius started to laugh softly.

"We already heard," and Calpurnia looked up at him and shook her head even as she smiled.

Vincent found he was starting to blush.

"I guess our customs are different from yours in more ways than one," Vincent said lamely.

"Yes. I think we will find that quite interesting," Julius replied, still smiling.

Vincent refilled his goblet and had started to take another drink when he felt something brush behind him.

"Ah, my daughter, Olivia," Julius said with a smile.

Vincent looked up and a second later felt as if he were choking, as he sprayed the contents of his goblet across the table.

"Your daughter?" Vincent gasped.

Julius leaned back and started to laugh as the girl, smiling innocently, sat down by Vincent, her dark hair still wet and shiny.

"Noble Vincent, you Yankees are certainly different," Julius said, wiping the tears from his eyes. "And I must say perhaps an interesting change."

Oh God, this job is going to be hell, Vincent thought, unable to reply.

# Chapter Three

Cromwell looked at the group and felt a ripple of apprehension. Of Jubadi and Muzta he already knew their intentions. If this campaign did not work as planned, the damned beasts would slaughter all of them. For that matter, he half suspected they'd most likely slaughter them anyhow even if they won. Only a fool would trust Tugars, Merki, or whatever it was the beasts called themselves.

Looking over at Hamilcar, leader of the Carthas, he could sense an ally in that concern at least. They were playing for time and knew it. There had to be a chink in their system which he could exploit. If worst came to worst he could always take the *Ogunquit* the hell out of here along with Jamie and the others. He would lose his Suzdalian and Yankee crew, they were being left behind for this campaign, but that would be their problem, not his.

Hamilcar returned his gaze without comment. All that needed to be said between them had already been said. At least the Merki would not feed upon him this year, and for that he thanked Baalk, to whom he had offered his last-born son in tribute for the reprieve. Everything that could be learned would be learned.

"The plan, then, is simple," Cromwell began, pointing to the map spread out on the table before the group.

"Tomorrow our fleet sets sail, my *Ogunquit*, eighteen gunboats, two mortar boats, Jamie's ships, and over a hundred and fifty Cartha ships. Aboard will be over twenty thousand men, the ships' cannons, thirty field guns, and three thousand muskets. We should reach Roum within seven days. Taking the city with modern weapons should be not too difficult.

"But we will not, at least in the beginning."

Hamilcar shook his head with disdain.

"You do not agree with our plan," Jubadi said coldly.

"We could take it with ease," Hamilcar replied.

"That is not what we want for the first several days. We are after bigger game," Tobias retorted. "Remember our goal is to bring Keane and his precious army out of the city. If Roum is under threat, they will rush to help. If the city falls at once, especially after our people declare themselves, Keane will not drive straight in. I know Keane and how he thinks. He'll act with near-fanatical determination as long as the fall of the city is a threat and not an accomplished fact. Our goal is to bring him out into the steppe."

Tobias pointed to the town of Hispania and the marker indicating the farthest extent of the railroad.

"Bring him to here and a day's march beyond."

With a dramatic flourish, he slammed his fists down on either side.

"And then cut him off. We'll show him how fragile a rail line really is. We'll strike first by burning their largest bridge. Five hundred raiders—that will be under Jamie and Hinsen. They can tear up track for miles behind him, leaving him stranded. The forces in Suzdal who are with us already know their parts. We'll force Roum over to our side just before he arrives, and then we will move out of Roum by ship, swing across, and take Rus behind him.

"Before he can return, Suzdal will be in our hands."

Jubadi nodded approvingly.

"There'll be some extra warriors going with you," Jubadi said quietly and looked over at Hulagar.

Tobias, unable to show his surprise, gazed suspiciously at Hulagar.

"I am sending Hulagar, my sons, some guards, and the Zan Qarth's shield-bearer along."

"My lord Jubadi," Tobias said quickly, "the key to our attempt is to not let anyone know that we are supported by you. The sight of a single Merki could change all of that."

"They will remain hidden throughout," Jubadi said sharply, his tone indicating that there would be no debate. "You have much to attend to before tomorrow morning, Tobias Cromwell. You and your men had best see to the final arrangements."

Tobias stood and looked nervously at Jubadi. The last-minute addition was disquieting. He tried to look Jubadi in the eyes, but again, as always, there was that sense of a taunting gaze, a judgment. He looked away and without comment stalked out of the room.

"He is not pleased," Hulagar said, laughing softly.

"Did he actually expect that we would let him build these ships and then go sailing off? The contingent will stay aboard the *Ogunquit* at all times."

"It is worse than the lower regions of torment down there," Hulagar said, shaking his head and reaching over to fill his goblet with Cartha wine.

Hulagar hesitated for a moment.

"Something is bothering you," Jubadi asked softly.

"It is not your other two sons, my Qarth, it is the Zan, Vuka."

"I want you there to learn, to observe all that happens in this new way of war. Vuka will someday be Qar Qarth. I want him to be there, to see how these cattle weapons can be fought."

"To send all three of your sons of the first consort," Hulagar said softly, "perhaps it is not the wisest to risk your lineage in such a manner."

Jubadi smiled and shook his head.

"I had three brothers. One died when thrown from his mount, the other two at Orki. It is the risk of all of us. I want all three of them there.

"And of course my shield-bearer, and the bearer of Vuka will be there as well."

"Vuka might not be easy with being trapped inside the furnace of that ship," Hulagar said, knowing he was pressing the argument.

"Then he must learn," Jubadi snapped impatiently.

Hulagar lowered his head in acknowledgment. He knew that in his position as shield-bearer he could perhaps force the argument, but the inner voice, the ka-tu known only to those who were shield-bearers of the Qarths, spoke differently. Perhaps it would be a testing for Vuka, to better learn endurance and, most important, patience.

"Just remember that Tamuka is his shield-bearer, not you," Jubadi said. "So do not interfere, my friend."

It was rare that Jubadi referred to him as a friend, and he could sense that the Qar Qarth was uneasy with his decision as well.

"Watch Tobias closely," Jubadi said, shifting the subject. "He is a coward, as are most cattle, so I have no fear that he will turn. After all, he believes that if he wins he will rule Rus on his own."

"Perhaps we should have told him in the beginning that we would occupy the town after he has taken it, and that the Tugars if they live to their promise will close on the eastern flank of Roum."

Jubadi shook his head.

"He can still rule, as we have always had cattle rule over our subjects. But I sense that these northern cattle would fight to the death if they knew we were coming as well. We must let them weaken each other first. Once they are under this Cromwell, and the buildings to make more weapons are secure, then we shall move in. He must not know. If he did, he might grow suspicious and perhaps even flee with the most dangerous weapon upon all the water of the sea. Let him finish this task first, and take control. By then my sons will know the ways of war and can take the ships to attack the Bantag on their own.

"Don't forget that when it comes to battle decisions, let him make them. He understands this new war better than I, and you, my friend, are a shield-bearer, not a warrior."

Hulagar nodded in reply, taking no offense, for Jubadi was right, he was not a warrior, he was far more, the controlling spirit of a Qar Qarth.

"Now send in the Zan Qarth. I must speak to my eldest son before he leaves."

Hulagar stood up, bowed low, and left the room. Had he heard the inner whispers correctly? he wondered. There was the faintest murmuring in his soul that the plan which had looked so flawless in all its complexities had somehow been altered onto a path he could not yet foresee.

"And I say that how you propose to spend this money is complete foolishness!"

Inwardly Andrew cursed the whole concept of democracy from top to bottom. It was bad enough that he had to appear before this Senate to argue the military side of the budget, but to take a grilling from the man across from him was almost more than he could stomach.

Mikhail, the senator from Psov, looked at him with open contempt.

"Senator," Andrew said evenly, trying to hide his building anger, "until such time as we are certain that the Tugars are truly gone and that the hordes to the south have swept eastward as well, we need to continue to arm, to improve our weapons, and to be ready for any and all possibilities."

"And bleed ourselves white in the process!"

"You forget, Mikhail Ivorovich, that it was the army under this man that saved us," Ilya of Suzdal growled, stepping forward from his desk to stand by Andrew's side. "But then again, you were serving on the other side."

"You bastard," Mikhail snarled.

"Senators, senators!"

Andrew slammed the gavel on his ornately carved table for attention. Ilya glared at Mikhail and returned to his desk.

"The issues of the war are past," Andrew said, as if lecturing to a roomful of children. "Remember, this is a Senate debate on the military budget, so let us please stick to the topic."

Sitting back down, Andrew looked about the room. This damn thing would have been a lot easier if Mikhail and the other boyars who had won election were simply dead, he thought grimly, regretting yet again his declaration of a complete amnesty for all those who took the oath of allegiance to the new Republic of Rus. He felt it to be a proper Lincolnesque gesture, which Kal, positioning himself to run for president, had fully agreed to. He knew that back home, once the war was over Lincoln would do the same, unlike so many heads of state who massacred the losing side and laid the groundwork of hatred for the next generation to fan into another conflagration. If the precedent was set now, it might very well help to hold the republic together long after they were all gone.

No one had expected that Mikhail, Boyar Ivor's half brother, would still be alive. It was only after the amnesty had been offered that he had emerged from hiding. Worse yet, he then proceeded to carry the town of Psov as a senator in an election which had obviously been bought.

Of the thirty-eight senators in their single-house legislature, eight were former boyars. The more radical revolutionary zeal had firmly taken hold in Suzdal and the now partially rebuilt Novrod. In the remote districts of Rus the peasants who had survived the pox and Tugar occupation had little understanding of their new government and thus simply voted in their old rulers. It would take the linking of these areas into the rail system, and a lot of education, Andrew realized, before they would understand just how badly they were now being served by representatives interested only in preserving some of their former power.

Andrew leaned back in his chair and surveyed the assembly. As vice-president under Kal he found himself in the curious position of running the Senate even as he testified, but the running was more like being a teacher, constantly interpreting and explaining the fundamental basics of a parliamentary system to men who had no tradition or knowledge of such a system. It had all sounded so idealistic and easy in theory but was sheer hell in practice. He found himself wondering what Tom Jefferson would say to all of this.

"I demand satisfaction for what Ilya said here. One such as he has no right. He is nothing but a peasant, as was his father and grandsire before him," Mikhail shouted, refusing to sit back down.

"But you are a bastard," Petrov, Kal's cousin and senator from one of the north wards of Suzdal, taunted in reply. "Your brother Ivor Weak Eyes, now he was born on the right side of the bed, but not you!"

"Senators!" Andrew brought the gavel down with such strength that the handle was sheared off, sending the hammer spinning out into the middle of the room.

The action at least brought a gale of laughter from the public gallery and a moment of silence on the floor.

"Senators," Andrew said softly as the laughter died away.

"Now first of all. The discussion of lineage as a means of insult is beneath the dignity of senators," Andrew stated with an admonishing tone.

Petrov looked at Andrew, his anger still showing, and sat back down.

"On the other side, everyone has a right to speak and say what he wants, outside the realm of personal insult. Station of birth no longer applies in this republic. One becomes a senator no matter who his father was."

Mikhail glared at Andrew and said nothing as a round of applause from the gallery, and from the common-born senators, thundered through the room.

"Next," Andrew said sharply, looking up at the gallery. "This is a meeting of your Senate and will not be interfered with. It is always open to the public, but if we allow you to shout and make comments, then in the end this room will be ruled by a mob. I will not tolerate such outbursts. If you have comments you may speak to your senators outside this room."

The citizens in the gallery looked at each other sheepishly and fell silent.

"Good. Does everyone understand the rules?" Andrew asked in his best professorial voice.

The men around him nodded their heads, some eagerly, like students excited with their subject, but the former boyars sitting around Mikhail simply looked about the room with open disdain.

"Fine. Now as secretary of war I was being questioned by Senator Mikhail of Psov about the proposed military budget for next year. Senator, do you wish to continue your questioning?"

"I think your idea for how much taxes are to be spent is nothing but lies."

Andrew bristled inside, fighting to control his temper, and he could see that Mikhail was truly enjoying taunting him like this.

"You say that it is lies. Would you care to explain," Andrew replied softly, looking over at Hans, who as general of the Suzdalian forces was white with anger.

"That President Kal is calling for what you call dollars, four million dollars in taxes."

"That is correct, President Kalencka has requested such a sum."

"Of which almost all of it, three out of four dollars, goes for your army and its projects."

"The army of the Republic of Rus," Andrew snapped coldly, "not my army, senator."

"Nearly two million of that sum goes for these factories, as you call them, to turn out yet more things, these rails and trains, which you also place with the army."

"That is correct. The rails will be so we can move men

and weapons quickly if ever our borders are threatened. As you know, we now have a treaty with the Roum, which almost all of you agreed to. When the rail line is completed, entire armies can be moved hundreds of miles in a matter of days, outracing even the speed of the horse-mounted hordes."

"And remember Manifest Destiny," Vasilia interjected. "It is a good dream, to spread what we are around the world, uniting all men under one system, free of boyar and of Tugar."

"Vasilia, you are out of order," Andrew said, even as he was thankful to hear his support.

"He is always out of order," Gavelo, former boyar of Nizhil, snapped, looking to Mikhail like a servant to his master.

"It is a means for certain men to get rich while others suffer," Mikhail said coldly. "Your factories have driven almost all the old ironmakers, the swordmakers, out of business, and made them poor. Already we have heard how Roum merchants will travel here, selling their cheap trinkets and driving yet hundreds more into destitution. Hundreds of merchants now look upon empty shops. Yet the circle of Yankees who run these new businessess and those who are friends of Kalencka grow rich, not only from the tax money, but from the profits that come from these factories."

The tack of Mikhail's argument caught Andrew off-guard. Why was this man sounding like a champion for interests not directly related to boyar concerns?

"The factories and railroads are owned by everyone, all citizens of Rus. The men who design and work them, Rus and Yankee, are paid by the government. Remember as well that all who work there are part of the army as well, yet paid to do work we all need. As time passes and the threat of the hordes disappears, we will change this, and if anyone wishes to set up his own factories he may do so. Anyone may do so. In fact, if a group of Rus citizens wanted to make rails and sell them to the government for a rate cheaper than we can now make them, all of us would be happy."

"Rubbish. You are already too powerful. I am therefore proposing two things here. One, that the budget for your army be cut in half immediately. The Tugars are gone, and we have no need for these new weapons your factories make. Next I demand that you end at once the requirement that all men must now drill one day of the week with weapons and for four weeks during the winter, for it is senseless to waste their effort. Finally, I demand that your government sell the factories to any who can bid the most for them."

"If you wish to do so," Andrew said coldly, "you may propose these changes at any time. First you must write what is called a bill and read it formally to all here."

"Another Yankee trick. Only they can read," Mikhail barked. "What need do boyars have of reading?"

"It is how the government runs," Andrew retorted. "Someday everyone will read. For those senators who cannot, we have scribes and readers. That is the law."

"The law you dictated when you set this government up."

Christ, I should have killed him, Andrew groaned inwardly.

"The Constitution and Bill of Rights cannot be changed," Andrew said evenly. "They shall always stand as they are."

That at least was one point he had lied about when he had sat down to frame the government charter. He realized from the beginning that he would have to create something absolute; otherwise, with the Rus's lack of experience, some strange monstrosity might evolve. Maybe on his `deathbed he'd tell them about amendments, but not before. At least for now the bluff was working.

Mikhail looked around for support and saw that beyond his small circle there was none forthcoming.

"After you or your appointed scribe reads your proposal, copies will be given to all senators. For one month it will be debated, unless a majority wishes to make the debate longer. This will give time for all citizens to be informed so they can make comments to their senators."

That at least was working, Andrew thought with some satisfaction. In this first year of the government the senators felt they must talk to their people before voting on anything. He could only hope this old intent of representative government would last.

"After all of that, you senators will vote. Then President Kalencka will decide to sign the bill or not. If he refuses to sign, you must vote by a two-thirds majority to defeat him."

"See, it is stacked against us. This whole thing you call democracy is a sham to trick the peasants about who the new boyars are," Mikhail snapped, and with a snort of disdain he rose up and stormed out of the room, the other former boyars following.

Andrew waited for the assembly to settle down and then looked about the Senate floor. It was almost noon anyhow, and Mikhail was simply grandstanding again. It was obvious Mikhail had timed his walkout when there was only a brief time left for the session anyhow. He had made the mistake of storming out before an important vote on railroad appropriations and had learned from the mistake.

"Gentlemen, the Senate is adjourned until tomorrow morning."

Taking the handle of his gavel, he struck the edge of his table and then leaned back with a sigh.

"Son of a bitch, I should have shot him when I had the chance," Hans growled, as he leaned over the table and shot a spray of tobacco juice into the small spittoon he had brought in for the hearing.

"My sentiments as well," Andrew said. "Ah well, democracy in action. I bet Abe must have wished the same more than once.

"What's on for this afternoon?" Andrew sighed, looking back to John Bullfinch, former lieutenant of the *Ogunquit* and now his personal adjutant and secretary. The boy had turned into an excellent aide, the one crew member of Cromwell's who had refused to desert.

"Let's see," Bullfinch said in his high-pitched voice, Adam's apple bobbing up and down. "Sir, you have a meeting with President Kalencka at two. Then an inspection tour of the new musket rifling works at three. Next, sir—"

"Next he has time with his wife."

With a smile, Andrew looked up. Sweeping past Andrew, she leaned over Bullfinch's shoulder and with a flourish picked up his pen and drew a line through the page.

"Meetings canceled by order of myself and the president. Kal ordered you to take the afternoon off," Kathleen said, shaking her finger at Andrew. Her green eyes sparkled with a mischievous light as she stepped past Bullfinch and came up to put her arms around Andrew.

"If I were president I would have had that Mikhail arrested and hung from the gate," Kathleen said sharply, looking over to Hans for support.

"Kathleen, it is a republic we've got here."

"And you were military dictator for over a year before that."

"Not any longer," Andrew sighed.

"Well, if you had given women the right to vote from the start, he'd have never made office."

"I think it's time for me to leave," Hans replied, rising to his feet.

"Hans Schuder, I don't know why you don't agree with me on this. With your influence I might have been able to persuade my husband to put that into the Constitution."

"I'm just a soldier, ma'am. Politics ain't my business," Hans replied lamely.

"A likely excuse," Kathleen replied with a grin. "But anyhow, my dear," she continued to Andrew, "you promised me a jaunt out of town a week ago. I've got the carriage outside, and I'm not taking no for an answer."

Andrew stood and looked down at his wife's figure with concern.

"I'm still nearly two months away, and Emil said the fresh air would do me good."

"Well, it looks like I've got my marching orders," Andrew said with a mock sigh.

Extending his arm to Kathleen, he left the Senate chamber, and passing down the main corridor of the capitol he paused for a moment before the doorway into the presidential offices, but she pulled him away and out through the open doors onto the broad steps facing the great square.

Suzdal was vibrant with life. A summer shower had washed through the town early in the morning, and with its passing a cooling breeze had risen up from the northwest, bringing with it the tangy scent of the great woods beyond. Andrew paused and with a smile of satisfaction looked around.

It was hard to imagine that it was upon this square that the 35th Maine and 44th New York had fought their last desperate action against the Tugars. Behind him the ruins of the old palace had given way to the offices of the new government. The Senate chambers, Kal's offices, and the meeting room of the Supreme Court were now housed in a square whitewashed building of fresh logs, adorned as usual with the scrolling designs and carved adornments that were the delight of the Rus. Walking down the steps of the capitol, Andrew returned the salutes of the honor guard from the 1st Suzdal who stood at the base of the steps.

Smiling, Andrew stepped out into the square. Merchant stalls lined the square, selling the traditional wares of Rus along with the dozens of newer products introduced since the war.

The tolling of a church bell echoed across the square. The crowd packing the marketplace fell into an expectant hush and looked to the top of the cathedral in anticipation.

Suddenly there was a cacophony of bells as the minute hand on the new cathedral clock marked the arrival of noon. Side doors to the clock opened up and a wooden bear emerged carrying the standard of Rus, and the crowd broke into appreciative applause. Behind the bear came a procession of cubs, each bearing the flag of the ten city-states, Novrod, Vazima, Kev, Nizhil, Mosva, and the others, and with the appearance of each flag, the visiting citizens cheered. The last cub carried the red-and-gold standard of Suzdal, and an ovation swept the square.

The bear and its cubs disappeared, and then a lone figure appeared. An ugly hiss went up at the carved likeness of a Tugar. The figure stood before the clock, and then from a door directly beneath the clock emerged the images of a Rus soldier with gun raised, flanked by a Yankee, pushing a small cannon. Puffs of smoke shot out from the cannon and the musket, and the Tugar fell upon its back and disappeared while a wild cheer went up from the crowd. The two soldiers retreated back into their niches. Finally a robed form appeared wearing a halo, and the crowd blessed themselves as the figure of Perm turned to face them and then, following the path of the bear and its cubs, disappeared from view.

The crowd broke into applause and then slowly started to disperse.

"I don't think they'll ever grow tired of Vincent's creation," Kathleen said admiringly. "It's the pride of the town. Nadia, Vasilia's wife, told me that the town council of Novrod is planning one that's even better. Having a good clock is becoming a real point of civic pride."

"And it's getting everyone used to clocks as well," Andrew said, nodding toward the row of clock vendors, who always did a brisk business at noon.

The issue of time on this planet had been an intriguing one to settle. It had started when an apprentice under Vincent had taken upon himself the task of repairing Andrew's rusty pocket watch, damaged like all the others in the tunnel of light. The boy had finally succeeded, and became a master craftsman in his own right by doing it. However, the day on Valennia seemed to be an hour shorter, a fact which Andrew found intriguing alongside the other curious point that a year was nearly forty days longer as well. There had been a lively debate on whether to have a twenty-three-hour or twenty-four-hour day. Vincent Hawthorne, who had first tinkered with clocks and introduced them to this world, finally won out for the twenty-four-hour system, arguing for the symmetry of it, and the fact that the gearing in clocks would be easier to calculate. Though Andrew realized it was not logical, he felt as if he were being cheated out of precious time in the one respect and getting it back on the other side.

Fumbling with his watch case, he went through the daily ritual of setting it ahead an hour and then slipped the cherished memento, a present back in '63 from the men of Company B, his first command with the regiment, into his vest pocket.

Leaving the steps, which had survived from the old palace, Andrew nodded his greetings to the throngs who called out good-naturedly to him, or in most cases still looked upon him with an admiration verging on awe. The giving of flowers was a Rus tradition he still was not used to, but Kathleen beamed happily as a group of children rushed up to her with excited giggles and presented her with a bouquet. Leaning over, she kissed the youngest on the cheek, and the blushing girl drew away.

Andrew stopped before the carriage and looked it over carefully before helping Kathleen climb up. It was almost as good as the carriages back home, with metal springs and light iron-shod wheels. Yet it was still more Rus than American and far heavier than what he was used to. It had an out-of-balance look with a former Tugar war-horse, larger than a Clydesdale, in the traces.

Driving a carriage with one hand still made Andrew nervous. He felt perfectly comfortable with his horsemanship when mounted. But then it seemed as if Mercury somehow sensed his master's disability.

Awkwardly taking the leads, Andrew swung the carriage around and started across the plaza. Reaching the middle of the square, he saw a line of stalls and eased the horse to a stop.

"I hope business is good for you today," Andrew called in Latin to a merchant wearing the long toga of the Roum.

A curious crowd was gathered around the row of half a dozen stalls, looking with wonder not only at the array of silver necklaces, bracelets, and embroidered linens, but also at the mysterious shopkeepers.

"Good, very good," one of the merchants replied haltingly in broken Rus.

"He's only the first of many," Andrew announced to the curious crowd. "Trade between his people and ours will only make us all better off. Just remember it's going to take a while for them to accept paper money."

"And ruin our own silversmiths, by their being here," came an angry voice from the group. "His prices are cheaper."

"Yours are too high, Basil Andreovich," came a taunting reply.

The protest instantly triggered off a debate, and knowing if he stayed it would turn into another lecture on the free-market system, Andrew forced a smile and got the horse moving again.

"They came in on the train this morning," Kathleen said. "Now that must have been a sight, a group of merchants from the descendants of the Romans, taking an American train to trade in a medieval Russian city." Leaning back, she started to laugh.

"It's only the beginning," Andrew said quietly. "It's the ideas I'm even more interested in. Those Roum, or Romans, whatever you want to call them, will go back home in a couple of days having made far more than they hoped for. They'll also have seen how our country runs. Once the railhead reaches their city, hundreds of them will make the trip. It's only the beginning. I think Rus furs and woodcarvings will get a high price over there, and the Roum will pay in silver. Bill Webster's screaming all the time that we need more hard currency."

The young secretary of the treasury was a wonder to him. Somehow he had forged an economic system, based largely on paper currency, which was working.

The fact that his face was on the dollar bill was a constant source of amusement to Pat O'Donald, who by luck of the draw had pulled the ten-dollar slot, while Emil held the five and Hans, who he knew was secretly proud of it, had the twenty. Kal had argued vehemently against the fifty-dollar position but appeared on it anyhow, and Casmar in winning the hundred had diplomatically insisted that the largest denomination should carry the image of Perm and Kesus. The hard part of it all had been convincing the Rus that the money held real value.

What took even more doing was setting up the first bank of Rus, and showing the people that they could safely put paper money in, and later on get it back with a hefty five percent interest rate. It seemed like some sort of strange miracle to them, and once the novelty caught on the bank was flooded with business, a fact which Webster rejoiced over as he loaned the money back out at six and a half percent for the dozens of individuals who approached each week with new ideas for businesses.

His next big innovation had been the stock market, a concept which Andrew found to be a complete mystery. The men from Maine had started off the craze, once he gave them the right to form private businesses when the state of military emergency ended. Nearly every man was a shareholder now in one concern or another. Several had grown rich in the process and more than a few had gone bankrupt; it was a passion every bit as strong as the incessant gambling that had always been part and parcel of the old Union Army.

"Paper, sir."

Andrew looked over at the Suzdalian boy running by his side.

He reined in the horse and nodded to Kathleen, who pulled out an iron penny and handed it down. The boy handed the paper up and looked at her with a wistful smile. Shaking her head, she pulled out two more pennies and tucked them into his hand.

"Perm bless you," the boy shouted and then ducked away into the crowd.

"Let's see what Gates has in his rag today," Andrew said, trying to take the single sheet out of her hand.

She looked at the paper and then quickly folded it.

"I guess what you expected, Andrew. He's screaming about the sewer-pipe controversy and denouncing Mina and the entire government."

Andrew groaned, shaking his head.

"Then there's the stock market prices," she said quickly, changing the subject, "and those disgusting advertisements of that Uri the undertaker—'We'll plant you on the road to heaven.' I tell you, those slogans are setting a real trend in poor taste."

Andrew laughed softly. Actually he rather looked forward to Uri's newest ditties and puns, as did the rest of the city. Gates's paper was turning out to be one of the best primers for reading in the entire republic, and Uri in the process had cornered the market on funerals.

"Come on, Andrew, let's get moving before someone finds a reason to call you back to work. I'll let you read the paper later."

He tried to read the headline, but she shook her head, folded the paper, and tucked it into her purse. With a snap of the reins he urged the horse back into a canter.

Leaving the great square, they made their way down the eastern thoroughfare, and passing through the gate of the inner wall, Andrew reined the horse back in.

A steam whistle cut the air, and through the outer gate of the earthen walls a train emerged trailing its billowing cloud of white smoke. The broad area between the old city walls and the outer earthworks had been cleared of the vast wreckage of the war and was now the main terminal of the MFL&S railroad. The northern battlements, wiped clear by the floodwaters which had broken the Tugar attack, had been rebuilt and strengthened. The ground between the earthworks and the old inner walls was now covered with a dozen lines of track for the city's growing shipping yards.

The train swung through a curve and glided into the open platform station with whistle shrieking and bells ringing.

"The twelve-o'clock express arriving from Novrod, Nizhil, Vazima, Siberia, and points east to Hispania now arriving track one," the stationmaster announced as he walked down the length of the platform, wearing a gray frock coat and top hat which somehow had become the standard garb of conductors and stationmasters. It was another incongruity which Andrew found touching.

Andrew reined in for a moment to watch the unusual spectacle. Dozens of workers arriving back from the railhead on their monthly leave came clamoring off the train shouting joyfully as their families rushed to greet them, while local travelers alighted, many of them looking about in wonder at the sights or nervously back at the train, which for nearly all the Rus was still a wondrous invention.

Andrew was delighted to see two Roum merchants climb down from the train, carrying heavy packs, both of them surrounded by curious citizens eagerly shouting questions to the confused pair.

"So unlike an American train station," Kathleen said with a smile.

"Just a bit," Andrew replied, looking at the strange collection of people who now swirled past him, more than one doffing his cap in respect and offering a sweeping bow with right hand touching the ground (a habit he had yet to successfully discourage), or if in the uniform of the Suzdalian army, snapping off a sharp salute. A contingent of half a dozen men wearing the Union-blue uniform of the 44th New York came past, and after the formal salutes to Andrew the men tipped their hats to Kathleen and passed on.

"It's more than just the people," Kathleen said, "there's a wonderful vibrancy to what we've helped to create here. You can sense it. These people have been held down for a thousand years, and though they drive you near insane at times, there's a childlike wonder to them. They actually believe that the world is now limitless, that nothing can stop them."

"All aboard, all aboard. The twelve-fifteen local now departing track one for all points east!"

"It is limitless," Andrew replied, his voice almost wistful. "Let's just hope that Mikhail and those who think like him don't somehow find a way to subvert it all. That's the problem with a democracy. It's great in theory but hell in practice. I could have held power, but in the end it would have simply created a new boyar, or worse a Czar."

"Let's not talk politics, or I'll counter with my suffrage work," Kathleen said, leaning into Andrew's arm and by her look making it quite clear that the topic was closed.

The train whistle shrieked, and with the harmonic cacophony of half a dozen bells mounted up front—a very Rus touch, Andrew thought as they played against each other— the train eased out of the platform, and coming through the switching yard gained steam on its run out the east drawbridge gate.

Easing his horse into a trot, Andrew guided the carriage on down the road and out through the massive earth-banked positions of the outer wall. With a practiced military eye he surveyed the dead field beyond the earthen embankments that protected Suzdal with a vast array of deadfalls, sharpened stakes, and brush entanglements.

Already there were some who were stating that the maintenance of such vast fortifications around the capital city of Rus was now a wasted effort. But for at least the next several years he wanted them in place. Similar fortifications were going up around the rebuilding cities to the east as well. To the southwest, a hundred miles of fortifications were going up along the banks of what was now called the Potomac River. It was a barrier line that stretched from the Inland Sea all the way up to the Great Forest, a line of nearly ninety miles across the great steppe, the forward defense system to be ready by fall if the Merki should plan to come. Next time, if there was a next time, it was his hope to hold all the major towns and meet whatever enemy approached on the border of Rus territory. To abandon everything and just hold the city was once acceptable, since the revolution had only taken hold in Suzdal and Novrod. Even then, Novrod had been abandoned, since it was obvious that the defenses could not be divided. But if there was a next time, the country would disintegrate if he tried that expedient again.

The people of Rus had suffered horribly in the war. Over half had lost their lives from the pox or at the hands of the Tugars, and every city had been devastated either by the Tugar occupation or in the final stand at Suzdal. The southern half of the city of Suzdal was the only urban area of importance to stay intact.

The Rus in the past had been used to disaster; their old cities burned of their own accord every generation or so. The rebuilding of homes this time had happened rather quickly, but rebuilding all that had been created since would be a heartbreaking task. To lose the vast factory complex would be a catastrophe.

Crossing through what had once been the Tugar lines, he silently looked at the great earthen mounds where tens of thousands of the enemy lay buried. Atop each of the mounds a tattered horsetail standard fluttered in the breeze.

Looking back to the city, he felt a surge of pride. The northern half of the town, wiped clean in the flood, was still being rebuilt, but along more modern lines, with broad open streets paved with stone. The Rus architecture was still evident with ornately carved structures of logs, but in an area now called the Yankee Quarter his men had laid out half a dozen blocks in a more New England style, with whitewashed clapboard houses and a small town green flanked by several churches, a meeting and armory hall, and a barracks for the men of the regiment and battery who were single or, still being married to someone back in the old world, continued to honor their vows. He felt a deep respect for those unfortunate men. To him the marriage vow was sacred and unbreakable and he had always despised someone who took it casually, yet he could understand their current situation and respected those who had decided to remarry here. Some of them, however, had never adjusted. There had been half a dozen suicides since the war, and more than a score of men were now trapped in a tragic cycle of drinking or blinding melancholia.

He felt that it was a real strength of his comrades that they had stuck together in this new world, choosing to settle in the same area of town, still bonded together by the work and military drill.

Yet in most of the men he sensed a growing acceptance of their situation. Many had come to realize that here in Rus, they had skills that instantly catapulted them to positions of authority, offering opportunities unheard of back home.

Vincent at twenty was a general, Ferguson at twenty-six was the chief engineer of a transglobal railroad. Webster, the financial wizard, at twenty-one was secretary of the treasury and would, Andrew suspected, be another millionaire like Commodore Vanderbilt.

Even Emil Weiss had become somewhat less irascible, since there was no one to disagree with his theories of medicine. Emil's pet project had been a wonder to the Rus. While still serving as military dictator, Andrew had rushed through a host of ordinances, the key one being a system of sanitation following Dr. Weiss's recommendations. Water now came in through the aqueduct that drew its source from the rebuilt dam. For right now, water was still being drawn from common cisterns fed by the aqueduct, but in another couple of years Emil hoped to have every home in the entire city fitted with wooden pipes and a remarkable innovation of water-flushing privies. Sewer and storm-drain lines were being laid, the progress coming most swiftly in the northern half of the city scoured clean by the flood.

The first completed section emptied into the Neiper just beyond the northwest bastion. Gates had been screaming in his paper, and rightfully so Andrew had to admit, over the fact that the hundred-and-fifty-yard section of bronze pipe designed to take the sewage out into the middle of the river had yet to be installed, and the waste thus was pouring straight out along the bank and floating down through the dock area.

Emil had become nearly apoplectic when Mina had refused to manufacture the section, claiming a severe shortage of the precious metal. He was glad he had not run into Emil since yesterday's announcement of that decision. In fact, he realized a bit sheepishly that he had actually been dodging the good doctor.

Cresting the low rise, Andrew reined in the horse, and alighting from the carriage, he offered his hand to Kathleen.

"This is your favorite spot, isn't it?" she said almost chidingly.

"Well, it does offer the best view."

"I was hoping for a place just a little more secluded for our picnic."

"In a moment, my dear," Andrew said, stretching and looking about. Below him, a mile away, the city of Suzdal was spread out on the bluffs rising up from the river. Turning to his right, he gazed with open affection at the base of power for all that had been created. The old dam had been replaced, and half a dozen factories were now laid out beneath it. Showers of sparks rose heavenward from the iron and steel mill, which was working at full blast, day and night, to meet the insatiable need for rails, forty tons a day for the drive eastward alone. The old emergency system of simply laying iron strips on top of wooden rails had been abandoned, once the rolling mill for proper rails had gone on line. Beyond the need for rails, there were the myriad requirements for farm implements, tools, rolling stock, the new rifled muskets, and the heavier twelve-pounder artillery which O'Donald insisted upon.

Above the foundries were the four blast furnaces, where over a hundred tons of ore and another hundred tons of coke and limestone flux were cooked down every day to meet the insatiable need for metal and yet more metal. Alongside the foundry the railroad workhouse was a bustle of activity. Boilermakers, working under Yankee engineers, were turning out ever more powerful locomotives, along with all the required rolling stock of flatcars, boxcars, ore and coal hoppers, and passenger cars. Various smaller buildings were located around the foundry where an endless variety of specialized items were made, including a number of private enterprises that consumed the five tons of iron a day Mina had allocated for commercial interests. Safely removed by several hundred yards was the powder mill and ammunition depot. The stockpile of ammunition expended in the war had been replaced, but the supply of lead and copper had dried up when all contact with Cartha was lost the previous year. Fortunately the copper would start coming in from the Roum for more telegraph wire, and only the previous month a prospecting team had reported the location of a supply of lead a hundred miles to the west of the ford, in the direction of the Maya.

He was tempted to start running a rail line in that direction, but they did not have the resources to go both ways as yet, and if the Tugars ever posed another threat, at least for the next several years it would come back out of the east and not from the west, where embassy and scouting parties reported a realm that was nearly desolate and empty from the plague and Tugar occupation.

From down the river he could see a vast raft floating into the dockyards, where a train with a long row of flatcars awaited the cargo. North of town up by the ford a giant sawmill operation was booming, drawing power from the river, cutting the two thousand ties needed every day along with the millions of board feet of lumber required for rebuilding the cities.

Above old Fort Lincoln, their first outpost on this world, was yet another factory complex. The original grist mill and sawmill were still running, along with the smaller foundry that turned out several tons a day, all of it spikes and footers for the rail line, while farther up were the mines for coal and ore.

Between the mills, the mines, the factories, and the rail-laying crews, nearly thirty thousand men were working. It was an impossible expenditure of labor in any normal sense, but labor had been squandered under the old boyars, and with the new farming mechanization it was possible to keep such a number employed and fed. All the men were actually part of the regular army of thirty thousand, and one day a week was devoted to drill as well. It was a system which Andrew found helped to keep a unit cohesiveness, rather than simply waste manpower in garrison life, at a time when an entire nation needed to be rebuilt and entirely restructured.

"What next?" Andrew whispered, looking with pleasure at all that had been created so far.

"Still dreaming more plans," Kathleen asked, pulling out the picnic basket and settling down by Andrew's side, conceding that their lunch was going to be on the hill.

"It's just that I've never been so happy before," he said quietly, looking over at her. "I thought the fighting would never end, either back in our old world or here. It was eating into my soul, the killing, the endless killing. At least I've lived long enough to see that the price might have been worth it in the end."

He looked over at her and smiled.

"I used to think that somehow I was a sacrifice for others. there was nothing in my life anymore. That maybe after me, there would be people who would live better, live in peace. Now I'm actually starting to believe some of it is meant for me as well."

Almost shyly, he reached out and placed his hand over her stomach, then with a start pulled back.

"Does she always kick that hard?"

"He wants to see his father," Kathleen said with a shy grin lighting her features.

"She."

"Maybe both, like Tanya and Vincent."

"God help me," Andrew whispered.

"No, God help me. Remember, I'm the one that'll have them. You'll just get to pace around in the next room."

He gave her a worried look, and, smiling, she leaned over and kissed him lightly on the lips.

Laughing, he shifted position to find a way that he could comfortably embrace her, oblivious of the fact that atop the hill they were visible to any curious onlookers.

For the moment at least, he felt safe.

# Chapter Four

The water swirled in a raging torrent, plucking with a greedy power, drawing him into its vortex with a hideous strength that could not be resisted. It was the same, always the same, and though his mind screamed to fight, his body would not.

He let go and the blackened flood pulled him under.

Oh dear God, how many times, how many times. This time he would let go. This time he would drown. And then the fire built within, the choking terror as the darkness washed around him.

No!

Gasping, he kicked his way up, the air in his lungs like fire, ready to explode, to shatter him into riven sparks of dying flame. With a shriek he reached the surface, thrashing, fighting. Kicking, he fought against the flood. The bottom, he could feel the bottom again. Splashing through the darkness, he floundered, fell, and as if running in mud, his mind numb with panic, he struggled toward the flame-engulfed shore.

The hands clasped around his legs.

God, make it stop! The shriek tried to burst out, but was silent, caught in his throat, as if his words were useless and would not be heard.

The hands grasped and pulled, grabbing his waist, dragging him back. Again they had him.

As if his eyes contained a will beyond his control, they looked down. Woodenly he turned and gazed back out upon the torrent.

It was a river of Tugar corpses, flowing into the darkness. Bloated bodies swirled past, pale and ghostly in the firelight. Bodies that writhed in agony, reaching out to him with taloned hands. Human bodies rolled by, with bloated stomachs, swollen features of the drowned. All of them, all that he had ever killed, all the tens of thousands, tumbled past him, gazing upon him with sightless eyes. The hands reached higher, pulling him down, dragging him back into their fetid embrace.

A graying corpse of a Tugar rose up out of the maelstrom clutching at him, pulling him back into the flood.

The blackened flood sucked him into the darkness, the hands grasped him, pulling him into their sodden flesh reeking of death.

"God, God forgive me!"

"General, for Kesus's sake, general, wake up!"

Vincent felt a slap across his face. The world returned.

He struggled for control, and this time he simply could not. A shuttering sob escaped him.

"My God, I'm in hell."

Gentle hands came around his shoulder. He could feel the bristle of a flowing beard against his cheek; it flashed memories of his father holding him when fear took hold of him in the night. Always his father would be there by the side of the bed, to scoop him up, to hold him and whisper the fear away.

"I'm in hell," he gasped, struggling for control.

"It's all right, son. You've done nothing wrong. It was only the dream again."

Shaking, Vincent struggled. He was the strength, the one that they looked to. It was always the same now. God, could he never be the frightened boy again? Because in his heart that was how he felt all the time. To all of them he was the general, or the ambassador, and most of all the hero, the one who had slain tens of thousands and saved them all.

"It's all right, son, I understand," the old man whispered.

How he wanted to break down, to sob, to pour out all the terror within to this old man who held him. Just for once to let go and retreat back. On rare nights, all so precious they were, there would be the one other dream. It would be years ago, long before all this had ever happened. He was still a student at the Oak Grove Quaker school in Vassalboro. The scent of apple blossoms drifted in the air, and lazily he could look out the window to the beautiful sweep of the

Kennebec Valley. The dream was laden with a bittersweet dreaminess, a longing back to an innocent lost time so long ago, of running through the high grass of summer, his dog bounding joyfully by his side. Oh, God, to somehow be there again, to smell the breeze and feel the lazy peace. Before he had gone off to war and lost his innocence forever.

The old man was rocking him gently, and his thoughts returned. The old man could sense the coming back from the terror, and gently he let go and sat back.

"It's all right, son," Dimitri whispered, "I understand. I've heard you before but knew you would not want me to know. I'm glad, though, that I finally acted."

Embarrassed, Vincent tried to look away, but Dimitri grabbed hold of him and forced him to turn back.

"Out there," Dimitri whispered, nodding toward the door, "it'll always be the same. I will be your adjutant, old Dimitri, and you will be the famous general. But you are only human, son. I know the burden. A man cannot be human if the killing does not haunt him.

"Old Dimitri will keep the secret of his young hero." He smiled. "And I think you even more a man for knowing this of you."

Vincent struggled to hold the tears back, which burned hot at what he had just heard.

Unable to speak, he could merely nod his head in thanks.

"Come, general," Dimitri said, his voice changing. "I had to wake you anyhow."

"What's wrong?" He felt himself instantly awake, the nightmare disappearing, coiling within to come back later.

"Roum is under attack, my general. I think we have a war on our hands. Marcus wants you at once."

"Jesus Christ, not again."

He clambered out of the bed, even as Dimitri shouted for the orderlies.

"What the hell is going on?" Vincent snapped, the nightmare forgotten, impatient now with even a moment's delay as Dimitri and two assistants helped him to get dressed.

"A messenger came in to Marcus about half an hour ago. Raiders hit the port of Ostia shortly after midnight."

"That puts them about five miles away," Vincent replied, even as he looked over at the clock ticking on the mantel. It was nearly three. Whoever they were, they could have done a lot of damage by now, or worse, could be moving inland.

"They're not Tugar?"

"Human, that's all we know."

At least that was a relief. During the winter, scattered bands had hit the southern and eastern frontiers of Roum, several hundred miles to the southeast. Several thousand had been taken, but then the feared enemy had seemed to disappear off the face of Valennia.

Vincent buckled on his sword and turned to look in the brass mirror. Even at three in the morning an ambassador had to look calm and collected, the perfect warrior-states-man—even if he was only twenty. Reaching down, he unsnapped his holster, drew out the revolver, and checked that the caps and load were all right. The precious weapon had been a present from Emil. It was a light .36 Colt, intended more to impress than protect and one of only a handful of revolvers on the entire world. He spun the cylinders and holstered the weapon.

"Have the regiment and batteries formed in front of Marcus's palace."

"I've already had the alarm sounded," Dimitri replied.

Vincent looked over and smiled.

"Good. We've got an alliance with Marcus, and I want him to know right now that we plan to stand by it. We don't know what the situation is yet—it might be some damn pirate raid. Something's been brewing with those Carthas. Maybe this is it."

"Let's go."

He stepped out into the darkened hallway, and the guards by his door snapped to attention. Vincent looked at them for a moment, they nodded, and his gaze shifted to Dimitri. Turning, he pressed on, Dimitri by his side. He was curious but did not want to ask.

"The men think you are refighting the old battles, soldier's dreams, nothing more."

Soldier's dreams. God, he was a soldier. O'Donald had called him one of the best killing machines on this planet.

"Let's go see if we need to practice our craft again," Vincent said, as if to himself, and leaving the palace they headed into the forum, which was already aswarm with men. To the south he could see the horizon glowing red. Again he was about to go into battle, and his stomach tightened with excitement and fear.

\*　　\*　　\*

Squinting, he looked across the water as the mist took on a flat opaque light, breaking and swirling. The small port of Ostia was before him, resting on the shores on the Inland Sea, the River Tiber forming its northeasterly edge after tumbling down through the final cataracts and proceeding to the coast.

Most of the city was shielded from view by a low ridgeline half a mile out from town. All he could see was the flames leaping into the air, and beyond that, out in the misty bay, half a hundred galleys moving in toward the city. It was going to need a lot of rebuilding after this experience, Vincent realized, watching glumly as flames engulfed the small port from one end to the other.

Vincent lowered his field glasses and offered them to Marcus, who looked at them with curiosity.

"It will enable you to see objects far away," Vincent said.

Marcus raised the glasses and gasped as he pointed them out to sea.

"Carthas," he hissed angrily.

"What the hell for?" Vincent said as if to himself. "If reports are right, they'll have their own horde arriving in another six to eight months. There's no sense to this."

Vincent looked back over his shoulder. The paved road leading down from the city and across the broad open valley behind him was covered with a long serpentine column of men, the city reserves, mostly armed slaves. The first and only legion of Roum, which had been drilling since the Tugars had been repulsed, was deploying out on the slope behind him, forming a battle front of nearly a thousand yards. Directly behind him stood the men of the 5th Suzdal, with the Novrod light batteries beside them.

Their advance out of the city had been covered by a hundred mounted warriors, who had pushed back the thin screen of archers sent out to meet them. So far Vincent felt it was going to plan, with his deployment concealed from the enemy. The only problem was that the next line of hills, a half mile forward, was acting as a screen for the Carthas as well. A long line of men occupied the crest, armed with spears and bows, but what they had hidden directly behind that low ridge was a mystery.

The Carthas had done a clean job of it, he thought with grudging admiration. They had cut the town off, and not a single inhabitant had gotten back to the city to tell them what was actually going on.

"This doesn't seem right," Marcus said coldly, still gazing through the field glasses.

"Why?"

"If this was a pirating raid, they'd be pulling out by now. They'd be fools not to know your regiment of Rus infantry and two batteries of artillery are here. With those weapons you can slaughter them like pigs and destroy their ships."

Vincent grimaced with a sudden memory.

"Maybe they have such weapons too," he said quietly.

"What?" Marcus asked coldly.

"Before the Tugars came, we traded some muskets, powder, and a field piece for copper, lead, and zinc."

"Were you mad?" Marcus snapped.

"No, just desperate."

With a snort of disdain, Marcus looked at Vincent coldly.

"We needed the metal if we were going to win. It's possible they figured out how to make more."

Vincent beckoned for the glasses, which Marcus returned. For several long minutes he scanned the crest of the hill, but all he could see was pikemen with a thin line of archers deployed halfway down the slope.

"Nothing, not a damn thing. They have every intention of staying, though—they're unloading troops as fast as those ships can beach."

"We're hitting them now," Marcus growled angrily. "Hit them while only part of their force has landed."

"Could it be that's exactly what they want us to do," Vincent replied, suddenly feeling very cautious.

"The longer we wait, the stronger they'll be," Marcus snapped.

"My plantations are down there. In another hour they'll spread down the coast and destroy the rest of my estates," Petronius, oldest of all the senators, shouted angrily. "I want action now."

"Gentlemen, it's too easy," Vincent replied. "They're sitting there almost begging us to attack. Let's wait until that fog lifts a bit more and we can see what we're up against. In the meantime we can send forward a screen of skirmishers to probe their line and try to figure out what they really have."

"I thought he was your ally," Petronius retorted. "I think he's just a boy afraid of a good fight."

Vincent looked over coldly at Petronius. The old man sat astride a horse, his heavy belly resting on the mare's back. His skin had a pale sickly hue to it, pockmarked from the smallpox, giving his features a hard, almost expressionless appearance, as if he were wearing a mask made out of old wax. He looked back at Vincent as if he were nothing more than the lowest of servants.

Vincent looked back at Marcus calmly.

"I'll not argue with you," Vincent said. "I've seen a long hard campaign against the Tugars, and got my rank through battlefield promotions, rising up from a private."

"A former slave, like the rest of his troops," Petronius said haughtily, his voice dripping with sarcasm.

"A free man, like my troops," Vincent snapped, looking back angrily at Petronius, regretting his statement, since it was diverting attention from what he wanted to say.

"All the same nevertheless," Petronius sneered.

Vincent looked back to Marcus.

"Let the fog lift off the ocean, see what's out there, and then attack."

Vincent could see a moment's hesitation on Marcus's part, and then he turned away.

"We attack at once. The longer we wait the more damage they will do."

Marcus looked back at Vincent.

"And what do you plan to do, my noble ally?" he said, the challenge in his voice obvious.

Vincent bristled at the cold disdainful looks of the patricians arrayed behind Marcus.

"The alliance stands, Marcus. My men will advance with you," Vincent replied stiffly. "I only hope for all our sakes you are right."

Trying to conceal his nervousness, Tobias Cromwell paced the deck of the *Ogunquit*, peering through the fog, which was brightening.

A small cutter appeared out of the mist, shooting across the flat calm water as the dozen rowers strained at the oars.

"They're getting set to advance," a messenger shouted as the cutter swung in beneath the heavy battery of guns.

"Damn this fog," Tobias hissed impatiently. And yet at

the same time he found himself chuckling inside. Hamilcar had seized on the advantage at once, advising Tobias to lie out in the mist along with the rest of his gunboats and Jamie's ships until the battle was joined. The additional surprise it might offer could have a telling effect, and he had realized the possibility. It was just the waiting that was so unnerving.

A low flat boom echoed across the water, and he instantly recognized the sound as a battery firing in volley.

It was almost time, and a smile crossed his features. The captives had revealed that it was only one regiment facing him, the 5th Suzdal, under that young Hawthorne. Damn it all, it would have to be him, Tobias thought grimly. Out of all the lot he had developed something of an admiration for the boy.

"Let's get some steam up," Tobias shouted. "We're moving in."

"Shake out that line there," Vincent shouted. "You look like a bunch of amateurs!"

The 2nd Novrod battery, a hundred yards away on his left, snapped off with another volley. Turning, Vincent watched as the shots hit into the Cartha ranks over on the next ridge. The enemy line wavered under the pounding.

Damn them, why couldn't they just break and run? But it was all too obvious they had seen gunfire before. He could remember the first time O'Donald had fired a Napoleon over the heads of the Rus when they had first arrived on this planet. The entire horde of them had broken and run. These men were used to what guns could do.

Vincent could feel the trembling inside. Is this how Andrew felt, standing thus before a regiment under fire, waiting to go in? But Andrew wasn't here now; this battle was going to be his and his alone. Success or failure was his responsibility, and the deaths, God help him, his as well.

The regiment was drawn up in perfect order, a battle front two hundred yards wide, a double rank of seven companies forward with three companies in column as reserve, five hundred and twenty men. To either flank Marcus had deployed his forces, nearly ten thousand men of Roum. Vincent looked at them critically as well. There were no fabled legions of Caesar here such as he had read of in the *Gallic Wars*. That was hoping for far too much.

Two thousand years of Tugar rule would never have tolerated such a thing. The Roum had become as servile as the Rus across that time.

At best they were an armed mob, carrying pikes, shields, clubs. The only disciplined formation was the imperial guard of the first legion, and even they left something to be desired as the ten block formations fifty men across and ten deep came up over the crest of the hill and started into their advance.

Vincent silently cursed as Marcus rode past him on the right, leading the advance, surrounded by his patricians. The best troops should have been kept in reserve—he should have sent the militia in first to probe the enemy and committed the best units for the kill.

Better to lose untrained militia than the few professionals on this field, he thought grimly. Turning his mount about, he looked back at his regiment again. It was madness to commit them like this, but it was politics now, not sound military sense, that had to guide him. In this first action he had to show Marcus the alliance was committed, an action that would kill more than one of his men in the next couple of minutes.

"We'd better get this moving!" Vincent shouted. He looked down at Dimitri, and at Yurgenin, who directly commanded the 5th, and at Major Velnikov, who commanded the 2nd battery.

"Velnikov, advance with my regiment and deploy at one hundred yards. Bugarin, your battery stays on the hill and will fire in support."

Velnikov looked over at his cousin and smiled.

"The glory goes to me, my friend," he laughed.

"Goddammit, we're not after glory here," Vincent snapped.

Velnikov fell silent.

Vincent looked down the line. The legion was up over the crest now, the first line sweeping past the regiment to either side.

"All right, men. These people are counting on us. Show them how free men from Rus can fight!"

"Fix bayonets!"

Steel rattled on steel as razor-sharp blades were locked into position.

"Present bayonets!"

With a deep-throated roar, muskets were dropped to the level, the sunlight gleaming on the burnished blades.

Turning, he pointed his sword down the hill. The color-bearers and guards stepped in front of the line.

"The 5th will advance!"

The drummers picked up the beat, and with parade-ground precision the regiment stepped off, flags snapping in the late-morning breeze. Spurring his mount, Vincent rode forward, Dimitri and Yurgenin riding by his side.

Onward they marched, the drum cadence marking the step, trampling through the high grass, crossing over low stone walls, aligning to the center, the line a precision cut across the open fields.

Forward the Carthas held their serried ranks along the crest of the hill, a wall of pikemen a quarter mile across, their leveled blades poised and waiting.

The range closed to four hundred yards, and inwardly Vincent prayed that somehow they'd break. The thought of stopping at one hundred yards and pouring measured volleys into their defenseless ranks left him cold and filled with loathing.

Yet as he looked over his shoulder he was swept up by the beautiful terrible power of men advancing with chilling precision, as if on parade.

"As terrible as an army with banners," he whispered, awestruck that all of this was his, the men looking at him as if he were the center actor on the stage, sword held high, pointed forward.

Through three hundred yards, and then two hundred, the measured tramp of the men thundered across the field, counterpointed by the shrieking of artillery rounds arcing overhead, plowing into the Cartha lines with deadly effect.

To his left he heard a wild shout, and looking over, he saw Velnikov galloping down the slope, waving his hat, racing ahead of the line, his six limbered guns bouncing and careening.

"Goddammit, Velnikov, stay with the formation!" Vincent roared, but he knew he wouldn't be heard. The damned artilleryman was after glory. The guns swung out not a hundred yards in front of the Carthas, the crews leaping off the limbers, untrailing the weapons, and swinging them around.

And in that moment the center of the enemy formation suddenly melted away, the pikemen casting weapons aside, streaming to the rear in what appeared to be a mad panic before a single shot had even been fired.

A wild shout went up from behind, and looking back,

Vincent could see his ranks starting to break, ready to surge forward.

With a roar of anger, he stood tall in the stirrups and held his sword straight out to one side, motioning for the men to hold, to keep formation.

The discipline held; the outward surge eased back.

Something was wrong now. It was too easy. Anxious, he looked down the line and saw the discipline break away as the legion broke into a ragged charge, Marcus and his patricians swept along by the weight of their own men pressing in from behind. Coming out of the low ground between the two ridges, the legion swarmed up the slope, cheering, waving their spears, disintegrating into the mad rush of a mob eager for blood, closing the last hundred yards to the crest.

The top of the hill was empty for but a moment. As if rising out of the grass, teams of men pushing wheeled carts crested the hill flanked by a double rank of infantry armed with muskets.

"Merciful God in heaven," Vincent whispered.

He could still get out, pull back. But he couldn't leave Marcus's people out here to be slaughtered. There was only one thing to do.

"Fifth Suzdal at the double!"

The first puff of smoke appeared from the cannon farthest down on the right and in an instant ripped down the entire length of the Cartha line, as forty guns opened up on the advancing army.

A slash of iron hail slammed into the 5th. Men dropped, tumbled into the grass, screaming in pain, as the canister cut bloody swaths through the ranks.

Yurgenin spun his horse around, tumbled from the saddle, and was still. Vincent looked back for a second, but the men were still coming on.

"We've got to get into range," Vincent roared. "Their gunners aren't that good."

Velnikov's battery kicked off its first salvo, and he could see great slashes cut into the lines of musketmen and gunners poised on the hill.

The range closed to one hundred and fifty yards, the regiment surging forward, battle flags forward, the men shouting hoarsely.

"A hundred yards, almost there," Vincent roared, and

then in a numbing flash that ripped down the entire Cartha line another volley slammed out.

His mount surged upward, screaming in anguish, rolling over. Scrambling madly, Vincent jumped clear as the one-ton animal slammed into the ground, kicking and screaming.

Shaken, he stood up and held his sword aloft.

"Come on 5th, forward!"

Dimitri, leaping from his mount, fell in by Vincent's side as their line closed in.

"Just a bit more! Come on, men, come on!"

The left flank passed Velnikov's battery as the six guns leaped backward. A Cartha field piece flipped into the air, tumbling over, and the 5th shouted with triumphant rage.

Sprinting hard, Vincent dashed ahead of the line, sword held high, as another hail of canister swept past, cutting down the regimental flag-bearer into a bloody heap. Instantly a color guard swept up the cherished emblem and pushed on.

Turning, Vincent looked back, and holding his sword aloft, he pointed it straight out to the side.

"Regiment, halt! Halt, dammit!"

Panting, the men drew up, the line holding firm, and he felt his heart swelling with a dark consuming pride. He had drilled them, taught them before the Tugars, and had trained them even for this, the day when they might have to face weapons like their own.

"Regiment, take aim!"

"Aim low, boys—remember, aim low!" Dimitri roared.

Vincent and Dimitri stepped back behind the ranks.

"Fire!"

A sharp volley ripped down the line, and through the smoke he could see dozens of the enemy go down.

"Independent fire at will!"

A blast of canister cut through the rank next to him, dropping half a dozen men. A young Suzdalian boy staggered out of the line, shrieking hysterically, holding his hands to his face as blood spurted out, running down his arms like a river.

Unflinching, Vincent turned away from him.

"Faster! Load faster!"

The first musket was shouldered and fired, followed within seconds by hundreds more.

"Pour it into them! Break them up, break them up!"

Stepping behind the ranks, Vincent walked down the line, shouting encouragement, pointing forward, peering through the smoke to see the effect. The enemy were still firing, the canister cutting out, slashing holes through his lines, his precious ranks of men. The flat hum of canister and musket rounds snapped through the air, counterpointed by the deadly return fire of the Suzdalian rifled muskets.

A deep throaty roar echoed from the left, and in the smoky gloom he could see Velnikov's guns engaged in their deadly work, pounding in solid shot topped with canister against the enemy artillery. But the damage was coming back out as well, for even as he watched, one of the guns spun around on its mount, a wheel careening into the air, sliced clean away from the barrel. In the milling confusion to either flank he could not see if the Roum were advancing or retreating; the mob was simply surging about.

Looking back, he saw the three reserve companies holding formation fifty yards back, the men standing ready.

"Dimitri!"

"Here, sir," and the old man came up by his side.

"When I give the word, I want the three reserve companies to go in at the double, moving them up directly behind the volley line. We'll volley-fire, and when the flags start forward, push them through."

With a salute, Dimitri ran down the hill, waving for the reserves to come forward. Vincent stalked back down the line to the center, positioning himself next to the flags.

"Hold for volley fire!" Vincent roared, and the order raced down the line. The men loaded and brought their red-hot weapons up to signal they were ready. The smoke lifted briefly, and he could see that the enemy had been staggered; gunners were down, the fire was ragged, holes were punched into the ranks of musketmen between the cannons.

"Companies A through G will fire and reload!"

"Volley fire present!"

"Fire!"

A snapping thunder leaped out

"Reload! Now, Dimitri, charge 'em!"

With a wild shout the three reserve companies shouldered their way through the line at the run, bayonets leveled, Dimitri at the fore, sweeping up the regimental flag-bearer and pushing him forward with the tide.

"Charge, charge!" The cry roared down the line at the sight of their comrades rushing in.

Vincent stepped forward, waiting the last precious seconds, making sure the men were reloaded. If there were any more surprises beyond that hill he wanted them ready.

Turning, he held his sword on high.

"Charge!"

Even as he screamed the command he heard the tearing roar of a heavy musket volley slashing out from just beyond the ridge. Forward, through the smoke, he could see the regimental flag go down. Like an ocean his command surged forward, caught now in the wild fervor of battle. He felt himself out of control, swept along by a tide he could not stop. There was nothing he could do now but run. The last yards seemed like an eternity.

The enemy gunners were starting to break, but some held grimly to their posts, their guns leaping into the air, the deadly canister cutting gapping holes in the line.

But it was too late, all too late. Before him he could see the reserve enemy ranks, hidden beyond the low fold of ground, rising up with muskets poised.

The three companies forward came staggering back screaming their rage, unwilling to break, yet forced, as if by some unseen hand, to fall away.

Another sheet of flame licked out, musket balls snicking past, filling the air with their deadly hum.

The 5th slowed, stunned, and then singly and then by the hundreds the men, no longer commanded, but guided now by the darker instincts of war, raised their muskets and fired back.

Dimitri appeared, staggering out of the smoke, dragging the wounded flag-bearer with him.

"It's a slaughter!" Dimitri roared. "They had a damn reserve in the high grass four ranks thick!"

"Pour it in!" Vincent screamed. "Pour it into those bastards!"

The two lines stood poised not thirty yards apart, firing blindly into the smoke, the only sight of the enemy the perpetual sheets of flame erupting from the other side.

Stunned, Vincent stepped back from the line.

I'm a field commander, he screamed to himself. What the hell do I do now? What the hell would Andrew do?

Taking a deep breath, he struggled for control, and gradually the clarity of thought returned.

A quick look down the line and he could see that though stunned, the regiment was holding, either through pride or in the shock of the surprise—they could not think of anything else but to stand and fire back. Andrew had told him how green regiments would stand out of sheer ignorance when veterans who knew better would turn tail and run. Whatever the reason, the 5th was holding for the moment.

He could see that Velnikov's guns were still in action, but the battery was now firing off to the flank, and in that instant he realized all was lost. The enemy muskets were not just arrayed against him. The sheets of fire from muskets and cannons were extending all up and down the line along a front of nearly six hundred yards. The Roum had already broken, and by the thousands were running to the rear. He could see that nothing would stop their panic until they were inside the city walls.

"Dimitri. Pass the word. Get our wounded out of here. Detail one man to each wounded who needs help. We're not leaving our people behind!

"Tell Velnikov to get the hell back up to the next ridge!" Vincent shouted to a trembling orderly, who saluted and raced down the line.

"Dimitri, the regiment will retreat by line," Vincent shouted. "First line to retire ten paces and reload. Second line will fire, then fall back twenty paces. We'll leapfrog back up to the ridge."

It was an unorthodox maneuver they had never drilled for.

Dimitri saluted, and, shouting commands, he started to race down the line.

The first rank started to fall back, and the Carthas, sensing the pullout, began to push forward.

"Second line, volley fire present!"

Muskets were leveled into the faces of the advancing foe.

"Fire!"

It seemed as if a shot couldn't miss, so close were the enemy.

"Retire twenty paces and reload!"

The discipline was still holding, but he could sense the near panic starting to build as the men turned and ran. For a moment, Vincent feared that they would simply keep on going. The men broke through the line behind them and continued. Vincent stopped with the first rank, praying that the company officers could maintain control behind him.

Turning, he looked back, and a moment of pure terror seized him. The Carthas were charging.

"Volley fire, present, fire!"

The enemy not a dozen paces away seemed to go down into a tangled mass, and the charge ground to a halt.

"Retire twenty paces and reload!"

The man next to him staggered backward with a grunt, holding his stomach and falling to his knees. Vincent reached down to pull him up.

"Leave me, goddammit!" the man shrieked.

The moment seemed to stretch into an eternity. He could feel his arms already going around his comrade, trying to pull him to his feet. From out of the smoke he saw a broken line of Carthas coming forward, bayonets leveled.

"Dammit, sir, leave me!"

He looked around wildly. The line was already disappearing back. He had to stay with his regiment. An anguish of self-loathing filled his heart as he let his hands slip away and the man slumped down out of his grasp. With a bitter curse, Vincent ran for his line, even as they presented muskets forward.

A sharp volley punched out as he dived into the ranks for protection. Coming up to his knees, he saw the wounded soldier still kneeling, and through the swirl of smoke a Cartha appeared, with bayonet leveled, and drove the blade into the man's back.

"You bastards!" Vincent screamed. For the first time he unholstered his gun, aimed it at the enemy soldier, and started to snap off rounds. The soldier's face exploded with blood as he staggered over backward and fell.

"Come on, sir, come on!" Someone was grabbing him by the shoulders, pulling him back. Still cursing, Vincent retreated with the line, following it back through the next rank.

Another volley snapped out.

The pressure was easing off, the enemy advance in front of the regiment breaking apart under the cadence of volley fire.

Vincent went back up the hill, getting behind his regiment as it retreated, the men working with deadly efficiency. The Carthas forward were no longer pressing in; their attack was stalled now in the bottom of the valley. He looked to his flanks, and his gut tightened.

The legion was gone from the field, and already the Cartha lines were lapping around the edges, the enemy leery of advancing, holding back, but nevertheless firing with ever increasing effect. And then over the steady roar of battle a deeper, rumbling shriek filled the air. Looking to his right, he saw the remnants of Velnikov's battery cresting the hill and falling in beside Bugarin's. A massive plume of dust lifted into the air directly in front of the cannons. The gunners ducked down, pointing excitedly back out to sea.

Racing up the ridge for a better view, Vincent turned out to face the ocean, and his heart felt as if it had been stabbed. The fog had lifted, and there upon the waters was a dark low craft, smoke pouring from a single stack. The vessel was squat and ugly, like a metal shed floating on the placid sea.

"Where in the name of God . . ." Vincent whispered.

A flash of light snapped from the side of the craft, instantly obscured by smoke. Long seconds passed, and then he heard the round shrieking in, its voice low and full of death, the sound sliding up higher and yet higher. The banshee roar ripped overhead, and for a brief instant he saw the round coming in. A blinding flash filled the sky just beyond his battery, and a thunderclap detonation ripped across the landscape.

Stunned, he looked back at the ship, riding with terrible menace, out of reach on the ocean nearly two miles away.

It had to be Tobias, he thought grimly. Somehow the bastard had made an ironclad and armed it with guns far more powerful than anything in the Rus arsenal. A sense of forlorn despair filled his heart. A flag was flying from the stern of the vessel, and disgust filled him when he recognized it as the national colors.

"Better a rebel flag, you traitor," Vincent whispered, his voice filled with loathing.

Numb, Vincent stood on the crest looking at the fleet while the battle disintegrated around him. The legion was gone, streaming back to the city in mad panic. The Carthas were advancing all along the front, and the Rus units were the only organized formations left on the field.

"It's lost," a voice shouted behind him.

Marcus, oblivious of the death snapping around him, reined in his mount, and Vincent could not help but feel an admiration for this man, under fire for the first time, and yet showing all the calm detachment of a veteran Union officer. The sight of him reminded Vincent of what he was, and what still had to be done. He forced the ship out of his mind.

"It's lost," Marcus said evenly, his features pale. "Get your people out of here."

"We'll hold them for a couple of minutes more on this hill. It's going to be hell at your gates with that panic." Vincent pointed to the terrified mob rushing back to the city. "My people are the only disciplined forces left."

"I'll not forget this," Marcus said, and leaning over, he gripped Vincent's arm tightly.

"I want you to see how free men can fight, even when it's someone else's war," Vincent retorted sharply.

Marcus drew his hand away as he gazed at Vincent.

"It's a different world now, Marcus, and you'd better realize it," Vincent shouted, pointing back to the advancing enemy and the ironclad ships beyond. "Now go over to Velnikov. Tell that old bastard to pull his guns up, to position two of them by each of the gates back into the city and put his last gun in reserve in the forum. I want Bugarian to split his battery, three guns on either flank of the 5th. After that, try to round up some of your cavalry to help screen our flanks, and see if you can dig up a horse for me as well. I'll see you back in the city. Now move it!"

Marcus looked down at Vincent, a smile crossing his features.

In a gesture that Vincent found to be almost amusing, Marcus saluted him, and then with a vicious tug he pulled his mount around and galloped off.

"It's not looking good," Dimitri cried, coming up out of the smoke, a retreating line of men behind him.

Vincent didn't respond. The enemy forward were now a good two hundred yards back, holding at extreme range. At least the pressure was off there. To his right, several hundred yards away he saw a column of Cartha troops cresting the ridge and starting to swing their line about for a flanking action. In a couple of moments they would be on him.

A thin smile crossed his features. Andrew had faced the same situation at Gettysburg, when the 35th had stayed behind to stem the rebel advance while the rest of I Corps retreated. Could he do as well?

"All right, Dimitri, we'll shake out into a long skirmish line, single-rank. I want the flanks bent back so the line is shaped like a horseshoe. Pull out Company A as a reserve in the center, artillery on the flanks. We'll pull back at a walk, wounded in the center."

Another shrieking howl tore across the sky, and not a dozen yards away a plume of dirt snapped up. Vincent held his breath waiting for the shell to explode and then ever so gradually exhaled.

"Fuses aren't that good. A dud," he laughed.

He looked back out at the ship again. There was nothing to be done about that now. But Andrew had to know what was happening here.

"I need a messenger!" Vincent shouted.

From out of the confusion a young Suzdalian came up to Vincent's side, his eyes wide with fear, a thin trickle of blood staining his blond hair.

"I'm a good runner, sir," the boy said, trying to control the fear in his voice.

"I want two of you!"

The boy beckoned for one of his friends to come over. The second one seemed younger than the first, Vincent thought, forgetting just how little difference there was between his age and theirs.

"Do you know where the telegraph station is in the city?"

"Yes, sir," the blond youth replied.

"All right, then. Have them send this message to headquarters back in Suzdal. 'Under attack by at least ten thousand Carthas, most likely far more, several thousand with muskets, thirty or more cannon. Led by Cromwell. *Ogunquit* converted to ironclad with very heavy artillery. Retreating to Roum. Expect siege within several hours."

"You got that, boy? Now repeat it."

The boy recited the message back.

"Good. Now both of you run like hell. If one of you gets hit, the other one has to get the message through."

The two saluted, turned and started off across the field.

With shouted commands, Dimitri pulled the lines in. It seemed to take an eternity. Behind the ridge, half of Bugarin's battery galloped across the back of the slope, the field pieces bouncing through the high grass. Velnikov's battery started out on its retreat, the drivers lashing their mounts, the gun crews running alongside.

Vincent felt a swelling of pride. By all rights the men should be in a blind panic, desperate to get the hell out and away from a fight that wasn't even theirs. The enemy formation on the right flank was starting to close in, a solid column of men advancing at the double. Bugarin swung his three guns around, and within seconds a sharp volley rang out, cutting a bloody swath through the formation.

"That's it!" Vincent roared. "Pour it into them!

"All right, at the walk, let's get the hell back to the city!" Vincent cried, and with a steady pace he started the regiment down off the ridge.

A thundering roar cut through the air, and with a soul-tearing shriek a heavy shell plowed into the ground directly in front of the line. Vincent held his breath, waiting for the detonation, as his men started to scramble away. Then ever so gradually he exhaled.

"Another dud," he laughed softly.

A thunderclap snapped out, cutting a bloody swath through his rank, bringing half a dozen men down.

"God damn you, Tobias," Vincent roared, looking back at the ship.

"A signal from Tobias. He's ordering us to break off the attack."

Hamilcar looked over at Hinsen, his eyes filled with rage.

"They're in a mad panic. We could be in their city before noon," he snarled darkly.

"It's not part of the plan," a voice growled behind him.

Hamilcar turned and looked back into the tent where the Merki had been concealed since landing under cover of darkness.

If only I could put you in front of a gun, he thought coldly, even as he washed all emotion from his features.

"Remember this is but the opening move," the Merki said sharply. "Maybe you could take the city, but once inside, your muskets could be overwhelmed in the narrow streets, and your artillery would be useless. Our purpose is a siege, not a storming."

"It was a good slaughter," Vuka laughed, shading his eyes to gaze across the field of battle. "But a waste of good meat," he whispered softly in Merki. Hulagar looked over at him coldly.

"Were those Yankees?" Hulagar asked, lowering the telescope provided by Cromwell and pointing to where the last of the 5th had disappeared but moments before.

"They were Rus infantry," Hinsen replied. "Prisoners report that Hawthorne is the ambassador. If that's the case, I'll bet they're his regiment, one of the best in the army."

"You know this Hawthorne?"

Hinsen's features hardened. The pet of Keane and Schuder, while everyone cursed at him. Everyone else got promoted, like Vincent, and until the last he was still a lowly private in the 35th, still kicked around by mick sergeants who wouldn't let him shit without permission. Well, it was the infantry and artillery he had trained that had smashed that goddam Quaker. Inwardly he hoped that afterward he'd find him dead on the field.

"I know him," Hinsen replied coldly.

"And you do not like him," Hulagar ventured.

"It was a pleasure to beat him today."

"His troops were good. Yours still need practice in this new war before you can match them on equal terms."

Hinsen suppressed an angry retort.

Hulagar looked back across the field. He had learned much in the last hour. The Roum were cattle; the fact that they had repulsed thirty thousand Tugars left him with even more contempt than before for Muzta's tattered horde. The Carthas had fought well enough for their first action. But the Rus had shown him something that would bear remembering. They fought as well as any of the Merki horde.

"I can see now why the Tugars were defeated by the Rus and Yankees," Hulagar said, looking over at Vuka and speaking in Merki.

Vuka gave a snort of disdain.

"They are still cattle."

Hulagar shot a quick look over at Hamilcar, who stood in silence, watching the exchange with a look of incomprehension.

"We will stand by Cromwell's plan," Hulagar said, turning away from Vuka to again face Hamilcar and Hinsen. "Order the men to advance slowly and keep the pressure on, but they are forbidden to break into the city."

With a nod from Hamilcar, the couriers galloped off.

"It is a good start," Hulagar announced. "Now let us see if they take the bait."

# Chapter Five

" 'Have retreated to the city. Cartha advancing to surround city for siege. Count three thousand plus muskets, at least forty field pieces. Twenty thousand or more infantry. Two heavy guns, at least fifty-pounders, repeat fifty-pounders, are being moved up.' "

Andrew paused for moment, looking around the table. All of the military staff were present, along with Kal and Casmar, prelate of the church, who besides his other duties with the church and the Supreme Court had become a trusted adviser to Kal. The room was Spartan, containing a simple long table with straight-backed wooden chairs surrounding it. Three of the walls were adorned with a variety of maps and dozens of charts and graphs representing the myriad of tasks associated with running the army, the industries, and the railroad, which administratively was still under Andrew's control as secretary of war. Out in the street below he could hear the chatter of the crowds in the great square, going about their afternoon business, oblivious to the crisis that was upon all of them. Andrew sighed, looked back at the telegram, and continued to read.

" 'Situation extremely critical, food supply in city only sufficient for two weeks. Casualties to 5th and batteries three hundred dead and wounded. Battery commander Velnikov dead. Three guns lost. Telegraph line soon to be cut, will reposition station beyond city to update our situation. Marcus expecting aid. Might capitulate if none forthcoming. Will stay here in city with men and hold until relieved.'

"Signed, 'Hawthorne.' "

Sighing, Andrew took off his glasses and sat back.

"Why in hell would Cartha attack Roum?" Hans asked, looking around the table.

"Cromwell attack Roum, you should say," O'Donald said coldly.

"Well, at least we know what happened to him," Emil said evenly.

"Yeah, and I wish to hell he had simply drowned," O'Donald retorted angrily.

"I suspect that there is a lot more to this than meets the eye," Kal said, finally stirring himself. "The Tugars came two years early on their march. They should in fact be arriving this fall, the same time that the Merki horde would arrive in Cartha. I suspect that there is a relationship between this attack and the Merki."

"In what way?" Andrew asked.

"I don't know yet," Kal said, extending his one hand in a gesture of confusion. "Undoubtedly they have heard by now what we have accomplished, and perhaps they are concerned."

"We are over seven hundred miles north of Cartha," Emil said, as if trying to reassure himself. "What concern should we be to them?"

"If a fox killed the hens in the next farm, maybe you would consider getting a club," Kal replied.

"So you believe there is a link here," Andrew said.

"I suspect it. Nothing more yet."

"Well, he would have needed a hell of a big works to convert the *Ogunquit*," John Mina stated, "if that ironclad is indeed the *Ogunquit*. And to cast heavy cannons—that takes a lot of skill and the factory to do it. He's made an arrangement with the Cartha, that's for certain. It's the only way that ship could have been turned out."

"Remember we did trade some guns and a field piece to them a couple of years back," Emil said. "It must have made them awful greedy for more."

"Could it be that the Carthas are preparing to fight the Merki?" Casmar asked hopefully.

"If they were, why waste their strength attacking Roum?" Kal replied. "None of our ambassadors to them has ever returned—we gave it up a year ago. If they wanted technical assistance we would have provided it."

"Then one possible assumption is that Cartha is attacking with the full knowledge of the Merki," Andrew said quietly.

"You mean that bastard Cromwell has thrown in with them heathens?" O'Donald snapped, his voice brimming with contempt.

"Their Namer of Time would have been there last fall," Kal said. "The Merki know what was happening."

"Then he might be supplying them as well," Andrew whispered, suddenly feeling sick with the thought. God, could it all be starting again? he wondered.

"We know so damn little," Andrew whispered, and he inwardly cursed himself for this lack of attention. Except for the fortification line to the southwest and the slow beginning of a rail line down to it, all their effort had been focused eastward, with the assumption that if the Merki were a threat, it would be next year at the earliest. Another year would give them an army with sixty thousand rifled percussion muskets and over four hundred field pieces, many of them the new and heavier bronze twelve-pounders. And more important, there would be the potential of Roum manpower to fill the ranks, along with the precious resources under their control. The thought of the Merki now having similar weapons was something he had never seriously entertained.

"Our last report from the forward scouting parties was that the Merki horde was still moving straight east, well over a thousand miles away along the shore of the inland seas," Hans said.

"How old is that report?"

"A week old."

At least they were finally getting copper from the Roum to start telegraph-wire production again. They had scraped the bottom just to string the line to Roum. He could see the next step would be an immediate running of line down to the watch posts on the southwestern frontier.

"And weapons?"

"Typical horde equipment, nothing out of the ordinary."

"This is curious," Andrew said, trying to relax, to focus his attention on what had to be done.

"The horde is still moving on its regular path and should be in Cartha sometime around midwinter. The Carthas mount a major expedition to attack Roum, led by Cromwell, and they're armed with modern weapons."

"Could it be the bastard is simply renegade?" O'Donald said hurriedly. "He somehow takes over Cartha for a while and gets metal and powder production going, maybe even thinks he can lead a rebellion against the Merki. Well, the damn thing blows up in his face and he, and those who want to follow him, get the hell out and move to set up someplace else."

"You know, there's something to that," Emil interjected. "He can't go south—there's more of them Tugar cousins farther south; hell, they're all over the place. Only here, up north, have we smashed them up. It's the only safe place for humans on this entire world. So he figures it's a safe bet."

"Damn fool," Andrew whispered. "We would have taken him back in."

"Not him," Casmar said softly. "He was always too prideful, and all could see that he and you did not get along. To come back after running away would have been beyond him."

"But his crew were mostly Suzdalians," Andrew replied.

"He could have always lied to them, kept them in the dark about what happened, and what you would do if they returned."

Andrew nodded sadly. He certainly could have used that ship, and even Cromwell, pain that he was.

"You know something?" Kal said with a sad chuckle. "The Merki have to cross the Inland Sea in their migration, and there's only one place, at the narrows between the northern and southern halves of the ocean. He might have plans within plans."

"So if he builds a base up here, he could sally southward come winter, and with that one boat bottle up the entire Merki horde on the west bank," Andrew whispered. "That means . . ."

"It means there's only one other path for the Merki to follow," O'Donald interjected, standing and going over to a map of the Inland Sea.

"If they can't cross at the narrows, they have to come north to get around."

"Straight at us," Hans snapped. "That bastard's inviting them to take us out."

Andrew looked around the room, suddenly unsure. There were too many possibilities.

"To what purpose?" Casmar asked.

"Father, he'll hold the winning card that way. He's got control of the sea, he can jump back and forth. If Roum surrenders—and remember we've already started upgrading its iron industry—he'll have a whole fall and winter to build more weapons, and then he can jump back to Cartha, stay in Roum, or even pick up the pieces after the Merki move on."

"If Roum surrenders," Andrew said quietly. All looked over at him. He picked up the telegram again and looked it.

" 'Marcus expecting aid. Will capitulate if none forthcoming,' " Andrew said evenly.

"Look, we don't know what the plan is," Andrew said, rising to his feet. "He could be in the employ of the Merki, but even if he is he might have his own plan anyhow. We can speculate endlessly about what his real purpose is. Gentlemen, we have to deal with the concrete, the crisis as it is here and now, and leave the speculation until we have more facts."

"We've got to move quickly," Hans said, standing up to join O'Donald by the map.

"That Marcus is a tough nut," Kal interjected. "He wants our weapons and our knowledge, but the last thing he wants is our revolution."

"And Tobias might be willing to offer the first two without the third," Andrew replied.

"If Roum surrenders, it could change our position in a drastic way," Hans said, peering at the map. "We'll be blocked in our expansion to the east and lose valuable resources, especially the mercury for percussion weapons and copper, zinc and tin, which would cripple our telegraph and any hope of breech-loading weapons."

"The weapons are one thing," Casmar interjected softly. "It's the other considerations, my friends. Before we even have gotten fairly started, we'll have a hostile neighbor. I've prayed that all our dreams will work, that men and women around this world can be united in a common dream of prosperity and peace, that we'll stand together against the hordes, that never again will any of us be cattle."

"If it's a Merki plot, father, they'll have turned not just the

Cartha but also the Roum against us. If it's a plot of Tobias's, we could possibly be in their path," Andrew said forcefully.

Only this morning he and Kathleen had awaked together in a world that had promised a peaceful place for their child to be born. He cursed inwardly. Was it all to start yet again?

"Gentlemen, it's also a question of honor," Andrew said softly. "We have pledged our word to Marcus. You're right, Kal, he is a tough nut, and he is definitely not interested in our social revolution. But I'll say this for the man—I think he is honorable. We have an agreement, and he'll wait to see if we'll honor it."

"So we go in," O'Donald said, his voice eager.

"Mr. President," Andrew said formally, looking down the table, "I'm recommending to you that we order a full mobilization of the army and send out an expedition for the relief of Roum."

"I've never had to face anything like this before," Kal said cautiously. "You handled it all last time."

"The procedure is simple, Mr. President," Andrew said, shifting to Kal's formal title. "As president you are empowered to mobilize the army pursuant to a treaty obligation and send the army out."

"And the Senate?"

"Watch out for that damned Mikhail," O'Donald said coldly.

"For now you could define this as a military expedition without a formal declaration of war. We are not invading anyone, or suffering direct attack. We're simply sending an expedition to relieve an ally."

Andrew paused for a moment and looked down to the far end of the table, where a gaunt, sad-faced officer had sat in silence.

"John, what will we need and how long would it take to get things moving?"

The group looked over at John Mina.

"What are you sending?"

"Twenty-five thousand men and a hundred artillery pieces," Andrew said sharply.

"Twenty-five thousand?" Hans interjected, "Sir, that's five divisions out of six, and the sixth has one brigade down on the frontier. You're stripping our defenses here to the bone."

"The Merki are no threat at the moment," Andrew

replied. "The threat is to Roum. Hawthorne reports they've landed twenty thousand already."

"He's just a boy," O'Donald said. "He could be overexcited."

"I trust his judgment," Andrew replied. "He took a good drubbing today and still kept his head about him. I think he's got enough sense to realize the danger of exaggerating."

"I agree with Andrew on that," Kal replied, "all personal feelings aside," and the group, relaxing a bit, chuckled softly.

"There could be more coming in," Andrew continued. "Remember, this is just the first day. There are a lot of unknowns here, and I want the numbers on our side. This is a political situation as well—I want Marcus to see what our strength really is, just in case he's wavering. If the numbers are on our side it'll mean fewer casualties as well in the long run."

"There's good wisdom in that," Casmar interjected. "With luck, such a force might scare those scoundrels off without a fight."

"I still don't like it," Hans said coldly. "Remember, he could always move the *Ogunquit* this way and his men as well."

Andrew looked over at his old mentor and smiled.

"I've thought about that. Remember with the rail line we can move troops back within a couple of days, while it'll take him at least five days to get here and longer for the galleys! We'll have the advantage. Once we push him out of Roum, no matter which way he turns our army will be there. While I'm gone, get some additional people working on the southwest bastion guarding the river approach just to make sure."

"What about old Fort Lincoln?" Kal asked.

"It's nearly five miles south of the city," Hans replied. "If he ever did run the *Ogunquit* past it, the men inside would be cut off."

"Regarding Roum," Andrew interjected, dismissing the concern about a strike against Suzdal, "we're not there first, my friend, but I want us there with the most. Besides, you and O'Donald will be here, and that's worth an extra division in itself."

"Now wait a minute, colonel darling," O'Donald roared. "If there's going to be a fight, and it looks like it'll be slam-bang artillery duel, I plan to be there."

"I'm leaving the 44th behind for security with you two in charge, but the 35th Maine goes with me. I'll feel safer knowing that."

"And you running off to see the action," O'Donald said with a huff. "You're the secretary of war—it should be Hans and me that go."

"I'm going up with the army, I have to. But I want Kal here with some backing."

Andrew looked over at Kal, who hesitated for a moment and then nodded in agreement.

"Now Kal," O'Donald said, a note of pleading his voice.

"President Kalencka," Kal replied with a grin, "and commander in chief, according to the constitution, Pat."

"You dirty scoundrels," O'Donald groaned, and mumbling a curse he leaned back against the wall and fell silent.

"Back to you, John," Andrew said, his tone making it clear the debate was over. "What do we need to move the army?"

John, who had already started to scribble furiously with a pencil, looked up at Andrew with a grimace.

"It'll take us to the limit, beyond it. If we had made the rail line a four-and-a-half-foot gauge instead of three-and-a-half, our rolling stock could have handled more. This is rough, mind you, but I figure we'll need over seven hundred cars and fifty locomotives to do the job. I'd suggest sending up twenty-five days' rations with the army. The men can pack eight days' rations each; the rest can be loaded in boxcars. Batteries you should strip down to one horse per gun and one caisson. It's moving the horses and feed that's the tough part. Moving one of those damn big horses and its feed is equal to moving twenty men."

"One horse per gun?" O'Donald interjected. "It'll slow us down."

"We did it in the last war," Mina replied. "That's the beauty of the old four-pounders—the men can man haul 'em if need be. Even stripping it all down it'll still come down to that number."

"Damn, that's a tall order," Andrew said quietly.

"We've got the locomotives, but a lot of them are older models, not able to haul much beyond fifty tons, five carloads. Ten out of our fifty engines are in for overhauls. We can cut that short and get maybe all back out in a couple of days. There are eleven engines on the line now hauling construction equipment east or heading back, along with the four engines working at the railhead. I can send up word for them to dump off their supplies, turn around, and head back. It's the rolling stock that's a problem. We've got just over sixty passenger cars for the entire line, and that's not even enough for one division. Boxcars and flats we've got just under two hundred of each. The one advantage you've got is that we've got over four thousand men working along the line. They're all regular army, their equipment is with them. Most of those are already at the railhead, so that'll cut things somewhat, but not enough."

"So we're short?"

"If we press in all the hopper cars and cabooses, and throw in the forty dormitory cars for the construction crews, along with crane cars, everything with wheels, and load them down to the maximum, we might barely squeeze it, though we'll still be a hundred cars short. We'll have to overload, it's that simple. But you won't get more than twelve, fifteen miles per hour at best with the engines hauling that much."

"Why not run half up and then come back and fetch the rest?" Kal asked.

"It'd be a logistical nightmare, sir. We can run fifty trains up that single track, that's the easy part. It's gonna be a hell of a sight, I tell you, damn near four miles of rolling stock and locomotives all on one line. Yes sir, a hell of a sight."

John fell quiet for a moment as if lost in a reverie, and the group waited patiently for him to continue.

"But try to start turning them around in that traffic," John said softly. "There's only a couple of sidings at the railhead and one turntable in Hispania. The next major siding and rail yard is at the Kennebec River crossing two hundred miles back. We'd have a real problem running them back through that snarl.

"There's another problem I'm not even sure we can handle. We're running three trains a day each way up that line. Our tank stops for water might run bone-dry. We're going to have to haul along all the buckets we can find. If need be we'll fetch water from the rivers and filter it with muslin.

"Fuel's another problem. We're going to run through a couple of thousand cord mighty quick. Just running up the line is going to damn near exhaust our stockpiles. Turning trains around, moving them back here, then running them up again would be out of the question. As it is, if I can scrape up a spare train, I might just load it up with firewood to be on the safe side. Remember as well, chances are at least one engine will act up, might even break down, especially some of the older models. We'll have to be ready for that. Otherwise it could tie up everything to beat hell."

"Can all this be done?" Andrew asked.

"How soon, sir?"

"Two days," Andrew said quietly.

Mina gave a sad exhausted smile. Andrew looked at his logistical chief closely. The preparations for the Tugar war had pushed him over the edge, but with his burden of responsibility he could understand how it had happened. John had never seemed to recover completely from the strain. Yet he was a genius in what he did, pulling together a vast industrial operation out of what had been a medieval agrarian society less than three years ago. All that had been accomplished, the arming of a modern force with thirty thousand men and two hundred field pieces, the building of nearly seven hundred miles of rail line, along with the myriad of other tasks, would most likely have been impossible without Mina's skills. Andrew just feared that he was using this man up too fast.

"I'd rather have a week," John said quietly.

"We don't have the time, John," Andrew said gently. "It'll take us two days to get to the railhead. We'll lose half a day unloading. Then it's still over forty miles of marching, another two days at least. That's over a week. Those fifty-pound guns will undoubtedly smash the city walls to dust by then."

"You know, this mobilization will shut down our industry for weeks," John said. "Everything will come to a halt, with all the men mobilized. We're way behind on threshing equipment for the fall harvest, along with pipes for the water supply. It's going to throw everything out of kilter. We might even lose part of the harvest as a result."

"We'll still have five thousand men here," O'Donald said glumly.

"He's got a point there," John replied. "The men of the first division are drawn from the ironmills and mines."

"They're our best division, all of them veterans of the Tugar war," Andrew replied.

"You're keeping me and Hans behind," O'Donald countered.

"Hell, three of the other divisions have a lot of Tugar fighters in them; it's just the fifth and sixth that are new."

"The first goes with me. I want the best troops in the army for this fight."

"At least leave the 11th Suzdal from the third division out," Mina pressed. "They're our locomotive and boiler makers for our new steam-powered sawmills and pumps."

Andrew hesitated for a moment. The request seemed logical, but some inner instinct, which had always guided him in the past, took hold.

"They come with us. I might need them," he said quietly.

John shook his head in disagreement but said nothing.

"Two days, John."

The major stood up wearily, taking his scraps of note paper.

"If you'll excuse me, sir, I'd better get things moving," and with a salute to Kal he walked out of the room.

"All right, then, gentlemen, I think we have a lot of work ahead of us," Andrew said, realizing that the power of the meeting had shifted completely out of Kal's hands and back to his. It was a strange feeling after a year, and he could not help but like the sensation again. Kal looked over at Andrew and smiled, as if reading his thoughts, and Andrew felt a momentary discomfort.

"In war a general must lead," Kal said, as if to convey that he understood.

"I'm sorry Mr. President," Andrew replied. "Does all this meet with your approval?"

"It's a bit like old times again," Kal replied. "I'm sure your Mr. Lincoln must have felt his generals were in charge at times."

"Oh, that McClellan, now there was a fine one for politics," O'Donald laughed. "Our little Napoleon."

Andrew remembered the rumors that had swept through the army after Lincoln had relieved McClellan after Antietam, suggesting the Army of Potomac might be instrumental in a coup. It had merely been a rumor, but it had made him decidedly uncomfortable with the political clique that had been in control of the army in '62.

"I'm your secretary of war," Andrew said, "and I never wanted the job of vice-president. But always remember, sir, we are a republic. Never let your generals tell you what to do."

"I stand corrected, then," Kal replied, still smiling. "I must remember we are setting precedents every day."

"The political situation," Casmar interjected. "We should address that."

"Well, for foreign policy I'll send a telegram to Marcus immediately, if the line is still up, letting him know what we're doing and that we will lift the siege in no more than eight days. That'll give him the backbone to stay with us."

Andrew smiled. Kal was showing his political abilities to the best with his statement. The note would be one of full support, but there would be a subtle threat as well not to change sides in it.

The two looked at each other and smiled.

"I think Andrew's suggestions are sound for our local politics as well," Kal replied. "Even a day is crucial. I think we'll have the necessary support. But for now this expedition is moving under a presidential proclamation of a military emergency—my scribe will figure out the necessary wording. Let us hope this affair will be wrapped up in a couple of weeks anyhow without any need for a full debate and a declaration of war."

Andrew was tempted to add a word of caution. Wars were always started with the promise they would end with just one battle. This campaign looked as if it just might turn out that way. But he had been fighting far too long ever to believe in optimism.

"Things never go according to plan," Hans growled from the corner of the room, "I hope all of you remember that in the weeks to come. I suspect what we're seeing now is the mask of something far more subtle."

Smiling, Mikhail Ivorovich looked over at his fellow boyars, Alexander and Petra. With a nod he dismissed the scribe who had just read the message. The three waited until the door closed.

"So he really has done it," Alexander said, a grin of delight crossing his features.

"How sure are you of this message?" Petra asked cautiously.

"All three came over that Yankee wire. The one that our dear president sent back," and Mikhail's lips curled with disdain, "went out not an hour ago. I've had my people in that telegraph machine office for some time. I pay them well for this information."

"I thought these plots of yours were only a dream," Petra said coldly. "I still find it hard to believe."

Mikhail bristled inwardly, struggling for control. Where was Petra when the boyars were overthrown? he was tempted to ask. The old man had pleaded illness and hidden away in Mosva. He was not there for the humiliation; he had evaded service with the Tugars and then reemerged after the revolution and amnesty of boyars offered by Kal.

"I have worked on this for over a year," Mikhail said quietly. "It is no dream anymore."

"And it's about time," Alexander said with a laugh, picking up a tankard and draining off the rest of the beer. With a cheery belch he leaned over and scooped up another drink out of the open barrel by the side of the table.

"I'm getting sick of this joke called a Senate," Alexander said. "By Kesus's hairy ass, I could see no sense in your counsel of cheating my way into this office. I'm ready to vomit with the babble of these goddam peasants who think themselves better than us."

"Why did you not send for the other boyars?" Petra said dryly. "Why did you bring just us two into this?"

"Because you have a small mouth," Mikhail growled. "When it comes time to make our move, then I will tell the rest, and not before. They only need to know enough to act out their parts for now. Their reason for acting will come soon enough."

"How can I believe the secrets you have revealed to me about your plots of the last year? What you have told is beyond incredible. How did you maintain contact with him when not even that damned peasant Kal could find out?"

"One of the Yankees was in the pay of our dear lamented prelate Rasnar," Mikhail said evenly. "After Rasnar died, this man was able to contact me and offer his services. I ordered him to leave the city at the end and to lay the groundwork for this plan. He has served me well. The agents have stayed in contact infiltrating in and out of Suzdal. It was far easier than any imagined."

"Lamented prelate, but not dear," Alexander retorted with a laugh. "He was as shrewd a bastard as I've ever seen. He'd steal the coppers from a dead peasant's eyes, he would. Too bad he didn't win. But I didn't trust him, the same way I don't trust you."

Mikhail laughed softly. "Spoken like a true boyar," he replied. "But at least we can trust each other more than these filthy peasants. How much longer do you think we can stand against them? Last year, before their railroads reached to our provinces, we could still exert some control on our people. Our old men at arms who survived the debacle of the Tugars were still our base of power. But now with these damnable steam machines, people from our provinces come daily to this filthy den of peasant revolt. I'm seeing it more every day. They come here, or go to work in those monstrosities called factories, and then go home strutting as if they were of noble birth."

"Last week I had some scum approach me in my palace and not ask to see me," Petra said coldly, "not ask to see me, but damn my eyes they demanded to see me. Told me they'd turn me out of the palace if I didn't do this voting thing the way they wanted. One of them said he was just as good as me, no less."

"The arrogance of 'em," Alexander said coldly. "I'd have killed him and hung his head from the city gate."

"And been up on murder charges," Petra retorted, anger rising in his voice. "Murder charges, can you imagine that? Us charged for killing some arrogant animal of mean birth."

"Poor Ivan," Alexander mumbled. "To think they actually arrested him. Hell, it's something that was our right. Why, in the old days there were no questions asked when we took a peasant girl for a little romp. Now they call it a crime and they're actually going to put him up on trial."

"He was a fool," Petra said with disdain. "Doing it like that in the middle of a tavern with his men-at-arms holding her down. Damn him, at least he could have done it back in his palace in private."

"And cut her throat afterward, so she couldn't tell about it," Alexander grumbled.

"Your plan had better work, Mikhail, or it's the end of us," Alexander snarled.

"They were fools enough to grant this amnesty."

"I doubt if they would have done it if they knew you were alive," Alexander replied with a chuckle. "If I had been them I would have cut your throat, amnesty or not."

"They're too weak," Petra retorted. "They think men must live by pieces of paper with rules written on them."

Such thinking was still a mystery to Mikhail. Every day he

sat in their foolish Senate made it yet more of an intolerable mystery. He knew they were destroying him. The open smirks on the filthy peasants who sat around him when they voted against anything he tried were like a wasting cancer tearing into his guts, eating him alive.

Yet there was support. There were eight former boyars and half a dozen men from the old merchant guilds in the Senate. He could sense their growing feeling of betrayal. Oh, the merchants had embraced this republic idea fast enough in the beginning. But these Yankee industries were driving more than one of them out of business. The others could see the way the winds were shifting.

The Yankee called Webster had created a thing he called incorporating, or some such foolishness. That was yet another mystery, how hundreds of peasants could turn in pieces of paper they called money, then receive other pieces of paper in return, and then overnight a new business would spring up, with prices that undercut the old families. He had gone to the building where these papers were traded back and forth, and left disgusted at the sight of mere peasants shouting and trading, wearing clothes that would have caused their death but a few years before. He was still enraged over how a filthy peasant had given him money for his crops before they had even been harvested. He had thought the man mad. Only to discover the bastard and the several hundred scum he represented had made twice as much as he had by the time it was done.

The old fortunes outside of the boyars were dying away. It was these new peasant upstarts who were now starting to dress in finery beyond their station. It was creating discontent, which he knew would play into his hands when the time came.

"They will have their surprise soon enough," Mikhail said with a cold laugh. "Then let them see how much power can be found in a scrap of paper."

"The line just went down, sir."

Vincent turned to look at the messenger.

"Anything come through?"

"We got this in just before it went dead," and the boy handed him a sheet of paper.

Vincent unfolded the piece of paper, scanned it, and then looked over at Marcus and smiled.

"Go on, read it to me," Marcus said coldly.

" 'To Marcus Licinius Graca, first consul of the people of Roum,' " Vincent said formally as if reading a proclamation.

" 'In two days an army of twenty-five thousand men and one hundred field pieces will depart from Rus to support you in your hour of need. Within eight days our forces will be at your gates to aid you in the destruction of our common foe. When victory has been won we will offer whatever aid is required to repair the damage.

" 'We are enraged that you, our comrades in this crisis, have borne the brunt of such a brutal and vicious attack, and we will stand beside you in your hour of need. Know that when the people of Rus make an agreement they will live by it to the death.'

"Signed, 'President Kalencka.' "

"Eight days," Petronius retorted with a snort of disdain. "What will they do to us in eight days?" He pointed across the field to a line of earthworks going up half a mile away.

Vincent looked back out to the siege lines going up. Thousands of Carthas swarmed along the ever-encircling line, throwing up a continuous circle of entrenchments and gun emplacements. They were playing a cautious game. Some of their light field pieces had been run up, opening a smattering of fire against the south wall. But the two heavy fifty-pounders had been held back so far, resting on a low hill over a mile away, far out of range of his remaining battery of nine four-pounders. Tobias wasn't risking moving them up to effective battering range until they could be well protected.

Then again, the whole thing had seemed far too cautious. Less than seven hours ago the entire army had been in rout, with the Carthas pushing forward. And then without any sense of logic their attack had ground to a halt while still two miles out from the city wall. At the time he had thanked God for the respite, since the chaos around the gates had been a nightmare.

But now, it just didn't seem correct. He should have pressed the attack and slaughtered all of them as I would have, Vincent thought coldly. There was no military logic in this.

"I like that closing line," Marcus said quietly, interrupting Vincent's thoughts.

"Sir?"

"The one about living by an agreement to death if need be."

"I know the president rather well, sir," Vincent said quietly. "He's a man of great honor when it comes to his word."

"Could he be saying something to us as well?" Petronius retorted coldly.

Caught off guard, Vincent struggled to catch Petronius's meaning.

"I think Senator Petronius is saying that there's a threat in that note to us as well," Marcus replied.

"I don't see it that way." Vincent replied.

"You are a rather guileless ambassador," Marcus said with a smile.

"It's their war far more than ours," Petronius interjected, the passion in his voice rising. "Those weapons they have are the same as yours. Without your deviltry my plantation would not be a smoking ruin. I for one think what is happening here is between you and them and we are innocents caught in the middle."

Petronius stepped before Marcus as if Vincent was not even present.

"Ask for terms," Petronius said. "We're all in agreement that we don't want the threat of what these Yankees bring. Now we know there is another source for their power. Their cannons are bigger—even that boy admits to it. Perhaps they will give us these things and the secrets of making them, and then we can say to hell with the Yankees and their peasants."

The half-dozen senators who stood behind Petronius nodded in agreement.

"They've given us nothing at all, except trouble," Catullus snapped.

"Today I lost three hundred men dead and wounded," Vincent retorted, his voice edged with a cold anger. "Those were the finest troops this world has ever seen. I trained them, and they were my friends and comrades, so don't any of you say we haven't given anything here. When I go home I'll have to see their families and try to tell them their husbands and sons died for something, and now you make a mockery of that."

Vincent knew his anger was taking control, but he had just about had enough. Dimitri, who was standing off to one side, though not understanding a word of what Vincent had said, could see his anger and made a subtle gesture for him to be silent, but Vincent ignored him.

"We broke the Tugars' back, we stopped the pestilence, and we paid the price. Half of our people died doing it."

"We didn't ask you to," Petronius retorted. "The world worked well enough before you came."

Vincent sensed all control slipping away. Part of his mind was screaming at him to remain silent, to remember what he was now, and to remember what he had once been. But the other part was driven by other memories. The thousands of dead in the streets of Rus, all the killing, the look in the soldier's eyes as he let go of him and ran only hours before. He wanted to kill Petronius, and the thought both terrified and excited him.

"Enough!"

Marcus was looking straight at him, his back turned to the senators, and Vincent could see the look of warning in the first consul's eyes.

"When you took command on the field today," Marcus began softly, "you proved yourself far more of a man than I had first believed. I could not understand before that why you had been given this post other than for your knowledge of our language. I believed you were sent to us merely because you had married the daughter of your president."

Vincent felt himself bristling, but the look in Marcus's eyes were full of warning.

"I know better now," he said evenly, and then he turned to look back at Petronius.

"By the way, I never bothered to ask, but where were you when our men ran away?"

Petronius glared at Marcus with a cold rage.

"You ran. I saw you far ahead of all the others riding back to the city," Marcus said accusingly, and then pointed back to Vincent. "While this man and his Rus soldiers fought to protect our retreat. You are not fit to wear the toga of a senator. The god Cincinnatus must look down upon you with disgust."

"You have no right," Petronius retorted.

"I have every right," Marcus roared.

"Out on that field this man took over. Took over from me when I did not know what to do. He ordered me and I obeyed him, since I knew he was right. I told him then I would not forget what he did. I will honor that word."

"The Senate will debate this," Petronius said coldly.

"Let them!" Marcus snapped. "But I plan to give them their eight days, and I'll crucify any man who dares to say either in the Senate chamber or the forum that we should seek peace with those people out there."

"We can bring you down," Petronius replied, his voice full of menace.

"The Licinius family has stood as first consul for four hundred years," Marcus snapped. "The legion will stand with me."

"The legion is a humiliated rabble tonight," Catullus hissed.

"My men aren't," Vincent replied, his rage having passed to a cold deadly calm.

"It's not your place," Petronius said tauntingly.

"Our treaty is with Marcus and then the Senate," Vincent replied. "We will not stand by while a revolution overthrows his government."

"Boy, you have no say in this," Catullus said. "You are nothing but an ambassador."

"I am a representative of my government," Vincent replied. "They'll back any decision I make here.

"And besides," he said, a thin smile lighting his features, "since I am married to the daughter of the president, he'll have to back me in anything I do, even shooting you as a traitor if I should feel like it."

His gaze locked on Catullus as he casually reached down and unsnapped his holster flap, exposing the butt of his pistol.

Stunned, Catullus looked around for support.

"This is an outrage against the body of the Senate," Petronius shouted.

"I see only six senators here," Marcus retorted. "Now if there is nothing else, I want you out of my sight."

The six looked at each other, as if something had yet to be done. Vincent stepped forward to stand by Marcus's side, hand still on his pistol. Dimitri came up to join him, leaning against the battlement wall with his musket pointed casually toward the ground.

"It's not finished," Petronius snarled, and turning, he stalked down the steps of the battlement, the others following behind him.

"I don't know a word of what you folks said," Dimitri

drawled out with a smile, "but I think they were planning to kill Marcus."

"What did he say?" Marcus asked, exhaling slowly as he turned away.

"Assassination, sir."

"They wouldn't dare," Marcus said with a cold laugh.

"Et tu, Brutus," Vincent replied evenly.

"Who's Brutus?"

"I'll tell you sometime," Vincent said. "But from now on I'm assigning ten of my best men as your personal bodyguard."

"It wouldn't look good, your men protecting me. Besides, they're only six out of twenty. Four senators are out on their estates, but the rest will support me. If they tried to kill me the other senators would bring them down. Never has a first consul been killed."

"There's always a first time," Vincent said, a note of irony in his voice.

"They're going back to the Senate right now," Marcus said. "I should be there and speak first to announce your father's promise. It'll stiffen the backs of the others."

"It sounds like an excellent idea," Vincent replied and then looked over to Dimitri.

"Pick out a detail. Put Boris in charge—he's got a level head on his shoulders. Tell him if anyone makes a threatening move on Marcus to shoot the man dead."

"Right away, sir," Dimitri said with a smile and a salute. He raced down the stairs.

Marcus started to form a protest, but the look of determination in Vincent's eyes cut it off.

"All right, then," and with a smile he turned to start down the stairs. Pausing, he looked back at Vincent.

"There was a clear threat in that telegram. Petronius was right in that, you know."

"I don't see it that way at all," Vincent replied evenly.

"Well, he'd better be here, or there'll be hell to pay," Marcus replied, and he continued down the stairs.

Vincent turned away and leaned over the battlement to survey the Cartha lines, bathed in the last glow of evening. The western horizon was awash with a red shimmering glow. Vincent felt he could never tire of the sunsets on this world, the large red sun shifting the twilight sky into a swirling pastel of light.

Well, he had learned another skill of being an ambassador

today—to lie convincingly. It had taken him a moment to read between the lines, while Petronius and all the others had realized it at once. Kal had made it all too clear that if they surrendered there'd be hell to pay. He could see the military logic of forcing Roum to stay on their side. If Roum should turn, there'd be the potential of an implacable foe on the eastern border, killing the hope of Manifest Destiny before it had truly started. The world of humans would be divided, and in the end the Tugars, the Merki, any one of the hordes would exploit it and bring Rus to its knees.

They had to keep Marcus in power, and Vincent realized that he was now the broker of that power. The sacrifice of the 5th and his own actions on the field had touched Marcus; something in the man had changed. His deliberate line about Rus preventing any form of revolution had apparently closed the deal. He could only hope now that the promise would not come to haunt him if Marcus should later prove obstinate regarding any hope of change.

It would be a fine balancing act now, yet another burden on top of the enigma of what Tobias had done here today.

A snap of light flashed from the hill, followed almost immediately by a second.

"Son of a bitch," Vincent whispered.

The seconds passed, and as the distant boom of the two heavy guns rolled across the city a high piercing shriek filled the air. A geyser of dirt rose up in front of the wall a hundred yards to his left. At the same instant a bone-numbing shock ran through the battlements, and leaning over, Vincent saw a section of wall half a dozen feet across rise into the air in a cloud of dust and shattered stone.

Shouts of panic echoed along the battlements, echoed by the distant cheers of the Cartha.

"He'd damn well better get here in eight days," Dimitri shouted, coming up to rejoin Vincent.

"We hold until relieved," Vincent said reassuringly, looking over at the old man beside him. He could see Dimitri take some strength from his words. How strange, he thought. This morning I was sobbing in his arms and now he's looking to me for strength.

Gradually the shouts died away and the field was silent.

"You know, it's curious," Dimitri said. "This whole thing."

"How's that?"

"They had us by the throat, and then let us escape."

Vincent nodded in agreement.

"And the telegram, sir. Their forces crossed the telegraph line hours ago. But they didn't cut it till that last message came back in. You'd think they would have dropped those lines the moment they got to them and kept both us and the president in the dark about what was going on."

"You know, I never thought about that," Vincent replied. Yet another piece that did not fit. Hans had told him that half the secret of victory was to be inside the mind of your enemy, to think like him, to live and sleep inside his mind.

Vincent raised his telescope one more time to survey the enemy line in the gathering twilight. For a brief moment he thought he saw a man dressed in blue standing beside the two heavy guns, but in the last light of evening he could not tell.

"Just what the hell is Cromwell up to?" Vincent said quietly, and with a sigh he turned away and started down the line to inspect the damage and to reassure the frightened soldiers of the legion.

Tobias Cromwell stepped away from the guns and looked down at the piece of parchment in his hand. Most of the message was garbled—the one member of his crew who could read Rus Morse code was far too slow to get it all down. But the intent was clear.

A cold smile of delight crossed his features.

# Chapter Six

"Andrew, it's time to wake up."

Ever so gently, she leaned over and kissed his brow. He stirred, mumbled something, and then rolled over.

I never thought I'd go through this again, Kathleen thought. But there was another part of her that had always known there'd be an endless cycle of this as long as he lived.

There were moments, such as now, when she quietly cursed herself for ever falling in love with him. War had been a near-constant companion of her life for over seven years, the only respite the brief interlude between the end of the Tugar war and now. But even that brief period, she realized, had always carried the threat. The feverish building, the drive to forge an alliance with Roum, the defensive lines off to the southwest. He was away more than he was home, and on every return he seemed to have aged just a bit more from the strain.

She ran her fingers through his hair, noticing the first streaks of gray along the temples.

And now he was off again. Would the nightmares come back to him because of this? Would he even come back at all this time? A shot of pain stirred through her, and absently she let her hand drift to her stomach. Well, *he* at least was certainly awake and kicking.

The distant call of a trumpet echoed up from the village green. The army was mobilized again, the old military routine intruding back into all their lives.

"Come on, Andrew, it's reveille."

His eyes opened, and she felt a brief stab of anger. The call of a bugle could bring him instantly awake, something she could not do.

"It's time already?" he asked, yawning and blinking the sleep out of his eyes.

Fumbling for his glasses on the night table, he looked over at the clock.

"Dammit, it's already four o'clock. You know I wanted to get up an hour ago."

"You needed your sleep," Kathleen replied forcefully. "It's going to be a long day."

He looked over at her crossly, but saw in her eyes there was no sense in arguing.

"I already told your orderly you'd be late," she replied with a huff. "You're not expected till four-thirty."

A faint smile crossed her features as she snuggled close to him, pressing her body tight against his side.

"We do have a half hour," she whispered.

"But the baby," he whispered, while at the same time looking back over at the clock.

"I might not see you again for months"—or maybe never, she thought to herself. Her hands drifted down his side.

"The baby," Andrew asked, as if suddenly caught in a struggle.

"Just be very gentle and he'll never know the difference."


"Regiment, atten-shun!"

Andrew stepped off the front porch of his house and out past the picket fence. The 35th was drawn up on the village green, battle flags hanging limply in the red light of dawn. The air was cool, washed by the thunderstorm that had passed through during the night. Birds chirped, and Andrew looked up for a moment. They were a breed peculiar to this world, looking to him like cardinals streaked with a broad band of shimmering indigo. Their call was a curious harmonic blend, each bird following the song of its companions in another key. It had a bright airy feel to it. In the distance he could hear the man-made counterpoint to their song, the distant cries of the train whistles and the deep rumbling of rolling stock.

The 3rd Suzdal, the first regiment out, part of Kindred's

division, would be leaving in fifteen minutes. It was time to get down to the station.

With a brisk vigorous pace, Andrew walked down the line. Many of the faces were Rus. Well over a third of the old veterans of the 35th were gone now, buried in the old military cemetery down by the abandoned ruins of Fort Lincoln or resting in some unknown grave between here and the ford. Another third were elsewhere this morning, in command positions with the Rus army, or like Webster on permanent leave as government officials. But those who were left were the old solid core of an elite unit, their pride obviously passed to the new recruits who had filled out the ranks, eager to serve as Yankees, happy to be privates when more than one could have been an officer in another unit. In many ways the 35th was the West Point of this world, the only unit in the entire republic that stayed as an active military formation and drilled year-round, exempt from the labors the rest of the troops were involved in.

Stopping before the colors, Andrew snapped off a sharp salute. An orderly came up to his side holding Mercury's reins. Andrew gave his old companion an affectionate pat, and reaching out with his one hand he grabbed hold of the pommel and swung himself into the saddle, the orderly passing the reins up.

Shouted commands echoed down the line as Andrew gave Mercury a gentle nudge. Drums flourished, the fifers picking up the song, and he smiled inwardly at their choice for this morning as the six hundred men burst into the opening stanza of "The Girl I Left Behind Me."

"The hour was sad, I left the maid, a lingering farewell taking,
Her sighs and tears my steps delay'd, I thought her heart was breaking,
In hurried words her name I bless'd, I breathed the vows that bind me,
And to my heart in anguish press'd the girl I left behind me."

The Rus, with their love of harmony, especially basses, wove the song into a strange romantic mystical web. The glory of war had deserted him long before, but for a brief instant it came rushing back to him, the leavetaking at dawn, the drums, the steady rhythmic tramp of the men behind him.

Andrew cantered past his house, the side of the road lined with the families of the 35th. With a flourish he pulled out his sword and saluted Kathleen, who stood on the porch of their saltbox-style house, complete to the white picket fence, a wonderful touch of Maine in this faraway place. He reined in for a moment, looking at her wrapped in a flowing robe, her pregnancy showing, her features flushed with a warm glow.

With a smile he nodded, urging Mercury into a canter, and continued on down the street. Reaching the Methodist church at the corner, the regiment turned right into Gettysburg Street, named like the old company street back in Fort Lincoln for one of the regiment's proudest moments, and started up the hill. For two more blocks they passed through the area of the city commonly known as Yankee Town by the Rus, the street lined with clapboard houses, most of them still modest single-story saltboxes and Cape Cods, though more than one of the men was planning a proper Victorian when the frenzied pace of industrialization had died off and labor wasn't so strictly allocated to essential needs.

A broad open boulevard marked the end of their village; the other side of the street was lined with the traditional Rus log homes. The streets were crowded with families watching the regiment pass. Most all the men who had been mobilized had reported down to the rail yards hours ago, their families staying behind to avoid the mad chaotic crush.

The drums thundered and echoed down the street, the men finishing their first song and shifting to the unofficial anthem of the army, "The Battle Cry of Freedom."

The great square of the city was before him, packed with the people of Suzdal. Four regiments were drawn up before the cathedral, the first brigade of the old first division. On their shoulders burnished muskets were poised; heavy blanket rolls draped over their left shoulders. Haversacks were crammed to overflowing with eight days of rations. Cartridge boxes and pockets were filled with a hundred rounds per man. Their baggy white tunics and trousers were a sad comparison to the blue uniforms of the 35th, but the men looked lean and tough from the hard labor of the mills.

The old veterans of the Tugar war looked proud at the approach of their commander.

Hans rode out in front of the formation, with Kindred, the division commander at his side. Both still wore their old Union Army uniforms.

As Andrew drew closer, Kindred turned to face his unit.

"Brigade, atten-shun! Present arms!"

As one the twenty-five hundred men raised up their muskets, the sound of hands striking wood and metal echoing through the plaza.

Andrew raised his sword, returning the salute of the brigade. Riding alone at the head of the column, Andrew sat upon Mercury, his eyes deep-set behind the thin wire-framed glasses, his features stern.

"What the hell do I need with a book-learning professor?" his regimental commander had once said on the day he reported to the 35th, an awkward, confused lieutenant who until a week before had been teaching history at Bowdoin College.

The memory of that moment forced a smile to his features. What would old Estes say to all of this now? For a brief moment he let the inner tension, the anxieties that had ruled his every waking moment since he had first come to this world, drift away.

There are moments like this that make it all worth it, he thought.

Hans swung his mount in to ride by Andrew's side. The two looked at each other for an instant. No words needed to be said, for both understood what the moment had stirred. War, which they knew as only those who had fought in it ever could, was sweeping them into its dreadful maw once again. But here, for this brief instant, what they had created from nothing could show its grandeur as well. Riding past the center of the square, Andrew turned to ride straight at the cathedral, where a platform had been raised upon the front steps. Upon the platform stood Kal, dressed in his presidential best of stovepipe hat, black jacket, and baggy black trousers, with Casmar by his side. The sight of his old friend sporting chin whiskers and wearing Lincolnesque clothes almost forced a smile. But there was a sad solemnness to Kal, and Andrew felt a moment of cold chill. The man seemed this morning to radiate a quality of troubled sorrow that stabbed Andrew's heart. He slowed for a moment and with solemn formality saluted a man who though a friend was also his president.

"God watch over you, my friend," Kal said, his voice echoing over the plaza. Andrew was stunned to see tears in the man's eyes.

Casmar raised up his hand, holding a branch dripping with water, and with solemn dignity made the sign of cross, the droplets sprinkling over Andrew.

The tableau held but for a moment, and with a gentle nudge Andrew urged Mercury forward, riding across the front of the cathedral and turning down the road to the main gate.

The tramping cadence of the regiments echoed down the street. The deep shadows of the street were suddenly pierced by shafts of red light from the rising sun directly in front of him. Back in the square the Rus regiments broke into "The Battle Hymn of the Republic," singing it in their own language, which seemed to add a deep richness to the words.

Andrew turned to look back. The sunlight reflected with a dazzling brilliance off the thousands of bayonet-tipped muskets so that the street seemed to be awash with a swaying column of fire.

Hans caught his look and turned as well. Finally the old sergeant looked back at him, his face filled with awe.

"And to think we helped to create this," Hans whispered.

"As Lee said," Andrew replied, "it is good war is so terrible, else we would grow too fond of it."

The troops continued down the road, passing under the main gate and out into the rail yard.

The orderly column behind him was a marked counterpoint to what appeared to be a mass sea of confusion. Every inch of track along the sidings was jammed with railcars of every description, most of them packed to overflowing, with men sprawled on the roofs of boxcars, sitting atop wood tenders, some of them piled into hopper cars, which Andrew could already see would be sheer torture to ride in.

Whistles shrieked, frightened horses neighed with terror, men cursed and yelled as they manhandled guns up onto flatcars and lashed them in place. Gangs of laborers sweated in the cool morning air, carrying boxes of rations, musket and artillery rounds, fodder for horses, entrenching equipment, cased and padded boxes filled with smithing tools for the guns so they could be repaired in the field, and the hundreds of other items necessary for an army to function.

Andrew saw John down by the station and cantered over to him. With a weary smile John looked up from the bulging sheaf of papers in his hands.

"Long night John?" Andrew asked.

"Haven't slept a wink in two days," John replied.

"Well, once we get out of here, you're taking a couple of days off."

"Like hell, sir," John replied evenly. "I'm going with you."

"Now John, I need you here."

"You need me in the field, sir. This is only half the job so far, and I'm not arguing with you over this the way Hans and O'Donald did. I know where my duty is, and I'll be on the last train out with or without orders."

"All right, John," Andrew said, unable to argue with this man who had a far better grasp of all that was happening than he could ever hope to master. "Now how's the loading?"

"A bit behind schedule, but I figured that would happen and planned some built-in extra time." He paused to look over at the large clock hanging in front of the station.

"The first train still leaves in eighteen minutes. We'll have thirty-one trains leaving out of here at fifteen-minute intervals for the rest of the day. Six trains are already pulling out of Novrod, and the rest will be leaving from the other cities just about now. Everyone is to hold to twelve miles an hour—most of the engines will be working to the maximum even at that—and there'll be three-mile intervals between each train. Your train will be twentieth in line."

"That still puts me over sixty miles back from the front," Andrew said uncomfortably, even though that issue had already been debated.

"General Barry is already up at the railhead, and our last report indicates the Carthas have made no move in our direction. If anything had happened during the night we would have highballed you up the line already."

This new form of warfare was something they had only talked about in plans and late-night debates. It had been decided then that a commander should be in the middle of the formation, in case a crisis developed at the rear of the column. Though he agreed with the concept it still made him feel uncomfortable. He had always led from the front before.

"Excuse me, sir," John said. "You're train number three—your staff is already aboard. Now I've got other things to attend to. Also now that the parade's over, could you get the boys of the 35th out of the way? It's too crowded here already."

Turning away, he stalked down the platform.

"General Kindred," and his voice shot out high and clear, "Your 7th Regiment was late getting here. I can't tolerate that."

Incredulous, Kindred looked down at the colonel.

"Now listen here, John," Kindred ventured.

"You might be a high and mighty general now, Tim, but you once were a sergeant in my old platoon. I want you to kick that colonel's ass. Now your other boys should know their tracks and engine numbers. Get 'em on board."

Andrew looked over at the thoroughly discomforted general and smiled.

"He's in command here more than I am," Andrew said, and turning, he looked around at the vast assembly.

"Just where the hell is engine number three?" Andrew whispered, looking over at Hans.

"Damned if I know. Just ride around a bit. The men will think you're inspecting them or something."

Andrew nodded in reply, then leaned over and grasped Hans's hand.

"This will be my first fight without you by my side," Andrew said.

Hans smiled.

"You're doing fine, son. Just remember, though, I still think there's something more behind all this than meets the eye. You're going to be way the hell out there on the end of nearly six hundred miles of track, so be careful."

Hans grasped his hand sharply and then pulled back and saluted.

"Give 'em hell, sir."

Andrew saluted in return, and pulling Mercury around just a little too sharply, he started off across the track, squeezing his way between the tail end of a caboose and the engine of the train behind it.

Starting down between two tracks, he immediately gave up trying to salute the endless line of men hanging out passenger-car windows, packed in boxcars, and hunkered down on the flatcars loaded with cannons and piles of boxes.

"At ease, men, at ease," he chanted over and over again. He paused for a moment with one group, playing the old game, asking a man about his family, shaking the hand of another, pausing to chat for a moment with a soldier who proudly showed off the scar from a Tugar blade.

Crossing over another set of tracks, he finally saw the military command car, still sporting the embarrassing tableau of him leading a charge. His staff stood alongside the track, looking around, taking in the sights. He was tempted to launch into a good chewing-out, but gave it up, realizing that all of this had too much of a grand holiday air to it, an experience unique to every last one of them.

When he drew up before them the men came to attention, saluting as he climbed down off of Mercury. He patted his old friend, offering him a lump of honeyed sweet before an orderly led the horse away to a boxcar where five other horses, all old veterans of the Civil War on earth, waited.

Andrew looked up and down the length of his train. The engine was the *Malady*, the new second model of locomotive which was now the standard pattern for the locomotives of the MFL&S Railroad. Twenty cars were strung behind it. The men of the 11th Suzdal were packed into the first ten passenger cars, then came the two cars for his staff, which was packed with maps, a complete telegraph station, old-fashioned Signal Corps equipment, and a complete operating station, which Emil was undoubtably fussing over.

The car behind him contained the only large tents for the expedition, again for Kal's hospital. Next came two of the new armored cars, the heavy twelve-pounders pulled out and replaced with the lighter four-pounders of two batteries which could be moved forward. The last six cars were packed with yet more rations and ammunition, the roofs occupied by the men serving the guns in the armored cars.

From the earthen wall that flanked the far side of the rail yard a field piece cut loose with a sharp staccato boom, and with a cold start Andrew looked up.

"Here we go!" a young orderly shouted.

The engine of the next train forward let down on its whistle with a high shriek, followed an instant later with a cacophony of shouted cheers, bells, and screaming whistles. White billowing clouds of woodsmoke rose up from the engine. A shudder passed through the cars, and then ever so slowly the engine started to inch forward. Andrew watched as the train commenced to gather speed. It reached the end of the siding, switching through to the main track and turning to head out the gate. The sharp snap of a musket volley rose up from the other side of the earthen wall as the honor guard of the 21st Suzdal fired a salute to the first train out.

"All aboard, all aboard!"

A fireman came running down the length of the train.

Andrew, joining the others, scrambled aboard the car. Barely was the last man up when a lurch shuddered through the car. Andrew grabbed hold of the railing for support as he stepped up onto the small platform.

The train inched forward, bell ringing, occupying the place of the previous train. Even as they rolled forward and stopped, a puffing plume of smoke marked the arrival of another engine coming in through the northern rail gate. Behind the train were half a dozen of the massive dormitory cars which had been run down only the night before from the end of the line in Roum territory.

"Five of those cars will hold a regiment," Emil said, coming out onto the platform to watch the show.

"Without them we'd be in a tough spot."

"Those things are filth-breeding dens of squalor," Emil said sharply.

"No worst than quarters aboard a ship like the *Ogunquit*."

"Whatever deviltry that Cromwell created, I'm certain he didn't think of proper sanitation," Emil sniffed, "but that's no excuse for us."

"I'm certain he didn't," Andrew said, unable to contain a disparaging laugh. "I've heard them ironclads are hell in the summertime. Hundred-and-fifty-degree heat belowdecks in a fight."

"Well, I hope they all fry in hell," Emil said. "A lot of good boys are going to be on my table in a couple of days."

"Let's hope it doesn't come to a fight in the end," Andrew replied. "Though I've never seen it, I think a battle won without a fight must be a rare pleasure indeed."

"Well, it'd give all these boys the five percent of pleasure that can be found in a war, the excitement and adventure, without the ninety-five percent of hell that makes up the rest of it."

The train behind them came to a stop, and within seconds the twelve hundred men of two regiments who had been drawn up along the earthen wall swarmed forward, laughing and shouting, struggling to grab the best places on the cars and avoid being stuck on the roof.

"You bring your microscope along?" Andrew asked, desiring a moment of light talk. Once the train got moving and his overexcited staff had calmed down a bit, the rest of the journey would be filled with long hard hours of work.

"God hear my prayer," Emil intoned piously, looking to the heavens, "I don't want to see a single lad get hurt, but if they do, I want to make slides of the infections."

"Now, you know I'm a firm believer in Semmelweiss," Emil continued, warming to his subject. "Studied under him in Vienna. He figured out how infection gets moved from one person to another. But he never went far enough. He understood the how, but never the why."

"And you think that microscope you made is the answer."

"I'm positive of it. There's a whole world of tiny creatures. I'm calling them sims after my old professor."

"Do you think he'd be insulted?"

"Good heavens, no. But as I was saying, it's these creatures I suspect, millions of them that grow in wounds and cause disease."

"Oh, I believe you, doctor, it's just that it seems hard to imagine."

"Believe it! Those damn fools with their miasmas and night vapors were a pack of butchering idiots."

Andrew knew better than to debate with his old friend. After all, though Emil had taken off what was left of his arm after Gettysburg, the doctor had assuredly saved his life in the weeks afterward.

"Now, we know boiling destroys them. I already proved that with boiling instruments and bandages. You remember how I killed off that typhoid outbreak in Novrod last fall."

"It was certainly a miracle," one of Emil's young medical trainees said, coming up to look admiringly at his mentor.

"It wasn't a miracle, it was plain common sense. People were getting sick. It turned out with a little questioning they were all drinking from the same well. When everyone started to boil the water, the outbreak died down."

"But you can't boil a man's arm or leg to kill the infection," Andrew said.

"That's the puzzle," Emil replied, his enthusiasm dropping somewhat. "I think it's the sims. If I could just find a way to kill them and leave all the cells of our body unharmed, I'd have the key to cutting our battle death rate to a fraction of what it is now."

The sharp blast of a cannon startled Andrew again. The *Malady* came to life, smoke puffing out of its stack, its bells starting in with a harmonic tolling. Another cheer rose up from the rail yard as a shudder ran down the length of the train and ever so slowly they started to edge forward. From the cars alongside on the next track men leaned out, waving and shouting. The train started to pick up steam, the slow thumping clatter of the rails rising in tempo. Standing erect, he found that he was striking a pose, playing the necessary part in this drama, the commander riding out to war on his iron horse, bathed in smoke and steam.

The car swayed as they reached the switch, clearing the head of the train alongside. For a brief moment he had a view back to the old walls of the city. Upon the battlement atop the stone-towered gate he saw two women dressed in blue. Kathleen and Tanya together. He raised his hand once, a sad restrained gesture, as if trying to convey not just to her but to the thousands of excited soldiers in the yard that after all this was not a joyful ride they were embarking upon.

The car arced through its turn, and the boxcar behind him blocked off the view. The train crossed through the gate and over the drawbridge moat. Another volley snapped out as they rolled past the 21st.

A waste of good powder, he thought sharply. For a brief moment he saw Hans looking up at him, his features grim, and then his old sergeant disappeared from view. The train crossed through the dead zone of entanglements and turning again started northeastward, running parallel to the outer wall of the city. The first switch shot past, the side track leading off to the east and the industrial works. The track was backed up with train after train waiting their turn to cut across the main line and into the city through the north gate for loading.

"How John ever pulled this together in two days is a wonder," Andrew said with open admiration.

"If it doesn't kill him in the end. That boy's heading for a serious bout of nervous debilitation. Don't use him up too quickly, Andrew."

"I've got to, Emil," Andrew replied sadly. "The same way I've always used up men when I had to."

The train, still gaining speed, clattered onto the trestle bridge across the Vina River, passing under the wooden aqueduct that came down from the dam. He looked at them appraisingly. Both the trestle bridge and the aqueduct were barely adequate temporary affairs. Trestles, Ferguson had explained to him, were easier for as yet unskilled laborers to build than a good arched wooden or iron bridge. The aqueduct was a crudely cobbled affair of upright wooden poles supporting a rough board trough, which lost nearly half its water before it reached town.

Andrew looked over at Emil, who gazed at the viaduct as if it was a treasured grandchild, who though ugly to the rest of the world was in his eyes the perfection of creation.

We're stretched to the limit, Andrew realized. The Suzdalians, used to the slavery under the boyars, now thought the schedule of six twelve-hour days a week was a luxury. But most of them still lived in the most primitive of conditions. Their old social system was shattered and they were still groping to find a new one, and thankfully were still imbued with a mad enthusiasm for their revolution. But the revolution was going to have to offer something back to them personally before much longer or the first faint cracks of strain might break wide open. He had been playing a conjuring game with them for too long already.

Yet there was far too much to be done. This mad frenzy of preparation and building might be able to hold for only a brief while longer, driven at the moment out of a terrible fear that another visitation like the Tugars might arrive, and a compulsion to drive eastward, to seek out new allies and markets.

Having crossed over the river, the train turned to the east, slowing significantly as it climbed the hills that rose up along the northern banks of the river. Andrew pushed the thoughts away and settled back to enjoy the countryside, bathed now in the full light of morning. A fold of hills blocked the factories to his right, marked now only by the columns of smoke rising up from the locomotives and the ironworks, which in spite of the emergency was still running with replacement crews.

The puffing chugs of the engine swirled skyward, filing the air with a faint but not unpleasant scent of woodsmoke. The fields to his left, rising up to the yet higher hills north of town, were rich with the fullness of summer, the wheat stalks golden and full.

A year and a half ago this area had been the camp of the Tugar horde, while the armies fought in the plains below. The forest had been cut back for several miles to feed their fires; stumps showed along the sides of the hills. A small farm village clung to the side of a knoll, the homes made up of yurts, their wheels gone, the heavy felt tents clustered around the burned-over ruins of the villagers' former homes. The thought of people living in the yurts had bothered him at first, until he had spent an evening in one. Built for nine-foot-high Tugars, the yurts were commodious and to his surprise remarkably warm.

Andrew noticed the tempo starting to pick up again. Going over to the side of the platform, he leaned out from the car, and behind him the wonderful panorama of Suzdal stood below. From a distance it still held a fairy-tale splendor, the southern half of the city which had survived the siege a splendid mix of onion domes and high wood-shingled buildings adorned with fantastic swirls of color, all of it dominated by the cathedral tower of stone, faced now with a proper clock. Looking farther north, he could barely make out the white church spires of the Methodist and Catholic congregations. From out of the gate another engine appeared, its smoke puffing high into the still air. Turning to look forward, he could see a smudge of smoke ahead hidden by low hills, the mark of the next train down the line.

This was a wonder, what they had created, and in his imagination he could picture the long line of trains thundering by every fifteen minutes, hour after hour. If only I had Hank Petracci's balloon right now, he thought, I could climb into the heavens and see this long steam-driven caravan streaking eastward. He stepped back up onto the platform and leaned back, admonishing himself for his flight of fancy. There was still a war to plan.

A flash of blue showed on his right, the broad upper reaches of the mill lake, its waters rippling with the first faint breeze of day.

It reminded him of the lakes up in the Waterville area of Maine, a cluster of fir trees on the far bank reflected in near-perfection by the water. The train rolled along the lakeside for several minutes, its passage kicking up flights of waterfowl nesting along the banks. The happy shouts of the men forward rolled across the water like waves. The train started into a more northerly curve to skirt around a low series of hills. To the right a branch line of track arced out, continuing along the riverbank to the city of Novrod twenty miles away, and from there on to Mosva and Kev before rejoining the main line to Roum nearly a hundred miles farther up the line.

Andrew looked over at Emil, who ever since leaving the city had been lost in a dreamy silence.

"There's something hypnotic about trains," Emil said. "They make you want to smile, to dream about faraway places, distant romances yet to happen, happy reunions in smoke-filled stations. The clatter of the rails is like a song, the landscape a tapestry rolling by."

"Why, you've got a touch of the poet in you," Andrew said.

Emil grinned shyly.

"Well, it's just they give me a happy-sad sort of feeling. I had always promised my Ester that we'd ride a train. This was before they came to Budapest."

It was rare for Emil to talk about her, and it caught Andrew by surprise.

"I always regretted that. The train line was opened, and she kept pestering me to take it with her to Vienna.

"And then the cholera took her away," he said softly, "so we never did go to Vienna like she wanted."

Fumbling, Emil reached into his pocket and pulled out a handkerchief. With a look of embarassment he wiped his eyes.

"So now when I ride them I think of her. How she wanted to have just one excursion on these new things."

"Maybe she's riding with you now," Andrew said, affectionately putting his hand on Emil's shoulder.

"That's what I'd like to think," he sighed. "Anyhow, I'd better go back in there and recheck my equipment. That numbskull Nicholas packed it."

"He's the best student you have," Andrew said, "Kathleen has nothing but praise for him."

"Now, now. It's Kathleen that's the best medical student

I have, and yes, damn him, Nicholas is second, but never let them hear you say that."

Andrew gave Emil another affectionate pat on the shoulder as he opened the door and went into the crowded staff car.

Having rounded the hills, the train turned due east. A scattering of trees edged their passage, the forward march of the great forest. To the south the ground drifted away in an undulating wave of low grass-covered hills to the distant horizon, etched clear in the morning air. The region they were passing through was the meeting place of the endless steppe and forest. He stood alone on the platform for one last moment, letting the rhythm of the train wash over him.

Taking a deep breath he turned away and stepped into the car, the questions engulfing him before the door had even closed behind him.

"Aunt Katie!"

The little boy raced down the platform, and kneeling down, she leaned forward, protecting herself from his exuberant embrace.

"You like the trains, Andrew."

"I want ride," Andrew shouted, and then struggled with an imitation of a whistle that came out with a spray that caused her to laugh as she pulled out a handkerchief and wiped her face, and then the smudge of grease off of his.

"Pick me up."

"You know she can't do that," Ludmilla said, sweeping up behind Andrew and lifting him into the air so that he shrieked with delight.

"Grandma, put me down. Katie carry me."

Kathleen stood up and kissed him on the cheek as he struggled with mock disdain.

Seeing Tanya, Kathleen went over and gave her a loving embrace.

"How are you doing?"

"I had to come down and see the last train leave," she said quietly.

"So did I," Kathleen replied. "Don't worry—Vincent's safe in the city. Andrew and the men will have him out of there in no time."

"Oh, I know that," Tanya said, and Kathleen could see the fear in the girl's eyes.

She held her friend close.

"You know something?" Kathleen whispered. "I think all men can be a pain in the ass."

Tanya looked at her wide-eyed.

"Here they get us pregnant, leave us with the babies, and then go traipsing off to their damnable adventures. And we get stuck at home, playing the dutiful wife, worrying ourselves sick over them. Back in America during the war we were supposed to knit socks to keep ourselves busy. Now is that fair?"

A sad worried smile lighted Tanya's features.

"At least Vincent and that president over there could have allowed me to go join him before all this started."

"Now, you know the twins couldn't have stood the travel," Ludmilla interjected, still holding Andrew as she looked into the carriage, where the two girls were fast asleep in spite of the commotion around them.

"You're right," Tanya said, loud enough for her father to hear her. "All men are a pain in the ass."

Kal looked over at his daughter with an air of mock injury while his staff, who had been standing at a respectful distance, looked at her with open shock.

Tanya looked back at Kathleen and forced a smile, though both knew that their bravado was hiding a terrible sea of fear.

"Time for us to leave."

Kathleen looked over and saw John, his face gaunt with exhaustion, come down the platform and stop in front of Kal.

"You've done a magnificent job, son," Kal said, his voice full of emotion. "All of you have. I'm not speaking now as president, but as a father to that boy up in Roum, and I thank you for this miracle you've created."

Kal stepped forward and clumsily put his one arm around John, hugging him in the older fashion of Rus. John nervously accepted the embrace, then stepped back and saluted.

"God keep you, John. I wanted to be here to see you off," Kathleen said, coming up to take his hand.

"Thank you, ma'am."

"John, it's always been Kathleen."

He nodded wearily, then walked back to the last remaining engine on the siding and waved.

The train whistle blew, triggering a delighted squeal from

Andrew, which was counterpointed by the high piercing wails of the twins. As the train edged forward, John leaped aboard the first car and clambered up the steps.

Ferguson leaned out of the cabin, snapping off a cheery salute as the engine rolled past, setting off a vast plume of steam, sparks kicking up out of the stack. The row of flatcars was piled to overflowing with the men of the 21st Suzdal and the eighth battery. The excitement of the early morning had died away, and the men looked somber, coming to attention, saluting as each car rolled past Kal, who had his hat off and over his heart.

Kathleen looked over at him. Good God, he was becoming like Lincoln, she thought as he anxiously looked at the men rolling past.

The caboose rolled by, a lone officer standing on the back.

"Don't worry, Mr. President," the boy shouted, "we'll all be coming back!" The train turned through the gate and disappeared from view.

The station was silent except for the crying of the girls. Kathleen came up to Kal's side and saw tears in his eyes.

"I kept trying to look into all their faces, to breathe a blessing of life to each and every one of them," he whispered. "But Kesus help me, I know some of them will never come home again."

He stood in silence, and Kathleen felt numbed by his pain, unable to help him, to dredge into her soul beyond her own fears and somehow reassure him that he was doing what had to be done.

"Now I know why your pictures of Lincoln always looked so sad," he said quietly as he blinked away his tears and a look of forced composure appeared.

Slowly he put his hat back on.

"Come, my family, let's go home," he said evenly.

Andrew, breaking free from his grandmother's embrace, raced up to Kal's side. With a smile he held up his hand, and Kal took it, so the two walked down the platform side by side, a sight filled with such poignancy that Kathleen struggled for control.

"Join us for dinner, dear," Ludmilla said, coming up and putting her arm around Kathleen's shoulder.

"I'd like that," Kathleen whispered.

"Well, they're all gone," a voice called.

Kathleen looked up and saw a burly thickset man, followed by a retinue of half a dozen others, come out of the city gate.

"He would show up now," Tanya hissed, drawing up alongside Kathleen.

"Yes, senators, they're gone," Kal said evenly, continuing on so that Mikhail had to step aside.

"I'm certain that with the great plans you and Keane made, this campaign will be a success," Mikhail announced, his voice loud enough that the people who had stood a respectful distance back from Kal could hear the exchange.

"Kesus alone knows," Kal replied, the concern in his voice evident.

"Unfortunately, Kesus is not here to advise us in person, so all of us good citizens must count on your judgment instead."

Mikhail hesitated and looked over at Kathleen and Tanya.

"And, of course, our friend Keane and your young son-in-law, whom you appointed ambassador."

"I have the fullest confidence in our army, which gained our respect by fighting to free us," Kal replied.

Kathleen could not help but smile at the barb in Kal's retort.

Mikhail paused for a second, taken aback by the veiled insult.

"Oh, I support the army fully, and pray for its glorious success. But I can't help but think that this is a different war, Kal," Mikhail finally replied, as Kal walked past him. "Without the folly of this railroad and the overreaching ambitions of some, it never would have been called down upon us."

"If you wish to debate it, the floor of the Senate is the place," Kal replied without looking back. "A good day to you, Senator Mikhail Ivorovich."

Mikhail bristled at the dismissal, and Kathleen could see he had hoped to draw out an argument in the street to play upon the fears of the families who had watched their loved ones leave. But he had scored his mark nevertheless, Kathleen could see, as she looked over at the anxious faces, as people turned to each other and started to whisper. By nightfall this encounter would be told of in every tavern in the city.

Kathleen, walking behind Kal, with Tanya by her side

pushing the carriage, looked over at Mikhail, who glared at her coldly.

"I hope you rot in hell, you lowborn bastard," she whispered in a barely audible voice, her words belied by a sweet, friendly smile.

She could see him coil up with rage.

"Come on, you coward," she whispered. "Wouldn't it look heroic, the brave Tugar-kissing Mikhail attacking a pregnant woman on the street."

His visage purple with rage, all he could do was glare at her as she walked by, a grin of delight crossing her features.

"Andrew should have hung him, amnesty be damned," Kathleen said evenly, looking over at Tanya, who smiled at her with evident delight.

I think before it's all over he still might have to do it, Kathleen thought to herself as they walked back into the city, so strangely quiet now that the army was gone at last.

# Chapter Seven

Numb with fatigue, Vincent stopped at the edge of the parapet and looked down. A section of wall nearly a hundred feet across was nothing but shambles. Another breach had been cut along the south side, from the massed battery of six-pounders, but this one was far worse, the sole work of the two heavy guns which were dug in not six hundred yards away.

Behind the breach, hundreds of slaves worked, building an earthen rampart to seal the puncture off. The defense line was crude, but could be efficient with the men of the 5th positioned around the hole, the battered houses lining the streets now linked with barricades of rubble. His command was stretched beyond the limit. A hundred men here, another fifty at the south breach, the rest held in reserve in the forum to be rushed to where the crisis would finally break.

The damnable problem was that the walls of the city were designed without any thought to gunpowder. They were too high and too thin, and worse yet there were no sections of the battlement wide enough for his field pieces to be deployed with enough safe clearance for recoil. He had tried to lash a gun in with short ropes to stop the carriage from rolling back. On the fourth shot the gun cracked a trunnion, putting it permanently out of action.

Their only weapons with any range were the twenty double-torsion ballistae, with a range of four hundred yards, useless against the enemy entrenchments.

He looked back out to the enemy battery. If only he had a couple of squads of snipers armed with scope-mounted Whitworths, they could play hell with the gun crews. If I ever get out of this, he thought coldly, it's something I'm going to make sure gets done.

"Everybody down!" a lookout screamed.

The slaves dropped their tools, scrambling in every direction. Vincent felt exposed, naked, but like a proper officer he had to show disdain for fire. With a measured casualness he turned his back to the enemy battery and looked down at the breach.

A high piercing howl filled the air. Stunned, he felt a rush of air, and for a terrifying instant thought that he was finished. A gaping hole appeared in a house facing the breach, followed a second later by a thunderclap flash of light and smoke. A side wall of the house burst open, spilling the shattered wall into the street, crushing three men who had dived into the gutter for protection. Roofing tiles sickled through the air, shattering against the side of the building across the street.

Terrified screams rent the air. Men came to their feet and in panic started to rush down the street, away from the explosions of death.

Vincent watched as a squad of legionnaires rushed out, shields up, blocking the retreat. Metal snicked out and a slave staggered back screaming, holding his side. The mob stopped, and then sullenly gave back, cursing, returning to their labors.

"Can you keep ahead of the damage?"

Vincent turned to face Marcus, who had come up behind him.

"You know, sir, it really isn't too wise for both of us to be together like this under fire."

"What you're trying to say is that you want me hiding back at the forum."

"Sir, if you should get killed, I think you know what will happen."

"Catullus and Petronius would like nothing better," Marcus said with a smile. "Can you hold them off?"

"It's still five days till reinforcements arrive," Vincent said quietly. "If they keep this hammering up, they're going to have a hole in our lines a hundred yards across. My rifles couldn't possibly hold a breach that wide. I've already lost nearly half my men as is."

"That's what Petronius supposedly said last night."

"Can you hold him off?"

Marcus looked over his shoulder at Boris and the rest of his bodyguard.

"You were right about the assassination," Marcus said quietly.

"What?"

"An hour ago," Boris said excitedly as he came up beside Marcus.

"Let him tell it—he saw it far better than I did," Marcus said with a smile, looking over at Boris and patting him on the shoulder.

"We was going down to the south wall. It was a crowded street, people milling about. Suddenly I saw this flash of metal. They were on him in no time. Well, Marcus here got the first one and no mistake. I got the second one with the bayonet," and he nodded to his blade, which was covered with dried blood.

"You never should have let them get that close!" Vincent roared angrily.

"If you're upset with him, don't be," Marcus replied soothingly, sensing the anger in Vincent's words. "He did a good job."

"They could have just been two madmen," Marcus said as if dismissing the subject.

"I doubt that," Vincent snapped in reply.

"Well, there's no way of ever proving it, so it's best to drop the matter."

Vincent stepped away from Marcus and drew up close to Boris, who looked at him wide-eyed.

"You got it half right the first time," Vincent said coldly. "You'd better make sure you get it completely right the second time. If he gets killed, this whole thing will unravel, and I'll have your head for it."

"Yes, sir," Boris said, his voice trembling.

"All right, then, we understand each other, Boris," and he turned away.

He hated to command this way. He had always done it before by sharing the hardships, ordering softly, leading by example. For the first time in his career he had threatened a soldier, and he found it distasteful. But there was no other way.

Vincent looked back down at the breech, where the slaves were back at work building the secondary wall.

"You know, Marcus, you have nearly two hundred thousand people in this city, yet only ten thousand under arms."

"What are you suggesting?" Marcus asked.

"When they storm this town, the advantage of weapons will be squarely on their side."

"If your people had delivered the thousand muskets that you promised, the odds would be better."

"Sir, we still have another division to arm at home. Once the surplus of weapons started we would have sent them."

He knew that was a lie. After seeing the slave labor in Hispania after the formal treaty signing, Kal had made it clear that he would not arm a government that could use those weapons against its own people. The old-style smoothbores were sitting in the warehouses by the thousands waiting for conversion to rifling. At the moment Vincent wished he had compromised on that issue and sent the equipment up.

"You have over a hundred thousand men in this city working like the ones down there," Vincent said, pointing to the gang of slaves, who looked up nervously at the two leaders gazing down at them.

"Slaves fight?"

"They fought tooth and nail against the remnants of the Tugars."

"Because they knew that if they failed, two out of ten of them would go to the feasting pits."

"They could fight against the Carthas. Their numbers would tip the scale."

"What for?" Marcus replied.

"For a chance at freedom, Marcus," Vincent replied.

"You said before Petronius that you would not support a revolution against me. What is it you are proposing now but a revolution?"

"I'm proposing a salvation for you. If you offered emancipation to the slaves of this city in return for their fighting, damn near every one of them would follow you. Hell, you're already viewed as something of a hero to them for turning back the Tugars. They'd follow you, Marcus."

"And my country would be destroyed when it was over with."

"Marcus, without them, you'll have no country."

"Don't push me," Marcus said coldly. "In five days' time your comrades will be here. They must know that out there, they'd be mad to stay and be caught by your army."

"Oh, they know we're coming," Vincent replied, thinking back to the mystery of why the telegraph line had not been cut. "I half suspect they want Andrew to come here with the army."

"Why?"

"I don't know. But I suspect all of us, you, Andrew, everyone is being maneuvered for some other plan."

"And don't maneuver me for your plans," Marcus said evenly. "I've come to like and admire you, young though you are. But you have the streak of a dreamer in you, Vincent Hawthorne. Maybe it is this strange absurd Quaker belief you carry."

"I don't know if I can call myself a Quaker anymore," Vincent said sadly. "I've killed too much to still claim my belief."

"Would you rather have lain down to the Tugars, or to those out there who we both suspect are the human mask of the Merki?"

"No," Vincent whispered, somewhat ashamed at giving an open voice to his denial of faith.

"My belief in freedom still stands, though," Vincent continued.

"And my belief in maintaining Roum as the eternal it has always been remains as well."

A thin smile creased Marcus's handsome but careworn features.

"I think we are at an impasse, my young ambassador," Marcus said, making it clear that the debate was finished.

Vincent suddenly noticed they had been standing on the battlement for some time, and not a shot had been fired from the heavy siege guns, or from the lighter weapons. Turning away, he walked over to the wall.

Across the field, alongside the battery he saw several horsemen. Pulling out his telescope, he raised it.

"It's Cromwell," Vincent hissed, offering the glass to Marcus.

"I'd give damn near everything to have a Whitworth," Vincent snapped, enraged at his impotence.

"Something's up," Boris announced.

One of the three horsemen broke away from the group, riding up over the battery ramparts, and started across the field. A white flag fluttered from his lance.

"What does a white flag mean?" Marcus asked.

"It's the symbol of truce. They want to talk."

Marcus looked over at Vincent.

"There's nothing they can offer, Marcus. It's a calculated move to play on our weaknesses."

"Let's first hear what they have to say."

The horseman drew closer, waving the flag over his head, slowing as he approached the wall. The lone rider came to a stop fifty yards out and held the flag up high.

"Come forward!" Marcus shouted.

Cautiously the man drew up before the breach, gazing at the ruins with interest.

"Boris, level your gun on him," Vincent ordered.

With a grin of delight, Boris stepped up to the edge of the breach and clicked the hammer of his weapon, the sound causing the rider to look up.

"You'd better have business with me or I'll order you shot," Marcus announced.

"I am seeking Marcus Licinius Graca, first consul of the Roum."

"I am here," Marcus replied sharply.

"It is the wish of my commander that you come before him in parley so that the differences between us can be settled without further resort to blood. He will promise your safety."

"Not yourself," Vincent replied sharply. "It's not done, and you don't dare leave the city."

"I will send an emissary."

"You have nothing to fear from us," the envoy retorted, his voice full of irony. "We pledge your safety."

"Like hell," Vincent replied. "Send someone else."

Marcus looked down at Vincent and smiled.

"Then it's you."

"Me? I'm the ambassador for Rus, not your envoy."

"Who should I send, then? One of my senators? This war involves you as much as us. And it's your Cromwell you'll be meeting. I'm sending you."

* * *

With bell clanging, the engine slowed to a crawl. Stepping out of the car, Andrew walked out onto the platform and nervously grabbed hold of the railing.

If there was one thing he couldn't stand, it was heights. Cautiously he peered over the side to the river valley a hundred feet below.

"Crossing the Kennebec, sir?" an orderly asked, looking out the door and then coming out to join Andrew.

"None other," Andrew said dryly, his stomach knotting as the boy immediately went to the side of the platform and leaned over.

"It sure is a long way down there, sir."

"More than a hundred feet, son. Now get back up here."

The young Rus soldier came up and looked at Andrew as if he were yet another boring adult who had cut into his fun.

"What's your name, boy?" Andrew asked, slightly embarrassed. It was getting so he couldn't even recall his own staff. They came on with him for several months, soaked up the training, and then went on to serve as adjutants in other regiments.

"Gregory Vasilovich, sir," and with a proud flourish he pointed back over the side. "My father helped build this bridge."

"Well, you've something to be proud of, Gregory."

The train swayed slightly and Andrew clutched the railing even tighter. Since there were no side rails to the trestle, it appeared as if they were crossing on thin air, and he felt as if at any second the train would simply tumble over the side.

"Don't worry, sir, it's as safe as they come. The biggest bridge in the world."

He had watched the construction with awe while it was going up. Over three hundred thousand board feet of lumber had gone into it. Ferguson had designed the five-hundred-foot-long structure with amazing skill. All the wooden supports and beams had been precut to a standard size at a sawmill in the woods fifteen miles north and then floated down the river and hammered together with wooden pins. The most amazing part of it was that the structure had gone up in under a month. Ferguson felt he was in a race with the legendary railroad engineer Hermann Haupt, who had worked miracles with the Union Army supply lines and had built a bridge of similar size in only three days. Lincoln had called that bridge the beanpole-and-cornstalk wonder. The name had stuck, and most of the men on the line now called this one the beanpole bridge, a name which at the moment did little to reassure him. Five other major bridges and dozens of smaller ones were needed for the line, but for Ferguson this was his proudest accomplishment.

The train inched along the bridge, and as they drew near the east bank of the river he saw two lines of men snaking up the side of the riverbank, bucket brigades, working at a furious pace. The train gained the far bank and with a slashing discharge of steam came to a halt.

"Fifteen minutes, fifteen minutes!" the cry echoed down the train.

"Mitchell, patch us into the wire, find out the latest," Andrew shouted back into the car.

Andrew climbed down the side and jumped to the ground, groaning and stretching. A mad scramble of men cascaded down from the cars ahead and behind.

The tank stop was an insane turmoil of activity. Another train was stopped ahead of them, still taking on water, while gangs of laborers were throwing wood up into the tender.

"Not on this side, you bastards! The other side!" a weary soldier shouted, coming down the track. His foot snaked out, catching a soldier on his bare backside as he started to squat down not ten feet from the side of the train.

"It's a goddam pestilence pit out there," Emil shouted, coming up to join Andrew, pointing to the other side of the train.

"Well, that's one thing we never planned for," Andrew said dryly. "When you're moving twenty-five thousand men, they've got to go somewhere."

At least his staff car and the passenger cars had privies. They were nothing more than small closets with the usual seat that opened straight down to the track. But for the men trapped on the other vehicles it must be getting rather difficult.

"God, what a stench," Emil grumbled and stalked off. Andrew, wrinkling his nose, found himself in full agreement.

A young telegrapher came past Andrew and leaped onto the telegraph pole, scurrying up it, trailing a wire behind him. Andrew watched him for a moment as he gained the crosstree. Hanging on with one hand, he unclipped the wire dangling from his back that led into the train and snapped it onto the main line.

"Hooked in!"

Andrew could hear the key inside come to life as Mitchell, the original organizer of the telegraph system, tapped out a signal. There was a moment's pause and then the return started to come in.

After several minutes the clattering stopped and Mitchell appeared in the window, leaning out to hand Andrew a piece of paper.

"So what's the news?" Kindred asked, coming up beside Andrew, wheezing slightly from his asthma.

"They've run out of wood a hundred miles back, hitting the last four trains. They're burning everything, including the boxcars, to get to the next station. A car farther up broke an axle, derailing the train. Nine casualties, one dead. It tied the line up somewhat while they manhandled the cars back onto the track. In the middle here we're running a couple of hours behind schedule. Water's running low all along the line. But we've lost only one train so far."

As he spoke, he nodded toward the rail siding, where an old first-model engine, its eight cars behind it, rested on the side with a broken driveshaft. The train had broken down several miles farther up the line. The next train had uncoupled its load, run up, hooked on, then pulled it back. Luck had been with them on that one. If it had let go midway between two of the tank-stop sidings it would have shot the schedule to hell.

"So far so good," Andrew said evenly, looking back up at Mitchell. "Send out my approval, then disconnect."

The whistle of the next train forward cut the air, the engineer playing out the opening bars of a popular and very obscene tavern song. Many of the engineers had mastered the skill of playing the steam whistle, and each had adopted a particular tune as his signature. It was something they never did when Mina was around, since he vehemently denounced the practice as a waste of good steam.

The telegrapher on the pole snapped the connection off, tossed it to the ground while Mitchell reeled it in, and scrambled back down the pole.

The last of the men came scrambling back, leaping aboard as the train started to pick up speed. The train alongside Andrew lurched forward, easing down the track and stopping underneath the water tank, replacing the engine that had pulled away. The hose dropped down, and Andrew watched as a slow trickle of water came out.

Looking over at the wooden tank, he saw the bucket brigade hanging on rough ladders, passing containers up and emptying the precious liquid into the tank in a never-ending battle to try and stay ahead. The one thing they didn't have was a good wind to keep the pump running when they needed it the most.

Soldiers shouldered past Andrew, coming up to the side of the tender and throwing logs up. From out of the cab the engineer jumped down, oil can in hand, setting to work while his fireman and the two brakemen raced down the side of the train, tapping wheels with hammers to check their tone for cracks.

From out of the crowd he saw a blue uniform coming forward. The heavyset mustached officer saluted.

"Stover, sir, commander 2nd Vazima. It was our train that broke down."

Andrew looked at him for a moment, racing through his memory.

"Cliff, isn't it?"

"Thank you, sir, it is," Stover replied with a smile. "I put the boys to work on the water gang, helping out the garrison here. The rest are cutting up a pile of leftover lumber for firewood."

"Fine. I'm sorry to say it looks like you're out of the fight. Your boys can stay on here as extra garrison."

The disappointment in Stover's face was obvious.

"It's an important job. Lose this bridge and we're all in trouble. We can't be sure what Cromwell might be up to."

"All right, sir," Stover said sadly.

The engineer came around from the other side of the train and leaped back into the cab. "All right, we're just about full!"

Andrew looked down the track and saw another train pulling in and stopping on the bridge behind them.

The engineer hit the whistle. This time it was a religious melody, which made Andrew smile at the contrast from the previous tune."

"All aboard!"

Andrew returned the salute of Stover and walked back down the line, dodging past the wood crew, which was furiously piling the logs in. Men scrambled past, saluting him, so that he had to walk with his hand constantly up. Climbing up the side of the car, he rejoined Emil, who was coldly looking at the south side of the track. Andrew felt his stomach churn at the sight and smell. Men were running past, some struggling with their trousers, to the shouted delight of their comrades.

The whistle sounded again, and ever so slowly the train started to move. One poor soldier slipped and went face-down into the muck, and a raucous cheer went up. The soldier stood up, a look of horrified disgust on his face at the filth which covered him from head to foot, and Andrew burst out laughing.

"Come on, Annatov, you worthless shit," a voice boomed, obviously from an enraged sergeant.

"Shitty Annatov, shitty Annatov," the chant rose up with hysterical laughter.

"Come on, boy," Andrew shouted. "Run for it."

The soldier looked over at him, saluted even as he ran, and gained his car, greeted now with loud groans of disgust.

"That poor boy will carry that nickname to the grave," Emil chuckled.

The way Emil said it sobered Andrew.

"I just hope he's an old man and can laugh about it in the end," Andrew said as he turned and went back into the car.

"The commander will see you now."

Vincent was seething. He and Lucullus, first tribune of the legion, had crossed through the lines and then been kept waiting out in the sun before a large canopied tent for over an hour. It wasn't until Lucullus had turned on his heels and stalked off back to the city, shouting an angry curse, that their escort started to scurry, begging them to stay, offering some wine and a cool place to sit, along with the promise of an immediate audience.

The tent flap was pulled back, and Vincent could not help but notice that it had the appearance of a Tugar yurt, something that made him feel uncomfortable.

As he stepped into the gloom, he saw a short rotund form rise up from behind a desk in greeting.

"I am Tobias Cromwell, commander of the fleet and army," he said in Cartha, the translator standing next to him converting his words to a reasonable Latin.

"Lucullus, tribune of the legion, envoy of the first consul," the old warrior snapped, coming to attention.

Vincent looked over at Cromwell with a cold rage.

"We have no need for introductions, Tobias," Vincent said sharply.

"You know you weren't invited to this meeting," Tobias replied. "That is why there was the delay. My staff and I had quite a debate concerning it."

"So your Merki masters slipped out the back when you were done, is that it?" Vincent retorted.

"Merki?" Tobias said, extending his hands in a gesture of innocence.

Without waiting for the offer, Vincent went over and sat in a chair by Cromwell's desk. Lucullus shot him a look of reproach and then sat down beside him.

"The purpose of this meeting?" Lucullus asked.

"To spare any more bloodshed," Tobias replied.

"Under what terms?"

"That you renounce your agreement with the Rus and forbid their railroad to enter your territory, that is all. In return you will receive the same type of weapon support that they have claimed they will provide. In fact, I am in a position to immediately give you one thousand of our muskets and advisers to train your men.

"If you should do this, the Rus army will have no legitimate reason to enter your territory and the conflict is over."

"That is it?"

"We will also agree to pay reparations for the damage to Ostia, to any family that lost a member, and also to the owners of the plantations destroyed. We did not want to do it this way, but we had to make a clear demonstration of our intent. This war is against the Rus, not against you and the rulers of Roum."

Vincent was seething with rage. The plan was all so neat, yet he could not say a word in response.

"And the disposition of your army?" Lucullus asked.

"We, ah, do have a military concern there. If we should leave immediately, their army will simply return in force. That would not be fair to you, our allies. We would turn west to meet them, we hope with you by our side, and would demand that they withdraw and tear up their rail line to the river which they call the Kennebec."

"Named after a river from your own home state," Vincent interjected with cold irony. "Remember you used to be a Mainer and Union man yourself once."

"Used to be, Mr. Hawthorne," Tobias replied in English, looking straight at Vincent. "Vincent, it's a different world we live in, and we'd all better adjust to that fact."

"Ambassador Hawthorne or General Hawthorne is my title," Vincent replied coolly.

"Excuse me, Ambassador Hawthorne," Cromwell said, the faintest edge of irony in his voice. "It's just that I remember you from different days.

"But back to you, Lucullus," Tobias said, ignoring Vincent for the moment as if he were not there. "Those are our terms. I will call a cease-fire until this evening, when I will expect your decision. Will you agree to a cease-fire in return?"

"We have nothing to fire back with," Lucullus said with a grim laugh, "so of course I will agree."

"One last thing," Vincent said quietly. "I have one question to ask of you."

"Go on, then," and there was a note of exasperation in his voice.

"Why?"

"What do you mean?"

"Why this effort on your part? Whether Roum and Rus are united or not is no concern of the Carthas and you."

"Your expansion is very much a concern of Cartha. And besides, we can offer a better deal to Roum. The same industries, but without the damn peasant and slave revolution you are secretly importing to them along with your products," Tobias replied in Cartha, the translator hurriedly turning it back to Latin for Lucullus.

"Stop skirting the issue, Tobias."

"Admiral Cromwell," he replied stiffly.

"As I said, stop skirting the issue. The Merki horde will be in Cartha this fall. Their Namer of Time should have been there last fall. Already some of the Wanderers have crossed through our frontier outposts with full reports of their where-abouts. The Merki know what you were doing in Cartha. They must know what is happening here and given their approval. You are nothing but a mask for a Merki plot."

Damnable Wanderers, Tobias thought coldly. A tight security net had been spread out, on his suggestion, but some-how the scum still managed to seep through.

"Could it not be that I am using the Merki?" Tobias responded evenly.

"How?"

"Vincent—excuse me, Ambassador Hawthorne—the Tugars were but a minor horde compared to the Merki. They are numberless. They can sweep the world before them."

"And they lost to the Bantag," Vincent said, venturing that a Wanderer report was true.

"Yes, that is the point," Tobias replied.

Vincent smiled inwardly. He had picked up a valuable confirmation of what had only been a vague rumor about a yet even more distant horde.

"The Merki can turn either way. They fear your mad expansion eastward. They are afraid that you are ahead of them in their march. That from Roum you will go to the Kathi, the Chinese people eastward. Now, the Kathi have been on this world even longer than the Roum. Their race is spread across the march of three hordes. There would be nothing to stop you moving east, since the Tugar no longer exist."

"No longer exist?"

"Oh, you didn't hear?" Tobias said with a smile. "They were annihilated six months ago. They fled southward across the march of the Merki, attempting to find refuge with the Bantag, who destroyed them."

Vincent looked closely at Tobias, not sure whether to believe him or not. If it was true, the situation had shifted once again.

"But as I was saying, the Merki are caught two ways. If they turn all their attention eastward they will cross the narrows of the Inland Sea."

"With your help."

"Yes, with my help," Tobias replied sharply. "They and the Bantag will fight, and the devil take the hindmost. But they are concerned about what you are doing. They fear Rus to a certain degree. Thus I have entered the picture with this agreement. Neutralize you and they can turn their attention elsewhere. They have even exempted the Carthas, if they will do this service.

"But if not," and his voice sounded weary and sad, "they will abandon their fight with the Bantag and come raging northward, taking the old Tugar territory."

"With you helping them?"

"I will survive in either case," Tobias said coldly.

"So I am to assume that you have our best interests at heart."

"You could see it that way."

"And I'm really supposed to believe this? Why did you not approach us in peace? We sent repeated envoys to Cartha. None ever returned, so we finally gave up."

"They will not deal with you. The Carthas were forbidden all contact."

Tobias rose up from his chair, indicating that the audience was finished.

"I'll await your reply in the morning," he said to Lucullus, and motioned for the two to leave.

Lucullus stood up without comment and left the tent. Vincent started to follow, then paused and looked back at Tobias.

"Captain Cromwell, a word alone, please," he said softly in English, looking straight into his eyes.

Tobias hesitated.

"You've done a lot I hate, but I still recall during the war when you saved my life by fetching my men and me out of the water after the Tugars overran us. For the sake of that, can we talk as two former comrades?"

Tobias smiled sadly and nodded for the translator to leave the room.

"It feels strange to speak English again," Tobias said wistfully. "That Cartha tongue was difficult to learn."

"Rus wasn't much better."

"I suddenly understand now why you're the ambassador. You're one of the few that can speak Latin."

"I never thought my language class at the Oak Grove school would ever help me in this way," Vincent said, struggling to sound relaxed, to somehow create the necessary atmosphere.

"You know, I never told you this, but I saw your school once. It looked lovely sitting up on that hill overlooking the Kennebec River."

"I hope it stays there forever."

"Oh, some goddam fool will get hold of it in the end and ruin it. I went to a school like yours—it wasn't Quaker, though. The headmaster was a weak incompetent. His wife was a conniving shrew and destroyed the place with her ambitions. It always happens that way," Tobias replied, his voice distant and cold.

"You seem always to see the worst. I try to look for the best."

"That's why we are different, Vincent. I'm a realist, you're an idealistic dreamer. I wish the world were what you believe it to be. I've learned differently," Tobias said slowly.

"And it has made you bitter and alone," Vincent replied. Tobias laughed coldly.

"What is it you wanted to say to me?"

"Do you honestly expect to survive in the game you are playing?"

Tobias leaned back on his desk and looked away.

"I think my chances are pretty good. I've always got the *Ogunquit*. Quite impressive now, isn't it?"

"Looks like the *Merrimac*," Vincent said with a voice that seemed to show a lack of interest.

"My inspiration, actually. I was an engineering officer for the *Cumberland*."

"You were in that action? How come you never told any of us?"

"No one would have been interested," Tobias replied sharply.

The memory of that shell from the *Merrimac* bursting in the middeck of his ship still haunted him. He had received his captaincy after that action. To a damned military transport ship. They had accepted his excuse for going over the side before the order had been given to abandon ship. But he knew the review board would never give him a combat command, damn them all.

"But I remembered that rebel ship. I saw the plans for her after we captured the naval yard. The *Ogunquit* is quite the ship now. Two-inch armor plating, twelve heavy guns—she's the toughest ship afloat on this entire godforsaken world."

"You made the conversion at Cartha."

"Gathering a little intelligence, general?"

Vincent smiled disarmingly.

"Can you blame me?"

Tobias smiled and shook his head.

"You've certainly come a long way from the day I fished you out of the drink. General and ambassador. Are you still a good Quaker?"

"I don't know anymore," Vincent replied, suddenly feeling on the defensive. "This world's changed all of us, including me and you."

"We've got to learn to live in it."

"You once were my comrade," Vincent said. "We found a way to live in it, and to help the millions of other people here."

"Do you honestly think your way helped them? Vincent, half the Rus died in that war. The Tugars would have taken but two in ten. Nearly six hundred thousand died who might have lived. I don't see that as helping them."

"We broke the back of the Tugars."

"We could have done it my way," Tobias replied, his voice rising. "Hide till they passed. Then come back and have twenty years to prepare. But your Keane had to interfere."

"My Keane? You never could stand to be under his command, could you?" Vincent said, trying to keep the accusation out of his voice.

"No. From the moment he came aboard my ship he showed me no respect. It's always been that way—officers who look at me and laugh inside because I'm too heavy, and short, and my voice is too high. None of them ever looked beyond that, to the ability I have locked up in me."

Vincent sat quietly. Watching Tobias, sensing the rage and fear.

"Andrew never blamed you for pulling out of the city," Vincent said softly. "The city was falling, and we were doomed. You had a means to get out, and every right to take it.

"And maybe even to carry on the struggle," he added, offering him an honorable excuse.

"I didn't find out till months later. Come back, you say? To what? A court-martial for desertion?"

Yet another review board looking at him disdainfully, excusing him yet in their eyes mocking him, saying he was not as much of a man as they were. The thought filled him with a cold anger.

"Oh, I can hear Keane's sarcasm, the laughing disdain of everyone as we come back. No, he would have used it as an excuse to strip me of the *Ogunquit*. I suspected him of that desire long before. I would come back and then there'd be nothing at all. I'd be someone living at the edge of his table.

Oh, he would have given me a steam engine to run someplace, on dry land.

"Dammit, I know more about steam than Ferguson or any of the others. I know more about heavy guns than any of you. All of you were busy giving each other promotions, and I was bypassed, as I've always been bypassed. Just as I was ignored when the entire navy was at war and they laughed and gave me a damnable transport when I begged them for a military command. I studied Ericsson's monitor designs, I knew them inside and out, down to the last bolt. I understood the big guns, the Rodmans, Parrots, Dahlgrens, better than anyone. But no, they gave the monitors and guns to their cronies instead. No, there was no going back to any of that, not to any of it, here or back with their damn navy."

He fell silent, his breath coming short and hard.

Damn him, Vincent thought. He had that knowledge and never offered it. He fought to control his features, to look calm, as if he were an elder, counseling another without a trace of judgment in his voice, trying to guide someone to the inner light, not by preaching but by letting him gradually see the folly of his own ways.

"You can still use those skills with us," Vincent said encouragingly. "You hold a balance now. We still need you, captain. Think of what you could build with our new mills. You could build your monitors and rule the sea for the Republic of Rus."

Vincent came up to Tobias, putting his hand on the man's shoulder, and looked straight into his eyes. He braced himself inwardly, forcing away the other memories, the rage he still felt over the slaughter of his troops. Perhaps he could still redeem himself here. Could end the fighting and give an advantage to the republic against the Merki.

"Kal is president now, I think you know that."

"That peasant is a shrewd one," Tobias said coldly.

"You're right. He is a shrewd one. He is running the show now, not Keane. Remember, he is my father-in-law. I've got influence.

"Captain, I'm promising you a way back. I'll stand beside you. You saved my life once and I never forgot that. I'm willing to pledge that to you now and support your side. I'm ambassador to Roum. I'm now in direct contact with you,

and as such am serving as an official representative of the Republic of Rus. I'm therefore, in that capacity, offering you a full amnesty, and return to your official status as commander of the Rus navy."

"Overstepping yourself, aren't you?" Tobias said, his voice barely a whisper.

Vince forced a laugh.

"I can get away with it. Besides, they need you, and the skills you never told us about.

"And your knowledge of the Merki," he added after a pause.

Tobias looked at him, their gaze holding. Vincent felt a surge of hope.

"Hell, captain, they even gave an amnesty to Mikhail."

"I know."

The way he said it made Vincent take notice. There was a touch of cold slyness in the response that was disquieting.

Tobias continued to look straight at him, and Vincent prayed inwardly, hoping that if he could do this, could end a war before it truly got started, perhaps he would be forgiven, the balance of blood paid off.

"Trust me on this, captain."

The moment seemed to hold into an eternity.

His gaze dropped, and standing, Tobias shook Vincent's hand off his shoulder and walked around the desk, putting the small piece of battered furniture between them.

"I can't," he whispered. He looked back up at Vincent, and there seemed now to be a wall around him.

For a moment he found that he had actually started to believe the boy. It was the eyes, though, looking into him, seeing what was inside him. He could imagine standing there with Keane, Kal, that damnable Irishman O'Donald, all of them looking at him, the way the others had. He was his own man now, finally; he never would let others judge him as they had before.

Vincent visibly sagged, lowering his head.

"Captain, you know you're a tool of the Merki. I don't know what your plan is with them. I do know that whatever you told me of those plans I wouldn't believe, the same way I don't believe what you told Lucullus and me earlier.

"They are implacable. It is a mortal fight to the death between the hordes and us. They still view us as cattle. And behind your back they view you as cattle as well."

Vincent could see Cromwell bristle and knew he had hit the mark. Tobias was definitely allied with the Merki and was not a simple renegade.

"They'll use you, they'll squeeze your knowledge from you, and have you kill your own kind to fit their plan, which you are not even aware of.

"You're simply a pawn to them. They'll promise you anything in return, but mark my words," Vincent said, his voice taking on a brutal sharpness, "in the end they'll lead you to the slaughter pits. All of us might go to the pits because of what you are deciding here, and any hope for our race will disappear."

"Get out of here," Tobias said, his voice barely a whisper.

Vincent could not believe how miserably he had just failed, when he had felt so close to changing everything only minutes before. He felt a sick numbness, a shocked bitterness that somehow his dream could be so thoroughly destroyed.

Damn you, God, he thought coldly, there was such a chance here to change this world, and You did not help me, give me the strength of words to do it. Do You even care? His world suddenly felt cold, empty, devoid of any hope.

His shoulders slumped in defeat, Vincent looked over at Tobias.

"Perhaps you were right about my school, about everything."

Tobias looked at him, unable to respond.

"If you change your mind, you know where to reach me."

"I'll not change," Tobias shouted, his features darkening. "Keane had his chance with me when we first met and destroyed it when he insulted me. I'll never give him that chance again. You can tell your Keane to go to hell."

Vincent drew himself up stiffly and saluted.

"Goodbye, Captain Cromwell," he said formally, and turned and walked out of the tent.

As he watched him leave, Tobias felt a painful tug, a memory of the boy standing on the deck of his ship, trembling with shock, demanding to be addressed as a colonel even as he fought back his tears. For a moment he had actually believed him. But he was only one, and there were all the others.

Collapsing into his chair, he sat in silence.

No, they would never have taken him back. There was only this course, desperate as it was. They would have to fear him; only then would they respect him. After all, it always was fear that drove him, he suddenly realized with a cold frightening detachment as if a gate into the blackness had been flung open. The screams of terror came back to him, the headmaster's wife beating him, and then the fear of the other thing the headmaster had done one night, and her finding them and taunting them both, beating him until the blood streamed down his legs.

The laughing taunts in the eyes of those around him, even when they smiled and acted like his friends. Only now would it ever stop. When he held the power over all of them, then they would tremble. Even the Merki would know that in the end. He would play their game, but in the end they would know his wrath, which he would vent upon them when all was done.

He suddenly felt sick to his stomach at the memories of it all. Doubling over in his chair, he vomited, gasping for breath, tears streaming down his face.

Staggering over to the back of the tent, he collapsed on his cot, and the blackness washed over him, leaping up out of the pit and dragging him again into its taunting embrace.

"There is nothing more to be said," Marcus shouted, looking down at the envoy, who was barely visible in the darkening shadows. "We refuse."

"You mean you refuse," the envoy taunted, and pulling hard on his mount, he turned and clattered off into the darkness.

"There'll be no going back now," Vincent said quietly.

"We just have to hold for five more days, if what your president promised is true."

Vincent could only hope that it was. So much can go wrong with any military operation, Vincent thought. Fortunately the several thousand men working on the rail line were also a brigade of infantry under General Barry. The moment the news broke, he must have mobilized them to defend the line. It was not knowing, though—that was the damnable part of it all. Andrew's lead elements could be disembarking even now. Or they could be tied up by some accident hundreds of miles away.

"It was a wise move not to reveal the true contents of the negotiations," Vincent said dryly.

Marcus laughed softly.

"Lucullus reported only to me. It was easy enough to change the demands to an absurdity."

"Thank you for sticking with us," Vincent added.

Marcus looked over at Vincent and smiled.

"I'm not so much a fool as to believe what your Cromwell offered. He is merely the glove over someone else's fist. I still cannot consider your suggestion to free the slaves. I intend to keep this system as my father gave it to me."

He paused for a moment and looked back at the city.

"If the gods willing I ever remarry and have another son," he whispered, "I would like to give the same city to him.

"But I do know that the Merki have turned their gaze in our direction," he continued, his voice suddenly gruff. "We will have to fight them in the end. You are our only salvation in that fight."

"Archers!"

The cry was picked up down the wall, and within seconds dozens of sentries were calling out the alarm.

Vincent ducked down low, pulling Marcus with him; there was no need to play hero in the dark. He saw the flutter of a white shaft arc lazily overhead and disappear into the street below. Another followed, and then yet one more. There was the clattering of hooves beyond the wall.

A rain of bolts shot overhead, disappearing.

Cautiously Vincent poked his head up. It was curious. The arrows were arcing high, coming down in a slow lazy curve. Gradually the volley died away, and then shouts echoed farther down the line from sentries calling a warning.

"Just harassing," Vincent said with a laugh, coming back up to his feet.

"First consul."

A legionnaire came racing up the steps from the street below, his hobnailed sandals striking sparks on the rough-cut stone. Saluting, he stepped forward, an arrow in one hand, a strip of parchment in the other.

"This message was attached," he said, handing it over to Marcus.

Motioning over to an enclosed turret, Marcus stepped inside and stood next to a flickering lamp and held the message up.

"The bastard," Marcus whispered.

"What is it?"

"He's appealing directly to the Senate, announcing the same terms, offering everything. As long as I am removed."

Vincent shook his head.

"He certainly knows how to play the game," Vincent said sadly, leaning against the wall.

Now what was he going to do?

Petronius stepped around the table and extended his hand.

"I always knew I could count on you in our hour of need," Petronius said with an eager smile.

Lucullus hesitated and then reached out and accepted the handshake.

"He is still my cousin, ruler of the Graca family. I would prefer no harm to come to him in all of this."

"But of course," Petronius said smoothly. "We of the patrician class certainly cannot go around murdering each other over these squabbles. It sets a bad example and might give the rabble the wrong idea."

"Yet these are new and different times, my friend," Catullus interjected. "Those of the Graca clan have ruled Roum for hundreds of years, and we certainly wouldn't want to change that. Now we will have you. Besides, Marcus has no sons now. At his age, if he has more offspring they will be weak and sickly. We need someone of vigorous blood who has already sired sons to rule after him. The legion, of course, will support you, since you are the first commander under Marcus."

"I must go and prepare," Lucullus said stiffly, and dropping Petronius's hand he stalked out of the room.

"A formal bastard," Catullus said as the door slipped shut.

"The Gracas are like that," Petronius laughed.

"How long have you been working on him?"

"Even before our contact was established with the Carthas," he said lazily, impressed by his own foresight. "Oh, I was glad when Marcus threw back the Tugars. Every twenty years they looted us dry, and twenty percent of our laborers disappeared. With them gone we have unlimited power.

"But when I saw what these Yankees really were, I knew we would have to fight them. I never said anything directly to Lucullus—he's too stiff, with that honor-of-patricians foolishness. But the seeds were planted."

Petronius went over to a side table, speared a sliver of honeyed meat, and munched on it absently.

"It's dark out now?"

"Should be."

"Good. The rabble will be getting their little messages. A truly ingenious idea. Make a reasonable offer which Marcus would most likely refuse, then turn the mob against him."

"Perhaps a bit too neat," Varius, youngest of the senators, said coldly.

Petronius cocked his head and gave Varius a quizzical look.

"Not backing out now, are we?"

Varius hesitated.

"I won't stop you, if that's what you mean. I no more like what the Yankees threaten than you do. It's just we should remember that Cromwell and the Carthas are not going through all this trouble out of the goodness of their hearts. We must consider what their plan is as well."

"Are you going to whine about the Merki or Tugars again?" Catullus snapped.

Varius looked over at Catullus and said nothing.

"The Yankees are more of a threat than the Merki could ever be. Just yesterday I had a slave put to death when I heard him whispering some Yankee nonsense about every man being equal."

"That kind of talk is dangerous," Petronius said sharply. "It could be the end of all of us."

"I agree with that," Varius said.

"Then we are not in disagreement," Catullus said with a soothing smile.

"And the Merki?"

"Well, if they should come," Petronius said, lowering his voice, "we all know that the Yankees cannot stand against them, especially with what Cromwell has given them, something the foolish Tugars did not have. Anyhow, if that is the case, then wouldn't it be better to be on the winning side?

"After all, they eat peasants, not patricians," Petronius added with a cold laugh.

Varius shook his head in disbelief.

"It is sometimes hard to imagine I am on the same side as you."

"But you already are, Varius," Catullus said, his voice

dripping with oily sincerity. "This time tomorrow, Marcus will be gone, and Lucullus will be in his place."

"Dear foolish Lucullus," Petronius laughed. "With the imagination of a block of stone. He'll be easy enough to rule."

"With Marcus alive and the Yankee soldiers in the town, there could still be a rally point," Varius cautioned.

"Poor Marcus," Catullus giggled.

"You did promise Lucullus he would be allowed to live?"

"Oh, did I?" Petronius said absently. "You know how dangerous the summertime is. Why, just last year my lamented wife came down with such a terrible stomach complaint."

"Tragic," Catullus sighed. "I know how heartbroken you were, Petronius."

"And the Yankees?" Varius whispered, his voice edged with disgust. "They'll fight you the moment they suspect."

"Such fools—they really should be careful of what they eat."

"If I did not believe this was to save the Roum we know, I would spit on you," Varius growled, and he stalked out of the room.

"Varius, just remember whose side you are on," Petronius snapped, his voice full of menace.

"I will. You have me in too deeply already," Varius retorted without turning back. "I'll remember to eat alone, though, in the future."

The two senators looked at each other and laughed.

# Chapter Eight

"End of the line!"

"Thank God," Andrew groaned, sitting up from his bunk and looking out the window.

It was early morning, the first faint streaks of dawn creasing the morning clouds. Fumbling for his glasses, he put them on. His mouth tasted gummy, and he smacked his lips with disgust. Gregory had received a chewing-out regarding the fact that his toothbrush had been forgotten. He was tempted to yell at the boy again, but in the gloom of the car he saw him peering back and felt it would simply be too cruel.

Gregory came back cautiously and held out a mug of tea. It was cold, but he gulped it down anyhow and felt a little bit better disposed.

"Help me with my jacket and sword, son," Andrew said, standing up. It was something about losing an arm he had never quite gotten used to. Dressing in a uniform alone and fumbling with the buttons was difficult with one hand, but the sword belt was simply impossible.

"It's going to be terribly hot, sir," Gregory ventured. "Maybe you'd prefer your four-button jacket."

Andrew was tempted. The jacket was the standard Union Army issue for enlisted men that went down to his hips, while the officer's jacket weighed damn near twice as much and went down to mid-thigh. Of course they were both wool, something that still struck him as insane for an army that had served in the scorching heat of the South. On the grueling forced march to Gettysburg he had seen hundreds of men go down with heat exhaustion. The steppes in the summer were going to be worse.

"I think I'll keep the officer's jacket on today," Andrew replied. The Rus expected their leaders to dress grandly, and today he knew he'd have to comply.

Gregory, shaking his head with concern, helped Andrew dress and then stepped back and nodded approvingly.

"Let's go out and see what's facing us," Andrew said. As he started through the car, his staff looked at him expectantly. Several were coming back in, looking somewhat wide-eyed, and from their expressions he knew.

Stepping off the platform, he hit the ground.

"God make it a dream," he whispered.

The side of the track was chaos for as far as he could see. The only semblance of order was with the men of the 35th, who under the sharp commands of their company officers were already falling into line from the train behind him. Looking to his own train, he saw men were still leaping off cars, wandering about, cursing, laughing. Officers and non-coms were shouting at the top of their lungs. A panic-stricken horse, eyes wide with fear, galloped past, several artillery men chasing it.

Grim-faced, he stalked down the length of the train, taking it all in. Reaching the back of the next train, he scrambled up on the caboose and looked at the ladder that led to the roof. Taking a breath, he grabbed hold and climbed up slowly. Reaching the top rung, he crawled up on the roof. To his amazement a soldier was stretched out on top sound asleep.

"Just what the hell are you doing here?" Andrew roared.

"Trying to get some sleep, damn you. Now leave me alone," the soldier groaned. He opened his eyes, blinked, and shot up. Before Andrew could say a word the man heaved his equipment over the side and leaped to the ground, disappearing into the crowd.

As far as he could see ahead, the track was jammed with trains. The grounds to either side were a mass of confusion. There seemed to be no semblance of order. Thousands of boxes of rations and ammunition were piled up haphazardly. Men were off in every direction, guns were rolled out by the track and none were deployed forward.

He was seething with rage.

"It certainly looks a mess."

Emil, puffing hard, came up to join him.

"It's an outrage," Andrew snapped.

"Remember, son, you are in command," Emil said quietly. Andrew turned to face the doctor, ready to explode.

"Don't turn it on me, Andrew Lawrence Keane," Emil said with a disarming smile. "Why don't you just sit up here for a couple of minutes and think about it?"

"Sit here?" he sputtered.

"That's right. Just sit here and join me in a little drink."

Emil reached into his pocket, pulled out a flask, uncorked it, and offered it over.

Andrew took a hard pull, shocked by the sharp potency of the vodka as it hit his empty stomach.

"You've been under a lot of strain. You've got to keep your calm about you. Get excited and your officers get jumpy. They get jumpy, then everyone gets on edge. It's been a couple of years since our last action. We've all got to get back in shape for it."

A whistle shrieked behind him. Startled, he looked back and saw another train sliding to a stop. Farther up the track he saw the small town of Hispania, its white limestone wall glowing red with the dawn. The railroad siding was aswarm with activity, and at least there he saw some semblance of order. Several batteries were drawn up, guns deployed in a defensive perimeter, a sharp line of freshly dug earthworks enclosing the area. A chain of men were hauling boxes up over the embankment and heading in the direction of a vast open-walled warehouse.

He started to breathe a bit easier.

"We've never tried anything like this before," Emil said evenly. "It's new to everyone, including you. Of course things are going to be a bit chaotic to start, but once we get the boys marching they'll fall back into the old routine.

"I'd better get started," Emil continued. "We need to find some wagons for the hospital equipment. I've also got to set up a base hospital here—we've already got some sick lads and quite a few injuries to take care of. I'll report to you later, son."

Andrew looked over at his friend and offered the flask back.

Emil took it and then tossed off a long drink before corking it. "Medicinal purposes, of course," he said with a grin and disappeared over the side of the car.

"Gregory!"

"Down here, sir."

"Get Mercury out, walk him a bit, then have him ready to go. Staff meeting in ten minutes. Send some runners up the line. I want brigade and division commanders here. Now move!"

"Colonel Keane?"

Andrew stepped over to the side of the train and saw Andy Barry.

"Get up here, Barry."

The old former sergeant scrambled up the side and, gaining the top, cautiously approached Andrew and saluted.

"Go on and report," Andrew said.

"Well sir, it's a bit out of hand here at the moment."

"I can see that," Andrew said quietly.

"Sir, the trains came in late, as you know. We had planned for them to get here yesterday afternoon so we'd have plenty of light. We just weren't ready to handle an army coming up to the end of the line like this."

"You don't need to make excuses, Barry," Andrew said, desperately working on forcing a disarming smile. "Well, straighten it out."

He could see the officer relax.

"You expected me to chew your ass off, didn't you?"

"Well, ah, yes sir," Barry said cautiously. "It kind of looks pretty bad out there," and he nodded up the line.

"It does, but well fix it up soon enough, won't we?"

"Yes sir," and Barry straightened up and smiled.

Damm it, I've been too long behind a desk, Andrew thought reproachfully. You start ruling by paper rather than face to face and you forget. He remembered the fat sleek officers of the Army of the Potomac, who sat in the rear lines or pranced about in Washington, controlling supplies, playing politics for promotions, currying favor, and by their stupidity and venality killing thousands of good men who deserved better and rarely got it.

Could I have become like that? he wondered. He could feel the tightness of the uniform that two years ago had hung loosely on him, like a jacket pulled over a tree limb. Don't forget this moment, he cautioned himself. It is far too easy, the older we get, to become what we once despised. Was this another price of peace, to lose the edge, or was it the price that war demanded?

"What's the report forward?"

"We pushed up a patrol all the way to the watch point the telegraph crew established, about ten miles outside the city, and reinforced them. So far they haven't sent anything up this way at all, sir. The rail bridge we were building over the Po is planked. I've got some engineers up at the Tartus working on a quick crossing—the bridge was only partially up. The bridges the Roum had on their old Appia Way are still intact."

"And they haven't moved anything this way?"

"Not a sign of 'em, sir."

"Curious."

"My thoughts as well, sir. I mean, hell, sir, if I was them, I would have screened up this way a whole hell of a lot further."

"It's almost like they're inviting us in."

"That's what me and a lot of the boys have been thinking as well."

Just what is Tobias up to? he wondered. He was starting to feel like a mouse being lured into a trap. There were far too many possibilities to sort out. The objective, at least, was still clear: to relieve Roum as soon as possible. His worst nightmare was the thought that the Carthas would take the city and then there would be a bloody fight to win it back, since it was impossible to leave a hostile force in control. The other possibility was far worse—that Roum itself might be hostile by the time he arrived. He suspected Marcus was less than enthusiastic about their alliance. If that happened, he knew what fate would be in store for Vincent.

He would have to push in as fast as possible. All he could see was to somehow spring the trap, if there was one, and then jump away in time.

"We've got our work cut out, Barry. We'd better get to it. Whatever supplies we don't take I want safely warehoused by evening. Colonel Mina will be coming up on the last train. Try to get some semblance of order with all these engines before he gets here. You know how he can be when he gets upset."

Barry gave a wry grimace and nodded.

"By the way, you're staying behind here with your brigade," Andrew said as if by an afterthought.

"Sir? We was hoping to go up with you."

"You're our construction crew, Barry. You and the boys are too valuable to lose on a volley line. And besides, I think it'd be best to leave a solid covering force at our rear, just in case."

Barry's features dropped with disappointment.

"You know it's for the best, Barry. I need you more here."

"Yes sir. It seems like I've worked my way out of being a soldier, that's all."

"You might get more soldiering than you want soon enough," Andrew said, not sure why the thought had even formed.

The senators looked from one to the other uneasily.

"This is most irregular," Scipio said coldly, coming to his feet. "Where is Marcus?"

"He was not invited," Petronius said sharply.

"Not invited, you say? We sit as advisers to him as heads of the twenty families. He is first consul, as his father was before him."

"And he has betrayed us. Come now, this war is none of our concern, it's Marcus they're after, not us. You just heard Lucullus describe the terms. The whole city knows them now. If we act, we can end this battle today."

"You're proposing treason," Scipio replied, looking about the Senate chamber for support.

"I'm proposing salvation," Petronius snapped. "It is Marcus who is the treasonable one for allowing all of this to start."

"They came here as invaders, they've killed hundreds of our people. Marcus is doing the only thing possible—fighting against them."

"And what about the Yankee invasion?" Catullus shouted. "It is they who are the threat."

"They could have come here sword in hand and annihilated us," Scipio argued. "They offer us trade, prosperity, and a common alliance against the hordes."

"And they talk about slaves being free," Petronius sneered.

"After listening to the likes of you, I think I would almost prefer that," Scipio shouted, coming to his feet.

"There is nothing more to be said between us," Scipio announced, his angry gaze sweeping the Senate chamber. "Those who stand against this madness should come with me, else you will be judged accordingly."

The senators looked uneasy, but none stood.

"Then my curse on all of you," Scipio barked. He turned on his heels and stalked from the chamber.

"We should stop him!" Catullus cried. "He'll warn Marcus."

"Let him," Petronius laughed. "Even now Lucullus is arresting our illustrious leader."

"They're abandoning the walls."

With a smile, Cromwell looked up at Hulagar and Vuka and smiled.

"Is it not happening as I said it would? The first formation will go in at daylight."

"This is merely the opening move," Vuka said sharply. "The diversion before the main course of the meal."

Cromwell looked at Vuka uneasily and saw Hulagar bristle at the lord's choice of words.

"Oh, don't worry about it," Vuka said with a sardonic grin. "Just a figure of speech, nothing more."

"It's still a success that will bring me pleasure," Cromwell replied.

"It is the other action I am more concerned about," Hulagar pressed.

"Hinsen is in control of that and should be in position by now. The last train has undoubtedly come in."

"That is the one we want, just remember that." Hulagar replied softly. "How much longer before we can expect them?"

"Perhaps as early as tomorrow night. Keane will force-march them."

"Is he with the army?"

"I'm certain of it," Cromwell replied coldly.

"All of them are in the Senate chamber at this very moment."

"Why are you disturbing me with this news?" Marcus growled sharply, looking angrily at Vincent and the trembling slave by his side.

"Julius and I have something of a friendship, Marcus," Vincent said evenly.

Marcus looked at the two and gave a snort of disdain.

"A friendship between a slave and one such as yourself?" Marcus said coldly.

"He is a loyal man," Vincent said hotly. "As good a man as myself."

"And by implication you are saying he is as good as me," Marcus said with a disdainful laugh.

"I'll not argue that now," Vincent retorted, "but you'd better listen to him. We don't have much time."

"Go on then."

With a groan Marcus came to his feet. Vincent was shocked by his nakedness, a manner of sleep all the Roum seemed comfortable with, but he would most certainly never adopt.

"The men who serve the Senate chambers," Julius began, "have been suspicious now since this evening, when those letters were shot into the city. About an hour ago my cousin Flavius—he works as a scribe—came and told me the senators were all meeting in secret at the house of Petronius."

"Let them," Marcus snapped.

"Lucullus was with them."

Marcus turned to look at Julius, a sharp interest now in his eyes.

"Go on."

"Flavius told me that a friend of his, Garba, was ordered to bring in some wine. Lucullus and the senators were talking. They fell silent when he came in. When he left the room, he lingered by the door. He heard Lucullus say that he would see to your arrest and that a cohort will surround the Rus soldiers and hold them there until the Carthas are in the city."

Marcus looked over at Vincent.

"How reliable is this?" he snapped.

"As the saying goes," Vincent said coldly, "I'd bet my life on it."

"I'm going up to the legion."

"I doubt, sir, if they will support you any longer."

"They are my personal army," Marcus shouted. "Of course they'll support me."

"They're scared men," Vincent replied. "They've suffered a shocking defeat. Petronius's people have been spreading some fairly effective lies the last couple of days. The bombardment is wearing them down even more. If they fight the Carthas they believe they'll die. This offers them a way out, and the fact that Lucullus offers this to them will decide the issue. Like it or not, Marcus, the Tugars were the base of your power. If any dared to move against you and your established order, the Tugars would help you in your vengeance. When you defeated them, your old system was bound to change. There is a void in the structure of power, and others are now eager to fill it."

"How can my legion, my guard, betray me?" Marcus said, his voice suddenly weak.

"Someday I'll tell you the rest of the history of the old Rome," Vincent replied evenly.

"Then it's finished?" Marcus asked, his voice distant.

"Not yet," Vincent said emphatically. "I'm calling the 5th in now to occupy your palace."

"But the walls."

"The hell with the walls," Vincent shouted. "It's your life I'm fighting for now."

"But when the Carthas break in they'll batter this palace down with their heavy guns, and you'll die, trapped in here with me," Marcus said, trying to force a sad smile. "Take your men and break out of here while there's still time."

"Quite heroic, Marcus, but it'll mean my army will just have to fight its way back in."

"For what? I'll be dead, Petronius will make peace with the Carthas, and you'll be fighting both of them."

"You have an army waiting to fight for you right now."

"Who?"

"The only people who will truly benefit by the defeat of those who serve the hordes. Free the slaves, and they'll fight to the death for you."

He tried to keep his features even, but the stunned look of Julius forced a smile to his lips.

"This was your plan all along," Marcus snapped.

"Never this way. We had hoped that in the end it would be peaceful. I'm afraid it won't be. You hold the decision, Marcus. I think you are noble enough that your own death might come second in your mind to that of Roum. The Carthas are but a mask for the hordes. I'll tell you bluntly—if the Senate defeats you now and throws in with the Carthas, we will fight to get the resources we need. But we are desperately few. Without your people by our side, both Rus and Roum will fall, especially now that we know they will have the same weapons we do. If you do not do this, all of Roum will perish in the end, for if I were the Merki I would annihilate any human who had tasted freedom or knew of the weapons we have."

"You ask too much," Marcus whispered.

Brimming with anger, Vincent came over and grabbed the man by the shoulders.

"Goddammit, Marcus, you don't have much time. You'd better act quickly."

Vincent felt as if he were about to explode with pent-up anxiety. It was all so straightforward and simple, and yet the man refused to see the truth.

"I don't think I can," Marcus whispered.

"Sir, the regiment's deploying into the palace. Ammunition is being moved over from our barracks right now— we're bringing it through the slave quarters."

"Julius, I want the basement slave quarters made ready for a hospital area. Our surgeon will tell your people what to do. Get some fires going right now. Take linens and start boiling them."

The man nodded.

Vincent turned and saw Dimitri standing in the doorway, with Bugarin beside him.

"I want men posted at every window. Get the guns inside and set up firing ports in the doorway. Take anything you can grab to build some fallback positions, on the far side of the courtyard. That outer wall will take some pounding. Once it goes, we'll fight from the courtyard. We'll hold the ground floor as long as possible, then retreat to the second. See if you can haul a couple of the guns to the second floor to fire into the courtyard.

"This building's good thick stone," Bugarin said with a grin. "It'll take 'em a while to batter their way in here."

"Now get to it."

The two saluted and left.

"So you're going to stay till the end."

"That's what I promised the president. I'll hold until relieved."

"What manner of men are you?" Julius said softly.

Vincent shook his head.

"At the moment, scared to death, Julius."

"You know you'll die here," Marcus said, the dejection in his voice a disturbing note.

"You still hold the key to that," Vincent snapped, "but I'll tell you right now your options are closing in. If we can hold till Andrew comes—and I doubt that—we'll prop you back up, but you'll be a puppet for our government."

Marcus looked sharply at Vincent, unable to reply.

"It's that simple, Marcus. I'm telling you the plain facts of politics. Rus is fighting for her life. We need what you've got. I wanted to see us work as partners, but if my regiment sacrifices itself to save your hide, personally I'll want the price paid back. You've lost your legion and your Senate. We'll run things after that."

"You'll run it," Marcus said dryly.

"The hell with it all," Vincent snapped. "I'm resigning this post and going back to Rus. Let someone else do the dirty work, because I've had a bellyful of it.

"Now if you'll excuse me, I've got other things to attend to."

Without waiting for a response, he strode out of the room to find Dimitri waiting for him in the hallway.

"Well?"

"The bastard refuses to budge," Vincent said.

"Something's forming up out in the forum. I came back to get you."

Cold with rage, Vincent stalked through the palace, pulling out his revolver and checking the load. Coming to the partly open doorway, he saw a formation of the legion gathering up in the early-morning mist.

With an impetuousness born out of an all-consuming anger, Vincent stepped out of the protection of the doorway and onto the marble steps of the palace, and looked coldly at the men who had stopped their advance.

"What the hell do you want, dammit?" Vincent shouted. "You should be back on the walls defending your city."

"The war's over," and Lucullus stepped out of the ranks. "We are here to arrest Marcus Licinius Graca on the charge of treason to the Senate and people of Roum."

"The traitorous dogs you call the Senate?" Vincent laughed. "As for the people, they should consider whom their Senate has sold them to.

"The Carthas are the envoys of the hordes," Vincent shouted, his voice carrying across the square. "Your Senate will sell all of you to the slaughter pits by this act."

"Out of the way, Yankee," Lucullus shouted and started forward.

With a flourish, Vincent cocked his revolver and pointed it straight at the advancing soldier.

"Don't you move a goddam inch," Vincent yelled, trying to keep his voice from cracking.

A hush fell over the square. From the corner of his eye Vincent could see several bowmen moving into position.

"Tell your men to back off," Vincent warned. "They might get me, but by the eternal I'll put a bullet through your head before I'm finished."

"I am commanding you to surrender your sword, Lucullus," a voice called behind Vincent.

A smile crossed Vincent's features.

"I'd advise you not to come out, sir," Vincent whispered, still keeping his weapon pointed at Lucullus.

"The hell you say."

Vincent felt someone brush against his shoulder, but he didn't dare to look.

"Lucullus is no longer in command of the legion," Marcus shouted. "Now return to your posts before the Carthas are in the city."

The moment held, neither side moving.

"The legion is no longer yours," a voice called from the square.

"Ah, Petronius, the heroic leader, hiding behind his men," Marcus sneered.

"To save the people of Roum from you."

"For the final time, I command the legion to return to its posts."

"The Carthas are in the city," a cry echoed up from a distant corner of the square.

"Back inside," Vincent whispered.

"Not yet," Marcus snapped.

"Then hear me now," Marcus shouted. "I declare that any man or woman who is a slave and who comes forward to defend our country will henceforth be free."

Vincent felt as if the world had shifted into a blur. He heard Petronius screaming to kill them, and saw Lucullus crouching low as if to race forward. The archers fired. Diving to one side, he knocked Marcus to the ground, snapping off his revolver as he fell.

Lucullus spun around, hitting the ground hard, while a wild angry shout seemed to echo up across the square. Hands came around him, pulling him back inside, even as he dragged Marcus with him. Gaining the door, he saw the dark-clad livery of the Carthas rushing forward through the square, the snap crack of musketfire echoing out.

A thundering volley lashed out from the palace, cutting

into the Carthas, and to his horror taking down a number of the legion as well.

Gasping, Vincent came to his feet and saw a red stain on Marcus's toga.

"You're hit!"

Marcus struggled to his feet, forcing a smile as he looked down at the arrow lodged in his arm.

"It could have been worse," he replied, his voice slurring slightly from shock.

"Well, you really went and did it," Vincent said with a smile.

"Too late, though," Marcus said coldly. "I should have done it the moment this all started."

"Well, at least you made the move. Now if we can only hold on. The people will rally to your support."

"I doubt if it'll do any good," Marcus replied, swaying slightly.

"Take him out of here," Vincent ordered. "Get the surgeon to fix him up."

Marcus offered no protest as several men led him away.

"What did he say out there?" Dimitri asked.

"He offered freedom to any slave that fought."

Dimitri laughed.

"A shrewd offer. Rather conditional freedom, I'd say."

Vincent could not help but smile as he realized what Marcus had actually said.

"It's a start, Dimitri, it's a start."

Vincent went back to the crack in the door and peeked out. The mob was still scattering in every direction. Not a shot was being fired from the palace, and he thanked God that the men were not killing any more of them. The Cartha detachment had pulled back into the forum, and from the far size of the plaza he saw a gun being moved up.

"The trick now is to hold," Vincent said, "and pray that these people help us."

God, it was worse than anything he had ever known in Virginia. Swaying in the saddle, Andrew was tempted to take another drink of hot water from his canteen but fought the urge down. The next river was still a good ten miles away, and the only thing around him was the steppe.

Raising his hand to shade his eyes, he looked around. The gently rolling hills were going from green to brown in the high heat of late summer. The grass was like a vast ocean, waving with the puffs of hot wind that swirled and eddied, bringing no relief from the torment.

He struggled with the nausea, knowing it for what it was.

I can't collapse now, he whispered to himself. There are still hours to go. I can't collapse now.

A fantasy danced through the mirages. It was autumn, a cooling wind coming in off the ocean of Maine, the icy surf crashing on the rocks foaming white, washing up over him and Kathleen. She was smiling, standing in the tall grass, with Ilya, his old border collie, by her side. How deliciously cool she looked, her white dress fluttering in the breeze, pressed against her body, showing every line and curve. She was standing before him, Ilya barking and dancing with joy.

"A cool drink of water, love?"

Laughing, she was holding up a pitcher, rivers of droplets falling. Coming closer. Her clothes had slipped away, showing the fullness of her breasts, the leanness of her slender thighs, a bewitching smile of love in her eyes.

"A cool drink of water."

"Oh, God, thank you."

"Sir. Colonel Keane, sir?"

"Thank you, love, thank you."

"Colonel Keane, sir!"

"Bullfinch?"

Confused, he looked down at his adjutant, his face bright red with the heat.

"Sir, you were talking. Are you all right?"

Embarrassed, Andrew looked about. His staff was behind him, walking down the dust-shrouded road. On the next rise ahead, a mile away, the mounted skirmishers were deployed. His eyes aching, he looked to either side. Behind him, wending their way down the Appia Way and the railroad embankment alongside, the regiments and batteries pushed forward, their flags held high, their forms shimmering and swaying like ghosts in the blasting heat.

"Colonel, sir," Bullfinch said, his voice insistent, "a message just came in on the telegraph line."

With an anxious face, Bullfinch handed the message up, and Andrew could see that he had read it.

His glasses could not seem to focus on the words, there was something wrong with them, and absently he took them off and held the telegram close. It was useless.

"Read it for me," Andrew said, letting his hand drop away, his glasses falling.

Bullfinch fell behind for a second and then appeared again, holding the glasses back up. Andrew absently took them and slipped them into his pocket.

"The message reads as follows, sir. 'Forward scouts report Roum fell this morning to Cartha. An envoy from Roum is at our station declaring our help is no longer required, that Roum and Cartha have signed an alliance.' "

Something stirred within. He felt as if he had been slapped.

Reining Mercury in, he came down from the saddle. As he hit the ground he felt as if his legs would buckle. He had to hang on to the pommel. With deliberate slowness he stepped away from Mercury and took the message from Bullfinch, and putting his sweat-streaked glasses on he read it for himself.

"Ten-minute halt," Andrew said, and wearily he sat down.

A bugle call sounded, was picked up and rolled across the steppe. All around he could hear the sound of exhausted men sighing, equipment clattering to the ground.

"You all right sir?" Bullfinch asked.

"I just need a couple of minutes," Andrew said quietly, ashamed at his own weakness. It was one thing he had never truly adjusted to during the war. The killing heat of summer would sap his strength, draining it away. More than once on the march he had thanked God he was an officer who could ride; otherwise he knew he'd have died on the road. The men of the 35th had never judged him harshly for it, but the humiliation of the weakness had always troubled him.

"It'll be night in a couple of hours, sir," and he looked up to see Hank Petracci, the balloonist, walking through the grass, giving him an understanding smile.

"Not soon enough, Jack. I wish we had your balloon along."

"It'd be a lot better than walking, sir," and with a friendly salute Hank went for several more feet and collapsed with a sigh into the grass.

A shadow came over him, and startled, he looked back as Gregory and another orderly unrolled a shelter half, drove poles in on either side of him, and in seconds set up a lean-to. Embarrassment be damned, he felt as if they were saving his life. He heard someone pouring water and then the shock of something cold running down his back. He had shed his heavy uniform jacket an hour ago at the last stop and had been riding in shirt sleeves and a vest. The cooling water on his neck hit with a shock, and for a second he felt as if he was going to faint.

"You're pushing a heat stroke, Andrew."

"Ah, my ever-hovering doctor, do sit down."

"I didn't save your life at Gettysburg just to have you kill yourself out in this godforsaken desert," Emil snapped, squatting down by his side and looking into his eyes. He nodded to someone standing behind Andrew, and another shower of water rolled down his back. He started to shake.

"Lie down, colonel," Emil whispered, placing his hand on Andrew's forehead.

"If I do that, I'll never get up. We've got to keep moving."

"The men have been dropping like flies for the last couple of hours. I've seen at least four of them dead."

Andrew held the telegram up for Emil to read.

"Damn them," Emil whispered. "So they sold out."

Andrew closed his eyes, though the shimmer of light still danced before him. He had to focus, to think clearly.

He lay back, and felt more water on his chest and opened them to see Gregory kneeling beside him, his eyes full of an almost motherly concern.

Andrew smiled weakly.

"I'll be all right, son."

"Drink some of this, sir."

Andrew brought his head up and started to gulp down a cup of water.

"Slowly," Emil snapped. "Drink it fast and it could kill you."

He let the water run over his parched tongue, glide down his throat. He felt his stomach knot up, and he struggled against the nausea, fighting to keep the precious liquid inside his body.

Think, damm it, don't let the weakness take you. He closed his eyes, wanting to drift into sleep.

Vincent, what about him?

Startled, he sat up. Emil was gone; Gregory and Bullfinch were sitting by his side.

"Did I fall asleep?"

"Only for a couple of minutes, sir," Bullfinch said.

"The telegram said nothing about Hawthorne," Andrew said. "We can't waste any time."

Taking the tin cup in Gregory's hands, Andrew slowly drained the rest of its contents, his stomach accepting it, every drop soaking straight into his body.

"Let's get moving," Andrew said, coming to his feet.

"Now Andrew," Emil said, coming back to his side.

"Don't 'now Andrew' me. We've still got Hawthorne and his men in that city. I know that boy. He said he'd hold until relieved, and by God he'll do it. Every minute is precious."

He walked over to Mercury's side and saw that his old friend was played out, flanks lathered with dried sweat.

"Bugler, sound the advance."

The clarion call went out, was picked up, and resounded off into the distance. Curses and groans filled the air as men struggled back up. Knots of men paused, bending over and picking up prone forms which they moved out of the high grass and over to the side of the road.

"I'm sending out an order to detail one man for every five who are down," Emil said with a tone that indicated he wouldn't accept any debate. "If they can get tent halves up for shade and we leave water behind, we'll save most of them. Otherwise they'll die out here."

Andrew nodded an agreement.

"Come on, Mercury, you and I will walk for a while."

Without looking back, Andrew started off, leaning on the saddle, willing one foot in front of the other.

The dream returned, Kathleen running before him, laughing, her naked body white, cool, inviting, her breasts rising and falling with each step, and he laughed at the foolishness of her running naked like this in the middle of steppe. It was snowing and she was running without any clothes on. Just how insane was that woman?

I'm riding again, he thought. The movement was slow, languid, as if she were beneath him, and then she was gone.

Vincent was looking at him with his old eyes in a boy's body. The boy was dripping with water.

"You told me to report to you at sundown, sir."

But no, that was during the war. Which war? It was the Tugars, wasn't it, or was it Gettysburg? No, that was Johnnie, dear Johnnie lying dead. Vincent wasn't even in the regiment then. It had to be the Tugar war.

"Why are you so wet, Vincent? You're in the damn city."

Wet. I'm wet.

He opened his eyes. It was dark. My God, have I gone blind?

There was a flash. Startled, he looked back, pulling out his revolver. Another flash in the twilight. There was laughing, splashing.

I am wet. He looked down and saw the dark water swirling about his legs.

"Where in hell am I?"

"It's the river, sir!"

Gregory was beside him, splashing water up at him as if he were a child.

Grinning dumbly, Andrew looked about in the gathering darkness. By the thousands men were wading into the coolness, laughing, scooping up handfuls of the precious liquid, falling over.

"How long?" Andrew whispered.

"What, sir?"

"I remember you making a lean-to, pouring water on me."

"Several hours back, sir," he said quietly. "At least I think so."

"Well, I'll be damned," Andrew whispered.

There was another flash of light, and he saw the fork of lightning on the far horizon to the west, and the first faint scent of a cooling breeze washed over him.

"Thank God, it's going to rain," Emil laughed, coming up by Andrew's side and with a dramatic flourish falling down to sit chest-deep in the river.

"Oh, my hand to God," he sighed.

Dumbfounded, Andrew looked around, and giving himself over, he collapsed into the water by Emil's side.

"Worst march I ever made."

"We most likely lost two, maybe three thousand from the heat," Emil said. "They're strung out on the road all the way back to Hispania. This rain, though, will save most of them."

"What's that?" Andrew asked, pointing to a flickering glow on the southeastern horizon.

"Didn't you notice that before?"

"Dear doctor, all I remember seeing is my naked wife running around in the snow," Andrew said with a sigh.

"You really were sun-struck."

"Guess I was."

"We've been seeing that for the last half hour. It's Roum."

"Then someone is still fighting in there," Andrew said, coming back to his feet.

"It certainly looks that way."

"Bullfinch."

"Here, sir."

"Any more messages?"

"They're hooking into the line now, sir."

"Well, get up there and be quick about it."

Going over to Mercury, Andrew swung into the saddle, the horse nickering as he pulled him up from drinking and rode back up to the riverbank. Pulling out his field glasses, he trained them on the horizon, hoping somehow he could see something. It was still nothing but a shimmering dance of light.

"How far have we gotten?" Andrew asked, looking over to Gregory.

"Just over thirty miles, sir. It was a hell of a march."

"Then it's thirty to go?"

"About that, sir."

"Andrew, I hope you're not thinking what I think you are," Emil said, coming up to his side.

"Pass the word," Andrew shouted to his staff. "Two hours' rest. Maybe that storm behind us will catch up. We'll march in the rain—at least it'll be cool."

"Not a night march, Andrew. Half your army will be down by dawn."

"Those are the orders," Andrew snapped, and Emil, seeing that it was useless to argue, walked away with a muffled curse.

"Sir, we just got a message in," Bullfinch shouted, running back to stand by Andrew.

Reaching into his saddlebag, he pulled out a pack of matches. He struck one and held it up, cupping the flame in his hand against the growing breeze.

"Hispanic Station reports Kennebec River crossing under attack. Forces unknown. Line west went dead twenty minutes ago."

Merciful God, they're behind us," Andrew whispered. Suddenly it all became clear, the pieces of the puzzle falling into place at last. He had been played for a fool.

He looked back to the west. They could be back in Hispania late tomorrow morning. The wood supply in Hispania was low, but they could still run fifteen or twenty trains back. It'd be at least another half day, more like a day, to get back to the bridge. And then what? he thought angrily. I'll be running from one end to the other and doing nothing but killing my troops for nothing.

He looked back to the east. If I force-march it, I'll be there by noon tomorrow. Maybe half the men will be ready to fight. The Carthas will be rested. I don't even know if I'm doing any good going that way. I can always send Barry's detachment up the line to find out what happened.

"We've been led down the garden path, Emil," Andrew said woodenly, handing the telegram down to his friend, who struck a match to read the message.

"I've got a suspicion there's more to this than meets the eye," Emil replied coldly. "That Cromwell always was a sneaking bastard."

"Sometimes being a sneaking bastard is a good quality, especially in war."

"What are you going to do?"

"There's nothing I can do behind me now," Andrew said. "If we've lost the bridge and our connection back home, we've lost it. Running back won't do a damn thing. I'll send Barry with a couple of trains up the line to find out what happened. Send a courier back up the road to Hispania. All men who fell out on the march are to marshal back to that city. They're out of the fight for here. Get Kindred to go back with them and organize a scratch brigade."

"His asthma is killing him in this heat and dust," Emil said with a worried tone. "It's a wise move."

"Andrew, if he diverted some of his strength to hit the bridge, why didn't he take it out before we crossed?"

"Because he wanted us to cross."

"What the hell for? He could have had Roum that way."

"I couldn't figure it out before," Andrew said softly. "Keeping the telegraph line open even as he surrounded the city. Not sending a force out to delay us. Not blowing the Kennebec bridge as the first act.

"He never wanted Roum," Andrew whispered. "The bastard's after Suzdal."

# Chapter Nine

"And I will have to ask, what has happened to our army?"

"The line's been cut, senator," Hans growled darkly. "That's all I can tell you."

"I suspect that you know far more than you're willing to tell us," Mikhail said with a gloating smile.

Hans struggled not to tell him to go to hell or better yet challenge him to a one-on-one shootout.

"Senator, we have that one telegraph line going east, that's it. The line got cut, somewhere between Siberia Station and the Kennebec River. As soon as I know anything more, I'll inform the president."

"And this Senate," Mikhail shouted.

"Senator, as commander of the Suzdalian army I answer to the president," Hans retorted. "I am here only upon his request."

"I am certain that Colonel Keane has everything under control," Senator Petra said, looking over at Hans with a friendly smile. "It is most likely a temporary inconvenience. It could even be from the lightning storms, which I have been told will disrupt this telegraph machine."

"Temporary inconvenience," Alexander sniffed. "Our army goes galloping off, to support an ally we don't need, and now this. I knew something would go terribly wrong from our president's ambitions."

"He's right," Mikhail replied. "Go out into the merchants' quarters and ask them if they like these sharp-nosed traders from Roum. I tell you, this railroad project of Kal's is going to destroy all of us. We have wasted labor and resources that could have gone elsewhere. Our people live in hovels since the war. Build them houses, not a railroad. What has it given us? If it was not for this railroad we would not have sent off our sons to fight in a war that is not our concern. The building of it is ruining us, and will bring in foreigners who will steal all of our money and make us bankrupt."

"First of all, I find Mikhail's sudden concern for housing the people to be truly a change of heart," Boris said with a sarcastic sneer. "We need the Roum," he shouted angrily. "They have three times the men that we do. They have the metals we need for our army. We need these things if the Tugars should come or, Kesus preserve us, one of the southern hordes should march in our direction."

"How long will you hold these false demons up to us?" Mikhail laughed. "Ten years from now this clique of our president will still be scaring us in our sleep with Tugar talk. They're gone, and the southern hordes have their own preserves."

"Gentlemen, if I may interrupt," Hans said, his voice cold with sarcasm.

"When we are finished," Mikhail retorted.

"I have business elsewhere, and I must assume at least some of the members of this august body can understand that."

"You are dismissed, if your business is so urgent," Mikhail said, waving his hand toward Hans as if he were an annoying fly.

Bristling, Hans stood up and stalked out of the room.

O'Donald stood by the doorway, his red beard matched by the anger in his features.

"Kal wants you now," O'Donald whispered, grabbing Hans by the arm.

The two officers marched down the corridor, their countenances so grim that all stood back at their passage, the hallway echoing with anxious comments as they passed. Reaching the door to Kal's chamber, they walked in, O'Donald slamming the door shut behind him.

"A telegram just came in," O'Donald said. "Kal wants you to see it."

Without bothering to knock, O'Donald opened the door.

"I got him for you," O'Donald announced.

Wearily Kal looked up from the desk. Kathleen stood in the corner of the room, her features sharp.

"Kathleen, darling," O'Donald said nervously, "you shouldn't be up and about like this. What would the colonel be saying now?"

"Shut up, you dumb Irishman. I'm fully capable of getting about."

"Dumb Irishman is it, the lass says." O'Donald laughed, falling back into English. "And herself an O'Reilly before she took the name of Keane."

"Will both of you please be quiet," Kal said, coming to his feet.

O'Donald winked as Kathleen angrily shook her head.

"Now if we've settled this little quarrel," Kal said, "perhaps I can get Hans's opinion on this message."

Kal handed a scrap of paper over to Hans, who quickly scanned the document.

"It's a fake," Hans said.

"Why?"

"I find it impossible to believe that Andrew actually walked into a trap as this thing says, that he was killed and the army crushed."

"The telegrapher said it had the proper code word opening and closing the message."

"Whoever sent this could have tapped into the line and found that out easy enough. I know Andrew. He can be a regular killer demon in battle. But he's got a level head to him."

As he spoke, Kal could detect the note of pride in Hans's voice.

"The colonel trapped and defeated," O'Donald snapped coldly. "It's a goddam lie, it is.

"Excuse me, ma'am," he added quickly.

"My feelings as well," Kathleen replied, but the fear in her voice was evident.

Sheepishly he looked over at her.

"If I'd known about this message, Kathleen, I'd never have made light with you. Please forgive me."

She came over to Pat's side and put her hand on his arm. Kal watched her closely. He had brought her here to break the news, praying that Hans would confirm it as a lie. Her features were pale, almost translucent.

"Kathleen darling," O'Donald whispered, "please will you sit down."

Wearily she nodded as he helped her over to a chair and then with an uncharacteristic gesture kissed her lightly on the forehead and took her hand.

"He's tougher than the lot of us," O'Donald said, trying to force a smile.

"I talked to the telegraph operator," Kal said quietly. "He says that the operator didn't have the fist of anyone on the line, whatever that is."

"The signal each man sends is slightly different. A good operator can smell that out," O'Donald stated.

"Then why send it?" Kal asked. "If we could read through it?"

"Well, sir, maybe they thought we'd fall for it."

"Doubtful," O'Donald replied. "That Cromwell isn't that much of a fool."

"Foolish in one area, though," Hans said. "It proves they have the bridge and at least cut the army off from us."

"A brilliant move," Kal said, walking over to look at a map hanging on the wall. "They've cut the army two hundred miles in the rear."

He traced his finger along the map to Roum.

"If I were Andrew," Hans said, coming up to stand by Kal, "there's only one thing I'd do now. He has to push into Roum and at least secure that base."

"Taking him farther away from us," Kal said quietly, looking over at Hans.

Kal let his finger trace down the coast of the Inland Sea from Roum back toward Suzdal. He paused and looked back at Hans.

"We're nearly defenseless here," Kal whispered.

"Damn him, that's it!" Hans snapped. "He could move everything back this way. I've worried about that, but always assumed that we'd keep the rail line open and shift our forces if Cromwell tried it. I never expected him to actually get behind us like this and knock out the bridge. Andrew and I expected he'd try to block us going up, never heading back."

"How long if they should try and move this way?" Kathleen asked.

"Even with the wind against them, four days, maybe five for the steam ships."

"Fifty-pound guns," O'Donald said darkly. "They'd cut a hole in the harbor wall in an afternoon with those. It'll be murder, it will—they can lie a hundred yards off and blast us to ribbons. If our army's cut off, they could bring their entire force this way and land virtually unopposed."

Kal returned to his desk and sat down.

"How long would it be for Andrew to get back?"

"God knows how many miles of track will get torn up," Hans said darkly. "They'll make Sherman hairpins out of 'em."

"What?"

"Burn the crossties," O'Donald said. "A grand sight it is, as long as it's the other side's tracks. They'll lay the rails on top of the fire and then bend 'em around the telegraph poles. They'll be useless. The bridge is gone as well. Once he gets back to the Kennebec, he'll have to march two hundred miles to reach our inner frontier."

"If there's any delaying force ahead of them," Hans interjected, "it could take two weeks. maybe even three, and remember we don't know how long it'll be before he even takes Roum back. Supply will be a nightmare—they've only got twenty-five days' rations with them as is, and if Roum has fallen there'll be nothing in there they can use."

"Can we send some men up the line to meet him?"

"We can't," Hans replied. "Don't forget the southern frontier. If I was them Merki, I'd be striking now. Thank God we haven't heard anything from their quarter yet. As it is, we've got a full brigade down there, and only one brigade in the city."

"What will Andrew do?" Kal asked wearily.

"I don't know," Hans said dejectedly. "He'll have to figure something out, and damn quick."

"So we're on our own here."

"That's it, Mr. President," Hans said, looking straight into Kal's eyes.

Kal sat back and closed his eyes. It had all seemed like some grand exciting adventure before. Before they had ever come, he was nothing but a bad reciter of verse for Boyar Ivor. Hiding behind a mask of foolishness, living off the table scraps of the boyars, hoping to wheedle an exemption for his family and friends when the Tugars came. "President" had sounded so grand, to be like the legendary saint

Lincoln. After all, the war was over. Never had he dreamed that this burden would be placed upon him in such a way.

"Mr. President," he had just been called, and he could see the cold judgment in Hans's eyes. Looking to see if at this moment he could ever measure up. He opened his eyes, looking over at Kathleen, hoping that she at least would offer support. But he saw none there—it was she who wanted strength from him, some reassurance that her husband was safe, and that he would have a place to come back to.

If only I could run away from all of this and hide. Take my family up into the forest, find a safe haven for Ludmilla, for Tanya and the three babies. Yet she would not go. He had sent her husband out to Roum. Was he already dead? Had he made his only child a widow before she was even really a woman herself?

All of them were waiting. Without a word he got up from behind his desk and walked over to the door. He stepped out onto the balcony overlooking the square.

The air was cool, the scorching heat of the previous week washed away by the storm of yesterday. But the city was subdued, somber, people in the square standing about in small knots, talking with heads lowered, looking toward the government hall. Seeing him on the balcony, several started to move closer. They would expect him to say something. It was always so easy before—he'd trade lighthearted banter and then return to his desk. But seeing them approach, he was filled with dread. They wanted to know, they were looking to him for an answer.

Finding no solitude, he retreated into his office and faced his three friends.

He had to do something. It must have been so easy for Lincoln, for after all he was a saint, he thought. I'm only a peasant playing at being a boyar.

But you outsmarted all of them, he reasoned. Think like a peasant, like the mouse dancing with the fox.

"I'm declaring a full mobilization of the militia to take place at once," Kal said quietly.

Hans smiled and nodded his head.

Somehow he felt reassured by the look now in Hans's eyes. It was such an obvious step—why did he not simply ask for it? Or is it that I have to say it all first?

"How many muskets do we have?"

"There are roughly four thousand of the old smoothbores waiting for conversion to rifling in the factory."

"Distribute them to the militia, but only to Suzdal and Novrod men."

Hans smile turned to a grin.

"Only trust the old guard, I say," O'Donald interjected.

"What about the Senate?" Kathleen said sharply. "For my two cents, Mikhail's in with Cromwell."

Kal nodded in agreement.

"I'm leery of disbanding the Senate and declaring martial law," Kal said slowly, as if grasping for each word. "I suspect that would be a bad thing. Your Andrew keeps talking about precedents that I set. If I should do that, then in years to come other presidents will do it lightly, until finally there will be one boyar and nothing else."

Hans groaned and pounded the table with his fist.

"You'll wind up paying for that," he said sharply.

"Did your Lincoln do it?"

"He wasn't fighting Merki," Kathleen replied. "They were rebels, but at least they were honorable men we fought against. This is different."

"I can't make it any other way," Kal stated firmly, and then a smile creased his features.

"But I also know who the fox is. I am not that much of a fool," he whispered, "nor an idealist. We will take care of Mikhail and his like when the time comes.

"Can we hold the city?" Kal asked, his tone making it clear that the topic was closed.

"I doubt it," O'Donald said. "If Andrew and the entire army were here it'd be impossible for them to land. The *Ogunquit* would do some damage, for certain, but a couple of regiments of good riflemen armed with Springfields could play hell with them every time they opened a gun port out in the river. Without the 35th, though, those big guns will certainly weaken us. It's the one thing we never dreamed of—an ironclad coming up the Neiper to shell us."

"What's more important?" Hans said his voice cold.

"I don't understand," Kal replied.

"The city or what it produces?" Hans continued.

"The factories, by God," O'Donald cried. "We lose the factories and we're naked. They take the dam, blow it, there go the factories and the north half of the city all over again."

"We'll have to hold both," Kal said quietly.

"But sir, I don't think we can. At least the factories are far enough away from the river. He won't be able to hit them from the ship."

"We hold both," Kal replied. "I've got to think of politics here, my friends. Abandon the city and the merchants will turn—they are unhappy as is. It is that simple. And we pray that somehow Andrew will find a way out of this for us."

"And pray as well the Merki do not move," Kathleen said quietly.

"Kalenchka!"

The door slipped open, and Kal looked up angrily.

"Dammit, Boris, does everyone feel he can just walk in here?"

"Your scribe tried to stop me, but it can't wait."

"Go on, then."

"Mikhail just announced on the floor of the Senate that Andrew's been killed and the army defeated."

"So he has already begun his game," Kal said quietly.


There was something about a good fire that always pleased him. Smiling, Jim Hinsen watched as the last trestle, still licked with flames, tumbled over, collapsing into the river, kicking up a shower of steam. For over a mile in either direction of the bridge a line of fires crackled and burned. Piles of rails were laid on top of the flaming ties, sagging under the heat.

He had always regretted getting drafted into the Army of the Potomac. Hell, it was Sherman's boys who were having all the fun, with the looting, the burning, and—he licked his lips dryly—the women as well.

It was his first command, and he loved that as well. Dropped off by Jamie's ships, which had immediately put back to sea, he had waited with his thousand men in concealment for two days, watching the puffs of smoke crossing the far horizon. Finally hours had passed without a sign of activity and he knew the time was right. Darkness was supposed to be their cover; the storm had only helped as they boarded ship and worked their way upstream.

The killing had been easy enough. They'd expected only a hundred, and the fact that a full regiment was there had been a surprise. But they'd been even more surprised than he at the sudden onslaught.

The Carthas still weren't all that good with the musket, but when it came to the bayonet on the end they knew how to use it. Jamie's cutthroats were another matter. More than one of them damn Rus had thrown down his weapon and been pinned screaming to the ground by his boys.

He even remembered Stover, and he smiled at the recollection and pleasure of seeing him again. The man had cheated him once at cards, and you never did that. It was almost funny how Stover had begged as Jamie's men held him down while he slowly sliced the lousy cheater's throat open.

Now the trick was not to get squeezed in this little game. They might always have an extra train back in Suzdal. Chances were they'd definitely run one down from Roum. So just keep tearing that old track up and keep a sharp eye out for the fun.

After all, I am the commander, he thought with a sardonic laugh. I'll have to stay here right in the middle, the others are the ones that'll get shot.

"Independent fire at will!"

Choking on gunsmoke, Vincent crouched low, peering through the rubble and confusion at the onrushing host. A bone-numbing crash snapped through the building, followed by a shower of debris cascading into the courtyard in front of him.

"Jesus Christ."

He dived to the ground, hiding behind a shattered column. The entire east end of the palace had been blasted open by the close-range bombardment; a gaping hole was all that remained of the section facing the forum. Musket balls snicked past, followed by a spray of canister.

"Fall back to the other side of the courtyard!" Vincent shouted, standing and pointing with his sword to the breastworks that lined the west side.

Dodging through the wreckage of Marcus's palace, the line of Suzdalian troops pulled back, their retreat signaled by the triumphant shouts of the Cartha infantry, who stormed up the steps and gained the broken wreckage of the outside wall. Running low, Vincent jumped over the breastworks and then cautiously peered up over a pile of shattered rock.

The enemy now held the outside wall not sixty feet away. A cannon next to him snapped off with a deafening blast, the canister shot disappearing into the smoke, the iron rounds shrieking as they careened off the rubble. It was impossible to see anything in the confusion.

An explosion filled the courtyard, and a section of wall above him erupted in a shower of dust and stone fragments.

"The bastard's laying those shots in right over his own men!" Dimitri shouted, crawling up to Vincent's side.

Another shot screamed in, slashing into the balcony above, sending down a rain of debris.

"The men upstairs?" Vincent shouted.

"Barricaded in."

"I'm going up to look."

Crouching low, Vincent ran down the length of the courtyard. The enemy were pouring in a stiff fire, shooting blind into the smoke, the bullets smacking into the marble wall behind him, slashing off stone fragments, the lead shot ricocheting. Turning through the doorway into Marcus's public audience room, Vincent came around the portal and, breathing hard, stood up.

The chamber was a shambles. The wall above had been cut through earlier in the day, the shell bursting inside, spraying the room with debris and killing several men, who still lay where they had been cut down.

Running across the audience chamber, Vincent hit the back door into the slave quarters, where the far wall faced out into the street. At each window a sniper stood, gun up, scanning for a target.

"Any pressure here?"

"They rushed the door again," a sergeant with a blood-streaked face said, pointing to a battered portal, torn apart by shot. Bodies clogged the entryway. "We gave 'em the cold steel."

Grinning, the sergeant held up a gore-streaked bayonet.

"Good work, soldier," Vincent growled, slapping him on the shoulder.

Going down the length of the corridor, he passed a quick word to each man, who looked at him appreciatively.

He paused for a second at the entryway into the basement. His stomach tightened. He could barely face the hospital, but there was no avoiding it. Bracing himself, he rushed down the stairs. The stench was overpowering, the room a cacophony of sobs and screams of anguish. In the far corner the surgeon was at his bloody craft, saw in hand, the boy on the table mercifully unconscious from the last of the chloroform. Olivia stood next to the surgeon, holding a tray of instruments. She looked up at him, her features pale, and an exhausted smile lit her features as she saw that he was still unhurt.

"They've gained the outside wall of the palace," Vincent shouted, his voice hoarse and cracking.

The cries dropped away.

"Any man that can walk, I need you back upstairs. If you can't shoot you can at least load muskets. I need you."

"Come on, lads," a gray-bearded private groaned, pressing a bandage to his side as he came to his feet.

With a shuffling gait, the private started for the door. One by one the men started for the door, several of them crawling. Vincent looked over at the surgeon, who gazed at him as if he had been the creator of this anguish.

I am the creator of it, Vincent thought. I could have accepted Cromwell's offer of a free passage out. He found himself half wishing the arrow he had saved Marcus from had found its intended target. Without Marcus there would have been no reason to stay and watch the rest of his command get torn to pieces.

Vincent nodded to the surgeon and raced back up the stairs. Turning the corner of the steps, he continued on up to the second floor and stepped into Marcus's private quarters.

For a moment he paused. The quarters were Spartan in their simplicity, he thought. He found the idea curious. In this world there undoubtedly were Spartans someplace or another—there was damn near everything else. A servant with a musket slung over his shoulder rushed past him, lugging a box of ammunition.

"Marcus?"

"Over in the north wing, noble sir," the servant gasped.

"Keep up the good work, soldier," Vincent shouted.

The man looked back at him and smiled.

"I'm a free man—of course I'll fight," he said as he disappeared into the south wing.

Running across the room, Vincent entered the shattered remnants of the library. Most of the far wall was blown in, exposed to the open courtyard. The racks of scrolls were shattered and in flames; thick acrid smoke was pouring up through holes gaping in the ceiling. Through the light rain and billowing smoke he could see the Senate on the far side of the plaza, several hundred yards away. A snap of smoke burst from the Senate steps. The hell with heroics, he thought, diving to the floor, covering his head.

A section of the library wall burst in, sending out a deadly spray of stone fragments. A high-pitched scream echoed through the room as a soldier staggered to his feet holding his hands over his stomach, blood pouring out between his fingers.

Vincent ignored him and crawled up to the line of soldiers manning the wall, firing down into the courtyard below.

The pressure was building, he could feel it, even as his own strength was ebbing away. Gritting his teeth, he leaped up over a hole in the wall and out onto the balcony. A ragged line of riflemen lined the porch, hiding behind splintered fragments of furniture, barrels dragged up from the basement, piles of marble wrestled loose from the shattered, smoldering building. Crawling down the length of the porch, he scurried into the north wing, which was choked with a thick blinding smoke. A section of the wall opposite him was down, flames licking up hungrily.

"They've piled up carts of straw along the wall," a company commander shouted. "We can't see a damn thing."

"Marcus?"

"Next room."

Vincent ran through the doorway.

"Marcus!"

"Over here."

Crawling low to see through the smoke, Vincent reached the shattered wall where Marcus was crouched down, loading a musket for a Suzdalian private next to him.

"We're making quite a team," Marcus said, looking over at the soldier.

The private looked back at Vincent and nodded. "Don't know what the hell he's saying, sir, but he can load 'em as fast as I can shoot 'em."

The private turned back, looking for a target.

"How are we?" Marcus asked.

"Not good. They've gained the outer wall downstairs and the rooms facing it."

"Well, you never expected to hold them forever. If they rush that courtyard we'll slaughter them."

"But those damn guns are smashing us to pieces. The

fire's hitting the east side of the palace now. By the way, you can bid your library a fond fairwell."

"Damn them," Marcus sighed. "I'll miss my Xenophon. It was my only copy."

"You had Xenophon's works?"

"Came from the old world, an original copy sealed in a bronze box. A priceless heirloom. Well, that's the price of war, I guess," Marcus said sadly.

"God damn it all to hell," Vincent cried, feeling almost as much anger over the priceless work as he did over all the losses of the bitter fight that was now over a day and a half old. He was amazed at the punishment the palace could take. It was a fortress in its own right. Without it his tattered band would have been overrun long ago.

"So much for the slaves," Marcus said sarcastically. "I haven't seen a one."

"Well, you certainly didn't give them any time to do anything about it," Vincent said. "The Cartha were already in the city."

"Did Julius and the others get out?"

"During the night he slipped out the back entry under the cover of the smoke. He promised to see what he could do. A lot of them volunteered to stay, though, and I put them to work."

"Surprising," Marcus said evenly. "A slave's loyalty is a strange thing."

"Free men and women," Vincent replied sharply.

Marcus looked over at him and smiled. "Well, it looks like your desire to free everybody will get you killed today."

A desperate shout rose up from the plaza. The sniper next to Marcus rose up, aiming. As he squeezed the trigger the man flipped over backward, a spray of canister slicing the air. Horrified, Vincent looked at what was left of the man's head, even as his body kicked and thrashed on the floor, as if not willing to admit that it was already dead.

"Damn them all," Marcus growled. Cocking a musket, he looked up over the wall. Vincent scrambled over to the dying private, pulled the musket from his hand, and stood up to join Marcus.

The square below was packed with a wave rushing forward, bypassing the opening into the courtyard and hitting the north and south sections instead. Ladders were raised, men scrambling up.

Vincent leaned over, pointing his musket straight into the face of an advancing Cartha, who looked up at him with desperate terror-filled eyes. Vincent squeezed the trigger. The man tumbled over, taking the ladder with him. Marcus fired a second later, dropping a man who with musket raised was preparing to shoot back.

The rest of the Suzdalians in the room poured out a hail of fire, but the Carthas kept coming, pushing the ladders back, scrambling up as the defenders paused to reload. The first man gained the top, leaping into the breach in the wall. One of Marcus's servants drove in low with a makeshift pike, slamming the man in the stomach, pushing him back over the wall.

"They're on the roof!"

Vincent turned and looked up to the hole in the ceiling. A Cartha stood above him, musket aimed straight at his chest. He felt as if the moment was an eternity, the payment of all his sins coming to fruition at last. The hammer of the musket slammed down, emitting a shower of sparks. Nothing happened. Shaking, he just stood there looking up at the man above him not twenty feet away.

To his absolute amazement, the Cartha lowered his weapon, looking at the open pan now exposed to the mist and the drizzle. A curious smile lit his features, and raising his hand, he waved, as if offering an apology for having just tried to kill Vincent, and then ducked out of view.

All around him men were pulling back, running for the doorway into the next room. Marcus, oblivious to the threat from above and behind, had already reloaded, and as the next man appeared in the gap in the wall he shot him at point-blank range, the hair on the man's head exploding into flames from the hot discharge of the weapon.

"Get back!" Vincent screamed, grabbing Marcus by the shoulder. Marcus turned, looking at him as if he had been disturbed from an enjoyable pastime.

"Above us!" Vincent screamed, looking back up to see another Cartha bringing his musket up. Throwing aside his musket, Vincent pulled out his revolver and fired wildly, causing the man to duck.

"Let's go!"

Together the two ran for the doorway, where already the

men were reforming the next line of defense. Stepping into the momentary protection, Vincent went over to the opposite wall facing the courtyard.

"My God, they're in the courtyard!"

Below was a scene of mad confusion, barely visible in the dark billowing smoke and hissing steam as the light rain continued to fall. Men struggled hand to hand in the rubble, slashing at each other with lowered bayonets, wrestling their foes to the ground, grabbing fragments of polished marble, smashing them down on their screaming opponents. Knives flickered in the fireglow, carving into human flesh. For a moment he saw Dimitri, regimental flag by his side, holding the broken stock of a musket, using it as a club, desperately swinging, holding back two Carthas who kept coming in low with leveled bayonets, looking for an opening.

Gazing down from above, he felt as if he were looking straight into the lower depths of hell.

A bullet slapped into the wall beside him, spraying his face with fragments, and everything turned red. Gasping, he staggered back, terrified to open his eyes. Hands grabbed hold of his, forcing them away.

Dimly he could see Marcus looking at him.

"Can you see me, son?" In spite of his pain he found for the first time a warmth in the cold stoic consul he had worked so hard to reach. The man gazed at him, frightened.

Vincent fumbled in his pocket for his sweaty handkerchief. As he wiped the blood from his eyes he felt as if his face had been washed in fire.

Pulling the handkerchief away, Marcus took it and gently wiped his face, shaking his head.

"You're going to look like a demon of the underworld after this," Marcus said. "You'll scare your children to death when you get home."

"Home?" Vincent started to laugh, looking back out to the madness in the courtyard below as the Carthas steadily pushed their way into the palace.

"If Hulagar discovers this?"

"Shut up about Hulagar," Vuka laughed. "I just want to see what the sport is. It's never been my pleasure to see cattle slaying cattle."

Tamuka, shield-bearer of Vuka, looked about nervously. These new smoke killers of the cattle left him uneasy. Cattle were without teeth, to be grazed and fattened for the kill. He did not like this thing that they could now do. Though the Tugar were unclean, they were still of the horse, the ever-circling riders of Valennia, who would at least ascend to the everlasting sky as servants to the Merki. Cattle would return to the dust that they came from, or go to the afterworld as food for the feasting tables. It was not right to make of them one who could kill even one of the Vushka Hush.

Tamuka drew his bow, nocking an arrow, slinging his quiver around from its riding position on his back to down alongside his hip. The escort around them, seeing his action, followed suit.

"We were strictly ordered not to let the cattle of Roum see us. You are here to observe how this cattle weapon fighting is done, not to play in it as well."

"I am sick of hiding from the vermin," Vuka barked. "I am the Zan, heir to the Qar Qarth. It is Hulagar who should take orders from me. He is not even of the Golden Blood. There is blood being spilled, and I wish to wet my blade."

The escort laughed at Vuka's words, and Tamuka bristled. Holding down a curse, Tamuka fell in by Vuka's left side, watching intently as they clattered through the gates of the city.

A sharp continual thunder rolled across the city. Streaks of flame rose up from the center of town, marking where the palace was being stormed.

"Shall we go, my friends?" Vuka said, pointing toward the center of the city.

Tamuka pushed his horse in front of Vuka and turned.

"My lord, I cannot allow it."

"Out of my way," Vuka said, his voice oily and dark, "or are you a coward?"

There was an expectant hush. Tamuka had been accused —by right he could draw sword. All knew he could defeat Vuka, yet all knew as well he could not, for he was sworn to protect Vuka with his very life.

"My lord, I am going to give you a choice," Tamuka said quietly. "If you ride in there and the Yankees see you, I must face Hulagar, shield-bearer of your father. He will surely take my head for allowing this to happen, and I will submit. If you must ride in, then strike me down first."

Vuka looked around at his followers, who gazed at him

intently. Tamuka could see that more than one would be indifferent if he should die. Several looked straight at Tamuka, and he could see agreement in their eyes especially from Ken, Vuka's youngest brother. Vuka as well could see it and cursed quietly.

"If you must see something," Tamuka reasoned, knowing that Vuka would indeed strike him if he did not desist, "then go down to the wharfs. There was a flurry of fighting there, at least."

Wordlessly Vuka nodded and turned his horse aside.

"My lord."

"What is it."

"My honor demands that you retract your words," Tamuka said, forcing a winning smile. "You were hot for blood, you smell battle, one can get excited. But I must have my honor if I am to ride beside you."

"You are with honor," Vuka said, a bit too quickly. The tension of the group slipped away.

"I think this way will lead to the docks," Tamuka announced, pointing down a side alleyway.

Spurring his mount, Vuka set out.

"You test me at times, my shield-bearer," Vuka snapped as he cantered off.

"As a shield-bearer must," Tamuka said under his breath. Especially for one as impetuous as you, he thought safely to himself. It was an assignment traditional to his family, which was trained not in arms as much as in wisdom and the thinking of ka-tu, the path of knowing. It was they who rode by the clan leaders, the commanders of the umens, and the members of the Golden Blood. Often they drifted in the paths of night thinking, the leaving of the body to gain knowledge. It was claimed by some, the masters of the old order, that they could at times even learn to decipher the mystery writings of the ancient ones, the star-walking gods, fathers of all who rode the endless steppe. The Golden Blood ruled, but it was clan of the white, the holders of the ka-tu, who thought. The bond was far more than that of a warrior protecting his lord. It was to be the voice of wisdom as well, to stop them from the madness of blood that power gave.

Hulagar would not have slain him, he thought with a smile. That was merely an idle threat. In fact, there was really nothing Hulagar could do to Vuka, other than to intimidate him by his presence. But it had worked, and he smiled.

Vuka might eventually become a Qar Qarth worthy of the name, but he prayed to his ka that that day would be long in coming.

Even as he pondered he cautiously watched the streets. Never before had he ridden into a cattle city and not seen the terror and obeisance. At their approach the cattle scattered. But after their passage the street filled behind them, and the sight made him uneasy.

In their barbaric tongue he heard the word "Tugar," over and over, and there was a sinister tone to their voices that was chilling.

Vuka galloped ahead, threatening with his sword, clearing the way. A woman dressed in nothing more than filthy rags refused to give way, raising her clenched fist. With a backhanded swing Vuka cut her in half, and laughing rode on. The others, as if seeing this as permission to kill cattle, after the long months of restraint under pain of death among the Carthas, now laid to, laughing at the sport.

Tamuka knew the enormity of this mistake, but there was nothing to do but ride after Vuka.

Clearing the end of the lane, they turned into a broad boulevard facing out into the river. Dozens of Cartha and Roum ships lined the quay, and gangs of laborers formed a steady stream, hauling baskets of grain out of the warehouses. A circle of Cartha pikemen lined the boulevard watching the Roum slaves anxiously.

A sharp explosion rent the air, and looking up the hill Tamuka could see a column of fire-clad smoke soaring straight up from the direction of the forum.

"Ah, Hamilcar!" Vuka cried as if addressing a pet that he was almost fond of.

The Cartha general looked up astonished at Vuka's approach.

"What the hell are you doing here?" Hamilcar snapped.

"Cattle, watch who you address like that," Vuka roared.

A bitter smile crossed Hamilcar's features, and he lowered his head. Tamuka could see the hatred in the man's eyes but said nothing. They needed this man, and though pledges to cattle were in the end meaningless, for now it was still a pledge.

"How goes the fighting?" Tamuka asked quickly, before Vuka could make an issue of the exchange.

Hamilcar turned deliberately away from Vuka.

"The palace is falling, but the price is far higher than I wanted. In the end I see no sense to it."

"If we could have taken the city without a fight, perhaps the Yankees would be caught then."

"A wild dream of Cromwell's, nothing more," Hamilcar replied. "Perhaps, though, it will still work."

Hamilcar drew up closer to Tamuka, dropping his voice.

"These people did not know you were here. This could cause trouble."

Tamuka found that he actually liked this pet who spoke so boldly, and nodded in reply. A sound like a distant wave upon the Inland Sea started to rise up, in seconds matching the thunder of the battle being fought up on the hill. He turned in his saddle and looked back from the direction they had just come, and he felt a cold chill.

Brimming with rage, Julius raced down the street, leaping over the bodies of the slain. It had been a maddening day and night. Few had heard Marcus's words as he wandered about the city, trying to raise support, dodging the Cartha patrols and the occasional legionary who had not melted away, and now stood with the dying Lucullus. As he spoke he felt seized with a mad desperation. No one would believe him, no one cared, for what was one master versus another. They would still labor and starve anyhow.

And then he had seen them, Tugars riding through the gate as if going to see the fight, to laugh and watch as cattle slaughtered cattle. So all the words of the Yankee were true after all, for even he had doubted them. Tugars, whom they had slain and driven away, were now back, riding through the open gate unopposed.

As he screamed the warning, the streets, which had been empty, filled.

"I am Julius, servant of Marcus!" he had cried. "My words are true. Fight the enemy, fight the Tugars in our midst, and we will be free!"

And finally they had listened, following him down the street, pouring into the alleyways, leaping over the dead and dying who had been cut down by the beasts, prying up paving stones, sticks of firewood, tools from the shops, anything to kill a Tugar with.

"We've got trouble," Hamilcar shouted, pointing toward the crowd that had started to spill out of the streets and alleyways.

From the direction they had just come from a dark angry shout went up, a mob spilling around the corner. Tamuka could see that more than one of them were from the legion.

Most of them had been rounded up easily enough the day before, the fight gone out of them by the occupation and the beautifully planned betrayal by the cattle rulers of this city. If that one knot of resistance had not formed, he thought, the city would have truly been theirs without much of a fight.

"Get that damn Petronius out here again," Hamilcar shouted and then turned back to Tamuka.

"The Yankee army—how far away?"

"Half a day at least."

"If only we could finish off that defense and secure this town, we might still have a go at it."

A dark chant started to echo up across the rain-shrouded street, the crowd slowing at the sight of the Cartha pikemen lining the plaza.

"Tugar, Tugar, Tugar."

"It's you that's stirred this," Hamilcar snapped, looking back at Vuka.

"I'll have your tongue if you speak like that again," Vuka snarled.

"He's right," Tamuka shouted. "They had no idea we were here. Remember, my lord, they've killed Tugars, and they thought they were free of us."

Petronius came out of the warehouse and paled visibly at the sight of the growing mob, but when he turned and saw Vuka looking back at him coldly the man started to back up.

Hamilcar came up by his side, and Tamuka saw the flicker of a blade behind Petronius's back.

Trembling, Petronius stepped forward and started to speak. The crowd fell silent for a moment, but only for a moment.

"Bastard, you sold us to the Tugars!" a high clear voice cried.

A single rock arched into the air, followed an instant later by a shower of debris.

"We'd better get out of here!" Tamuka shouted.

"Tugar, Tugar!"

The chant was hate-filled, speaking of centuries of rage.

A paving stone arched through the air, landing in front of Tamuka so that his horse shied. Sawing at the bit, he swung the mount around.

"Get out of here!" Hamilcar shouted. "I'm burning the warehouses and pulling back," and turning, he disappeared into a crowd of soldiers.

Standing in his stirrups, Tamuka looked around. The only way open was toward the line of ships along the quay. But once there, what? None of them knew how to make such a thing move. The Carthas started to break away, running south, back toward the forum.

"This way!" Tamuka shouted, pointing in the direction of the fleeing soldiers.

Vuka, shouting with battle lust, fired bolt after bolt into the cattle, laughing as each shot slammed home.

"This is not a game! They can kill us!"

As if to add emphasis to his words, Kan, youngest son of the Qar Qarth suddenly spun around on his mount, his helmet gone, blood streaming down his face. Horrified, Tamuka watched as the terrified horse ran straight into the advancing mob. With the frenzy of wolves the cattle leaped upon the youngest brother of Vuka, tearing the hair from his body, stabbing at him with sharpened sticks, pelting him with rocks.

Kan shrieked in terrified anguish. The mob pulled him down. Desperately he struggled with his blade, backing up against his horse.

"Kan!" It was Vuka, screaming in anguish for his brother. Tamuka cut in front of Vuka, grabbing the reins of his horse, pulling him around.

"Run, my lord!"

"Vuka! Tamuka!"

Tamuka looked back. A cattle had leaped upon the back of Ken's horse. Holding up a heavy stone, he brought it down, screaming with maniacal rage, splitting his foe's head, spraying those around him with blood.

Kan disappeared, the cattle surrounding him, their arms

rising and falling rhythmically, the wooden stakes and stones flashing pink with foaming blood.

"Now, my lord!" Tamuka screamed, viciously spurring his mount into a gallop, Vuka's horse following behind him. Cartha or Roum, he did not care now, as he pushed southward, riding the cattle down, desperate to escape the advancing mob, the memory of Kan's death seared into his soul.

"Move it, dammit, move it!" Andrew roared. The city was now in sight. The center of the town was in flames, smoke and steam swirling up into the low-hanging clouds overhead. Before him the Cartha skirmish line was pulling back a mile or more away.

Turning, he looked back over the plain. His army was strung out for miles down the Appian Way. At best he could throw four or five thousand men into the advance. But something told him he'd have to strike now.

Pulling out his field glasses, he looked down toward the coastal plain. The blackened city of Ostia was barely visible through the mist.

White dots moved on the broadening waters of the Tiber, and it took him a moment to realize that the fleet was already putting out to sea. Barely discernible on the horizon he could see a dark squat shape, surrounded by a dozen beetlelike forms.

"So he really did it," Andrew whispered.

Looking back to the road between Ostia and Roum, he saw a long antlike column moving southward.

"Damn them, they're getting away," he whispered.

A flicker of light snapped up inside the city. Swinging around, he saw a flashing column of smoke rising up from the flaming ruins of the palace.

Long seconds passed and then a fluttering boom, like distant thunder, rolled across the plain.

Torn, he looked back to the harbor. He could still cut some of them off. But his gaze returned to the palace.

"Just a little farther, men, just a little farther!" Andrew shouted, pointing his sword toward the city. "Now move it!"

He urged his men on as they started down the broad open slope.

"Quick march, quick march!" Andrew shouted.

At every step his command seemed to melt away, men

stumbling, dropping into the high wet grass, some gaining their feet and staggering on, others looking up in anguish, so close to the end and yet unable to continue.

If they face me now, there'll be hell to pay, he thought.

But there was a dark desperation to it now. Every minute could spell the difference.

The clatter of musketry started to rumble. Mercury faltered, shaking.

A moment of concern filled him for his old comrade, and reining in, he leaped down from the horse.

"Someone get that saddle off!" he cried, and falling in with his men he pushed on. The regiments were mingled together. The identification now was only one of sheer physical strength to endure the end of the forced march in less than thirty-six hours.

All equipment was gone except for muskets, ammunition, and canteens. Everything else had been dropped miles before, during the long rain-soaked night.

Gaining the outer works of the Cartha, Andrew scrambled up on the embankment for a better look. The palace was a ruined shell, flames pouring out of it.

He must have made his stand in there, he thought coldly. Damn that boy, he would fight to the end like that. A knot of men from the 35th swept past, regimental flag and the old national colors held high. Andrew leaped down from the breastworks and fell in beside them, his hat gone, hair rain-soaked and plastered to his brow, sword held high.

Gasping for breath, he continued the pace, fearing that at any second a line of Cartha musketmen would appear on the shattered battlements to block his advance.

"For the breach!"

The men were starting to break into a run, staggering with their last ounce of strength, some now racing forward to somehow claim the honor of being first in.

It was a foolish madness, but Andrew felt it seize him as well, the end of nearly seven days of heart-tearing fear.

The first man gained the top of the rubble, holding his musket high in triumph. A flag went up over the parapet, the Suzdalian soldier waving it. A ragged cheer went up from the exhausted men.

Scrambling up over the parapet, Andrew saw a scattering of bodies. The streets were empty. Climbing down into the street, he paused for a moment. It could still be a trap.

"Skirmishers forward!"

But the discipline would not hold, not now, not after all they had endured. The men pushed forward, running down narrow alleyways, guided by the towering beacon of smoke in front of them.

Andrew caught up, shouldered his way forward. A shout started to echo up, and scattered knots of people appeared, holding up their hands, racing forward to embrace him. Andrew pushed his way through, pressing on. The alleyway started to broaden out, and without warning he found himself standing at the edge of the forum.

The vast square was a field of carnage. Hundreds of torn bodies littered the pavement. The sound of shouting and gunfire echoed from farther on, down by the docks. He hesitated for a second and then turned and ran for the steps of the palace.

"Skirmish line across the square. Take the Senate building on the far side. Thirty-fifth Maine to me!"

The men started to fan out, a knot of blue-clad soldiers spreading out around Andrew.

"Merciful God," he whispered, slowing as he climbed the steps. The building was a burned-out shell.

Reaching the top of the steps he looked into the smoke-shrouded inner courtyard.

Feeble cries rose up out of the carnage. Wounded and dying Carthas, numbed with shock, looked up with fear in their eyes. The men of the 35th moved in cautiously, kicking weapons aside.

"Thirty-fifth Maine!" Andrew shouted as he stepped into the courtyard, climbing over the smoldering rubble.

Picking his way through the ruins, he pushed into the building. The carnage was shocking, even to his battle-hardened eyes.

"Thirty-fifth Maine!"

From out of the smoke he saw a shadowy form emerge. Cocking his revolver, he stepped forward.

A Suzdalian private emerged, blood streaming from a chest wound. Another man climbed out from behind a pillar, his hair scorched, his eyes hollow, filled with a vacant distant stare.

Andrew continued to push in.

"Vincent!"

A feeble shout went up. More and more shadows rose up, coming forward.

"Colonel Keane."

Dimitri came forward, his face white with rain-streaked dust.

Coming to attention, he saluted. Andrew brushed the salute aside and grabbed the man by the shoulders.

"My God, you're still alive," Andrew said, finding that he was shaking.

"I guess we are, sir," Dimitri said, his voice coming far too loud. "They laid some barrels of powder up when we holed up in the back and then blew 'em off."

Numbly, Dimitri looked around.

"Vincent?"

"What was that, sir?" Dimitri shouted. "They blew 'em off, and then nothing. We was waiting for the next charge, and now you're here."

Dimitri reached down, fumbling at his uniform, brushing it off. "Where's the general?" Dimitri shouted hysterically. "I can't find the general!"

"Somebody take care of him," Andrew yelled, and patting Dimitri on the shoulder he wandered into the back of the palace.

"Vincent, goddamm it, Vincent, where are you?"

Soldiers looked up at him numbly, some with dazed foolish grins, others beyond caring, yet others caught in the pain of dying, or already still in death.

"I said I'd hold till relieved."

Andrew turned. For a moment he couldn't even recognize him. The boy's face was puffed and torn, blood seemingly seeping out from every pore. Yet he knew it was he with Marcus by his side, still holding a musket.

"Goddam you!" Andrew cried. "You scared the hell out of me."

"We scared the hell out of ourselves," Vincent said, trying to force a smile out and then grimacing from the pain.

"Fifth Suzdal along with the second and third Novrod batteries reporting, sir."

Andrew shook his head.

"You certainly have a way of turning up alive," Andrew said. "Damn, if this ever happens again, I think I'll just let you handle the situation and not worry about it."

Vincent shook his head in disagreement.

"Sir, I think next time I'll just stay home."

Andrew looked over at Marcus.

"Excuse me, sir, he's an old friend."

"And I'm just the ruler of another country," Marcus said dryly.

"I meant no insult," Andrew said stiffly.

Marcus smiled.

"I'm alive because of him," Marcus said, breaking into a smile. "You can take as long as you want."

"Where did they go?" Vincent asked.

"I'm damned if I know. I saw them pulling out. There's still some fighting down by the docks."

"Fighting?" Vincent asked, his voice edged with excitement. "I thought they had us. We were back into this corner of the palace when they blew off that charge, then nothing."

Pushing past Andrew, Vincent raced into the courtyard, Marcus and Andrew following behind him. Gaining the steps of the palace, Vincent drew up short, looking back excitedly at the other two.

"I told you they'd fight!" Vincent shouted, pointing out into the square.

A huge mob was swarming across the square, and at the sight of the three a tremendous shout went up.

"They fought for you," Vincent cried, gazing back at Marcus with a look of triumph in his eyes.

"The trick will be now to sort out who did and who stayed at home," Marcus said, his features even.

"Go ahead and try it," Vincent retorted with a mischievous grin. "Just remember that when your own Senate and legion turned against you, they didn't."

Wearily, Marcus shook his head.

The crowd pushed forward, and several knots of people shouldered their way up the steps.

Vincent felt a wave of revulsion at the sight of what was left of Petronius, but said nothing as the corpse was hurled unto the steps. Another group came forward, and at the sight of their burden he turned cold.

A dead Merki was nailed to a cross, followed a moment later by two more. Vincent saw Julius leading one of the groups. Their gaze held for a moment, and Julius nodded grimly. Struggling under the weight of their burden, they pushed the crosses up, anchoring them in place with piles of rubble.

Vincent looked up at the bodies hanging above him. To his horror he saw that one was still moving, its terror-filled eyes looking down at him. It was too much to take, especially a death in that manner.

He fumbled for his pistol to put the creature out of its anguish, enemy though it was.

"No!" Marcus snapped.

Vincent hesitated and turned his gaze away.

"Let them hang there till they rot," Marcus shouted, and an angry roar went up in response.

Vincent looked over at Andrew, who stood silent, looking up at the dying Merki.

"Now you know who the enemy really is," Andrew said sharply, looking back at Marcus. "Now you know why we need each other, because they'll be back."

"You'd better say something," Vincent prompted, looking back out at the crowd.

"You've certainly cornered me this time," Marcus said with a cold smile.

Nodding, Vincent drew back.

Marcus looked over at him sharply and then turned to face the crowd.

"As of today I reaffirm our alliance with Suzdal in the war against Cartha and the Merki horde they serve."

He hesitated for a moment.

"As of this moment, slavery is banished from Roum."

"Glory hallelujah," Vincent breathed, his eyes shining with a childlike enthusiasm.

"There—are you satisfied?" Marcus said.

"More than satisfied," Vincent replied.

"Damn you, boy, and I thought I could maneuver you like a playing piece on a board."

"You've never dealt with a New England Quaker before," Vincent said innocently.

The saying of the word "Quaker" caused his heart to knot, and he looked back at the cross and then to Marcus.

"One last thing."

"Go on, then."

"Would you outlaw torture as well?"

"Anything. Just don't bother me anymore, for right now I think I need a drink."

Marcus, ignoring the cheers, went back up the steps,

pausing for a moment to look at the ruins of what had once been his, and then disappeared back into the smoke.

Vincent watched him leave.

"Colonel Keane!"

Vincent looked over his shoulder and saw a private from the 35th come up the steps.

"What the hell is so all-fired important?" Andrew snapped, still smiling over the exchange between Vincent and Marcus.

"Sir, I was in the Senate building. I saw this big scroll of paper pegged to the wall. I knew you had to see it."

Andrew took the parchment and unrolled it, Vincent stepping over to join him.

"Colonel Keane," it read in English. "You've got what's left of Roum. I and my friends will take Suzdal in exchange. I'll be certain to forward your regards to Kathleen and young Hawthorne's woman as well. Checkmate. Cromwell."

"So now we know," Andrew whispered. "It's only just begun for us."

Vincent turned away. Cocking his revolver, he went up to the cross, the Merki still looking down at him in anguish. The creature laid its head back, a high quavering chantlike song escaping its lips.

He squeezed the trigger.

He had intended it before as an act of mercy, but not now. Vincent watched with cold satisfaction as the Merki trembled sagging down on the cross. He cocked the revolver and aimed again.

"He's dead, Vincent. Leave it be," Andrew said, coming up to his side.

Smiling, Vincent squeezed the trigger anyhow, slowly emptying the revolver into the dead body on the cross.

The rhythmic pounding of the steam engine below deck caused the deck to vibrate as the *Ogunquit* came back to life.

Hot with anger, Cromwell turned to look back at the Merki. "We could have had him," he shouted.

The crew scrambling across the deck preparing the ship for sea paused, stunned to see a human, a Yankee, scream in rage at a Merki.

Hulagar said nothing. Vuka started to step forward.

"You were wrong," Hulagar snapped, extending his hand for Vuka to stop.

"How dare you berate me!" Vuka hissed in Merki. "And to do so in front of cattle!"

"We could have taken the city. It just might have worked. You destroyed that. Tamuka has told me everything."

Vuka looked over at his shield-bearer with cold hatred.

"You are no longer my shield-bearer," Vuka growled.

Tamuka smiled inwardly. He sincerely wished that he had left Vuka to his fate. The Merki horde would then have had another as Qar Qarth when Jubadi finally rode to the ever-lasting sky.

"As you wish, Zan Qarth," Tamuka replied.

"I will draw your blood for this insult," Vuka snapped.

"You cannot," Hulagar replied sharply. "Tamuka saved your life—it was spoken so by your brother Mantu, who survived. You now owe him your life in return. By the law of your own blood, you cannot challenge him until such debt is returned."

Vuka turned back to face Hulagar.

"Nor me," Hulagar said evenly. "I am shield-bearer to your father. It is forbidden for a son to challenge his father, his brothers, and his bearer."

Vuka, impotent with rage, stood motionless.

"Do not shame yourself in front of us, and the cattle." There was almost a note of pleading in Hulagar's voice.

His features dark with blood, Vuka turned away and stalked to the rear of the ship.

Cromwell, who had watched the exchange, uncomprehending of the words, could see nevertheless that something was seriously wrong between the son of the Qar Qarth and Hulagar. He knew as well that the wrath would be shifted to him before all of this was done.

"There is nothing more to be said," Hulagar announced. "We did not lose too many. We have lured the Yankee army east, now we turn west to the real prize."

Without waiting for a response, Hulagar walked away, going up to stand beside Vuka at the stern rail.

"Not too many," Hamilcar snapped. "Two thousand dead and wounded, half of that from that mob that damn Merki triggered."

"And two heavy guns lost," Cromwell replied. "Along with twenty ships lost along the Roum dockside. I don't like this—it leaves them something behind. Either we should have taken the town and held it as I had hoped, or fired it to the ground and left them nothing. We did neither."

"They are cut off now. At least we know Hinsen took care of that."

"He would," Cromwell replied. There was something about him that had always made him feel uneasy. It was good to have him out of the way.

Walking over to the starboard railing, he looked back at the shoreline. The last of his ships were pushing off from shore.

Checkmate, he thought with a smile.

The note was a good parting gesture, a little something to get under Andrew's scalp, to make him reckless. But he almost regretted the other part. There was something about Vincent that still haunted him. At least he would never laugh. Even when he knew the boy had somehow understood, he had not laughed. The thought troubled him but for a moment. Something started to stir, a memory coming up. Just what was it? Vincent had left him, that was all he could recall now. There had been something else then, but all he could remember was waking up later, the sour taste of vomit still in his mouth.

He forced the thought away.

In less than a week he'd be in Suzdal. That was being prepared as well, and for the first time in days a smile of delight crossed his features, the disappointment of before washed away, along with the dark foreboding.

# Chapter Ten

"We are certainly in one hell of a mess," Andrew said.

The mood in the room was subdued, the exhaustion still evident on all their faces.

"Doc, why don't we start with you. I want to know the condition of our men."

Emil shook his head.

"The 5th and the two batteries are skeletons. Eighty-five percent casualties for the regiment, and the numbers are almost as bad for the batteries. They're out of the war."

Emil paused, looking over at Vincent. His face was swollen and pockmarked. But what worried him was the eyes. There was a coldness to them now that was disturbing. Andrew had told him about the incident with the Merki. Something had gone dreadfully wrong with the boy, but there simply wasn't time to talk to him now.

"For the rest of the army, I've never seen a march like that one," Emil continued. "It was worse than the Gettysburg Campaign, and it certainly rivaled anything old Jack ever did. As near as I can reckon, nearly a hundred men are dead, almost all from the heat. We lost some more, the usual accidents, falling off trains, accidental discharge of weapons, or killed last night in a tavern brawl."

Emil looked over at Marcus.

"When soldiers from different sides get together," Marcus replied, with Vincent translating, "especially after the events of the last week, there's bound to be some tension."

Emil shook his head in disagreement and continued.

"The entire army should have at least three more days of rest before you can even think of moving them, Andrew. They're played out. At least a thousand of them will be laid up for a week. Try anything before that and those men will get sick by the thousands. As it is, you can thank your lucky stars the Carthas weren't in the mood to put up a fight."

"That's what I was hoping for," Andrew replied. "The mere fact we were coming on so hard was the pressure on them I wanted.

"We paid a price, though. We've got just over nineteen thousand effective in the city," Andrew stated, looking down at the latest roll-call reports. "Kindred reports four thousand at Hispania, with fifteen guns. We had five hundred at the Kennebec bridge, two hundred each at the Penobscot and Volga, and another five hundred spread out at the tank stops. Counting our casualties, we've still got over a thousand men somewhere out there on the road.

"Gentlemen that doesn't leave us much, when you consider our new situation."

"What about the legion?" Emil asked.

Andrew looked over at Marcus.

"I've disbanded it," he said sharply. "They're politically unreliable."

"Don't throw the baby out with the dirty bathwater," Emil replied.

"I'll sift through them. The tribunes are under arrest. The rank and file can be used to train the new regiments as they form up." He paused. "Once we get weapons."

"That'll be some time," Vincent interjected. "We've got to get Suzdal secured first. But for right now you should start training new infantry units without delay. Arm them with pikes, with anything. There's no promising that Cromwell won't be back after we leave."

"Leave? I've pledged an alliance. Now you're going off again and leaving us hanging out here. I need support."

Andrew looked over at Marcus.

"If Suzdal falls, we might as well burn everything and head into the woods," Andrew said quietly. "There'll be no stopping them then. The battle has to be fought there. Everything we can give you is back there."

"So he has outmaneuvered you," Marcus said, his voice almost sad.

"He certainly has," Andrew replied bitterly.

"Then how do you propose to turn it around?"

"I'm still not sure," Andrew admitted. "That's why I've called this staff meeting. All I can think of now is moving the army back to Hispania, entraining, getting to the ruins of the Kennebec bridge, and then marching the rest of the way back."

"It'll damn near be impossible," John Mina interjected.

"How come, John? I need to hear this."

John held up a sheaf of telegrams and papers.

"Several reasons. We moved up here with twenty-five days of supply, and we've used eight of them. I've already checked the warehouses here. The Roum campaign against the Tugars destroyed a lot of livestock. Fields didn't get planted. These people barely squeezed through last winter. We can get grain, even move what little beef and pork they have up the rail line. But that's where the problems start."

He held up a telegram and started to read.

"From Kindred. 'As per your orders a recon train was sent up the line. Repeated cuts in telegraph line fifty miles east of Kennebec. Train stopped thirty miles east of Kennebec, reports line of fires on tracks. Contact severed, no report since.'"

"Damn them," Andrew cursed, slamming the table with his fist.

"We can assume," Mina continued, "that they've disrupted maybe upward of sixty miles of track by now, so the line stops a good two hundred and fifty miles east of our inner frontier. That's the minimum distance we'll have to walk to get back."

"At a standard march of fifteen miles a day, we could still cover that in less than twenty days," Emil said hopefully.

"Let's assume we try that," John said, warming to his subject. "The army's going to need nearly thirty tons of supply a day to keep moving. We can't turn these boys into packhorses loaded down with eight days of food. Soldiers always act like soldiers—they'll eat it up or throw it away, especially if it gets hot. And there's precious little to forage. That steppe is as good as a desert for infantry.

"For one day's march away from the railhead we'll need thirty oxen wagons just for the bread supply. I've already checked—the Roum don't have many heavier two-team wagons, and horses are too damn precious and few. Going with oxen will mean our rate of march will be limited to ten to twelve miles a day, because the beasts can't do much more than that. Now, assuming we bring the meat up on the hoof, for two days' march away we'll need sixty wagons."

"I don't follow that," Vincent said.

"Simple. The wagons for the first day have to turn around, and it'll now take them a day to get back. But you see, it'll get worse the farther we go. When you're four days away, they'll be four days' worth of wagons moving up, and four days' worth coming back, and we're still only forty-five to fifty miles away. We're talking over two hundred wagons at this point. Start talking about a wagon supply line two hundred and fifty miles long and you start to see the nightmare of it."

The group was silent, stunned by the contemplation of this logistical nightmare. John smiled like a schoolmaster who had just presented his students with an unsolvable problem.

"Now you see why I preferred a line assignment to being quartermaster and industrial coordinator," he said quietly.

"We have to assume that the Carthas are roaming this territory. If they cut out only one wagon train, the army will start to get hungry very quickly. Cut the line completely, and within three days the army will be starving. You're going to need security the length of the line. Remember how Mosby with just a couple of hundred men played hell with our supplies in '64? It'll be the same here. We've got precious few mounts. For all we know, those damn Merki supplied horses to Cromwell. There could even be Merki or Tugar raiders out there.

"I'm therefore suggesting that we'll need a regiment and a couple of guns to guard each day's supply coming up, and at least a hundred or two to protect the wagons going back."

"That's a hell of a lot of men," Andrew snapped. "You're talking about twenty regiments or more. Goddammit, man that's half our effective strength, just to cover our bloody tail."

"I'd want more than that," John pressed. "We'll need to protect the rail line all the way back to Roum as well. All you need is half a dozen riders breaking in, cutting out four or five lengths of rail, or worse yet setting them up to break when a train hits, and the whole thing will unravel.

"And there's the final point I haven't even added in yet. There's a good fifty-mile stretch without flowing water to speak of. Figuring two quarts will keep a man going for a day—"

"That's really pressing it in this heat," Emil interjected.

"Even at that minimum," and he paused for a moment to look at his notes, "the men can carry a couple of days' worth of water with them. But after that we'll need two hundred wagons, each hauling a thousand pounds of water, just to take care of the men. The maddening part of it is, we'll need an extra fifty wagons of water just to take care of the oxen hauling the water in the first place across the four-day march. For our horse, figure another hundred wagons of water. What makes it worst, though, is that when our supply line hits that dry stretch, the food load per wagon will drop significantly, since we'll need to load a quarter ton of water for each ox on the food-supply wagons as well. We traveled light with horses coming out here for the artillery. Going back, though, we'll need to haul all our ammunition for artillery and infantry as well if you want to fight a battle at the end of this. That'll come up to hundreds more horses, wagons for the equipment, tons of water for the animals. It's turning into a regular geometric progression.

"Finally, just where the hell will we get all these wagons, and the draft animals? It'll take weeks to bring them in from all over Roum, and harvest time is coming up damn quick. It could cripple these people if we took their transport. Even if we found them, we've got a little over two hundred flatcars to haul them up to the railhead. That'll mean running ten trains a day up and down the line for days just to move enough wagons to get us fairly well started. We're not even counting the bulk food, the thousand of barrels for water, the wood for the engines, and marshaling the men."

"In other words," John said quietly, "it's impossible."

"You made it look almost easy the last time," Andrew said sadly, shaking his head.

"I had contingency plans drawn up months ago," John replied. "We were operating out of our main base. Our rations were already prepared, boxed, and stockpiled, unlike the bulk we'll be hauling this time. One train per day can haul more than a hundred wagon loads and keep our entire army supplied. Four trains operating on a secured line could supply this entire army from a base five hundred miles away. The train has revolutionized supply and mobility. Our whole plan was based upon a secure supply line straight to Roum.

"Cromwell has destroyed that with maybe not much more than a thousand men."

"Or Tugars," Marcus said, shaking his head in disbelief.

"I heard somebody once say that amateur generals study tactics, professionals study logistics," Andrew said ruefully. "I was too busy fighting ever to worry about the details of this."

Andrew looked over at Mina with a renewed appreciation. He could sense that they were far more alike than he had originally thought. At night sleep would often come hard as he imagined all the possible situations he might one day face on the battlefield, and how to get out of them. John most likely did the same thing, juggling numbers, and forever tormented with just how thinly stretched they really were. Why the hell didn't I contemplate this possibility? he thought ruefully. Cromwell was the loose cannon. But he had always assumed the bastard had simply sailed south and disappeared. Never in his worst nightmares had he imagined Cromwell selling out to the Merki, arming their lackeys, and creating a fleet of ironclads to be used against him.

"Before the railroad, it was really rare for an army to operate much more than fifty miles from its base of supplies," John said. "Any farther and it starts to become unmanageable. The only alternative is to forage for nearly everything, the way Billie Sherman and Napoleon did. We're going to have to go five hundred miles, and there ain't more than a couple days' forage in that whole blasted distance."

"Is there any hope General Hans could be forcing his way up the rail line? The break might only be sixty miles across if he did that," Emil said.

"I can't run my army out on a limb based upon a hope," Andrew replied. "He's got only one fully trained division on hand. And besides, we stripped the rail yard clean of everything we had.

"So that's it, gentlemen," Andrew said wearily. "Our first alternative is out. Cromwell must have figured this one out quite nicely. Now we've got to think a better way to do it."

A knock on the door interrupted the conversation. Andrew smiled as Chuck Ferguson came into the room, walking rather stiffly with Lieutenant Bullfinch by his side.

"Pleasant trip?" Andrew asked, smiling at Ferguson's discomfort.

"Sir, I've never been on a horse in my life, and then you

order me down here from Hispania in less than a day. I'll never go near one of those beasts again as long as I live."

Going over to an empty chair, he gingerly lowered himself down, a grimace cutting his features as his backside finally hit the hard wood.

"Anyone got a drink?" he groaned.

Emil looked over at Andrew, who nodded approvingly. Reaching into his jacket pocket, Emil pulled out a flask and slid it across the table. Chuck tossed back a shot, and seeing Andrew shake his head he refrained from a second.

"That's a bit better. I thank you, sir."

"I'm going to pour the rest of that on your butt as soon as this is finished," Emil said, taking the flask back, to a round of gruff laughter breaking the tension that had followed Mina's depressing report.

"Other suggestions, gentlemen?" Andrew asked.

"How about swinging north, and running along the edge of the forest?" Emil asked. "It'll only add sixty or so miles to the march. The forest will be easier on the men than the open steppe, and we might be able to cut the water-supply problem if we sent out advance teams to locate some streams for us."

"The forest would be hell if they've sent some guerrillas up there," Andrew interjected. "At least out in the steppe we can see them coming. And besides, we'll still need some type of bridge to get across the Kennebec and Penobscot.

"I was afraid Mina would kill my first idea," Andrew said. "John, what would it take to run some rail up, rebuild the track up to the Kennebec, and bridge the river?"

"We've got a good forty miles of rail stockpiled at Hispania," John replied. "We could lay several miles a day if we said the hell with proper gauging and crosstying. The bridge, though—that's the problem. We'll need to cut another several hundred thousand board feet. We could be talking months, and that's just for the Kennebec. We'll have to assume the Penobscot is down as well. Back home, General Haupt had his bridging material stockpiled in precut sections. We haven't had the luxury of time for that.

"The alternative would be to not worry about the bridge and man-haul a couple of locomotives across along with the rolling stock to make up the supply trains. The army can still march."

"That sounds crazy," Emil interjected.

"Not that hard, really," Mina replied. "But it'll still tie us up for weeks, and all the time they could be tearing holes in the track faster'n we can fix 'em. Don't forget there's still the question of protecting the entire rail line. As for that bridge, it'll be several months before we see a train rolling across that river again. The worst part of it now is that every single locomotive is on this side of the river.

"And once we get far enough west, our entire rolling stock might be vulnerable. Lose those precious locomotives now and we're truly doomed."

"One if by land, two if by sea," Ferguson said quietly.

"What do you mean?" Andrew said, the beginning of a smile lighting his features.

"Well, sir, I've been doing some thinking."

"That's all he ever does," John said with an approving laugh.

"Now, I ain't no student of military thinking. Engineering is what I was studying in college before this war got started. But you haven't even talked about the strategy of what we're facing against Cromwell."

"Ferguson, are you actually about to propose what I think you are?"

Ferguson smiled and nodded in Andrew's direction.

"That's why I wanted him with me at this meeting," Andrew said, visibly relaxing now that he sensed Ferguson had indeed come up with a solution.

"Just what the hell are you two bantering about?" Emil asked. "Frankly, I still like my forest march idea."

"I think our Mr. Ferguson is saying we should build a navy," Andrew said quietly.

He had been hoping against hope for this idea. He had ordered Ferguson up from Hispania with orders to consider the problem. The question now was if it was within the realm of the possible.

"Cromwell has all the advantages, and he's outmaneuvered us at every stage so far," Andrew stated.

The letter still was a sore spot. Cromwell's threat to his wife and Vincent's he took as a low blow which he hoped even Cromwell would back away from. But that single word "checkmate" had seared him. Cromwell had always been in rivalry with him from the moment they had met. Now that he could actually play that rivalry out, Cromwell had bested him at every turn. The note bothered him far more than he was willing to admit to himself.

"Gentlemen, he expects us to march back—that's the only way we can go. If we do that, he's laid his plan out accordingly. We have to do the unexpected."

Vincent, who had been quietly translating the combined Rus and English conversation for Marcus, interrupted.

"And there's no guarantee that once we get back to Suzdal he simply won't just turn around and come straight back here."

"Roum can't take another attack like this last one," Andrew replied. "We have to guarantee Roum's safety even as we try to save our own hides, and don't anyone forget that. The only way we can block his navy is to somehow build a counter."

Marcus smiled openly as Vincent translated.

Andrew could see the man start to relax. He could understand the tension there. After all, it had looked as if the army was simply going to turn tail and run home again.

"A navy?" Mina asked. "Chuck, I've always liked your work. Hell, it was you that thought up the railroad, and you've designed most of the machines we've got around here. But by God this is entirely different."

"Let's hear him out," Andrew said. "Then we'll see if this boy is insane or not."

"I sent a telegram down to John Bullfinch here before I left Hispania. He checked and told me we've captured over a dozen Cartha galleys. We also have eighteen Roum galleys and a couple of dozen transport ships as well. Those transports are big grain carriers, fat and beamy."

"Damn fools should have burned them all," Bullfinch said with a smile.

"The free people of Roum stopped that," Andrew said, looking over at Marcus and smiling.

"The Cartha ships are fairly good—two banks of oars with two men on each blade, a couple with three banks," Bullfinch continued. "The larger ones will take two hundred rowers, and carry maybe an additional twenty or thirty men each. All total, we've got enough ships to carry maybe four thousand men."

"We could use them to run down to the Kennebec or Penobscot and take the supplies up that way," Mina said excitedly.

"One ironclad parked off either river would end that right quick," Andrew replied. "Cromwell's navy could blow those ships out of the water."

"So what good are they?" Emil asked.

"We use them to make our own navy," Ferguson announced triumphantly.

"How?"

"Now, my history isn't so good. But I had to take a couple of courses in it, though heavens knows why an engineering student needs to waste time on such things."

"Remember, I was a history professor before the war," Andrew said quietly, "so let's not get into that debate, because, son, you square-headed engineering types will lose it."

The room exploded into laughter at Ferguson's embarrassment.

"As I was saying, sir," Ferguson continued, "they were the best damn courses I ever took."

"That's better," Andrew said approvingly, in his best professorial tone.

"Well, sir, I remember how these Roman fellows," and he nodded toward Marcus, "were fighting a war, I can't remember which one, though, they always seemed to be fighting."

"First Punic War," Vincent said in Latin.

Andrew smiled approvingly, like a teacher who was pleased with an able student. "The Carthaginians had complete naval superiority, since the Romans had never fought at sea before. The Romans captured a Carthaginian galley, took it apart piece by piece, then used the parts as templates. They set up an assembly line, the first in history, and built an entire fleet, while the Roman soldiers practiced rowing by sitting on benches on the beach."

Marcus's features creased into a delighted smile.

"Our father gods built that first fleet. The fleet our ancestors rode to this world was the second one. That is how we came here to Valennia, according to the Tale of Varius, during the great war of the Cartha."

"Tale of Varius?" Andrew asked, his curiosity aroused.

"It described how our fleet fell into a vast ocean of light and came here when they set off to defeat the Carthas. They were caught as well. After coming here they sailed south while we took this land as ours. It is all written down."

"You knew of this, then?" Marcus asked excitedly, looking around the table.

Andrew nodded.

"Then tell me. Did our father gods, did the great Cincinnatus win?"

"You destroyed Carthage," Andrew said, though he would never admit now that personally he had always sided with the Carthaginians in their hundred-year battle with Rome.

"Just as he said it," Ferguson mumbled, looking over at Vincent with a grimace for stealing his story. "Anyhow, I'm thinking we take one of those Cartha ships apart, right down to the last peg, and number the pieces. We've got hundreds of wood carvers in the ranks—they'd be a natural for this. Then set up an assembly line. We'll add some improvements, though. We've got more than enough iron for nails, so we'll just hammer the siding on."

"They'll leak like sieves," Bullfinch objected. "And where are you going to get all that seasoned timber?"

"The hell with the seasoned timber. We'll build them green—that's most likely how the Romans did it anyhow. And so what if they leak like sieves. We'll bail all the way to Suzdal. We'll only need them to get there and fight the Carthas. We can build better ships later."

"Where in God's name are you going to get all the lumber?"

"There's a sawmill up the Tiber at the edge of the forest that was starting to turn out crossties for the railroad. We can turn out the planking and ribs in a matter of days. They've got a good stockpile of lumber already cut and waiting to be sawed into crossties."

"Just fine," Emil said coldly. "So we build our ships, set sail, or row them, and then we meet the *Ogunquit* or one of those damn gunboats and you'll have a sea of splinters and twenty thousand drowned men."

"We make ironclads," Ferguson said softly.

"You've got to be mad," Mina shouted.

"Maybe it'll take some madness to save our hides," Andrew said forcefully. "Go on, Chuck, I'm listening."

The room fell quiet.

"Sir, what did Cromwell do? He cut the top deck down from the *Ogunquit* and converted it to an ironclad. The same way the rebs did with the *Merrimac*. We can do the same to those fat grain transports, for starters."

"Those things aren't designed to carry the weight," Bullfinch objected.

"Then we'll make them so they can. Hell, you can have a flush deck like the *Monitor*, with a slope-sided gunhouse on top. If I had the time I'd even take a crack at a revolving turret, but even Ericsson took four months with his first one, and I figure we don't have the time.

"So we give them a flush deck, and just build a small gun turret in the middle. It doesn't have to move at all. We just square it off and cut a gun port into each side."

"I heard how out on the Mississippi they were building gunboats from scratch in thirty days," Bullfinch said, warming to the subject.

"You think you could do the same?" Andrew asked.

"Well, there's only one way to find out, sir," Ferguson said with a grin.

"Wait a minute," Mina cried. "Just where the hell are you going to get the armor, the power plants, the guns, the ammunition?"

"They're all sitting in Hispania right now, sir," Chuck said quietly.

John started to sputter a comment and then, throwing up his hands in dismay, sat back.

"I figured it out riding down here, sir, on that damn Apple or Appi Way or whatever you call it."

"Appian," Vincent said quietly.

"Right, Appian. Anyhow, we've got twenty miles of roadbed running alongside of it already, coming down from Hispania. Once we hit the end of our roadbed, we just jump over to the Appian Way, and run track straight down it right into the heart of the city and down 'to the docks.

"We take the locomotives and run 'em all down, tearing up the track behind us as we go. Once they get to the docks, we'll tear the engines off the wheels, swing them into the gunboats, and you've got your power. The new-model engines should make those things go like hell. You'll have sixty miles of rails and ties for armor and anything else you might need in the way of iron."

"Merciful God, Andrew, are you really going to let him do this?" John shouted. "Chuck, you and I've been fast friends for years, but this is the parting of the ways," he went on heatedly. "You're talking about destroying all our work."

"John, I don't want emotional appeals," Andrew said quietly. "If there's something wrong with the plan, then tell me."

"All right, Andrew," John replied excitedly. "The best run for our tracking crews was just over a mile and a half in a day. At that rate it'll take thirty days to get here."

"I agree," Chuck replied, "if we lay the track to be permanent. This is temporary. Throw down the ties, don't bother to spike except for every fourth or fifth tie, just enough to hold the track in place. There's forty miles of track stockpiled in Hispania. Cannibalize the other twenty from the line.

"The hell with gauging work. That Appian Way is pretty damn straight—I heard these Roum, or Romans, knew how to build roads. I figure we could run four miles a day, at least if we had shifts going day and night, and could have the rails and engines in town in under fifteen days."

"John, is it possible?" Andrew asked, cutting him off before he could object.

"Sure, it's possible," John replied, "but likely, I doubt it."

"But can it be done?" Andrew insisted.

Mina looked over at Chuck coldly, and then slowly nodded his head.

"All right, you've got the rails and engines into the city. Then what?" Mina asked.

"Now, I did some figuring in my head. Our rail comes out to twenty pounds a foot. That rounds out to a little over a hundred tons to the mile.

"How much you think those transport ships can haul, Bullfinch?"

"Oh, maybe several hundred tons each."

"Then we've got it," Chuck said. "We deck over the ship with rail iron just packed straight in and spiked down. Build up the gunhouse with more rail iron several layers thick backed with railroad ties. Make it eighteen feet square, the same length as the track, to keep it simple. Armor will weigh about a hundred and fifty tons, total.

"Now we take the engine right off the wheels and cab. Hell, we do that all the time back in the shops. I don't know much about ship's propulsion—you'll have to help me here, Bullfinch."

Bullfinch looked over at Ferguson with a grin. "A fleet, a

goddam fleet to kick that damn Cromwell under! Hell, I couldn't stand the bastard the first day I signed on board the *Ogunquit*, and it's gone downhill ever since."

"Stick to the topic, Mr. Bullfinch," Andrew said with a smile.

"Sorry, sir," Bullfinch said, his voice charged with excitement. "We can go two ways, sir. The easier to build is a paddle wheel. But the problem is you've got to build armor up all around them. The propeller is definitely the better way, but I know damn little about them, their size in relationship to the engine and the weight of the ship. Cromwell knows all of that; I certainly don't. I could make a guess. I did see one of Ericsson's monitors in dry dock. The propeller on her was a good eight feet across. But it'll be risky.

"Now hooking the engines in is another thing. You've got small cylinders on them set to high ratio. Ship engines are a lot bigger, with slower rotation. You'll need to build some reduction gears. There's no way you can crank a paddle wheel a couple of hundred times a minute."

"John, can we build the gears?"

"Tough in the time you're asking. Do it with leather driveshafts to reduce the power into the propeller. We could take some train wheels and cut them and notch them. It might work."

"Should we go for both systems, paddle wheel and propellor?" Andrew asked.

"It's good engineering, sir," Ferguson replied. "When you've got an emergency job like this, build two different systems. That way if one fails the other still might come through."

"Vincent, how many armored ships did he have?"

"I saw thirteen smaller gunboats sir, each carrying one or two pieces. The *Ogunquit* was the monster, though—at least ten pieces."

"We've got enough to build ten of each," Andrew said quietly. "But that still leaves the *Ogunquit*. Ferguson, you have any answers?"

"Give me several months, sir, and I could build something to match."

"We don't have several months," Andrew replied sharply.

"Then how long, sir?"

"How long for the boats?"

"Thirty days for the ironclads. With luck we could have seventy or eighty oar ships for transport."

"Then I'm giving you thirty days."

"So you're actually going to do this madness," John gasped.

"John, unless you have one hell of a better suggestion, I'm going with it."

"What about the guns, Andrew?" John replied. "We can't very well go up against their gunboats armed with four-pounders."

"Can you cast up bigger ones?"

"Well, we did capture the two fifty-pounders. Terrible pieces, by the way. I think I could pull it off. That foundry can turn out several tons a day. We'll need to cook it up to six or seven, and damn quick."

"I'd suggest carronades, sir," Bullfinch interjected.

"What's that?"

"Been using them at sea since the Revolution, sir. They're short-barreled pieces. They're smaller, so they can be worked better in the gunhousing Ferguson was talking about. You only need half the metal of a longer gun."

"What's the trade-off then?" Ferguson asked.

"Range. They aren't much good beyond three or four hundred yards. Those heavy guns can lay into us a mile off. But you can load them a lot faster, and for the amount of metal in a forty-pounder barrel you could cast a two-hundred-pounder carronade.

"Remember, sir, most of the action between the *Monitor* and the *Merrimac* was at a hundred yards. Sometimes they were actually touching."

Andrew looked over at John.

"If you can give me the iron, I'll cast them. But I'm going to have to make them extra thick to be safe, and the bores will be crooked as hell—there's no way I can ream them out correctly.

"At the range Bullfinch is talking about, though, it won't much matter whether they can shoot straight or not."

"What about powder?" Emil asked. "Those big guns will burn powder like there's no tomorrow."

"Same thing as the last time around. We'll dig the latrine pits for the nitrates. We'll get the charcoal from wood. What about sulfur?" John looked over at Vincent, who shot a quick question to Marcus.

The consul sat back for a moment and finally smiled and answered.

"They've got some springs down in Brendusia," Vincent said with relief. "A hundred miles down the coast and about twenty inland."

"There is one major question, though," Bullfinch interjected. "How thick is his armor?"

The group looked over at Vincent hopefully.

"There's no way to know," Vincent replied. "The handful of prisoners we took were simple line infantry armed with pikes. None were aboard the *Ogunquit* or any of the gunboats, and they all said those ships were wrapped in secrecy."

"Any suggestions, then, Mr. Bullfinch?" Andrew asked.

"For right now maybe it'd be best if Colonel Mina and myself argued that one out, sir," Bullfinch said. "Going with fifty-pounders would be the easiest. We already have those two guns we captured, along with a couple hundred rounds of ammunition. If we could coax it up to a larger caliber, I'd feel better, though."

"It's going to be a question of metal and what I can do," John said. "I've never worked with heavy calibers before, and there isn't going to be any time for trial and error on this one.

"I'm nervous to try anything beyond a fifty-pounder. At least we have the template from those two pieces Cromwell made. We know they work. The carronades will carry less punch. The big question is how much armor Tobias has. If he sheathed his vessels for proof against twelve-pounders, we'll sink him for certain."

"I wouldn't think he's that stupid," Andrew replied.

"Neither would I," John said. "But the simple fact of it is, you're asking too much already. I'll take a look at going up to a seventy-five-pounder. Give me a day to plan some calculations and maybe I can squeeze out enough artillery to put one gun on each ship. The truth is, we won't know our power till we engage him."

The group fell silent for a moment at the lack of certainty in their enterprise.

"What about all the rest of our guns?" Andrew finally asked.

"Ah, I haven't forgotten those," Ferguson replied. "We'll have nearly a hundred ships. We've got a hundred guns. It's simple.

"The sides of their galleys and ours will only be a couple of inches thick. Four-pound shot, even a concentrated musket volley, will be devastating at close range."

"Then we'll follow this plan, though there are some refinements I'd like to throw in," Andrew stated.

"What's Roum's part in this?" Marcus asked quietly.

Andrew leaned back and laughed.

"Marcus, without you it'd be impossible. How about for starters five thousand men to help with the rail line and another ten thousand workers for the boats, both groups working shifts around the clock?"

"Around the clock?"

"Never mind, you'll learn. Next we'll need thousands of people digging for saltpeter, refining the sulfur, cutting the wood. Just ask John after the meeting—he'll help you get organized."

"And for the fighting?" Marcus said coldly.

Andrew suddenly realized that except for Bullfinch and a handful of men out of his whole army, operations at sea were a mystery to all of them. Without the Roum they'd truly be lost.

"Good God, sir, we'll need your people there most of all. I expect your people will captain most of the ships and be a fair portion of crew."

"Then you need us for fighting after all," Marcus said with a grim smile.

Marcus sat back, a look of contentment crossing his features.

"You helped save my city. I want to return the compliment so that both Roum and Rus know this is an alliance of equals."

Andrew smiled in return. If the Merki should come in strength, it would be Roum manpower that would make the difference, if such a thing was even possible, now that the Merki knew the secrets of powder weapons and steam.

"You said you had some refinements of your own," Marcus asked. "What are they?"

"There again we'll need your help, Marcus. We have to deceive Cromwell. If he even suspects what we are doing, he could run back up here in a couple of days and make life hell. I want our surprise to be complete.

"First I want to lay out a security net at least fifty miles out from this city. That'll take thousands of men on patrol.

It'll be important that the men assigned know absolutely nothing of what is going on inside the city in case they are taken prisoner, so they should be picked and assigned out immediately. Next and most important, I want Cromwell to think we are coming back by land.

"Therefore we are going to detach at least three or four trains and start pushing them west. We'll make a couple of them armored, like the one we made for the Tugar siege—we have two armored cars already for that. We'll need a work crew of a couple of thousand and security all along the line. I'm putting Kindred in charge of that—I'll give him a brigade of Rus troops, and we'll need several thousand Roum. I don't want any legionaires in this—all we need is one to desert and our game is up.

"We'll push up the line, repairing track, and we'll even try to get an engine manhandled across the river. All the time we'll push our security net out along the rail line."

"You're hedging your bets, aren't you, Andrew?" Emil said quietly.

"I have to," Andrew replied. "As Ferguson said, in an emergency, have two plans in case one doesn't work. We'll use Hispania as a base of supply for that operation. We'll cannibalize the track from Hispania running west to repair sections farther up."

"You're giving me two headaches," John said.

"The second one will be smaller, John. Kindred's got good sense. Delegate some of your staff over to him. I want Kindred to make a rough-shod armor train out of anything he can find, and run it up the line tonight with a regiment in support. We start putting the pressure on now."

"What about weapons for my people?" Marcus asked.

"I'll release twenty-five hundred of our rifled muskets, taking them from the crews that will be on the ironclads. Vincent, you're responsible for setting up training of the Roum infantry. Pull out a couple of sergeants and officers from every regiment and put them in command."

Andrew paused, looking back at Marcus.

"Would you object to our men leading your infantry, at least for this campaign?"

"I can't argue with that," Marcus replied. "After all, my men will be commanding most of the boats."

"A fair enough trade, then."

Andrew sat back with a sigh.

"Then we're agreed on our course of action?"

He looked around the table. Only Ferguson and Marcus were smiling. The rest looked around at each other with stares ranging from confusion to outright disbelief.

"Gentlemen," Andrew said coldly, "the survival of Rus, of everything we fought for, is riding on this. All our families are back there. If we don't do this, it's all over. I'm asking for a miracle, and I'm expecting you to give me one. If we fail, by the time we stagger back to Suzdal, there'll be nothing left for us."

"We'd better pray that Hans can figure out a way to hold for thirty days," Emil said quietly.

"If anyone can do it, it's Hans," Andrew replied sharply. For the first time since leaving Suzdal he realized that some inner instinct had played out correctly again. Bringing up the brigade of foundry and mill workers for the campaign and leaving Hans and O'Donald behind was perhaps the only smart move he had made so far.

"Gentlemen, let's get to work. John, figure out your delegation of labor. Vincent, you start the training and help Marcus with organizing his labor forces. Ferguson, you start drawing up plans. The rest of you officers are at the disposal of Mina, or Ferguson. I want a survey run before nightfall of every soldier in the army for specialized skills in ship-building, gun casting, powder making, and carpentry, and send them over to John, who will work up the necessary teams. A quarter of the rail workers go to Kindred, the rest on getting track down to Roum. All foundry and steam engine workers should get down to the mill at once.

"Mr. Bullfinch, would you be interested in being admiral of the ironclad fleet?"

The boy looked at Andrew with open-eyed amazement.

"Nothing like a quick promotion to make your day, is there, John?" Andrew said with a smile.

"An honor, sir," Bullfinch said excitedly.

"You were closest to Cromwell, and you're the only naval officer from our old world," Andrew said. "Just remember, son, if you fail, we are all going to fail."

Bullfinch gulped nervously and said nothing.

"Any questions?"

"There'll be a million of them before morning," Ferguson said with a soft laugh, and the group, most of them shaking their heads, laughed in agreement.

Andrew looked over at Chuck and nodded a silent thanks for breaking the tension.

"Dismissed, then."

The group rose up, most of them rushing over to John and already shouting questions as he went out the door.

Andrew leaned back in his chair and looked over at Emil.

"Someday our luck is going to run out with these mad schemes."

"We've been running on luck since the day we got here," Andrew sighed. "By all rights old Ivor should have wiped us out the moment we arrived here. It's been borrowed time ever since."

"You never even mentioned the Merki," Emil whispered. "If they should march on us now, they could be in Suzdal before we even get there. It's been over a week now since we've heard any intelligence on them."

"Emil, if they turn north, there's precious little we can do. And absolutely nothing we can possibly do here at all. There's no sense in worrying the men about it. I prefer they just focus on Cromwell and we'll have to hope for the best."

"But you'll worry yourself sick about it," Emil said.

"Of course," Andrew replied softly. "If they hit us, Suzdal will fall, and it will be my fault for falling into this trap."

"You did the right thing based upon what we knew at the time."

"I should have thought of this. My thinking had never factored in their having control of the Inland Sea, and all that it implied. I'm an infantry officer from the Virginia campaigns; the combination of naval warfare never entered my mind. And goddammit I should have thought of it."

Emil extended a consoling hand, patting Andrew on the arm.

"You've always done your best and beyond."

"It might not be good enough."

Emil hesitated, and Andrew could see that Emil was barely holding his role of counseling father. He looked down for a moment and then spoke in a barely audible whisper.

"You really think this one will work?"

Andrew smiled and said nothing.

"By the way, Andrew, that Roman fleet they built. Marcus said his people came through with the second one. Whatever happened to the first?"

"It got wiped out."

Andrew stood up.

"Now if you'll excuse me, Emil, I've got a lot of work to attend to," and nodding a goodbye he slowly walked out of the room.

"I still like the forest march myself," Emil whispered as he reached into his pocket, pulled out the flask, and took a long slow drink.

The night was quiet. Breathing deeply, Kalencka leaned back on the parapet and looked out over the river. In the dim light of the twin moons he watched as the Neiper flowed quietly down to the sea.

How I loved this as a child, he thought with a wistful smile. It was before he had ever seen a Tugar, when he was still living in a world of innocence. His father would sit with him by the banks of the Neiper, spinning out the stories he told in the court. The adventures of Ilya Murometz, the lay of Igor's campaign, the revenge of Olga, the tale of Ivan Ivanovich, who rode about the entire world. Their fishing lines would be in the river and he'd imagine how he could climb down the line and see the world of fish below and swim away with them down to the inland sea and off to faraway adventures.

A light breeze rippled across the water, and the moonbeams flickered with a golden-red light. Turning about, he looked up at the Great Wheel, dropping down now back into the southern sky. So where did we all come from? he wondered. Emil had made a telescope and he had looked into the night sky with it, to see that the wandering star Alexandra was like a tiny moon, waxing and waning, that Saint Stanislav had other even smaller saints circling about him. And at the heart of the wheel, the stars were so thick they were like snowflakes floating in a blizzard.

Did the tunnel of light leap to those distant places? Muzta had said as much to Vincent, claiming that the tunnel was a Tugar thing. But how did they make it? Why did it snatch away humans only at certain places, and why did hundreds of years sometimes pass before yet more came, as the Yankees did?

It is a pleasure to dream of such things, he thought wistfully. Perhaps one day when I am no longer a president I can build a tower and sit in it at night, and look through the telescope thing and ponder.

Reaching out, he put his arm around Tanya, who snuggled up close to him.

"Do you think they're still alive?"

The spell of the moment drifted away. He could only console himself in silence. Andrew, the only one he could now whisper his fears to, was gone. He was truly alone now.

"I'm certain of it, dear."

"How can you be certain?" she asked, her voice almost childlike.

"Kesus and Perm will watch over them and us. They would not have allowed us to build this new life, only to take it away from us."

"But I've heard terrible things."

Inwardly he cursed. Mikhail had a fair part of the city in an uproar. Kal had explained both in the Senate and out in the Great Square how the telegram must be a lie, sent by Cromwell to confuse and demoralize them. But the silence from the east was now five days old. The only word was that the enemy were working up the tracks, destroying them as they came. Hans had finally ordered a precious regiment to force-march east, along with several thousand militia, to contain them. Yet from Andrew there was nothing, nor from Vincent either. He looked down the length of wall. At his approach the workers had drawn back to a respectful distance to give him this moment of peace. But farther away they were hard at work, throwing up dirt on either side of the log barrier, reinforcing gun emplacements, dragging barrels of water up onto roofs to stop fires.

Yesterday, at his order, all but essential personal were requested to leave the city, and more than ten thousand had started out to Novrod or friends in the countryside to weather out the storm. Reports were already coming back of a growing panic throughout the republic, and Mikhail's words were only adding to it.

"Mikhail's lies are just that, Tanya, nothing more than lies."

"Yet they are working," Tanya said. "People look at me as if my husband were already dead."

Kal found himself wishing that the constitution had been written differently, that senators could be arrested. Yet Mikhail had walked the line closely, never uttering outright treason, only crying that they were doomed, that the army was no more, and it was the fault of the president alone for stripping them of their defenses.

"We'll just have to pray a bit harder," Kal said, kissing his daughter on the forehead.

"Praying won't solve what's happening now."

"Daughter, sometimes prayer is the only thing we can do. I have no way of knowing what Andrew is doing, but I'm certain he is planning something."

If he is indeed alive, Kal thought to himself.

"Mr. President?"

"Over here," he said wearily.

A shadowy form stepped forward past the guards who were now his constant companions.

It was Hans, and he felt his stomach knot up. It could only be one thing if he was being sought out like this at three in the morning.

"They're here," Kal whispered.

Hans nodded, and leaning over the wall he shot a stream of tobacco juice down into the darkness of the river.

"Telegram just came in from our outpost at old Fort Lincoln. Enemy ships sighted at the mouth of the Neiper."

"Then it's begun," Kal said, trying to make his voice sound forceful.

"They'll start up the river at dawn sir, and be here by midmorning."

Kal leaned against the wall and looked up at the heavens. With a deliberate effort he put his hat on and then turned to face Hans.

"Hans, it's going to be a very interesting day," Kal said, and putting his arm around Tanya he turned and slowly walked away.

Jubadi Qar Qarth closed the flap of his tent and looked over at the shield-bearer of his son.

"Why were you sent as the messenger? Why are you not at the side of my son?" he asked nervously. "What has happened?"

"Your son is well, my Qarth," Tamuka replied, bowing low. "But I no longer serve him. He has sent me away. Hulagar felt it best that I therefore come back as messenger to you."

"There is much to tell in your simple statement, shield-bearer. If Hulagar entrusted you as messenger, then your honor stands high with him. Therefore my son has lacked sufficient reason to dismiss you."

"It is not important," Tamuka said. "The report of the campaign is."

"You are a diplomat," Jubadi said, reading all he needed to know in Tamuka's reluctance to bear an ill report of the Zan Qarth to his father. "Now tell me what has occurred."

Tamuka spoke quickly, reviewing the action, and making it a point not to speak directly of the debacle his son had created in the final hours.

"I have lost two of my sons," Jubadi whispered.

Tamuka nodded.

"How did they die?"

"As warriors, slaying dozens," Tamuka lied. How could he ever tell him the truth? Kan, the one who had held so much promise, had been dragged down and beaten to death. Young Akharn had been dragged away still alive, a Merki taken prisoner by cattle, a fate that would cause him eternal humiliation in the everlasting sky, where all would taunt him for such an end without a shred of honor.

"They will ride the night winds, their heads high with honor," Tamuka said forcefully. "May I ride beside them with such glory when Bugglaah reaches down to grasp my soul away."

Jubadi looked into his eyes, sensing that all was not told, yet he knew he would never ask more.

"It is done well enough," Jubadi said sharply, turning away for a moment. "You are to go back," he said.

"My Qarth?"

"I want you back there. I want no more sons lost to these cattle. You are shield-bearer—your father served my father as such."

"But Vuka," Tamuka said evenly.

"The hell with Vuka's words," Jubadi growled. "There is still Mantu."

"Yet only as he lives may he be the Zan Qarth, the heir to your rights."

"Only as he lives," Jubadi shouted. "Do you think I don't know what happened up there? Did I not have read to me Hulagar's dispatch before I spoke to you?

"You are loyal, Tamuka, but your loyalty now comes to me, and through me to the horde of the Merki. And I ask you, if I should die today, if it should be my heart that Bugglaah touches next, would Vuka be fitting as Qar Qarth?"

Tamuka was silent.

"Answer me!"

"No, my Qarth," Tamuka whispered.

"Then you know what to do."

Horrified, Tamuka looked at Jubadi. He could see the cold anguish in his Qarth's eyes. Feeling ill, Tamuka turned away. Such a thing had been done before by a shield-bearer—it was placed so upon them to protect the blood of the Horde, for a Qar Qarth that did not serve well could be death for all. Yet such a Qar Qarth, even one who had proved his worthlessness, could turn to his bearer when needed and thus would still rule, though another would speak into his ear with guidance. Vuka had turned his bearer away, denying all blame for what he had done. If he had acknowledged his mistake and learned from it, this would not now happen. Thus had the forty clans of the Merki created peace, preventing the bitter wars that had torn them asunder when clan chieftains had felt themselves oppressed by one not fit to lead. The Qar Qarth was either a true Qar Qarth or he was dead, and another of the Golden Blood ruled instead.

"You are asking me to kill him," Tamuka said, trying to control the trembling in his voice.

Jubadi, his back still turned, was silent. The minutes slowly slipped past.

"If he atones and proves himself different, perhaps not," he finally whispered, and then his words fell away.

"Mantu will rule instead," he said, his voice edged with a sense of finality.

"Mantu is with him even now," Tamuka replied.

"Then you know who is to be saved, shield-bearer."

"He will suspect," Tamuka said.

"Of course he will. If he has honor, he will know it is time to die."

Jubadi paused and with voice choking turned to look back at Tamuka.

"Give him that chance, to die with honor so that his soul may ride in contentment."

Hulagar paused for a moment.

"Unlike my other two sons," he whispered.

Tamuka did not reply.

"They are tormented now because of their brother," Jubadi snarled. "Kan, who was the light of my joy, will be humiliated forever because of him."

Jubadi slammed his fist into his side, his eyes bright with tears.

"Do not do it by your hand if you can avoid it."

Tamuka nodded in agreement. Vuka could not strike him because of the blood debt; to do so would curse him into the darkness forever. Thus he could not defend himself either if Tamuka were to strike him.

"My Qarth, let someone else go in my place."

"Don't you see?" Jubadi said. "He must suspect now that he has had time to think. If another shield-bearer came he would fight him. I will not order him to die, for never should a Zan be forced. Your mere presence will tell him what his only path will be to seek death with honor, or to somehow so redeem himself in the judgment of you and Hulagar that he may still live.

"But if he refuses, if he does not redeem himself and yet will not seek death in battle?"

"Then you will kill him," Jubadi said coldly.

"Can he not atone without this?" Tamuka argued. Though Vuka had failed, still Tamuka could remember him with fondness, as they rode together against the Bantag, his courage a shining torch.

"I doubt that now. He is not that cunning," Jubadi whispered. "I will say no more on this."

Jubadi walked back over to the entrance to his tent and beckoned for Tamuka to follow.

Coming back out into the bright sunlight of midday, Tamuka followed respectfully behind the Qar Qarth.

"Walk beside me. I must tell you the messages to take back to Hulagar."

Jubadi spoke with a clear voice, as if the conversation of but a moment before had never occurred.

"You will leave today. You must tell him that it will be yet some weeks before the two umens can ride north."

Tamuka looked over at Jubadi with surprise. This was part of the plan he had never known, and he felt it best to admit it.

Jubadi chuckled softly.

"Only Hulagar knew of this. I did not want our loyal cattle to know. I promised him rule over the Rus if he took that realm for us. Would he actually be so foolish as to believe I would let him stay there, owning all the secrets of the Yankees?

Once the city of the Rus fell, our umens were to sweep up and occupy them. Those who could would work in their machine places making us weapons; the rest would go to the slaughter pits."

"But the promise of injunction with the Carthas and to the Rus if Cromwell subdued them?"

"Promises but to cattle. The Carthas we will keep awhile longer. The Rus can feed us for this winter season."

"Cromwell has served us well," Tamuka said, keeping his voice neutral.

"He is only cattle nevertheless."

"Yes, of course," Tamuka replied.

"Tell this only to Hulagar. The four umens we had first talked about will not move. We were defeated at the place of the broken hills by the Bantag twelve days ago. We lost half an umen of warriors."

Tamuka was stunned.

"It cannot go on much longer like this," Jubadi said darkly. "Already they are crossing the Inland Sea at the narrows, pushing to cut ahead of us. As yet they know nothing of our Yankee weapons. I am saving them for when the time is right. But I need my warriors here, to cover our southern flank, forty days' ride to our south and west, protecting our people as they come forward. So tell Hulagar there will still be two umens but they will be late."

"As you command, my Qarth."

The two continued down the streets of Cartha, the guards of the Vushka deployed around them. Tamuka saw that the ship he had arrived in but hours ago was waiting for him. His stomach rebelled at the thought. The Merki were never intended to ride upon the waters, it must be so, for Yesha, the goddess of torment, seized him the moment the ship would move, and his own pahk, guardian of his body and soul, was rendered powerless to protect him.

"I want to show you one other thing before you leave. The Tugar Muzta spoke of such a thing, and the cattle Cromwell told us how it could be made. Yet another, the one named Hinsen it was, gave us the final idea."

Turning, Jubadi pointed to a large high-roofed shed. Walking up to the side of the building, Jubadi entered it, motioning for Tamuka to follow.

Tamuka stepped into the darkness, and it took several long seconds for his gaze to finally pierce the shadows.

Uncomprehending, he looked up, and then ever so slowly the monster started to move.

Unable to hide his fear, he leaped back, reaching for his blade.

"Don't!" Jubadi shouted. "There is some mystery inside it. If your blade should strike a spark we will all die."

Trembling, Tamuka slowly walked forward, underneath the belly of the monster. A large box hung down from the creature. Out of the back of the box a bright metal spear projected with four blades sticking out from the end.

"I do not understand," Tamuka whispered, going up to touch the blades, which were dull.

"Nor do I," Jubadi admitted. "Part of it comes from a barrow of the ancestors."

"You dared to disturb such a place?" Tamuka asked.

"Our chanter of the days of the ancients spoke of such things as you see inside that box. One of my pets saw a like such thing that Cromwell had fashioned, and the Yankee Hinsen came to beg of it. The proper prayers were called, and we took it."

"I fear it will disturb our fathers' dreams doing such a thing," Tamuka replied.

"Our fathers want us to survive," Jubadi said forcefully. "Tell Hulagar what you have seen here. If there is need we will use it."

Tamuka nodded, looking at the vast demon with a cold fear.

What are we becoming? he wondered as he followed Jubadi back out of the shed.

As he passed the spear he reached out and touched the blades again.

The propeller slowly spun as Tamuka turned and walked back out into the sunlight.

# Chapter Eleven

"Telegram again from Fort Lincoln."

Kal looked over at Hans, who wearily came up the steps of the southwest bastion facing out over the Neiper.

"Go on, Hans, what is it?"

"The signal station reports large contingents of Cartha infantry are disembarking down the beaches at the mouth of the Neiper. *Ogunquit* and ten ironclad gunboats passed the fort fifteen minutes ago."

O'Donald pointed to a cloud of smoke hovering over the river valley beyond the bend of the river.

"That must be them."

"The station is shutting down. The men along with the militia contingent are retreating up the mill road to protect the mines."

O'Donald looked over at the knot of senators standing to one side of the bastion, who had stopped their arguing to listen to Hans.

"Isn't there anything you can do?" Boris asked, a note of pleading in his voice.

"The twelve-pounders are the heaviest we've got," O'Donald replied.

"A shocking state of affairs this is," Senator Petra sniffed. "Why didn't Andrew make bigger guns?"

"Because they are expensive," Kal said slowly as if repeating himself for the hundredth time. "We believed the

Merki would come at us with bows, and the light artillery is best for field actions against them."

"Somebody then has made a terrible mistake," Mikhail retorted.

"We have all made a terrible mistake," Kal replied.

"There's a boat coming around the bend," Hans announced, happy to divert the group for at least a moment.

The vessel was a small Cartha ram, its banks of oars rising and falling with a rhythmic pace, its lateen sail taut against the southwesterly breeze, a large white flag flying from the mast.

The vessel came on at a swift pace, the distant chant of the rowers rising ever louder, a counterpoint to the senators, who fell silent at its approach. The vessel slowed as it approached the outer circle of earthworks that surrounded the city. The captain of the ship swung in close to shore, knifing through the shallow waters, the crew racing to drop sail. A Cartha warrior, dressed in purple, scrambled up into the shrouds, and cupping his hands he faced the bastion.

"I am a messenger from the Carthas," the man cried, his command of Rus almost as bad as O'Donald's, "sent to seek the rulers of the republic of Rus."

Kal stepped over to the bastion.

"You are speaking to the president of Rus," Kal replied.

"I am ordered that this parley must also be represented by the Senate."

Mikhail shouldered his way past O'Donald, the two brushing each other, their mutual hatred causing Mikhail to pause for a moment and grin darkly before he came to step up beside Kal. The other senators swarmed forward to join him.

"The Senate is here," Mikhail shouted.

Kal looked over at him coldly.

"I bring all of you an offer of a peaceful settlement," the messenger stated. "Know first of all that your army fought gallantly but was defeated and made prisoner before the city of Hispania. We ambushed them as they marched at night and routed them. Several thousand are prisoners and will be exchanged when a peaceful settlement is reached."

"I wish to see proof of that," Kal replied.

"Then go to Hispania," the messenger taunted. "Your Colonel Keane was buried there with honor, as was your son Hawthorne. With your permission I will send a man ashore with a token."

Kal nodded.

A Cartha stepped up to the side of the vessel and leaped into the water, a package tucked under his arm. Surfacing, he quickly crossed the narrow distance, and coming up on shore he gingerly picked his way through the maze of entanglements, waded through the moat, and then scaled the side of the earthen embankment.

O'Donald stepped up to the man, who looked around nervously, and snatched the long package out of his hand.

"Now get out of here, you filthy dog," O'Donald snapped.

Kal looked over at the artilleryman and nodded for him to open it.

The oiled leather casing was pulled away.

"It's a sword," O'Donald said quietly, and he held the blade up to look at the engraving down the side.

" 'General Vincent Hawthorne, presented by his old comrades of the 5th Suzdal. As He died to make men holy let us die to make men free,' " he read.

Tears clouded O'Donald's eyes.

"The boy—damn them, he was still only a boy."

Hans came up and took the sword away.

"You filthy blackguards!" O'Donald screamed, coming up to the side of the parapet. "I'll cut your livers out!"

"Pat, step away," Kal ordered, coming up to stand by his friend.

"This is a parley that still might give us peace," Mikhail shouted. "Get this loudmouthed drunkard out of here."

"O'Donald, go take a walk," Hans said, the gentleness in his voice not hiding the fact that it was a command nevertheless.

"Yes sir," O'Donald growled, snapping off an angry salute. He walked past Mikhail, throwing his shoulder in to knock the man aside.

"I'll have you for that," Mikhail growled.

"Anytime," O'Donald hissed, "and I'll cut your goddam jewels off and cram them down your throat."

The group looked at O'Donald, stunned by his rage. Hans started to speak but then fell silent as O'Donald stalked down the ramp and disappeared into the magazine.

"I demand he be arrested, for threatening a senator," Mikhail cried.

"I didn't hear anything," Hans said evenly.

Mikhail turned to look at Kal.

"He's the best artilleryman in the country," Kal said quietly. "If he's to be arrested it'll be after the war."

Without waiting for Mikhail to reply, Kal turned away.

"This is no indication that you have defeated our army," Kal shouted, struggling to control his voice. "It merely shows that but one of ours has fallen."

"My commander extends his sympathy at your loss," the envoy replied. "You can believe or disbelieve, but the facts are the same—your army will not come back."

"Is that your message, then?"

"There are the terms, which my commander believes your people will find generous."

"Go on then and get this over with."

"The Republic of Rus will declare an alliance to the Empire of Cartha. The president is to resign and go into retirement. A new president will be appointed by our commander."

"You mean Cromwell will be dictator."

"You did not hear me correctly," the envoy snapped. "A citizen of Suzdal will rule as appointed by him. We ask nothing else. There will be no arrests as long as all laws are obeyed. The prisoners of war will be returned home."

"I see before me the lying mask of the Merki horde," Kal replied, raising his voice so that the soldiers lining the battlement could hear.

The envoy laughed.

"Do you think us mad? The Merki have their own concerns, or have you not heard? They are at war with the Bantag horde, who ride thousands of miles away to your south. They are being defeated. When the time comes we will stand against them as you did against the Tugars."

"Then why not come to us in alliance instead of with guns?" Kal argued. "United we could stand against them."

"And destroy our customs, our lives, the way you attempted to pollute the Roum, to use your machines to cheat and betray our power? We are not such fools. Your power must be shared with us. I ask as well, are there not thousands who were rich but are now poor because of your Yankees? I ask the people of Suzdal to look around them and see who controls the great machines, who lives in the spacious new houses, who wears the finery while thousands starve. What good was your railroad to Roum but to make more wealth?"

"I believe nothing of what you have said," Kal replied. "Our army still exists and will return, and you are but the pets and cattle of the Merki."

"Pets and cattle would not create what we have wrought," and the envoy pointed back down the stream, to the plumes of smoke rising into the air, the ships still concealed by the river bend.

"You cannot possibly stand against our power," the envoy boasted. "If you resist we will smash down your walls within days. We have guns that can fire exploding shells into your city, setting it ablaze. And all the time that your city suffers because of the foolish pride of but one man, I hope that your Senate sees the truth.

"I was sent here to spare your lives. I see now that it is useless. When you or the new leaders that follow you change their minds, you will know where to find us."

The envoy signaled to his rowers. The water foamed as the double banks of oars bit into the muddy waters and the galley swung back out into the main channel.

A puff of smoke ignited on the deck of the ship. A rocket snaked upward, rising above the river, bursting with a sharp red light.

Seconds later a dark sinister form started to emerge from around the bend of the river.

"Get O'Donald," Hans shouted, looking back down to an orderly waiting at the foot of the bastion. "Senators, this is going to get very hot in a couple of minutes. Unless you want to be part of the action, I suggest you go into the bomb-proof shelters or back into the city. If you stay, stand clear of these guns."

"I'm staying," Boris announced, looking over coldly at his comrades. "I fought with the old 1st—a little action isn't going to scare me off."

Hans watched with a grim amusement as the group divided. To a man the former peasants who had fought with the army went up to join Boris, while the boyars hesitated and then with muffled curses walked over to join Mikhail at the far side of the bastion.

O'Donald came walking back up the ramp and looked over at them coldly.

"Now if only Cromwell will oblige us with one good shot," O'Donald whispered.

"I should confine you to quarters for what you said," Hans snapped, and then his features softened. "Ah, the look in his eyes, it was priceless, Pat."

The two laughed softly, coming up to join Kal.

"So there's the devil himself," O'Donald said, leaning on the earthen rampart. "It's an ugly thing, to be sure."

"And the most powerful ship in the world," Hans replied.

"Well, we'll see what my Napoleons can do," Pat said.

Stepping back from the wall, he looked down the line. Twenty Napoleons were lined up, the original four of the 44th New York, and the sixteen new guns made over the last year.

"Here come some more," Kal said quietly.

O'Donald looked back and saw two low squared-off craft turning the bend. Both vessels continued across the river, turning about just off the far bank.

Pat raised his field glasses.

"They're anchoring. Hell, that's nearly three-quarters of a mile away."

The *Ogunquit* continued to struggle upstream against the current, smoke pouring from its cut-down stack.

"A hell of a lot like the *Merrimac*," Hans said, leaning over the wall to send out a stream of tobacco juice.

"Lot more weight on her now," O'Donald replied. "That old *Ogunquit* could put on some steam—she must be carrying a heavy load of armor."

O'Donald raised his glasses again.

"Eight hundred yards. I want her a hell of a lot closer."

The ship continued on, the tension building. Pat looked back at his artillerymen, who looked at him with grim expectation.

"Don't worry, my lads," O'Donald shouted. "We'll give him something to think about." O'Donald paused. "By the devil's hide he's opening the gun port."

The three looked at each other nervously.

O'Donald looked around to see his gun crews standing by their weapons, pointing toward the ship.

To either side the infantry lining the log walls were crouching low, all of them looking at O'Donald with open fear.

"Here it comes," Hans replied.

O'Donald turned back. The entire front of the ship was

wreathed in smoke. Intently he peered forward. A deep-throated hum, like the sound of an approaching train, filled the air, rising in pitch.

For a brief instant he saw it, the dot growing larger, coming straight at them.

"To the left!" Hans shouted.

The ball screamed past, arching high overhead. O'Donald swung around to watch. The round dropped, slamming into the capitol building. A shower of logs, splintered like broken twigs, soared into the air. There was a pause and a thunderclap echoed, the southwest corner exploding outward, a rain of logs spilling down into the street below.

"Fifty-pounder be damned," O'Donald cursed. "He's got a hundred, maybe a hundred-and-fifty up forward."

"Range is six hundred. I'm opening up! Batteries mark your target!"

Gunnery sergeants who had been peering down the length of their barrels stood with arms outstretched, motioning with extended hands for their crews to move the pieces left or right. With a calm professionalism, O'Donald walked down the length of his old battery watching as his men again practiced their craft. Sergeants stood up holding their right arms up to signal the gun was ready. The number-four man came forward on each piece, set the friction primer into the breech, and stepped back, holding the lanyard taut.

O'Donald looked up and down the line, fist raised, a half-smoked cigar clenched between his teeth.

"By file on the right!"

He brought his fist down.

"Fire!"

The first Napoleon leaped back, and the bastion was wrapped in a cloud of sulfurous smoke. One after the other the fire raced down the length of the bastion.

"Reload!"

O'Donald, with Hans and Kal by his side, stepped up to the bastion wall as the smoke eddied around them and parted. A geyser of water snapped up off the starboard bow of the *Ogunquit*. A shower of sparks ignited on the forward armor plate, followed an instant later by two more. Another geyser shot up near the water line, and then the shot went careening off. Geysers erupted, sparks snapped, and rolling back across the water came a kettledrum-like rumbling of iron striking iron.

O'Donald watched intently, cigar clenched tight, cursing under his breath.

"Damn, it hardly dented him," O'Donald gasped.

"Batteries independent fire!"

"Maybe when he closes," Kal said hopefully.

O'Donald stepped back from the wall, not bothering to reply.

"The gunboats!" Hans shouted.

Puffs of smoke seemed to soar straight up out of the two ships.

"Goddam mortars," O'Donald said. "I always hated those bastards."

The veterans of the 44th stopped in their work to look up; the Suzdalian gunners paused, eyes wide with terror. After several seconds the men of the 44th went back to work with their reloading.

"You can see where they're going," O'Donald shouted, pointing up at the clearly visible shot rising higher and higher. "They're heading into the city. Now get back to it, damn all of you."

Kal looked over at O'Donald, who stood with arms folded watching the mortar shells, which were now directly overhead. The twin spheres seemed to hover in the sky and then with alarming speed started to drop. O'Donald turned.

"This side of the square!"

The shells dropped down. One suddenly lit off with a brilliant flash while still several hundred feet up, the fragments screaming outward. The second one dropped behind the wall with a dull crash. O'Donald shook his head.

"Lousy fuses."

The Napoleon alongside him kicked off, and a ripple of fire swept down the line, the gunners leaping forward, rolling the recoiled weapons back up into position.

O'Donald watched now with a cold professionalism. It was interesting work. The targets before had always been rebs, or Tugars, never an ironclad. He chewed on his cigar, watching the shots hit, his stomach tightening with the cold realization that he was doing little more than burning powder.

"Hold fire to a hundred yards!"

"We're not going to stop him," Hans said quietly.

O'Donald looked over at the old sergeant.

"Unless we get lucky, I'm not holding much hope."

Several long minutes of silence passed, the *Ogunquit* coming on relentlessly, while behind it a parade of ironclad gunboats appeared in its wake.

"The rest must be armed with regular cannon. The other two are mortar boats, hundred-pound shells at least."

At two hundred yards the forward gun port opened again.

All along the wall, gunners and infantrymen ducked down. O'Donald, as if showing his disdain, stood erect, Hans and Kal by his side.

A snap of flame shot out, followed instantly by the scream of the shell. A section of the old city wall a hundred yards behind them exploded in a shower of splinters. Screams of agony rent the air. As if in counterpoint the mortars fired again, the gunboats behind the *Ogunquit* following suit.

"It's gonna get hot!" O'Donald shouted.

A hail of iron roared in, the bastion beneath his feet rocking from the impact, a fountain of dirt erupting directly in front, the ground leaping beneath his feet. For a brief second he saw the mortar shells, and his stomach tightened. The rounds tumbled down, one slapping into the dockside rail yard and tearing a section of track into the air, the other hitting the river where the Cartha envoy's ship had stood but moments before, the shell detonating, lifting a plume of water up that showered down over the bastion.

Stunned, O'Donald looked around.

"All right, let him have it again. Aim for that gun port and keep pouring it in."

Wiping the muddy dirt from his face, he trained his field glasses on the ship as the Napoleons opened fire. Round after round slammed into the forward armor, the shot bounding off, the water around the *Ogunquit* kicked into a raging foam. Hammered dents appeared, but nothing more.

"Pour it in, pour it in."

Relentlessly the black iron ship came steadily forward, staying in midchannel.

"He's going to run the length of the city. Forty-fourth and fifteenth battery, swing your guns around to the west side. Sixteenth and seventeenth, hit those damn gunboats!"

Gunners grabbed hold of their weapons, lifting the prolongs, leaning into the wheels of their one-ton pieces. Boris and the peasant senators joined in, shouting and cursing.

The *Ogunquit* was less than fifty yards away. From the height of the bastion O'Donald looked down on its armored roof. Guns were run up to the bastion wall, crews cranking the elevation screws up, the barrels dropping down. The *Ogunquit* stood abeam of the bastion. Five gun ports along her starboard side swung open.

The two sides seemed to fire at once. A showering wall of dirt washed over O'Donald, and his ears felt as if they were about to be crushed in. Guns leaped alongside him, and ricocheting shot screamed across the water, crashing into the trees on the far side of the river. Through the smoke he saw part of a gun-port cover spinning through the air. Turning his glasses, he watched as the other gunboats came on relentlessly, shot screaming past, the Neiper white with foam. The *Ogunquit* slowed as if daring O'Donald to do his worst.

"Keep pouring it in," he shrieked. "Aim at the shattered gun port."

The battery crews worked in a fevered frenzy, powder boys shouldering their way up from the bomb-proof magazine below. A shot from a gunboat screamed past, its hot breath washing over O'Donald, staggering him, the round slamming into the capitol.

"Mortar!"

O'Donald looked up for a second, even as out of the corner of his eye he saw the *Ogunquit*'s guns being run back out.

Turning, he looked back at the black ugly maws of the heavy guns. They were firing up, he thought with relief. The bastion on the low bluffs gave him a good thirty-foot advantage.

"O'Donald, they're going to hit," Hans shouted, pointing heavenward.

At the same instant the *Ogunquit* fired.

Grabbing hold of Kal, who throughout the battle had stood by O'Donald, watching the action as if he were attending a play, Pat dived for the scant protection of the earthen wall.

The air was slapped out of his lungs as the sky overhead darkened with showers of earth. A humming scream filled the air, the darkness penetrated by a blinding flash. Stunned, Pat looked over at Kal, whose eyes were wide with terror. Looking down the line, he saw a gunner tumble over the side of the bastion, shrieking in anguish. An upended gun teetered for a moment on the edge of the parapet and then ever so slowly tumbled backward into the fort.

Yawning to clear his ears, O'Donald stood up. The sixteenth battery was a shambles.

"A direct hit," O'Donald shouted, coming back to his feet and running down to help pull out the wounded. Men staggered past him. Torn bodies littered the bastion. What was left of a corpse, the upper half of the body gone, lay spread-eagled against the wall, blown into the dirt by the explosive force of the shell.

"Clear the wounded back to the hospital! The rest of you keep at it!"

Turning, he looked back at Kal, who was kneeling over a body. Going up to the corpse, O'Donald was horrified to see Boris's bloodied face looking up at him.

"Oh, goddammit," he whispered.

Turning away, he saw a knot of men running back toward the city.

"They would live," Hans said, coming up alongside O'Donald, brushing the dirt from his uniform.

"She's moving up to the city," O'Donald yelled, pointing to the ironclad, which was again under way.

"They're running their entire fleet right under my nose and I can't do a bloody thing about it!"

Raging, he slammed his fist down, beating the bastion wall with impotent rage.

"Get your guns out of here," Hans said. "That last mortar shot was a lucky hit. But eventually they'll pound this bastion to rubble."

O'Donald nodded sadly in agreement.

A heavy shot from a gunboat screamed past, but he barely noticed its passage as it passed on into the city.

"O'Donald, I've only got one good brigade and a bunch of raggedy militia to hold this city, and the factories."

Hans paused for a moment as if wanting to say something, looking over at Kal.

"Mr. President, I'm sorry, but I need to talk to you."

Woodenly Kal got to his feet.

"He was one of my oldest friends," Kal whispered. "He was with me from the beginning of everything."

"I know, Mr. President," Hans said softly.

A gunboat drawing abeam the fort fired off its single gun, shaking the bastion, showering the group with dirt.

"What is it that you want, Hans?"

"Mr. President, there's nothing we can do to protect the

city. We'll have to ride this one out and pray his ammunition is limited. The Cartha infantry will be up here by midafternoon. I don't think they'll try to storm the place—we've at least got the advantage in numbers, maybe even muskets."

"I know that, Hans. We've already gone over it," Kal said quietly.

"And I think Cromwell knows it as well. He must have a plan for winning this with that consideration in mind. I'm therefore advising you to declare martial law and immediately arrest Mikhail and the boyars."

"So you're telling the mouse to become the fox?" Kal shouted, trying to be heard above the batteries, which were again returning fire.

"You and I know who that envoy was referring to."

"If I should do that, then those who follow me will do it even more easily," Kal replied. "Even your Lincoln did not do such a thing."

"He got pretty damn close," Hans yelled.

A thunderclap roar echoed over the river. Turning, the group watched as the *Ogunquit* fired a volley straight into the capitol. A section of its roof flipped into the air. Overhead a mortar round screamed down, exploding inside the city.

"The moment he makes a traitorous move I will have his head," Kal said forcefully, "but not before."

Kal looked down at the sword which Hans was still holding.

"May I have my son's sword, please," he said quietly.

Hans gently passed it over. Kal took the weapon clumsily in his left hand and held it up for a moment, looking at the script engraved down the blade.

"The boy was trying to teach me to read his English. I never was too good at it," he said quietly.

"It doesn't mean he's dead," O'Donald said. "That Vincent's got the lives of a cat, he does."

"Thank you, Pat," Kal said, smiling even as his eyes clouded over. "I'd better go back to the city."

Pat drew up, saluting Kal as he started to turn.

"Why, Pat, I think that's the first time you've saluted without being told to," Kal said, and turning away he walked down the bastion ramp, oblivious to the thunder of war and the guards that fell in closely around him.

Pat looked back at the battle still being waged. Two of the gunboats had already run past, and the *Ogunquit* was already several hundred yards upstream. In the shambles of the bastion the remaining guns continued to play at their hot, deadly game.

"That man's either a saint or a fool," Hans growled.

"But don't you know," O'Donald replied ruefully, "sometimes they're one and the same."

Grinning with satisfaction, Tobias tore the top hatch open and stuck his head out. A gust of hot air rushed up around him, and the men below cried with relief as cooling air finally rushed in through the open gun ports.

Cautiously he peered around. There could always be snipers on the shore just a hundred yards away. He turned to look back. Dark pillars of smoke rose up from half a dozen places. A thunderclap of fire snapped out from the last gunboat in line, the shot slamming straight into the inner wall, cleaving away a section of logs.

A fantasy that he had held for years had finally been fulfilled. He had led a fleet in line, run past a battery, and shelled an enemy city from one end to the other, losing but one man in his entire crew.

As he breathed in the cool air, the memory of the horrifying noise of heavy guns firing, the clouds of smoke, and the drenching suffocating heat was washed away. An entire city had stood in terror of what he had just accomplished.

He climbed back down the ladder.

"Even I am impressed," Hulagar announced.

Tobias looked straight into his eyes and saw that they were filled with an awed wonder. The nine-foot-high Merki had finally resigned himself to sitting on the gun-deck floor, unable to stand in the cramped fighting space. Tobias was pleased at not having to look up at the Merki.

"How is our ammunition?" Hulagar asked.

"We'll have to be conservative now. We put on the big display running up. The fleet will turn about and run back down, all ships firing two salvos, and anchor off the bastion to give support to our infantry moving up. The gunboats are ordered to fire one shot an hour. I want to keep a good reserve if we need to put the pressure on later or for an emergency. We've got eight thousands rounds with the fleet— there's no sense in using them all up at once."

"Arrows are the same," Hulagar replied. "A wise commander knows that."

Tobias felt himself beaming inside. Here was a Merki show-ing open admiration.

"Now we just wait for the rest of the plan to unfold."

Grinning, Tobias nodded, and leaving Hulagar, he strolled aft to prepare the ship to come about.

Hulagar watched him, a smile crossing his features.

He found that he almost liked this pet, for after all he was only a pet. It was strange in a way. He was forced to allow this one to address him as an equal, to wring from him every secret, to let him play out his game. It would almost be a shame to kill him.

The thought caused his attention to shift. Vuka sat across from him in the reeking darkness, their gazes locked.

"This is not war," Vuka said. "It is the devices of Karn the Dark One."

"It is war nevertheless—a war we must learn to survive."

"War is the glory of the charge, the wind in your hair, a fleet horse, the fear in your enemies' faces as you ride them down. There is no glory here."

"War is victory, nothing more," Mantu replied. "The glory comes afterward when your enemies are dead and you can talk about it while their bodies turn to dust."

Vuka fell silent, looking craftily at Mantu and then back to Hulagar.

His rage had slowly cleared. It had always taken too long; Tamuka had implied that often enough. Inwardly he cursed himself now. Not for what had happened in the cattle city. When there was blood, it was his right to wet his blade. It was afterward that he cursed, and he felt a cold stab of fear, and fear was a new thing to him.

Lowering his head as if to sleep, he looked over at Hulagar through barely opened slits. There again, Hulagar was watch-ing him. Again he had been a fool for speaking, for acting before thinking. The words that Mantu had uttered should have been his, weak and addled though they were.

He watched carefully, nodding his head as if weariness from the maddening noise had deadened his senses. Hulagar's gaze at last dropped away from him and shifted to his brother beside him.

There, his expression had changed, the harsh judgment leaving his face.

So it would be Mantu. Why had Hulagar sent Tamuka back to his father? Could the unthinkable be even now planned for him? He cursed himself again. Even as he had turned on Tamuka he knew he might be sealing his own fate. The mere fact that Hulagar had so openly berated him before his brother was a deadly warning which his ka, his fighting rage, had driven him to ignore. Who might it be? Hulagar could not, nor could his brother, for fratricide was the most heinous of crimes. Who would be sent, if indeed his father had pronounced the judgment against him, to strip away his right as Zan Qarth and bestow it on someone else?

A thought slowly formed. Who would the someone else be? Surely not Yojama, the slow buffoon, nor Qark, nor Toka, who drank of the fermented milk till he vomited nightly.

He stirred as if stretching, leaning his head back against the side of the ship, his eyes still barely open.

He needed to buy time, to redeem himself. He knew his father would hesitate, he knew his father's weaknesses, the foolishness of having warmth for one's offspring. How he had played that in the past, laughing inwardly as his father made himself appear stupid in his eyes.

He must buy time, must delay the judgment which must be done in such a way that he would die with honor, for he knew his father would never send him to the everlasting sky to be an object of scorn.

If the judgment was to be done.

He looked over at Mantu through veiled eyes. He would be the one to be chosen in his stead, he knew that with all certainty from the way Hulagar still looked at him.

His plan started to form.

# Chapter Twelve

"You two on the third bench, pull with the others!"

The two Suzdalian privates looked at the Roum drillmaster standing above them not understanding a word that had been said.

"Now just what the hell am I supposed to do? Here I'm waving this damn stick in thin air, and you're screaming at me," one said.

Andrew stood to one side and looked over at Dimitri, who seemed to turn an impossible shade of scarlet.

"Excuse me, sir," Dimitri said stiffly.

Breaking away from the group, the old colonel stormed down to the row of benches.

"Now listen here, you bastards," Dimitri roared in his best parade-ground voice.

The Roum ship captain looked back at Dimitri with evident relief.

"When that man over there says jump, you jump!"

"But he's speaking that Roum gibberish," the protesting private cried. "How are we supposed to understand him?"

"You learn his bloody language," Dimitri shouted.

The men started to grumble.

"Ten days have already passed. We don't have much time if you want to see your homes still standing when we get back. So, Perm damn all of you, learn it! And learn how to row these ships."

"We're sitting here on dry land," the private snapped back. "It's like learning to ride a horse by sitting on a log."

"Or loving a woman by using your hand," another soldier said, and the group broke down into gales of laughter.

Dimitri let a smile cross his features, and waited for the jokes to die away.

"Very funny, Lev, very funny indeed."

Lev looked around proudly.

"You have a daughter, Lev?"

"You know I do," Lev replied, "and I didn't use my hand to make her."

The group started to laugh again.

"Fine, just fine," Dimitri said quietly, putting his arm around Lev's shoulder. "While you're sitting here on these benches," Dimitri said, letting his voice rise slightly, "think about a Cartha using something other than his hand on your daughter."

Lev fell silent.

"Or better yet, a Merki taking her to the moon feast—she's just about the right age."

The group was silent. Lev looked around, his features pale.

"You'll get your turns on the practice ships," Dimitri shouted. "Exactly one half day of it. The rest of the time you're here on the beach waiting for the rest of our fleet to be made.

"So, damn all of you, think about what's happening back in Suzdal. And when this Roum fellow shouts, you'd better damn well listen.

"If you make a mistake in battle," Dimitri said, stabbing a finger into Lev's chest, "everyone on this ship might die, and your daughter as well, so think about it."

Without waiting for a reply, he turned and stormed off.

"He was a damn good sergeant before he became a colonel," Andrew said approvingly, looking over at Marcus.

"I didn't understand the words, but I got the meaning," Marcus said with a smile. "I think sergeants and centurions must all be born from the same blood and nursed on vinegar to sour their tempers."

Andrew laughed in reply. He wondered how his old sergeant was doing. Hans must be up to his neck in it right now.

"Let's go on," Andrew said, urging Mercury into a brisk canter.

Across the broad field that less than two weeks ago had

been occupied by the Cartha they rode. Well over half his army, ten thousand men, and an equal number of Roum were arranged in a hundred groups. Rough outlines of ships, patterned after the captured Cartha quadriremes, were marked off with stakes, rows of benches lined up inside.

Less than a thousand oars had been made so far. The rest were waving boards with weights on the end, and in more than one "ship" the men simply held their hands up going through the motions.

"Oars?" Andrew asked, looking over at Mina, who awkwardly rode with the group.

Nervously dropping the reins, he pulled out the heavy sheaf of notes from the haversack dangling by his side.

"Two hundred and ten yesterday."

"We need eight thousand," Andrew snapped. "We've got only a thousand so far. You should be up to three hundred and fifty a day."

"Andrew, I've got over a thousand men on it. It's the tools that are short. We've even got people using hand knives carving down the wood as fast as they drag it out of the forest."

"Couldn't we shift some of it onto the sawmills?"

"The mills are running twenty-four hours a day to supply the lumber for the ships. It's one or the other. The oars are more labor-intensive. Ship planks and ribs are best left to the machines."

Andrew didn't say anything, just looked back out on the field at the men sweating under the noonday sun. It was a bizarre sight, the men lined up across a quarter square mile of field, moving back and forth rhythmically, the chants of the ship captains echoing, the incessant drumbeats marking the time.

It was hard to imagine these skeletal outlines as ships rowing into a possible battle.

"Well, Admiral Marcus Licinius Graca, there's your fleet," Andrew said, trying to sound cheerful.

Marcus nodded approvingly.

"I'll be like our father gods," he said, his eyes aglow. Andrew tried to let his enthusiasm build. After all, for a history professor this was like some grand experiment to recreate the fleets of the ancient world. He looked over to where a corvus, the famed Roman ship's drawbridge, which had helped them to win the First Punic war against the superior sailors of Carthage, was set up in the bow of one of the outline ships. The weapon had apparently been forgotten on this world, but at his own suggestion it would be incorporated into every ship.

The long plank, with a spike on the end, was upright, held in position by a single post driven into the ground. The men behind it were still rowing at battle speed. The commander shouted and a crew of men released the pulley holding the corvus, which slammed down into the earth, the metal spike burying itself in the turf.

The artillery crew at the front simulated the firing of their four-pounder while the men behind them dropped their oars, the Rus soldiers picking up their muskets from under the benches, the Roum militia drawing knives and daggers. The front ranks leaped upon the corvus, racing across, the rear ranks crowding in behind them.

The commander, seeing Marcus and Andrew, raised his sword in salute and then went back to shouting at his men, kicking and pushing them, sorting out the confusion in the back.

To Andrew it looked like a godawful mess, but he could see the excitement in Marcus's eyes.

Angling his mount up the ridgeline, he reined in at the top, stood in the stirrups, and looked northwestward. The plumes of smoke were now visible across the distant plain.

"How far to go, John?"

"Ahead of schedule there at least—two days to go."

Andrew nodded approvingly. He had been up there yesterday, and John was working a minor miracle. The four-mile-long procession of trains was steadily inching along the Appian Way. Nearly sixty miles of track, along with thousands of crossties, were piled aboard the overloaded trains. As the last car of the last train passed, labor crews ripped up the track and then carried it four miles forward, laying it down ahead of the first locomotive. Ferguson had been quick to point out that by this method, nearly eight miles of track and ties would actually be manhandled all the way into Roum, providing the additional space aboard the locomotives to bring down the stockpile of rations and the machine shop equipment of Hispania so desperately needed when it came time to install the locomotive engines in the boats. Over ten thousand men were engaged in this job alone, and supplying them with food and water was taking up nearly every wagon in Roum along with an additional thousand laborers.

"Let's get down to the dockyards," Andrew said, swinging Mercury about and leading him down the hill and back into the city.

Going through the shattered main gate, Andrew and his entourage edged their way through the swirling confusion in the streets. A long line of ox-drawn carts clogged the artery, piled high with food, heading out to the railhead. Reaching the forum, he could not help but look over at the flame-scorched ruins of the palace. The three crosses still hung there, the bloated bodies of the Merki raising such a stench that he pulled out a handkerchief to cover his nose.

The old battlefield smell, he thought grimly. It had hung like that over Suzdal for weeks, and in the trenches before Petersburg, and the hospitals of Gettysburg. It was a smell he felt he'd never be able to wash out of his life. It would cling to him, from war to endless war.

A cold thought struck him. Would he wind up like that someday, hung before a Merki tent as a trophy, or would they clamor around to devour his flesh and fashion a drinking cup from his skull, the dreaded Yankee dead at last?

He could see the advantage of what Marcus had done. Every person who passed through the forum could see the reason that their lives had been turned upside down in this day and night labor.

Passing the Senate building, they rode down the hill and out to the dockyards. The river was a swarm of activity. A raft was moving slowly down with the current, piled high with fresh-cut timbers. Along the shoreline on either side staked areas had been marked out for each of the eighty ships. Crews of laborers were busy at their respective sites.

A fifteen-foot-high tower of lashed logs, surmounted by a canopy, stood in the middle of the dockyard, and riding over, Andrew dismounted and looked up. Taking a deep breath, he awkwardly started to climb up the ladder. Gaining the top, he smiled as Mina's staff turned to face him and saluted.

Glad to be under the shade of the canopy, Andrew walked over to the long table that lined one end of the tower and looked down on the rough plans spread out before him.

Mina came up beside him, with Marcus and Emil in his wake.

"There have been some kinks in the line, sir, but it's actually starting to work," Ferguson announced.

"What number are we at?"

"All the keels are down, rib parts ten through twenty are up, and twenty-one through twenty-four are being dropped off now by the raft."

Ferguson pointed to a swarm of laborers working off the side of the raft, hauling out identically cut sections of wood, carrying them up the muddy beach, and dropping them alongside one of the work areas.

Ferguson nodded proudly.

"We're finally getting the system down now," he announced. "I thought we'd just simply assign a couple of hundred men to each ship and have them build it up from scratch, but John's idea was a hell of a lot better."

"What are we doing differently?" Andrew asked.

"Well, sir, while you were up checking the rail line," John said, "Chuck and I here had an argument, and I won."

"I'm willing to admit it when I'm wrong," Chuck said, "since it usually only happens maybe once or twice a year."

"I started to think about our job here," John continued, ignoring Chuck, "and it got me to thinking.

"As we took that Cartha ship apart, I changed some things. It's not going to have the sweeping curve fore and aft. The damn thing's simply going to be a straight-sided box, with an angled-in bow and a flat stern. To design that I simply took the middle section of ribs and planking and made them the same all the way down the length of the ship. All the ribs except for the first three and the last one will be identical. The same now stands true for all the planking, which will be cut in ten-foot lengths."

"Sounds logical enough," Andrew said.

"It makes building these things a hell of a lot simpler. Well, that kept my thinking going. If nearly everything is identical for a fair part of each ship, why not have the labor identical for each man? Every part is numbered now. Rather than having eighty teams working on eighty different ships, I have ten teams working on eight ships each. As each part comes in, the team installs it on ship one, then goes to ship two and installs the same part again, and so on up the line.

"Behind them comes an inspector to double-check the job, along with a team to correct mistakes, then come caulkers and tarrers, and then another inspector."

"It's working, too," Chuck interjected. "The problem is that we're actually outpacing the sawmills. I just thank God we had that lumber stockpiled to be cut into crossties and for bridging material or we'd be sunk before we even started."

"The gunboats?"

"That's a lot tougher now," Chuck said, reaching under the table and pulling up another set of drawings.

"No two of those grain ships are alike, so each one's a custom job. The biggest one, Bullfinch tells me, draws over seven hundred tons, and the smallest we'll use draws about two hundred and fifty. The others we're tearing apart for the wood. The decks are being cut down and reinforced. We're taking the sterns apart, rebuilding half for stern wheels, the other half for propellers."

"Can you make it on time?" Andrew asked.

Chuck looked over at John.

"Too many unknowns for that one," John said evenly.

"How about the guns?"

"There's a balancing act there," John said. "We're making the molds right now, and letting them dry. If there's even a hint of moisture in them when we start the pourings, the whole damn thing will explode. Andrew, there's a hell of a difference between casting a four-pounder and casting a seventy-five-pounder."

"Cromwell did it."

"He had over a year. He might have made mistakes, had molds blow apart—he had all the time in the world, and we don't. The fact we're going with carronades makes it easier— pouring two tons per mold is a hell of lot easier than ten tons. Some of the guns will be bronze. We're collecting every scrap of bronze in the city. It's a lot easier to work, with a far lower temperature—that'll give us a chance to make our goal by making a couple of extra bronze furnaces."

"What about shot and powder?"

"The shot's the easier part. I've cast up some molds for the balls, and they're being turned out right now. I wish we had some exploding shells as he does, but I don't have the equipment or time to turn them out. But I've also got a little improvement Cromwell won't have. I'm trying an experiment that might involve a little risk, but I think the advantages will outweigh it. I've made some molds for wrought-iron bolts rather than round shot."

"What's the advantage?" Andrew asked.

"O'Donald would love them. Wrought iron's a lot tougher and a bit heavier. When our cast-iron round shot hits his armor, it might punch through, it might not—in fact, the rounds might even shatter.

"The bolts are simply that—they look like rifle shells but are solid and made of wrought iron. They'll weigh out at nearly one hundred pounds. The trade-off is that our guns might burst from the strain of firing them. What I want to try is this. Once we get some rails in and the tools from the Hispania rail yard to work with, we're going to heat some rails up red-hot and hammer them into sheets. After the guns come out of the molds, we're going to take the sheets and wrap them around the breech. As the metal cools it'll shrink and compress in, reinforcing the gun. Remember, we've got a lot of ironworkers here who know their trade."

"Like a Parrot rifle," Vincent interjected.

"Exactly."

"This wasn't part of the plan, though," Andrew said cautiously.

"Sir, we're making this up as we go along. We'll test a gun, and if it blows, well, we've lost a gun. If it doesn't, we might have an edge."

"I guess we're doing everything we can," Andrew said quietly.

Andrew walked away from the group and looked back westward.

There were too many unknowns in all of this, and his senses rebelled at that fact. Warfare on land he understood perfectly—he had had two and a half bloody years of schooling in that craft before coming here. But in this game, Cromwell had all the advantages. He understood his ships, what went into them, how they were to be sailed and fought. On his side, all he had was a young lieutenant, and the Roum, who had been driven from the Inland Sea by the Carthas centuries before he had arrived. Cromwell also knew where all the parts of this vast puzzle were laid. The only thing he could hope for so far was that his plans for this fleet were unknown. The key trick was to keep convincing Cromwell he was trying to move back by rail, that he was still thinking like an infantry officer rather than like a sailor.

A shudder ran through the train, bringing Tim Kindred to his feet. An instant later the high-pitched scream of escaping steam and a deafening explosion washed over him. The windows on the car shattered, spraying the corridor with shards.

A wash of steam eddied past the car. A rifle shot snapped out, and then a ragged volley.

He looked over at the frightened corporal by his side.

"Come on, outside now, they've got to see you!"

Tim grabbed the shaking soldier by the shoulder, pushing him forward, shoving him through the door first.

"Now act your part, dammit!"

"They're shooting!"

"Don't you think I know that?" Tim roared.

Trembling, the corporal climbed down the steps, Kindred following in his wake.

Hot steam washed around them, and already he could feel the rapid change in the air, throwing an alarm signal straight into his lungs.

"Come on, boy, out into the open, and for God's sake try to look brave."

Kindred pushed his way through the hot fog and out into the sunlight. The engine ahead had been blown, the rush of steam still swirling straight up and billowing outward.

"Artillery piece, sir!" shouted a soldier running past Kindred and pointing up to the ridge.

A concussion snapped past him as the artillery inside the armored car sent off a volley. On the low ridge less than two hundred yards away he saw a flurry of activity, a horseman galloping away. There was another puff of smoke, and a brief fraction of a second later the shot slammed into the car he had just left.

A ragged volley swept along the ridge, bullets slapping into the car. The corporal started to duck.

"Goddammit, boy, stand up straight and don't move a muscle or I'll shoot you myself."

The corporal looked over at him fearfully and came to attention.

"That's better. Now just stand there."

"Skirmish line forward!" Kindred shouted.

From out of the boxcars soldiers started to pour out, hitting the ground, firing back at the puffs of smoke. A bugle sounded, and from the train behind a dozen mounted soldiers leaped their mounts off the flatcars and started to gallop up the hill, swinging out to take the enemy in the flank.

Intently, Kindred watched the enemy line. The firing had already stopped. Raising his field glasses, he was shocked to see a soldier with a telescope looking straight back at him.

"Don't move," Kindred hissed.

The soldier turned and disappeared down behind the slope.

The skirmish line started forward at the run, sweeping up the side of the hill. He had to press them hard, but inwardly he was praying for something else.

The men crested the hill, while from the next ridgeline over he saw thirty or more horsemen riding hard silhouetted for a moment and then disappearing from view.

"Sound recall," Kindred shouted.

Wheezing heavily, he walked down the length of the car and stopped in front of the locomotive now wreathed in flames. Two torn and bloodied bodies lay in the cab. Looking at them for but a second, he was grateful for their sakes that it had been quick. Death by scalding was something he did not like to contemplate.

One of the skirmishers came running back down the hill and, panting hard, drew up and saluted.

"They had one of our four-pounders up there, sir. It must have hit the engine and blown it open."

Kindred merely nodded, looking down the track. The handcar which had been running a couple of hundred yards ahead of them, looking for breaks, was still intact, the four men aboard hunkered down behind it, peering up cautiously now that the shooting had stopped.

"Get the work crews started," Kindred said, looking over to his staff, his voice barely above a whisper. "Push this engine off the track. Have the locomotive behind us push our cars up. Detail off the next unit of a hundred for security right here, and have them start making a sod fortress like the others."

Stepping away from the track, he looked back down the line. Now there were only four locomotives. They had encountered the first cut in the line nearly a hundred miles back, derailing a train. It had taken five days to move up the last stretch to this point forty miles east of the bridge. In the beginning it had just been a track shoe pulled loose, or the connector between two rails unbolted, or an entire rail gone, hidden away in the high grass.

He had laid out nearly five thousand men as security behind him, most of them terrified Roum militia, each group of a hundred beefed up with twenty Suzdalian regulars. It was still far too thin, only fifty men per mile, and every night someone had slipped in to at least cut the telegraph wire they were stringing back out.

It simply amazed him. Three, maybe four hundred men at most could play absolute hell with a rail line, tying down ten times their own number.

Training his field glasses westward, he could see the thin speck of the wrecked train that had been jumped thirty miles this side of the Kennebec. It would be there that the total destruction of the rail line had begun.

Maybe by the end of the day they'd reach it and he could settle down to the task of pushing rail up. Andrew might think this was nothing more than a feint, but by damn it wasn't to him. A slow rage had been building with this guerrilla warfare, and before it was done he would relish the chance to catch those bastards by the throat and see them hanging from the nearest telegraph pole.

"Excuse me, sir."

Kindred looked up and saw the corporal still standing at attention.

"Can I stand at ease?"

"Go on inside, boy. Get that jacket off and stretch your arm."

Kindred started to laugh as the six-and-a-half-foot-tall soldier climbed back into the bullet-pocked car. Now that was a touch he had thought up on his own. Finding a Suzdalian soldier as tall as Andrew had taken some doing. The poor lad had suffered the torments of hell, his left arm stuck inside an officer's jacket, waiting for days for some sort of action against the raiders, just so he could stand out in the open and be seen and shot at.

Kindred looked back up at the crest of the hill. A fit of coughing took hold, doubling him over as he gasped for breath. Damn this asthma, it'll be the death of me yet, he thought. His hat tumbled down in front of him, and as he picked it up he saw the neat bullet hole in the crown.

Smiling, he put the hat back on.

Maybe I'll get lucky yet, he thought with a sad smile. A death by a bullet beats asthma any day.

Jubadi looked up coldly as Muzta Qar Qarth of the Tugar horde entered his tent.

"I thought you would be on the frontier of the Roum," Jubadi said darkly, dropping all pretense of the formalities of hospitality.

"No, I am here, as is obvious," Muzta replied with a cold smile, "and might I add as one protected by your pledge of blood."

"You need not remind me of my own words, Tugar," Jubadi bristled, "but I must now remind you of yours."

Muzta, laughing softly, strode up to the raised dais in the middle of the tent and sat down by Jubadi.

"Remind me then," he said quietly.

"You were to have an umen of your warriors posted in the hills that flank the Inland Sea, there to await the word from Hulagar to sweep up and pin the Roum when the time was right. Instead you are here. Hulagar did not find your support. He found nothing."

Jubadi came to his feet.

"Nothing!"

Muzta nodded, leaning over to pick up a sliver of meat.

"That is obviously so," Muzta said quietly.

"Do you realize that the army of the Yankees is now in Roum? There is nothing to occupy them there, and all my forces are now in Rus."

"And you promised me the cannon you were making, you promised me a thousand of the Yankee guns, you promised me food. Who has to feed my people while my ten thousand rode on campaign?" Muzta snapped.

"Your food was waiting for you in Roum, the food that you should have taken the first time you were there."

Muzta leaned back and laughed darkly.

"You have yet to truly fight them. I have and I know. Before, we could slaughter the cattle by the hundreds of thousands every year and not one of the hordes would be slain. The price of food has gone up, Jubadi Qar Qarth.

"You did not tell me that the Yankee army would be in Roum, you led me to believe that they would be in Rus, that you would fight them there and I would sweep up Roum after their fall.

"So I began to think. Here were the foe that I must admit defeated me when I had six times the number I now have. I was to attack them again. And what would I have to show for it?

"The rest of my warriors die, and the Merki horde ride

into Rus and eat till the grease runs from their mouths while Tugar corpses litter the fields. Beyond that it would be you who would hold all their secrets, their places that make machines, that make the guns."

"The plan changed," Jubadi said evenly. "I did not expect the Yankees to move as they did. I thought we would take the Roum city, our army acting as a barrier while you took their lands to the east."

Muzta leaned over, laughing and holding his sides.

"And what military purpose would that serve? If their capital city was yours, the outlying provinces would be no threat. No, Jubadi, I saw your plan, and my people would be defenseless."

"Then why did you come back if you refused to do what I asked?"

Muzta held up his hand and smiled.

"We still need each other, Jubadi. I want the Yankee weapons, and you still need the strength I have. Tell me, is it true you lost half an umen to the Bantag?"

Jubadi silently nodded his head.

"You know they will reach their place of crossing the Inland Sea within sixty days."

"I know that."

"So they will cross the sea ahead of you and turn north. They harry you through the passes of the great hills. Slowing you down. What will you do?"

"That is none of your concern. Are you a spy for them?"

"There is no need for you to hide it, actually. You will take those ships of iron that float, and block the Bantag to the south, and use the cannons to slay them when you have captured all the weapons of the Yankees. It is easy enough to see."

Jubadi said nothing, watching with hawklike eyes as Muzta leaned over and took another slice of meat.

"If the Bantag defeat you, they will be hungry for me as well," Muzta continued. "That is why we need each other. I tell you now, Jubadi, before my people will move to support you, I want the guns and the stinking smoke that powers them. I want the right to harvest of the Carthas when the time comes. Then I will turn to strike the Roum when the Yankees have ridden back to the west.

"I must admit your trick was a good one, though it insults me that you thought I would actually believe it."

Muzta started to laugh softly, and Jubadi, a smile crossing his features, started to laugh as well.

"The guns will be yours, Muzta Qar Qarth."

When I defeat the Yankees I will not need you, Jubadi thought even as he smiled, as long as I have kept you close by for the kill.

"Then we are agreed."

"When do your umens ride north to strike the Rus?" Muzta asked as if in an afterthought.

"In another ten days, but they will only be one now."

"You are late."

"The Bantag. They were forced to cover the westernmost passes longer than I had planned for. Even now they should be pulling eastward. They will come to the coast and relieve the Vushka, who will go north. We will be in Rus in not more than twenty days."

"Still, you will have their city and I will have nothing."

"We will share in its wealth, Muzta Qar Qarth."

"But of course," Muzta said with a smile.

Without another word, Muzta Qar Qarth stood and walked out of the tent.

So he does not know, he thought with an inward smile. It is amazing how we can all so happily betray each other, for surely Jubadi will betray me as I will him. Even as the cattle who had once been a ruler from the Roum had slipped away to his spies on their southern border to tell him how the Yankees were again making their machines, iron floating machines that would fight the ones of Cromwell.

We will all play our games and lie, and there will still be a place for the Tugars when all is settled.

Ignoring the salutes of the guards of the Vushka, he swung into his saddle and cantered away.

"Their people are in position," Hamilcar said, as Tobias climbed up to stand on the deck.

"It's the perfect night for it," Tobias said quietly, pulling his oilskin coat up to ward off the steady downpour of rain.

A flash snapped over the river to the north, followed several seconds later by the bursting of a shell inside the city. The bombardment was taking its slow methodical course, tearing down the walls, spreading terror, harassing. The southwestern bastion had long been abandoned except for some infantry who were solidly dug in and would occasionally trade their one-ounce musket balls for a fifty-pound shell.

The land action was as he had expected as well. He knew he'd never have the numbers to seize the city and the factories by assault. This was a battle of minds, and so far he knew the tide was surely turning in his direction.

When humans fought Tugars, there was only one alternative, victory or death. But when humans fought humans, there were always a hundred shades in between.

The walls of the city were less than seventy-five yards away, so close that he heard a guard sneeze on the battlement. A moment later there was a muffled scream and at the same instant a snap of light shot up, the rocket bursting over the river.

"Now!" Hamilcar screamed.

The water on either side of the *Ogunquit* foamed as hundreds of oars from three galleys bit into the river, the ships swinging out from behind the ironclad and racing toward the shore.

A musket snapped off, the report a dull pop. Several more fired from the bastion, and then there was silence.

"Their powder's wet!" Tobias laughed.

Cries of alarm sounded, racing up and down the wall.

"Fire!"

The *Ogunquit* rocked beneath his feet. The five shells were aimed high, arching over his men and on into the city. The line of gunboats opened with a ragged volley. From the gun flashes he could see the galleys hitting the docks, the men leaping out, racing for the shattered wall. The bastion was already overrun, the column of a thousand men pushing straight in toward the gate, which was already open.

Smiling in the darkness, Tobias looked over at Hulagar.

"I told you Mikhail would have the way open. Already we are in the city."

"You have done well, Tobias."

To his surprise the voice in the darkness was Vuka's. Something had changed with that bastard, he thought, barely taking notice of Tamuka, who stood by Vuka's side.

# Chapter Thirteen

With whistle shrieking, the locomotive inched forward, the rail beneath her creaking under the weight. With a loud vent of steam the engine braked to a stop.

Chuck Ferguson leaned out of the cab.

"Unhook 'em."

A brakeman leaped down from the tender and pulled the pin connecting the engine to the twenty-car train, and stepping back, signaled that the engine was clear. Looking forward, the switchman waved that the line was open. Edging the throttle back up a notch, Chuck inched the locomotive into the siding. To either side of the engine was a heavy scaffold made out of uncut timbers. The train inched up the incline and then leveled off, the timbers of the rotating roundtable groaning under the weight. A signalman stood to one side of the cab, holding up his hand, slowly waving him forward. He held both hands up with wrists crossed, motioning for him to stop.

"Shutting down!" Ferguson shouted as he closed off the damper and turned open the vents.

God, I never thought I'd make it, he thought, wiping the sweat from his face with an oil-streaked handkerchief. Climbing down from the cab, he stepped back and looked up at the crane that the engine would now power. The engine would be jacked up in place and the drive wheels would be connected to overhead pulleys, which would power the crane hoist.

Once the crane was hooked onto a locomotive the entire

engine would be raised up and the turntable would be rotated, swinging the locomotive off the track to the first station, where the steam engine would be disconnected from the chassis. Lifted again, the engine would be swung over the dock, then lowered into the gunboat resting alongside the dock, while the chassis was pushed away down a side track. As the gunboat was towed away, the turntable would swing back and start the process all over again.

Walking away from the engine, he stepped back out onto the track. Hundreds of laborers were swarming over the flatcars, which were packed with the precious tools that had been stripped out of the Hispania workshop, and hauling the equipment over to the dockside, the work crews from the rail line shouting orders at the uncomprehending Roum workers. Without those precious tools, lathes, and forging equipment, Ferguson realized, the job facing him would have gone from improbable to impossible.

Looking back up the rail line that ran the length of the dockside, he shook his head in disbelief at what they had accomplished in just thirteen days. It was packed from one end to the other with steam-venting trains, boxcars piled high with supplies and crossties, flatcars stacked to near bursting with rails. The procession turned at the end of the dockyard, going over the rubble of several houses that had been smashed down to make the curve manageable and up the hill to the forum, a passage that would be impossible to climb and was damn near a killer to slide down. From the forum the trains were backed up all the way out of the city and on across the practicing fields beyond.

It was a hell of a tangled mess.

Four miles a day, five and a quarter miles in this final run—the pace had been killing. Not even old Hermann Haupt could beat that. But then again, he had to concede, Haupt didn't have over ten thousand workers on his line.

The job still wasn't done yet. The rail line would be driven on for another four miles, straight through the wall and most of the way down to Ostia. As the cars were unloaded, their purpose for the campaign was finished; the second engine in line would serve to push the empties on down the line and out of the way of the construction.

"You've done a hell of a job, Ferguson," Vincent said, coming up to slap him on the back.

"Yeah, but there's one problem."

"What is it?"

"I never really thought about it till now," Ferguson said, shaking his head, "but getting all these cars back up and out and then all the way back to Suzdal after this war is over is going to be one hell of a job. The entire rolling stock of the M FL&S will be sitting on a siding with nearly eighty miles of empty space separating it from the nearest piece of track to home. Except for the five locomotives with Kindred and the two working here, all our motive power will be stripped and sitting inside the ships. This railroad will be crippled for months after the campaign is finished. There isn't an engine around that could pull a single car back up the forum hill."

"You sound like you're already planning for after the war."

"I've got to."

"You think we'll actually win this one?"

"My job's the engineering, and Mina's my logistics boss—that's all I worry about for now. I'll leave the rest for Andrew. Come on along—I'm going over to check our first gunboat."

Leading the way, Chuck climbed up over a growing pile of crossties and stepped out onto the dock. Directly below him a heavy grain ship was tied up to the quay, men swarming all over the vessel. Climbing down a ladder, he leaped onto the deck.

Workmen looked up, nodded a greeting, and then continued with their labor.

"She seems awful high out of the water," Vincent said.

"We'll be loading on nearly a hundred tons of rail and another hundred tons of wood for armor. Add in the guns, the engines, crew, and ammunition, and it'll be over three hundred and fifty tons by the time we're done. All I can say is, Bullfinch had better be right with his displacement, or we've got problems."

Leaning over the open deck near the stern, Ferguson looked down below.

"We've got the mounts framed out for the two engines. The driveshafts to the propellers will be hooked into the engines by leather belts. Bullfinch kicked up a holler over that—said if they get wet we've got real problems—but there simply isn't enough time to make the gears to match the engine strength to the ship."

"There's a lot of space forward in the hull, from the looks

of it," Vincent said, getting down on his knees and bending over to look below.

"Firewood, Vincent—though to save on space, we'll be towing some barges with additional wood. The rest is for the crew and ammunition. Come on, let's go forward."

Ferguson stopped for a moment to look admiringly at the blockhouse resting amidships. Climbing up to the top of the six-foot-high wall, he sat down on top, even as the workmen around him continued with their tasks.

Vincent climbed up to join him.

"We've yet to close this over. We won't do that till the guns are put in."

He reached down and slapped the wall beneath him.

"A double layer of rail ties, two feet thick on top, sloping down to three feet thick at the bottom. We're going to double-layer the rails over the outside. The bottom row will be bolted straight into the ties, facing out. The top layer will be reversed and strapped in with U-bolts. If I had a couple of months more and a rolling mill I'd turn these into plate. There are going to be gaps and spaces between the rails, but they're still equal to several inches of armor."

"Think it'll keep the shot out?"

"It'll be as noisy as hell in there, but they should stand against fifty-pounders. We're putting a single layer of rail ties across the entire deck, then a layer of rails. On top of that we'll lay down planking so footing on deck will be easier. Along the sides we'll build a belt of rails down to a couple of feet below the waterline in case any shots skip in low.

"The trick is going to be how these damn things handle in anything beyond a flat calm. The hulls are deep, but there's a lot of weight topside, rather than down below the waterline. I think they'll roll like tubs. Again, it's a question of time, and not knowing much about ships—that's Bullfinch's department, but personally I wish I'd studied the subject more. Remember, railroading was what I was interested in."

"You don't sound too optimistic," Vincent said quietly.

"Give a good engineer a problem, the right tools, and a little time, and he can figure it out.

"As for everything else, I'm just the engineer, Vincent. The colonel gave me a job, and by damn I'll do it for him. I'll leave the strategy of winning it to him, and the fighting of it to you."

"Somehow I wish we could trade places," Vincent said, his voice distant.

Chuck looked over at Vincent and laughed.

"You've got to be kidding. I've got sixteen days left to build the gunboats. Even with two engines in each ship I'm not sure if the power ratio will be right. Now if those damn things go out there and break down, or worse yet, simply slide under the water and sink, this whole world's gonna remember me for Ferguson's Folly. I'll take your job any day."

"How long were you with the 35th?" Vincent asked softly.

"You mean back home? I joined in '62. Lord, did my parents kick up a squawk."

"You were an engineering student. How come you didn't go into the Engineer Corps? They'd have made you an officer."

Ferguson shook his head ruefully.

"My best friend, Frank Smith, he had his heart set on going into the 35th and kept telling me I wouldn't see any fighting if I went into the Engineers."

"You wanted to fight?"

"Sure, didn't you? Hell, everyone's talking about how you're the best damn fighter in the army."

Vincent lowered his head.

"So you joined the 35th, then?"

"Just before Antietam, same as the colonel. Was in every fight since, though I kept getting sick all the time and the colonel kept trying to talk me into taking a job in the rear."

"Why'd you stay if you had a chance out?"

"'Cause a reb kilt Frank," Ferguson whispered. "He wasn't in his first fight more than five minutes, Antietam, and then he was dead."

Ferguson paused for a moment.

"I liked killing rebs," he said softly. "At least I thought I did."

Chuck looked closely at Vincent. His face was still puffy and pockmarked, but the infection was finally going down.

"Something troubling you, Vincent?" Chuck asked softly.

Vincent stood in silence.

"I heard how you pumped six slugs into that Merki, even after he was dead," Chuck finally ventured.

"I liked it," Vincent replied, looking back up, his eyes shining. "Watching the bullets hit into him, his body jerking. I'm starting to think there is no God, that we are nothing but born killers, that everything I ever learned was a sham."

He sighed. It was finally out, something he found he could not bring himself to say to Andrew or Emil. Dimitri had looked at him differently since the fight, like a worried father. They all thought so differently of him, the noble soldier, imbued with the idealism of the cause. He barely knew Ferguson—maybe that was part of all of this.

Chuck shook his head sadly.

"I haven't fired a gun since we got here, except when we did that final charge in the square and we figured it was lost. They say I'm too important to go stopping an arrow or bullet."

"You'll get over it, Vincent."

"Did you?"

Ferguson looked around at the mad bustle of activity.

"I finally found something else," he said softly.

"I don't want to," Vincent said coldly. "I thought I did. I even told Andrew I had had it with fighting. But when I saw that Merki the hatred just exploded out of me. I get this strange almost tingly feeling when I think about doing it again."

Vincent looked over at Chuck with an empty vacant smile.

I'm sitting with a madman, Chuck thought sadly.

Cresting the low grass-covered hill, Gregory paused, reining Mercury in. Climbing down off his mount, he stiffly bent over, every inch of his body aching.

Shading his eyes, he looked northward. On the far horizon he could just see the high hills of the forest, and he longed to be back there, under the coolness of the trees, breathing in the tangy scent of the pines. Going over to the water skin, he untied the heavy bag and brought it around, opening it so Mercury could drink.

How much farther? he wondered. He had gone into the edge of the forest, riding through the scattering of trees for three days. Once, he had seen them, half a dozen riders, mounted on their heavy horses, crossing the steppe behind him a few miles away.

For three days the horizon had been dotted with fires every couple of miles. Those bastards burning the rails, he thought coldly. Yesterday he had forded the upper reaches of the Penobscot and seen horse tracks in the mud on the other side. Were they looking for him? he wondered. But since this morning the fires no longer showed; he must have swept beyond their reach. All he had to do was to continue southwestward till he hit the rails and then ride hard to the next water-tank stop. Surely it would be guarded and a telegraph line would be there to send the message in.

"Let's get going, boy," Gregory said, lowering the water sack and pulling it shut. Mercury nickered in protest, nuzzling around for more. Gregory, laughing softly, reached into the saddlebag and pulled out an apple and offered it as a substitution, which Mercury greedily took.

That the colonel would entrust his horse to him was an honor almost equal to that of carrying the message all the way back home. Surely he'd get a promotion for it once this war was over.

Slinging the bag up, Gregory climbed back into the saddle, groaning as his backside hit the hard leather.

"Let's be off, then."

Urging the horse forward, he continued across the flat plain, barely noticing the gentle rise of the ground beneath him. With head lowered he continued on, nodding wearily, trying to stay awake, not even noticing the crest of the hill and the slow dropping away into the next grassy swale.

There was no pain, just a numbness slamming into his side.

Mercury turned, ears flattened, breaking into a run.

He tried to draw a breath, but somehow it just wouldn't come.

There was a crack, a puff of smoke in the grass.

I'm shot, he realized with a cold panic. By Kesus, I'm shot!

And then the pain hit, blinding him, each surge of Mercury's gallop sending a stab into his heart.

He looked to his left and saw the two horseman coming out of the high grass, their horses moving from a canter into a gallop.

They shot me.

He reached down to his side and drew away his hand. It was covered with blood.

The two horseman drew out their swords, their taunting laughs drifting across the wind.

The message, the colonel told me the message.

He kicked Mercury hard, and the horse leaped forward. He bit his lips to keep from screaming, but the scream came anyhow, the cry lost across the vast empty steppes.

The great square of the city was empty, as if the city of Suzdal were dead. After the bitter fighting of the last five days, the silence was even more disturbing.

But it was no ghost city he lived in now. Suzdal was locked in the throes of a civil war, as if a family were trapped inside its own home, arguing over who would possess it, both sides threatening to burn the house down around the other.

A pennant was raised in front of the cathedral, and at the same moment a side door to the church facing north swung open. Kal knew that a door to the south side of the church had just been opened as well.

A line of skirmishers raced out of the buildings to either side, forming a cordon. Four men stepped in next to Kal, their height all but blocking his view.

"Be careful over there," Hans said sharply.

"Don't worry about me—not even that dog would dare to defile the pledge of Casmar."

"We'll just keep a sharp eye, and don't forget the revolver in your jacket."

Kal nodded absently, reaching up to pat the gun tucked in under the stump of his right arm. He had argued hard against that precaution, but Hans had finally closed it by stating he would physically prevent Kal from going unless he complied.

A priest appeared in the doorway and held his hand up.

Kal stepped out of the building, the guards edging in around him, the men moving at a trot, so that Kal had to run to keep up with their long-legged stride. Panting, he reached the doorway. The old ways coming back, he bowed to the priest, his hand sweeping the ground.

"Mr. President, it is I who should bow to you," the priest whispered nervously.

Kal nodded to the guards, who turned and withdrew back across the street. The priest ushered Kal in, closing and bolting the door behind him.

"Forgive me, Mr. President, but I must," the priest whispered, and he reached out and gently patted Kal's side.

The priest hesitated and looked down into Kal's eyes.

Feeling a bit sheepish, Kal unbuttoned his tunic and took out the revolver, which the priest gingerly took and set on a side table.

"I'm sorry," Kal whispered.

"These are terrible times we live in," the priest replied and then beckoned for him to follow.

The church held the old familiar smell of candles and

incense, and he breathed deeply, the fragrance drawing his memory back to far simpler days, when as a lowly peasant he stood in the back of the cathedral, listening to the choir chant the high service to Perm and His son Kesus.

Stepping into the nave of the cathedral, Kal genuflected, making the Orthodox sign of the cross, and then continued into the south wing, down the long corridor of private chapels, and stopped at last at the door into Casmar's office.

A doorway down at the far end of the corridor opened and a priest appeared, two men behind him. Kal looked away, ignoring their advance.

In the doorway before him Casmar appeared, dressed in the full robes of archprelate of the holy church. His purple cassock was embroidered with silver thread; the scarlet lining shimmered as if it had an inner light of its own. His high cap was encrusted with gems, and the cross atop it was of solid gold. It seemed strange to Kal to see him like this. He had grown accustomed to the simple black cassock which Casmar had always preferred and wore both in church and as a justice of the court.

Kal bowed low again, and noticed from the corner of his eye that Mikhail did as well, while Cromwell merely stood to one side, arms across his chest.

"I have pledged this holy church to the safety of the three of you," Casmar said formally. "Just remember that, for you stand here upon consecrated ground."

Kal felt a twinge of guilt for the revolver but said nothing as he stepped into the room, following behind Mikhail, who had shouldered his way forward.

Casmar went to sit at the head of the table, and Kal, noticing only one chair on the side facing the door, went over to it and sat down opposite his two opponents.

"It was Mikhail who approached me for this conference," Casmar said. "I agreed to act as the mediator and guarantor in the hope of ending this senseless bloodshed that has engulfed our city once again.

"Therefore I have granted him the privilege of speaking first."

Mikhail looked over at Cromwell and then turned to face Kal.

"It has been six days since my forces freed the south part of the city," Mikhail began. "I think it is time, Kalencka, that we end this foolishness. As president of the state of Rus

I am willing to offer you terms to prevent our city from being burned to the ground."

"I see it as six days since you betrayed your country and let in his army," Kal retorted, pointing over at Cromwell. "President, you say? When did you hold an election? Your people are nothing but your old retainers, disgruntled merchants, and the Cartha army that backs you up."

"Betrayed our country? Ten senators were with me in this."

"And twenty-four are still with me. The army stands with me as well."

He had believed too much in his dream that laws above all else could rule men. Vincent had taught him that, with his shining innocence. Yet there had never been a proper answer for one question—what could one do with those who laughed at laws, even as they warped and twisted them to hide behind? Mikhail had done it all so efficiently as a senator. The idea of a corrupt senator, a senator who could sell out his own people and do so without compunction, was beyond his understanding. He could see now how such men could make laws to protect themselves, how they could even kill someone, perhaps even an innocent child or woman, and then turn their power to protect themselves like the boyars of old. If he survived this crisis, which he now truly doubted, he would make sure that never again would such a man as Mikhail survive in office.

"What army?" Cromwell said coldly.

Kal looked over at Cromwell with open hatred.

"You betrayed your own kind as well. You are nothing but a servant of the Merki. My people know that. That is why they will fight you to the last."

Cromwell shook his head sadly.

"Andrew Keane was a fool. When we fought the Tugars, they had two hundred thousand warriors. If it had not been for a miracle all our bones would now be bleaching in the sun," Cromwell snapped. "The Merki have twice that number. You might not believe anything else I say, but believe that, Kalencka. I am here for your salvation, not your destruction."

"Then why have you set about to destroy our city?" Casmar said.

Cromwell sighed and settled back in his chair.

"Everything I say in this room I will deny outside of it," he said evenly. "I have struck a deal with the Merki."

"You're mad," Kal roared. "So you are their servant."

"Not their servant," Cromwell snapped. "I serve no one."

"But your own interests," Kal retorted.

"If you wish to see it that way, then do so. But hear me out."

Kal started to stand up, but Casmar held out his hand, beckoning for him to sit down.

"Go on, then," Kal said sarcastically. "I am eager to hear what the Merki Namer of Time wishes to say."

"Last year the Merki granted exemption to the Carthas if they would serve them in building this fleet."

"Which you taught them how to do."

"Yes, damn you, I did," Cromwell retorted angrily. "I met with their Qar Qarth, Jubadi. They knew what we had done to the Tugars, and it was their plan to wipe us from the face of the earth unless an alternative was reached."

"I'm eager to hear this," Kal growled out bitterly.

"They refuse to deal with you, or with any of the army that fought against the Tugars. They had to be put aside, and though I was reluctant to do so, I agreed."

"And killed my son-in-law."

"For that I am sorry," Cromwell replied, and Kal sensed an almost genuine regret in his voice. "But here is the agreement. The city will surrender to me, and Mikhail as a former boyar will be the ruler, a ruler as in the old days. The Rus factories will make arms for the Merki to be used against their rivals to the south. For that we will be granted exemption. In another two years they will be a couple of thousand miles away to the east and we will be spared.

"If we do not agree to that, they will sweep northward and slaughter all of you."

Kal sat in silence.

"For God's sake, Kal. You have only half the population you did before the war. They are twice as strong as the Tugars. Besides that, they learned from what we did to the Tugars. They won't make the same mistakes, and most of all there will be no miracles as there were last time. The odds are simply too great. Andrew must have been mad to think he could actually defeat them."

"With the alliance to Roum we would have had the manpower and resources to do so."

"The Roum did not want you. Your alliance was shaky at best, and they would have sold you away the moment the

Merki came. Besides, they are now firmly allied with us. You are cut off, your army is gone, and if you do not agree quickly, the Merki will be at your gates."

Kal was silent, looking over at Casmar, who sat expressionless.

"You have no alternatives left, Kal. If you wish to fight for Suzdal, we will destroy it from one end to the other if need be in order to take it. The rains of earlier this week prevented the shells from touching off any major fires. But it's been hotter than hell these last four days, everything is drying to tinder, and if a conflagration gets started you'll have nothing left at all. Tell me, do you really think you can rebuild this city again, raise another army, rebuild your weapons, throw us out, and then beat off the Merki alone?"

"I have no other alternative," Kal whispered.

"You're mad," Mikhail laughed.

"No, it is you who are mad," Kal replied. "At least now I have something within the law that will see you hang from the end of a rope when this is done."

"Remember we agreed there would be no threats in this meeting," Casmar interjected, and Kal, looking over, saw the disdain in the prelate's eyes for Mikhail even as he defended him.

"Your offer, then?" Casmar asked, looking over at Cromwell and ignoring Mikhail, who bristled but said nothing.

"Acknowledge Mikhail as president. The army, the navy, and the industries are under my direct control as head of the confederation of Rus, Roum, and Cartha. With such a force I will play the game with the Merki, and if need be I can stab them as well if they dare to betray me."

"And how would you do that?"

"I control the *Ogunquit*, they do not. With it I control the sea, something your Keane never appreciated. As for yourself and any who wish to follow you, you may move to Vazima on the border or even to Novrod to do as you desire. You may serve us or not, but I will give all of you your lives."

Kal laughed sadly and shook his head.

"I refuse."

"The offer has been made. You know now that there is no chance whatsoever of your winning."

"I faced that before, I'm willing to face it again. I've been a free man since the Yankees helped us to throw down the boyars. I would not go back to living under you, the Merki, and especially under you," and he pointed a shaking hand at Mikhail.

"Do you have any counterterms to offer?" Casmar said quickly before Mikhail could respond.

"Only this. Get the hell out," Kal shouted, coming to his feet.

He silently cursed the priest who had searched him at the door. If he had the revolver now, injunction or not, laws or not, he would shoot the two of them as they sat there.

"We can still save ourselves," Casmar snapped, slapping the table with his fist.

Kal, shocked by the display of emotion from the normally jovial, soft-spoken priest, turned to face him.

"Talk some reason into him, your holiness," Mikhail said, grinning with a cold delight at Kal's rage.

"I'm trying to talk reason into all of you," Casmar retorted.

Kal looked over at the prelate and said nothing.

"We are all agreed that the Merki, the Tugars, whatever they call themselves, are the common foe. As people who acknowledge the healing grace of Kesus, whom even you, Tobias Cromwell, acknowledge, as do the other Yankees, we stand alone in this terrible world.

"Think what we could do united. Tobias Cromwell, keep your fleet, and let Rus add her strength to stand by your side. Mikhail Ivorovich, if there are people, be they boyars, merchants, or peasants, who wish to acknowledge you, let them go with you. Rus is a great land—surely those who believe as you do can be given a place, and given a proper share of your old wealth. The factories will serve all three together, building up our strength against the Merki if they should come. Let the free people of Rus, who were once slaves, have what they have built, which includes this city that they raised from the ashes. Do not destroy that again with your quarreling, and let Kalencka, and those who acknowledge him as their leader, have at least this. Do this thing and we can still save ourselves, for surely we are like children fighting against each other in the dust, while the dread comes down upon us all."

"And of the thousands these men have killed?" Kal asked coldly.

"They can never be brought back," Casmar said sadly, "but if we let that divide us now, all their families will die in the end, and surely as their honored spirits sit above us, they would not want such a fate to befall their loved ones merely to avenge their deaths."

Kal shook his head sadly. If Vincent was truly gone, he knew that the boy would want him to do whatever was necessary to save Tanya and the children, even if it meant denying the wrongness of how he had been slain.

Oh, Kesus, Kal prayed silently, is this all we are? Is this the reality of my hope for the Union?

He looked over at his two rivals.

"The original terms still stand," Cromwell replied. "If you do not agree, Kal, I regret to say I will shell your town into an inferno."

Mikhail laughed and came to his feet.

"Peasant, I have planned this from the beginning. You idiot, if the tables had been turned I would have hung you from the nearest tree, and you like a fool invited me into this crippled thing you call a republic."

Laughing, Mikhail stalked out of the room. Cromwell paused for a moment, looking back at Casmar as if to say something. Kal looked at him with hatred. Cromwell's eyes hardened, and he slammed the door shut behind him.

"Would you have agreed?" Casmar asked sadly.

Kal stood silent, looking at the priest.

"Would you?"

"I'd best get back to my lines," Kal said evenly. "If they return first they might fire on me as I cross the street."

Bowing low once again, Casmar slowly raised his hand in a blessing over Kal's head. Putting his hat back on, Kal opened the door, and with a sharp swift gait that conveyed his rage, he walked out of the room.

The priest who had escorted him fell in alongside. Kal said nothing, though he could see in the young man's eyes a burning curiosity to know. Crossing the nave, he hurriedly genuflected and went to the door.

"Mr. President, your gun," the priest said, shakily holding the weapon out.

Kal snatched it away.

"For the good of all of us, you should have let me keep it," he said coldly.

The priest lowered his gaze. "It was forbidden by the pledge of the church," he whispered, and stepping forward he unbolted the door. The four guards dashed across the street, the skirmish line swinging out to either side.

Kal stepped in between the men, and they started off at a run, half-carrying him along.

Barely had they stepped out into the street when a puff of smoke erupted from the bombed-out ruins of the capitol. The volley of canister swept the street, knocking a skirmisher over. One of the men pushing Kal simply let go, collapsing behind him. A sharp volley rang out from the buildings lining the opposite side of the street, screaming over Kal's head. Within seconds he reached the open doorway before him and ducked inside, the guards pushing in after him. The skirmishers to either side rushed back to the protection of the alley.

One of the guards looked back out to the street and saw his wounded comrade, the priest bent over him. A musket ball smacked the pavement by the side of the priest as he struggled to pick the man up.

"Those godless Carthas," the guard roared, and he raced back out, coming up alongside the wounded man. Together with the priest he dragged the man through the door, the air around them hot with bullets.

"Good work, soldier," Hans said, clapping the man on the back.

"These people have little respect for priests," Kal said, looking over at the white-faced man.

"On second thought, maybe I should have let you keep the gun after all," the priest gasped.

"What was the offer?" Hans asked.

Kal nodded for Hans to follow him. Pushing their way through the crowd of soldiers, they went into the back room of the house and closed the door. The senators still loyal to the republic gathered around Kal, shouting questions. He stood in silence until they finally calmed down.

"It's as we expected," Kal announced. "Surrender, or the city will be burned. Mikhail will be president, but he'll merely be Cromwell's puppet. I should add that Cromwell admitted that he has sold himself to the Merki."

"Then there's no hope," Vasilia groaned.

Kal looked around the room.

"We're going to fight it out."

"With what?" another senator replied. "Almost all our troops are holding the entrenchments around the factory.

The city's held by the militia. If the Merki, the Tugars, whatever it is they call themselves, are supporting this, we're defenseless."

"We can fight with our bare hands if need be," Kal stormed, slamming the table.

"And we'll die in the end anyhow."

"Have you all gone soft?" Kal shouted. "You've tasted freedom, and after but two years of it you are becoming weak.

"You sit in front of me and whine, 'We'll die,' " and he raised his voice to a sarcastic falsetto. "You're senators, damn you—act the part. Our people have struggled to build this country, and you, all of you, should represent what is best in them, not worst."

"He's right," Vasilia said softly. "Have we forgotten what we are?"

"We'll still lose," the second senator said. "We must face that fact. Cromwell has crippled us, for the Merki to finish."

"Like hell he has."

Startled, Kal looked up to see O'Donald standing in the doorway, cigar clenched between his teeth. O'Donald stepped back, and Kathleen came into the room. At her presence the men stood.

"Will all of you sit back down? You know I can't stand this polite foolishness at times like this."

"May I ask," Kal said softly, "why the two of you are here?"

"Oh, you mean we weren't invited," O'Donald laughed.

"Pat, you're drunk," Hans snapped.

"Hans, you know I can drink you under the table—I've proved it often enough. It takes more than I've got in me to get me drunk."

"Well, my senators," Kathleen said evenly, stepping before O'Donald to cut off the argument, "how did the meeting go?"

"The offer we figured upon," Kal replied awkwardly.

"And will you people sell out to it?" she said coldly, looking around the room.

"I'll fight to the end," Vasilia said sharply, and a nervous chorus of agreement echoed around the room.

"Well, I'm glad to hear that," Kathleen retorted. "I'm not in the condition to thrash any of you, but I'm sure as hell Andrew would if you should turn cowards now."

Kal looked over at her wide-eyed.

"I should have come here first with it," O'Donald said, going over and putting his arm around Kathleen, "but I felt her ladyship here should hear the news first."

O'Donald held up a scrap of paper.

"A telegram from water stop Bangor on the Volga River. 'Messenger from the army of Rus arrived here. Message is we are coming back. Tell Kathleen I love her.' Signed, 'Colonel Andrew Lawrence Keane.' "

"Damn that boy, I knew he'd turn up," Hans roared, slamming the table. O'Donald, grinning with delight, pulled a cigar out of his pocket, walked over to Hans, and stuck it into the sergeant's mouth.

Smiling, Hans bit the end off and started to chew. "I've been meaning to ask you. Just where the hell are you getting your tobacco?"

O'Donald smiled. "When the Carthas stopped trade last year I got suspicious, so I bought up every cigar I could lay my hands on."

"He even sent his love," Kal said quietly, looking straight at Kathleen.

Kathleen looked around the room. Her hand dropped to her stomach, and a look of pain clouded her features.

"Lassie," O'Donald cried, putting his arm around her.

"Outside," she whispered.

Kal came to his feet, rushing over to her, Hans following him. O'Donald reached down and scooped her up, carrying her out the door.

"The rest of you stay here," Hans growled, slamming the door shut behind him.

O'Donald moved swiftly down the alleyway and disappeared around a corner. Kal, pushing after him, came up short as O'Donald turned, smilingly wickedly.

"Now put me down, you oaf," Kathleen said.

"There's something more, isn't there," Hans said, leaning up against the wall and exhaling nervously.

"Well, we had to get you out of there," O'Donald replied.

"Andrew's not the type to send love notes by military telegram," Hans said quietly, "but you scared the hell out of me anyhow."

Kal looked over at Kathleen and winked.

"He had to code it," Kathleen said. "O'Donald suspected it too. There was another sentence: 'My love to our two new sons, Revere and Longfellow Keane.' "

Kal looked at Kathleen in confusion.

"But?"

"We'd never hang names like that on our boys," Kathleen said, laughing. "It took me a couple of minutes to figure it out, though. Paul Revere and Longfellow, who wrote a poem about him."

"Who are they?" Kal asked.

"One if by land and two if by sea," O'Donald said, "and I'll be damned if I remember the rest of the poem."

"It means he's coming back by sea," Kathleen said.

"How, in God's name?" Hans said. "The *Ogunquit* will blow him out of the water."

"Maybe he's making another *Ogunquit*," Kal said evenly.

"With what?" Hans replied.

"I don't know. We might have to hold out another week, or it could be months. I don't know."

Kal walked away from the group for a moment.

A flurry of explosions washed across the city, rocking the ground beneath his feet. A whistling moan passed overhead, and looking straight up, he saw a mortar shell hovering above, slowly arching its way back down.

Kal looked back at Hans even as the detonation of the shell boomed across the town.

"What's the most important thing to hold, if we want to continue the fight?" Kal asked.

"The factories, of course."

"Are they in danger now?"

"Well, it's good defensive ground surrounding them. But if they should gather all their forces in one place they might punch through."

"Suppose we put every musket and gun we have in there."

"It'd give us a better shot at it."

"Then I'm abandoning the city," Kal said forcefully.

"What?"

"We've got to be realistic. We've got a little over twelve thousand men under arms here in the city. All the rest are with the army. The rest of our manpower is spread out across all the rest of Rus, working on the farms. I wouldn't be surprised if out in the villages they don't even know there's a war on.

"We're spread too thin. This city is going to be burned out from under us anyhow. So let them have it. The warehouses are nearly empty anyhow—the harvest has yet to come in. The military supplies have all gone up with the army. If we give the city to Mikhail he'll think he's won."

"It makes some sense," Hans said dryly. "I've thought of it, but politically I never figured you could do it."

"We know he's coming. We'll put every man we have in the factories and hold out. Who knows—it will at least stop the shelling, and maybe we can capture the city back intact when the time comes."

"It means he'll turn the guns on the factories," Hans said.

"They don't have the range, and we hold the high ground around the works and the dam," O'Donald replied. "Except for those damn mortars. The buildings might get smashed up, but if we sandbag all the machines and tools they should be able to ride it out. The only thing that scares me is a direct hit on the powder mill, but if we sandbag that up and clean it out, it won't do much damage. Besides, I think he won't shell them—he wants the buildings and machines intact for his masters."

"I'm going back in there now and tell those senators we're pulling out starting tonight, and if they don't like it the hell with them," Kal said grimly.

Kal paused and looked around at his friends, a grim smile crossing his features.

"What was it your Grant said? Andrew told me and I can't remember it."

"That bastard Grant," O'Donald replied. " 'I intend to fight it out on this line if it takes all summer.' "

"That's it," Kal snapped, and sticking his hand in his pocket, he stalked back down the alleyway and back into the building.

"You know," Kathleen said with a smile, "get rid of that stovepipe hat, stick a cigar in his mouth, and I think he'd even look like the man."

Smiling, Jubadi reached out and grabbed the horse's reins. Suvatai, commander of the Vushka Umen, stunned by the singular honor thus shown to him, bowed low from the saddle before swinging down to land by the Qar Qarth's side.

"The people, do they feed well?" Jubadi asked, putting his arm around Suvatai's shoulder.

"The pasture lands have been safe. The horses give milk, the game is plentiful," and Suvatai paused.

"But?"

"There is grumbling in the tents. The last of the cattle from Han have been consumed, and they look hungrily at the Carthas that we pass. Our diet of horse flesh is repugnant."

Jubadi nodded thoughtfully.

"They will have cattle again to feast upon, but for now they must be patient."

"So they have been ordered."

"The rest of the Vushka Hush—how fare they?"

"A week past they camped with the horde, and there was happiness again for at least one night in some of the yurts. The next day, as you ordered, they pushed on. Even now they ride hard, but three days behind me."

"I will give them one day here in this cattle city, but no more."

"Is it east, then?" Suvatai asked.

"North. I will send them against the Rus."

"One umen?" Suvatai asked disbelievingly. "The Tugars sent over twenty, and look what became of them."

Jubadi laughed.

"Cattle are weak. Do you not remember the tales of our father ancestors when the Yor appeared through the tunnel of light?"

"We were all raised upon the tales," Suvatai replied with a smile. "Did not your mother threaten you with them as did mine?"

Jubadi laughed softly.

"Yet there was a lesson to be learned. For the Yor came to Valennia to dispute this land our father ancestors had claimed before them. Did not the Yor have the weapons that could kill with nothing but light a hundred times farther than the bow? And we were even weaker, for the cattle had yet to appear, bringing to us the gift of their flesh and the horses upon which we ride to replace the yurts without horses upon which our fathers rode. And yet we defeated them. For all the hordes, the Merki, the Tugar, the Bantag, even the Panor stood together, for the Yor bickered among themselves over which of them would be Qar Qarth over us, and we turned them upon themselves and then slew them.

"That is the lesson I learned from my mother, and not the fear that others might have. We have turned the cattle against themselves."

"Still, I wish," Suvatai said softly, "that I had but one of the weapons of the Yor to use against them."

Jubadi shook his head.

"They were cast into the sea. Our fathers chose well with that, and I do not wish even now for them, for we would turn such evil against ourselves. The Yankee weapons at least are different, and kill but one or two and reach but little farther than the bow. The Yor could slay a hundred. With our warrior spirits we would all die in the end. There is no honor in such slaying."

"But I have heard rumor that you violated the mound of an ancient."

"It was permitted," Jubadi snapped in reply. "You will see what it will do for us when the time comes. But don't worry about such things. The cattle have gelded themselves—they are slaying each other even now."

"Good, very good." Suvatai laughed. "But it is a shame to think of the meat they are wasting, which they will shove into the ground or leave rotting beneath the sun."

"There will be more than enough to harvest, both of Rus and of Cartha, when we are done with them," Jubadi said with a grin. "But come, I have a surprise for my commander of the Vushka Hush."

Leading the way into the tent, Jubadi stepped aside to look at the grin of delight on Suvatai's face.

"But I thought there was an injunction against cattle."

"Yet the Qar Qarth must keep up his health and that of his commanders."

Grinning, Suvatai walked up to the woman chained and gagged in the center of the room. He looked over at the brazier, glowing hot, the embers cherry-red.

He pulled the dagger out from his belt and held it up.

"Let us cut the meat slowly," he said, his teeth glinting in the firelight. "I've always enjoyed it when they see their own flesh being devoured."

Sitting by the fire, Jubadi leaned back and laughed.

# Chapter Fourteen

"Let's get her going and turn it left!" Ferguson shouted.

"Ah, excuse me, Chuck, it's ahead slow, full rudder to port," Bullfinch said, shaking his head as if repeating yet again a lesson to a child that would not learn.

"Now why the hell can't you just talk English or Rus like everyone else?" Chuck said in an exasperated tone.

"The pot calling the kettle black," Andrew said. "Chuck, half the time I don't understand a damn word you're saying."

"It's plain enough to me," Chuck mumbled under his breath.

"Just get the show on the road," Emil said, looking cautiously down the open hatchway to the two locomotive engines below deck.

"Why don't we just drop this port and starboard at least?" Andrew said. "We've got only one steam sailor in the whole crowd. All the ironclad commanders are infantrymen from the 35th, and in the heat of battle it might confuse them."

Bullfinch shock his head sadly.

"If you insist, colonel, but it goes against tradition."

"I insist, Admiral Bullfinch," Andrew said, still smiling, "Now come on, we're dying of curiosity."

"I hope that doesn't become literal," Emil sniffed.

Bullfinch uncorked the speaking tube and blew through it.

"Ahead slow, turn hard left."

A heavy blast of smoke shot up out of the twin funnels behind the gunhouse. A shudder ran through the ship. Ferguson winced as a loud clattering groan came up from below deck.

From beneath the armor-covered paddlewheels astern the water foamed. Andrew could feel the deck start to shake, and then ever so slowly the *Suzdal*, first ironclad of the Republic of Rus, turned its bow out into the Tiber River.

A wild cheer went up from the shore as the tens of thousands who had labored for the past thirty days stood in open-mouthed amazement at what they had created.

Marcus looked over at Andrew, his eyes bright.

"I never thought it possible," he shouted.

"You know something? Neither did I," Andrew replied quietly.

"Let it run down to the canal on the current," Bullfinch said. "I don't want to give her full steam in this channel. If we mess up, we might run her aground."

Sitting on top of the gunhouse, Andrew felt himself relaxing for the first time in weeks. One of the new galleys, its crew wishing to show off, swung out from the opposite shore, the water foaming as their blades bit into the river. Zigzagging in a slightly erratic fashion, the boat swung up alongside the *Suzdal* and then sprinted ahead.

"They're the ugliest ships I've ever seen," Marcus said, shaking his head.

Having lived most of his life along the coast of Maine, Andrew had to agree. He was used to the sleek clipper ships coming off the ways up in Bath and his own Brunswick. The boats looked like little more than long boxes, flattened off astern. At least the bows looked businesslike, angling in forward like a sharpened tooth. The long corvuses, suspended from a single pole, hung forward and aft, the sharpened spikes atop the boards shining evilly in the sun. The green-wood ship rode low in the water, giving little freeboard. As a last-minute measure, carpenters were cobbling in another length of planking all the way around each of the ships to provide a little extra protection. He thought of Polybius, who had described the Roman fleet built in the same manner and mentioned that by the time the Romans reached Sicily the ships were barely afloat.

"At least they float," Andrew replied.

"Barely," Emil said. "And remember, there's not one boy in ten aboard those ships who can swim a lick."

"Don't worry, Emil, we'll be running close to shore the entire route, and every soldier has a life preserver."

"A dry board," Emil said, shaking his head.

At least it's better than aboard this ship, Andrew thought. There were only three hatches up from below, one into the gunhouse, the other aft next to the ventilation shafts into the engines, and a larger one forward to take on wood. If it was rammed this ship would go down like a bullet.

"All engines stop!" Bullfinch shouted. "Helm to the left, linesman forward, prepare to take tow into the canal."

Bullfinch looked over at the circle of men who stood around him.

"Now, all of you are going to be captaining a boat like this in another day or two. We're not going to have any time for lessons. We're not even going to allow you to pilot them on the river down to the canal."

Andrew could see the looks of relief on the faces of nearly all the men.

"Remember, you've got quite a few hundred tons of mass moving along. It's the same as those railroad engines you drive. Turn the power off and she'll still keep going. In an emergency you can go into reverse, but we don't know if these ships will handle the strain, so be careful. Remember as well, you've got to keep headway—if you just float with the current you'll have no control at all.

"And another thing. You've got clear visibility standing on top of the pilothouse like this, but under fire you'll be inside the pilothouse," and he pointed to the four-foot-high projection that ran the width of the gunhouse. "It's going to be cramped in there. You'll be sitting, and sealed off from the gunhouse directly below you, except for the speaking tube. You've been inside it already. It's an oven, and you'll only be able to see the action through the two-inch-high slits. It's going to be an entire other world. I'd suggest for starters you learn to handle your ships out here like this, using the extra speaking tube installed outside. But as soon as possible, start doing all your work inside."

The captains in training, nearly all of them former railroad engineers along with the three former sailors in the 35th, nodded, most of them furiously taking notes.

Lines snaked out from shore as Bullfinch conned the ship in on the last gentle burst of speed from the engines. The galley, having dropped astern, pulled a hard maneuver, the starboard rowers backstroking while the portside rowers dug in, spinning the ship about inside its own length. The men let off a hearty cheer and then turned to race back up the river.

"They're learning pretty well," Andrew said encouragingly.

"Faster than I believed possible," Marcus replied.

"Each oar is shared by one of my men and one of yours," Andrew said. "It's a good arrangement. Our people will learn a lot from each other that way."

Marcus nodded.

"Still leery about giving them their freedom?" Andrew asked.

"When you consider the alternative," Marcus said dryly, "I had precious little choice in the matter."

"When this is all over with, we can talk about government," Andrew ventured. "I served as a military dictator for well over a year, but we made the transition to a different form."

"Your Vincent's already been lecturing me on it," Marcus said with a wry smile, nodding over to the side of the gunhouse where Vincent sat alone.

Andrew looked over at the young man. He had a gut feeling about what had happened to Vincent back in the forum. But Vincent simply did not want to talk about it, so there was little Andrew could do but wait until he opened up.

"Get those lines out here!"

Bullfinch, leaping down from the gunhouse, raced forward, Ferguson by his side, shouting imprecations at the lock operators. The deck crew worked nervously under the gaze of Bullfinch as the canal operators tossed out cables, which were secured to the *Suzdal*. Dozens of men armed with long poles that were padded at one end waded into the water, fending the boat off from the rocky side of the channel.

Shouting and swearing, Bullfinch paced the deck, leaning over the side, watching as the boat inched into the narrow confines of the lock. The teamsters on shore started to whistle and snap their whips, and the long line of oxen moved forward. The lines went taut, the oxen digging in, and then like a long spring recoiling the boat slid forward again, the lines going slack. The boat drifted down the channel at a slow walk, the cut through the rocks rising up and nearly forming a tunnel, and after fifty yards dropping away.

"This is something we never dreamed of—raising and lowering ships through closed rooms filled with water,"

Marcus said, watching as the *Suzdal* drifted past the outer lock gate, which swung shut behind the ironclad.

"I'm just glad we helped you make it last year," Andrew said. "Otherwise we'd be stuck trying to build all of this in the ruins of Ostia."

He had not sensed any movement, but already the shore seemed to be rising and the men that he had been looking down on were now at eye level, gazing at the ship with gap-mouthed amazement. On the far side of the lock he could hear the cascade rushing out. The sheer rock side of shale alongside him dripped with water that glistened with the sunlight.

After twelve feet of drop the outrush of water slowed. The lockkeeper, looking down from above, waved, and his crews swung the heavy doors open, the *Suzdal* gently flowing out with the last of the running water. Another team of oxen were waiting, lines were hooked on, and the last two hundred yards of the tow led the ironclad back out to the river, the rapids now behind them.

"All ahead slow," Bullfinch called, climbing back up onto the gunhouse. The paddles dug into the water, the shuddering vibration started to run through the ship, and as they turned into the main channel the shore to either side drifted by. To his right, Andrew could see the long line of abandoned railcars, stretched out along the rough-laid track. It was a strange sight, as if he had cast off the devices that had helped him for so long, to leave them in the growing weeds.

If this campaign fails, he thought sadly, they'll most likely stay there forever, slowly rusting and falling back into the earth that they were forged out of.

The flame-scorched walls of Ostia were passed, and he could see the grim features of Marcus as he gazed upon the ruins of what had once been his main port.

"With the canal open to Roum, you don't need to rebuild here," Andrew said. "You could put docks up on the left bank of the river across from your capital, and we could even help you build a bridge across. An arrangement like that would be a lot easier to defend in the future."

"You mean they'll be back?"

"From the looks of things, we'll be fighting them, the Merki, and God knows who else for some time to come."

"Next time I'll be ready for them," Marcus snapped.

They passed close to a bar at the south side of the channel

and left the river behind as the shoreline turned away to the right, revealing the broad open stretch of the Bay of Tiber and the Inland Sea beyond.

A light chop started to develop, and for the first time Andrew felt he was truly aboard a ship again as the deck started to roll ever so slightly beneath his feet.

"It's most likely running about two feet a bit farther out. Let's see what she can do before we get into some waves," Bullfinch said, looking around at the neophyte captains, who smiled anxiously and said nothing.

Bullfinch blew into the speaking tube.

"All engines, ahead half speed. Keep the helm steady as she goes."

"I'm going down below to keep an eye on things," Ferguson said, and with a salute to Andrew he climbed on top of the pilot house, pulled the iron lid open, and squeezed through, descending into the gun deck and from there on into the engine room below.

The vibration picked up noticeably. The water astern foamed, and the breeze from forward started to pick up. Bullfinch knelt down on the deck, putting both hands down, and after a moment looked over at Andrew.

"Pretty rough vibration for half speed. It's what I was afraid of. Over a period of time it could really start to shake things loose, spring leaks. We're going to have to be careful."

He stood up and looked astern and then faced back to the captains.

"We're sliding to port as well—the engines are nowhere in synch. With this kind of rig we'll have problems like that. You're going to have to learn how to inch your RPMs up and down on one engine or the other to keep her moving in a straight line. Remember, there's one advantage. If your rudder gets blown away, you can always steer with your screws or paddles. If you lose an engine you can use the rudder to still keep yourself going straight."

Bullfinch leaned over and blew into the tube again.

"Bring up the revolutions on the port—excuse me, you lubbers, I mean left—engine. Do it slowly and I'll tell you when to stop."

Moving over to stand directly in the middle of the ship, he watched as the slip to port gradually corrected. He raced back to the tube.

"Hold it there! Mark your gauge on the left engine. That's your half-speed setting."

Bullfinch looked back up.

"That's how you do it. It feels like we're doing a good three knots, maybe even four."

The boat cruised along for some minutes, and Andrew felt the tension start to run out of him. The damn thing was actually working!

Bullfinch edged them up to three-quarters speed, and the vibration turned into a pounding shudder. The seas started to rise a bit, and a spray of water rose up every time the *Suzdal* slammed into a wave.

A galley, one of the small twenty-oared vessels of Marcus's original fleet, came running down from farther up the channel, the crew pulling hard, the forward prow plowing up twin furrows of foamy white. The boat swung around wide with a gracefulness that spoke of practice far longer than the four weeks the army had had on the beach.

Coming in alongside, the galley kept even with the ironclad.

"Any reports from the sentries?" Marcus shouted, cupping his hands to be heard above the pulsing thunder of the ship.

"That same ship was out there again, but we chased it back over the horizon!"

Andrew breathed a sigh of relief. The picket ships had been covering the area out for nearly thirty miles. A week ago a fast Cartha galley had been sighted. They could never close with it, and it had always refused battle, retreating when the squadron approached. At least it was out of sight this morning. How much longer can we keep Cromwell in the dark? he wondered. If he should come back with the *Ogunquit*, he could plug up the canal entrance and their whole plan would be for nothing.

"There's our target!" Bullfinch shouted, pointing in toward shore.

Taking up his field glasses, Andrew saw the raft anchored several hundred yards out to sea, a large square structure built up on one side with several layers of railroad ties faced with a double row of rail iron.

"Here comes the reason we're doing this," Andrew said a bit nervously.

"I'm going down to the gun deck," Andrew announced, climbing awkwardly up on top of the pilothouse.

"You know, we're still not sure of those guns," Emil shouted.

Andrew smiled but said nothing as he inched his way down the ladder.

He paused for a moment inside the cramped pilothouse, looking straight up at the cloud-studded sky above. Taking a deep breath, he hung on with his one hand, letting his legs drop through the hatchway into the gun deck below.

He fumbled for the ladder set into the aft side of the gunhouse and then slowly made his way down to the lower deck. Once through the hatch, he stood back up, forgetting the clearance, and cursed soundly as his head slammed into the ceiling.

The men looked over at him and smiled but said nothing.

"Ready to try a shot?" Andrew asked, annoyed at himself and trying to regain his composure.

"That's what the boys have been looking forward to, sir."

Andrew smiled at O'Malley, one of the old gunners of the 44th, a battery commander now who had come back to his old job of manning a single piece.

The carronade, the first one off the line, had been proofed four days ago, almost before it had cooled from the rough improvised turning that John had worked out, from a cylinder boring machine taken out of the Hispania shop.

Andrew walked up to the weapon and looked at it appraisingly. It was a short, squat, ugly affair, lacking the grace of O'Donald's treasured Napoleons. The barrel was only four feet long. The inner tube was built up with bands of heated iron that had been wrapped around the breech for reinforcement. The outside of the barrel had not been turned, and its surface was pocked with roughnesses that were already starting to gather rust.

The weapon lacked trunnions and was secured to its crude carriage by a large ring, fashioned out of a rail and forged into the barrel underneath. Inelegant as it was, the entire affair had a deadly look nevertheless.

Andrew leaned over, looking through the forward gun port. In the narrow square he saw the target raft standing slightly off to port.

A whistle sounded next to him, and he reached over and uncorked the speaking tube.

"I'm going to steer straight at it," Bullfinch announced. "When you people are ready to fire, signal me. From then on your gun crew will swing the piece to train on the target."

"Let's try one at four hundred and see what happens," Andrew announced.

"Run out!" O'Malley shouted. The gun crew leaped to their stations and hauled in on the block and tackle so that the carronade rolled forward, the mouth of the gun barely projecting out of the port.

O'Malley crouched down behind the piece, sighting down the barrel. Grabbing a handspike, he levered the breech of the gun up.

"Pull out the quoin a notch!"

A gunner stepped forward, took hold of the heavy triangular block under the breech, and slipped it back. O'Malley nodded and let the barrel down.

"Stand clear!"

Taking hold of a linstock that was passed up to him, he stepped to one side and brought down the flaming taper attached to the end of the pole, touching the small pile of powder at the breech.

A shot of flame snapped straight up, scorching the ceiling. With a thunderclap the carronade leaped back, smoke instantly filling the entire deck.

Choking, his ears ringing, Andrew stepped in front of the gun, peering through the gun port. O'Malley shouldered up alongside him.

A fountain of water shot up a hundred yards forward of the target and more than fifty yards to the right. A chorus of groans could be heard topside.

O'Malley looked back at him sheepishly.

"Point-blank range, sir—that's what we'll have to go for."

Gasping for air, Andrew nodded.

"Load her up!" O'Malley shouted.

A gunner pulled up the hatch set in the middle of the deck. A boy stuck his head up from below and passed up a powder charge, which the gunner ran forward. The boy closed the hatch as he returned to the darkened magazine below.

The *Suzdal* continued forward, the target growing ever larger.

This was one hell of a lot slower than four-pounders, Andrew realized. A land battery could get off six or seven rounds in the time it took them to load one.

The sponging done, the powder charge was rammed in, a heavy shot was taken from a rack set into the wall, and two men lifted it into the breech, the rammer pushing the round into the bore.

The gun was finally loaded and run out again.

The target was less than a hundred yards away.

Andrew went over to the speaking tube.

"Stop the engines. I want to see what we can do up close."

The pounding from below dropped away, and the *Suzdal* drifted forward silently.

"Clear the topside," Bullfinch shouted. "We might have fragments."

There was a scurry of feet above as the men dropped over the side and ran for cover behind the gunhouse.

"All clear!" Bullfinch shouted.

The *Suzdal* was less than fifty yards from the target.

Andrew nodded to O'Malley.

"Fire!"

The gun leaped back, and even over the explosion Andrew heard a reverberating crash. Eagerly he ran up to the gun port. The raft was rocking back and forth as if ready to pitch over.

At the corner of the target he saw a tangle of rails slammed into the wood backing, the end of one sticking straight out like a broken straw.

The *Suzdal* continued to drift in.

Andrew stepped over to a side gun port and crawled out, Marcus helping to pull him through.

"It's terrifying," Marcus whispered.

Andrew ran down the length of the ship as the bow brushed past the bobbing raft.

A mist of steam was rising off the smashed-in side. The bent rails were twisted in, and the two in the middle that had absorbed the brunt of the impact were snapped in half.

The *Suzdal* floated past the raft, and its back side came into view.

Several of the crossties were buckled inward, huge cracks laced the timbers, and a light shower of splinters lay across the raft and floated in the water beyond.

"It didn't punch through," Andrew said, his voice displaying his disappointment.

"Well, thank God for that," Emil said. "Remember that's a model of our armor."

"Suppose his is the same?" Andrew replied. "And don't forget we've got carronades—he's got long guns that punch a hell of a lot harder."

"It's too late to change it now," Emil said. "We're planning a sea fight, and he wasn't—his armor could be a lot thinner."

"We can always increase the powder charge and use the wrought-iron bolts," Bullfinch said.

"That's risking the guns and the crews," Andrew replied. "We don't have a weapon to spare to proof out the heavier loads."

"We might have to use them anyhow," Marcus replied.

Andrew nodded absently, and forced a smile.

"It'll do the job," he said encouragingly, looking back at the novice captains. "Now let's take her back in. Bullfinch, put her up to full speed. I'm going belowdecks."

Andrew walked astern, passing the gun turret. The two smokestacks were still billowing white plumes, and as he stepped past the air vents he felt the sharp downward rush of air into the boilers, drawn by rough fans powered by pulleys.

Reaching the aft hatchway, he took a deep breath and went below.

The boilers to either side of him were shimmering with heat. The dark, smoke-filled confines were like a furnace. Before he was halfway down, huge leather belts to either side started to move slowly, picking up speed. A loud incessant chatter rumbled through the engine room, counterpointed by the gasping bellow of the steam engines and the hissing whine of the drive belts. Reaching the deck, Andrew felt as if he had taken a bath; his uniform was already soaking.

Ferguson came up out of the stygian darkness illuminated only by the light from the open fireboxes and several dim lamps.

"I thought the gun deck was hell," Andrew shouted.

"That's just the front porch of purgatory up there," Ferguson shouted. "Now you're in hell."

A whistle shrieked, and Ferguson uncorked the voice tube and put his ear to it.

"Ahead full," Ferguson roared.

Andrew looked over as the engineers, stripped to the waist and standing to either side of their now wheelless locomotives, slowly pushed their throttles forward. The firemen standing behind them were throwing in more wood.

The sound started to climb, and Andrew looked around nervously. Driveshafts slammed in and out, spouting steam; the leather belts, hooked onto wooden wheels turned by the shafts, hummed and shrieked. Looking up, Andrew saw the belts disappear up either side of the ship into wells set into the stern, where the driveshafts for the twin paddle wheels were set.

"Hang on!" Ferguson roared.

The heat started to climb, and the thunderous pounding slammed into Andrew like hammer blows. He felt as if the world were shaking apart.

The whistle sounded again, barely audible.

Ferguson leaned in and then turned, cupping his hands.

"Raskov, helm hard left. Charlie, throttle your engine back a notch."

Between the two engines Andrew saw a short Suzdalian soldier spinning a steering wheel which was hooked into the rudder by two heavy ropes.

The ship started to heel over.

"Just what the hell is Bullfinch doing?"

At the same time he noticed a distinctive up-and-down motion start to take over. Terrified that he would fall into the belts, he staggered forward, grabbed a heavy wooden upright, and hung on for dear life, desperately trying to hide the fact that he was scared half out of his wits.

"Straighten the helm!"

Raskov nodding and with a half-terrified grin spun the wheel back, and Andrew felt the heeling ease off. But now the up-and-down motion became even more pronounced.

Sweat was pouring off him in puddles, and he felt his stomach start to tighten.

A loud shriek cut through the engine room, and Andrew looked up.

"It's the belt on the right side," Chuck shouted. "It's slipping—we'll have to tighten it. Throttle it back to half speed!"

Chuck stepped closer, looking into Andrew's face.

"I think you'd better go topside, sir!"

Still hanging on to the post, Andrew looked aft to the narrow catwalk between the whirling belts. The deck rose up and then dropped away again.

"Where's the other way out of here?" Andrew gasped.

"Hey, Harry, take over the watch!" Ferguson shouted, as he grabbed hold of Andrew's arm. "Come on, sir."

Leading the way, Ferguson started forward, walking between huge piles of wood. In the dim light Andrew saw several men laboring to haul the split wood aft, feeding the voracious appetite of the boilers. Reaching a heavy door, Chuck pulled it open and guided Andrew through, then pulled it shut behind him. The thundering of the engines dropped away, but the intense heat was still there. A dim light from a single candle, sealed into the wall and framed with glass, was the only illumination inside the narrow coffinlike room.

"Powder room's on the other side of the door," Ferguson announced. "We built this double-door system in case a spark might be floating around from the engines.

"You mean if something goes wrong the only way out for the men aft is either up between the engines or through this narrow doorway?" Andrew whispered.

"That's about it, sir—we didn't have time for anything beyond that. There are openings on either side of the powder magazine that lead up to the forward wood storage and quarters, but that's the long way out.

"If we get rammed aft or a shot takes us below the waterline, we won't need the escape hatches anyway. The moment that cold water hits the boilers, it'll flash to steam. If a boiler gets ruptured, everything inside will come pouring out." His voice trailed off and he shrugged his shoulders.

Ferguson said it so matter-of-factly that Andrew could only stare at him. He leaned closer, looking up into Andrew's face.

"Come on, sir, I think we'd better get you topside quick."

He pounded his fist on the next door, and a moment later it swung open and the powder boy peered out at them.

"Coming through!" Ferguson announced as he half-carried Andrew through the doorway.

He could feel the deck swaying beneath him. In the dim glow of the single candle locked behind glass, Andrew saw the stacked pile of powder, each canvas-wrapped charge sealed inside a wooden bucket. The room was barely larger than a closet. There was a sour smell in the room, and the powder boy's face was a dull green.

"Get me out quick!" Andrew gasped.

Ferguson reached over and blew into the speaking tube up to the gun deck.

"All flame secure?" he shouted. "All right, open that damn hatch—I'm bringing the colonel up."

The doorway above flew open and O'Malley looked down, his hands reaching into the darkness. Andrew grabbed hold of the ladder and tried to step up, but with the rolling of the ship, after the first couple of steps up he found he simply couldn't let go with his one hand to grasp the next rung.

"My God, I'm in hell," he groaned.

"Hang on, sir," O'Malley said. Andrew could sense the slightest touch of amusement in the artilleryman's voice.

Leaning into the hatch, O'Malley grabbed hold of Andrew's wrist.

"I've got you, sir. Come on up."

With trembling legs, Andrew half climbed and was half lifted out. On the gun deck, the air which he had thought was so damn hot hit him like a cold shower.

"Look out!" Andrew gasped as he raced for the starboard gun port. He stuck his head out the hole, and everything came tumbling up in one convulsive heave.

"Goddamm it, you idiot, watch where you're puking!"

Groaning, Andrew looked up.

"Even though I'm a doctor, I still hate it when someone pukes on my good shoes."

"Well, look out," Andrew gasped as the next wave hit.

"Haven't got your sea legs yet?" Emil said with a bemused voice.

"Shut the hell up," Andrew groaned as the convulsion passed and he collapsed forward, half in, half out of the gun port.

"Come on, son, let's get you out of there. You're a pitiful sight."

Struggling feebly, Andrew tried to crawl through the gun port, until O'Malley pushed him from behind and he slid down onto the still-rolling deck. Disgusted with himself, Andrew came up to his knees realizing he had landed in his breakfast.

From either side of the gun turret, he saw a crowd looking at him.

"Goddammit, don't all of you have something better to do?" he roared.

The deck cleared in an instant, but from the other side of the turret he could hear whispered laughter.

"Jesus Christ," Andrew sighed, standing up and leaning against the armored siding.

Emil, shaking his head, pulled out a handkerchief, and, started to wipe Andrew's face.

"You're a hell of an infantryman, but you'll never make a sailor," Emil said, chuckling and shaking his head.

"Emil, it was hell down there. It must have been a hundred and fifty degrees."

"Well, I heard in the old *Monitor* it'd get up to a hundred and ninety."

"Anyone who signs aboard an ironclad must be insane."

"Somebody's got to do it," Emil said. He went over to the side and rinsed out the handkerchief.

Like a father worrying over a sick child, Emil unsnapped Andrew's uniform and helped him out of his wool jacket, vest, and shirt. With a look of mock disgust, he tossed them into the gun port.

The cool wind hit Andrew with a shock, and he started to shake.

"Let's get you around aft out of the breeze."

Putting a solicitous arm around Andrew, Emil walked him back around the turret and helped him sit down. At his approach the men who had been gathered there drew respectfully around to the port side. Kneeling alongside Andrew, Emil rubbed the back of his head with the handkerchief.

"How the hell am I supposed to lead a battle when I don't dare go belowdecks?"

"You're the general, the admiral, whatever you want to call yourself. Men like you stay topside and strut around in your dress uniform. Let the boys who can handle it work below."

"I've never led like that before," Andrew sighed. "I've always done what I expected the lowest private to do."

"Some things you just can't do, Andrew. This one will be different. There's no charging line, with you running out front. Hell, I've always thought you were a madman for fighting like that anyway. You're lucky you only lost this," and reaching over, Emil patted the stump of Andrew's left arm.

"Ever since I signed on with the 35th I was always afraid you'd be carried in dead on me some day. There weren't many colonels who survived more than one or two fights doing what you did."

Andrew smiled weakly.

"And I was usually scared half to death," he whispered. "But it's the only way I knew. I'd be terrified and I'd see that same terror in some young boy's eyes, like Vincent's when he first fought, and I had to try to take that terror away from him."

"And you always won."

"Even at Gettysburg," Andrew said absently. "The arm was worth it for what we did there."

"Don't worry, you'll do all right in this one too."

"I damn near pass out and then throw up, and we're in a near-flat calm sea. Suppose the ocean's kicking up when we meet him? I'll be puking my guts out. And another thing. I got inside that closed-in turret, the heat was damn near maddening, and I couldn't stand it. The thought of fighting from in there is terrifying.

"I'll be cut off from all my men, the 35th will be scattered across all these ships, and I won't be able to see them, to look into their eyes, to know what they are thinking, and to judge from that whether they can stand what I want them to do."

He paused for a moment.

"I don't know a goddam thing about ship fighting, and Cromwell knows everything."

"Ah, son, so that's it as well," Emil said, sliding down to sit alongside his old friend.

"Checkmate," Andrew whispered. "So far he's beaten me at every turn. He's forcing me to fight him on the one field where he'll hold all the pieces. Even against the Tugars I had a good idea of how they'd fight. After a while I felt as if I could even get inside the head of their general, that gray-coated one."

The deck rose up and then dropped away, and Andrew groaned.

"This, this is all a mystery."

"It's just something new," Emil said quietly, leaning over to wipe Andrew's face again. "You've got Bullfinch, and thank God he came over to us from Cromwell. He'll be aboard with you. The boy's a good one, a bit high-strung perhaps, but I think he'll hold together.

"And you've got Marcus as well. Remember, there'll be nearly a hundred galleys behind us, and he's grim-faced for vengeance. The boys will fight all right when the time comes."

Emil stood up and leaned over.

"The same way you will, son."

A loud cough followed by a deliberate clearing of a throat came from around the side of the turret.

"Give me a hand up, doc," Andrew whispered.

Emil leaned over and pulled him up.

"Do I look all right?"

"A bit green," Emil said, shaking his head. "And lord, you do smell, but otherwise you're all right."

Emil stepped away and walked over to the side of the turret and nodded.

Bullfinch peeked around the corner.

"Sorry to disturb you, sir,"

"It's all right, Bullfinch. What is it?"

"Just wanted to report, sir, we're getting back into the river."

Andrew looked up and saw the bar had been passed and the shoreline was closing in. Suddenly he noticed that the rolling had dropped away.

"It did get a bit rough out there, sir," Bullfinch said.

"How rough?"

"Oh, maybe three feet or so."

Andrew shook his head.

"Boy, I'm from Maine, I've stood on the shore and seen men sail in fifteen-foot seas. But thanks anyhow."

"Well, sir, this certainly isn't the Atlantic. You'll get your sea legs in a day or two. Besides, in this tub I wouldn't want to try anything much beyond six feet at the most."

"Thanks," Andrew said woodenly. "Now how did we do?"

"Ferguson said we're really slipping the belt on the starboard engine. She shakes like hell at anything over quarter speed. I figure though at half speed we were running at just under four knots. If we keep it at that setting we should be able to reach Suzdal in just under six days. Since the galleys are going to have to row all that distance, it should match up all right."

"You did well, son," Andrew said, reaching out to pat Bullfinch on the shoulder.

"Thank you, sir." Bullfinch beamed.

"Emil, tell the rest of the men to come back here. Bullfinch, pilot the ship in."

The boy drew up and snapped off a salute, and with chest

puffed out he scrambled up the outside ladder to the pilot-house above.

The men started to file back, looking at Andrew cautiously.

Andrew felt somehow naked without his uniform jacket on and his shirt off. He had always been embarrassed by his pale, narrow chest, with ribs showing, and suddenly he felt extremely self-conscious. He saw that more than one of the men were sneaking looks at the stump of his left arm, which had been cut off just above the elbow. His right hand slipped up to cover it for a moment, and he saw the men avert their eyes. Drawing himself up, he let the hand drop.

"Colonel Mina, what's our situation?"

"Eleven ironclads are outfitted, with all stores aboard. The boilers have been run up and brief tests have been run in the river.

"Seven are having the finishing touches put in now. They're just waiting for the guns to be mounted so we can seal off their turrets. They'll be ready over the next two days.

"The last three are doubtfuls, colonel. The hull cracked on one of them and it's leaking like a sieve, the second is so out of balance I'm afraid she'll roll right over, and an engine on the third one was mounted in the wrong position. We're going to have to rip the deck off, hoist it up, and reset it. It might be ready in five days—if so it'll sail and try and catch up."

"The galleys?"

"Number seventy-two was coming off the ways as we left. We'll finish twenty-eight more over the next two days—eight more than originally planned for, but we had the extra parts. Stores are being loaded aboard the ships as we finish them."

"Thanks, John. As always you make miracles look commonplace."

"You can thank Ferguson and Bullfinch," John replied. "I'm just logistics. They're the ones who figured out how to do it."

Andrew nodded and looked over at the novice captains.

"Gentlemen, tonight we'll start to run the rest of the ironclads down the canal, and you'll anchor them along the ruins of the Ostia port. There'll be teams of galleys to tow you, since I'm not trusting any of you to run these ships in the river. You're going to be on your own. I'm giving you one day to practice with your ships out past the bar. Again you'll be towed out and then back in. Shake them down and find out how to handle them and also to repair anything that goes wrong.

"Now don't go busting anything," Andrew said, forcing a smile, and the men laughed nervously.

"Because if you do, it means you're going to be left on the beach," he said forcefully, "and I'll have one less ship. One ship might mean all the difference when we finally meet Cromwell."

The smiles were gone from the men.

"We sail for Suzdal in three days."

Crawling back down behind the stand of bushes, the scout slipped into the hole he had fashioned for himself, pulling some loose branches down around him.

The last patrol had been close, far too close. If one of the men walking through the low dunes had not turned aside to relieve himself, surely they would have stumbled right over him.

The scout smiled at the memory.

Why the hell they were doing all of this was beyond him. The only sense he could see in it all was that at least his family would not face the feasting pits of the Merki. At least now he could leave this place once night fell and run the long miles down the beach to the place of rocks. When the Wheel of Heaven reached its highest place in the night sky the galley would be there again. With the news he had of the ship that looked like the devil devices Cromwell had made, perhaps now they could go back to the Rus city.

He smiled at the thought of the loot to be taken there, and slipping deeper into his hole, he went to sleep.

# Chapter Fifteen

"It is good to feel the fresh wind on one's face again," Tamuka said softly, looking up at the pine trees that swayed gently with the night breeze.

"The ship of the cattle is a hellish place," Hulagar replied. "Such things were never meant for such as us."

"And yet we need them now," Tamuka said, stretching his long limbs with a groan. Sitting down, he leaned back against the trunk of a tree and looked back across the river. The city was quiet tonight, the lights darkened so that it looked as if it were inhabited only by ghosts.

Why was it that cattle chose to live thus, clustered together in stinking hovels, hidden behind walls, living with their own stench? The endless steppe of Valennia held such beauty when the rolling hills of winter turned scarlet with the sunrise as if the world were afire, or when the twilight settled across the encampments and the voices of the chanters rose to the everlasting heavens as the first light of the night appeared in the cloudless sky. How could cattle live so, when the grass of the vast fertile plains of Constan rose as high as a horse's head, so that when they rode it appeared as if the umens were but floating effortlessly through the green waves?

Or when the mark of a circling had been completed and the roof of the world rose up out of the endless plains, when Barkth Num, the place where the spirits of the ancestors could touch the world, first appeared, a tiny sliver of white rising up out of the endless sea of green, when still ten days' ride away.

How could these cattle live, Tamuka wondered, without

ever having gazed upon the things that he had seen? His thoughts turned to the day he rode alone into the high sacred hills of Barkth, yet still a quarter circling away, where the fires of the sky danced between the peaks, the rocky bare teeth of the world jutting to the heavens.

He smiled at the memory of the fear within when first he had approached the sacred place, for it had been his passage time, when all who had been born in the previous circling and could wield bow and lance went alone to dwell for thirty days in the high mountains, to fast and seek their ka, the inner spirit of the warrior. Smiling, he remembered the night of fire in the sky, the ancestors riding above in glory, sweeping across the endless heavens, the manes of their horses flickering and dancing, their arrow shafts streaking down with a fiery light. It was on that night that they had granted him their talisman, the fiery light dropping down, striking the high ice-clad mountains with their light. By the glow of the fire he had climbed in the night, finding the still-warm fragments of their arrow.

Reaching under his leather armor, he felt the small pouch of tanned cattle hide, the talisman safely locked within.

Hulagar, sitting beside him, smiled.

"Thinking of Barkth?"

Though Tamuka was nearly a circling younger than himself, still Hulagar looked upon the young shield-bearer with a certain awe. The mark of the ancestors had been granted to him. He had been chosen as a shield-bearer before his twelfth spring, the year before they had at last returned to the high mountains, the place where according to the chanters the ancestors had first come to Valennia ten thousand circlings ago.

"In another five years we'll be there again," Tamuka replied with a smile. "It will be strange to see it again, the roof of the world, the place of rest."

"I had often prayed I would look upon it once more," Hulagar replied, "to perhaps be honored among the honored and to have my bones rest there, rather than to be scattered across the endless sea of grass."

"Hulagar, you talk foolishness. Perhaps in the circling to come, when we return once more, and your coat is gray, perhaps then."

"Our world is changing," Hulagar sighed.

"The war with the Bantag? It is but a passing thing,"

Tamuka replied. "It has always been thus, but it will pass. Yes, it is true they press us now. My sire would chant to me of the days of his youth when the Bantag were cast down by Gorgath, the grandsire of Jubadi, and the steppe was red with their blood. So it has always been. A circling ago it was the Tugars who pressed us as well—even I have memory of our defeat at Orki. And now the Tugars are but beggars."

"At the hands of cattle they were made such," Hulagar replied. "Over there, before that city, they were destroyed, and now you and I hide in the shadows of night and gaze upon that accursed place where cattle cast down brothers of the horde."

"You sound fearful," Tamuka whispered.

"I am fearful," Hulagar admitted.

Tamuka looked over at the shield-bearer of the Qar Qarth and nodded respectfully. No warrior would ever admit his fear, not even to his own ka. Yet Hulagar was a shield-bearer, as was he, trained by the small circle of his brotherhood to look for a truth within even when the truth created words that would bring scorn from others. For how else was a Qar Qarth to be guided in his limitless power, unless one rode by his side who could clearly see all things?

"Speak to me of your fear," Tamuka said, turning to face Hulagar.

"There was a great change in our clans, a hundred and fifty circlings ago," Hulagar started, half speaking, half chanting his words, so that Tamuka shivered, for it was a sign that a spirit had entered Hulagar and was guiding his words.

"For we knew that the tunnel of light, the path of the ancestor gods, those who walked between the stars, reached beyond to many places. Things that were strange to us would suddenly appear, things that would shrivel and die under the light of our sun. Yet other things such as the Ewa who walk like us and are the cattle of the Pao beyond the Bantag realm, or the dreaded Yor, whom we cast down. Strange plants, the fruit of the Desar, the very trees of this great forest, these things came to us. And the cattle would come as well, always the cattle. Yet all were the same yet different, coming it seemed from many places, but we did not know these things, for we of the horde dwelled in Barkth, chanting for the return of our ancestor gods, who left us here ten thousand circlings ago."

Tamuka nodded at Hulagar's words, for thus was the

fabric of the songs sung in the evening before the fires, the women and children of the horde sitting about the circles, the warriors standing behind their kin.

"And then came the cattle that brought us the horse, the sacred gift sent by the ancestor gods, and we took this gift and rode forth upon the endless circling of the world, freeing ourselves, forever riding toward the sun, our eyes searching ever forward, to search for the path to the stars, to bring the world of Valennia into our hands as we came to know what was our birthright. No longer did we grub in the dirt for our food, for the ancestors had sent us the cattle. They had sent us all that we desired, hearing our prayers, the horse for our strength, the cattle to be our servants and food.

"They set us free."

Hulagar sighed, his eyes closed, and Tamuka could see the spirit still lingered within, and patiently he waited.

"I hear a voice of fear whispering in the wind," Hulagar sighed.

Tamuka felt the hair of his body prickle, and he let it pass through him, for he was a shield-bearer, one who must look within, and he did not retreat from Hulagar's words.

"The cattle have changed," Hulagar sighed. "The balance of the world has tumbled down. The Visu, the bird that sings, now devours the hunters of the air, the mouse leaps upon the throat of the fox. The cattle are changing, and we must become like them, and they are becoming like us. The balance is dropping away. Our ancestors who ride the sky look down in fear, they call to us in warning, for here is the placing of ending forever. The joy of the everlasting ride, the freedom of all that we are, it is slipping away into the night. We come back to Barkth, and will we ever ride again in innocence?"

Hulagar fell silent.

The screech of a night hawk cut through the air, and Hulagar stirred, opened his eyes, and looked over at Tamuka.

"We are all fools if we think we can put away such things as that," and he motioned toward the *Ogunquit* anchored in the middle of the river.

"Then annihilate all the cattle," Tamuka said dryly, "so that not one of them is left alive to remember such things. At least then we will eat well for a season or two. When next we circle this way, we can bring new cattle from other lands. There are far too many of the Constan already—let us drive a million of them east to bring back these lands. We did such things in our past, moving great herds of them, placing them around the world to do our bidding."

"Two years ago, the infection was only here," Hulagar said, pointing back across the river. "If the Tugars had not been such fools, they could have ended it, and we would not even be aware.

"Now there are three people of the cattle who know how to make machines, machines we do not understand. No, Tamuka, this knowledge will spread like a fire before us. Think you—if you were a cattle, how would you feel if rumor came that we could be so easily slain?"

"To think like a cattle is loathsome," Tamuka said evenly.

"Yet you are a shield-bearer—you must learn to think like all creatures to serve your Qarth."

Tamuka hesitated.

"To think like a cattle, Hulagar? I must strip away all that I am, to no longer know that I am the chosen of my ancestors, the destined masters of the never-ending steppe. That alone I can walk into a cattle dwelling and choose who will be taken for my table to nourish my kin. That alone I could walk among ten thousand of them and they would tremble at my presence, and if I commanded all would bare their throats to my blade."

Tamuka's face wrinkled with disgust.

"How can they bear to live?"

"Yet they think, they feel, they cry pitifully when we lead their kin to our pits," Hulagar said evenly. "Therefore they can hate us, and yes, they can even dream of what they can do to us if but given the means."

"I think more for the feelings of my horse than for them," Tamuka replied.

"As do I," Hulagar replied. "My horse is the companion of my ka, destined to ride with me in the ancestor world. Cattle are but nourishment for my stomach, destined to feed me in the next world as well.

"But cattle now make weapons, horses do not. Across this great world they are as numberless as the stalks of grass. Ten times our number, a hundred times our number perhaps. The knowledge that was bred in that city will leap out."

"I have heard," Tamuka said, "that when those in that city thought they were to be defeated, Muzta Qar Qarth still offered them quarter, that the required number would be taken for the pits, and the others could still live as they always had."

"And they refused," Hulagar said forcefully. "Their leader, Keane, said they would all die rather than continue living under the yoke. I have heard that too.

"That is our thinking, Tamuka. That would be our response if the world were truly turned about, and the cattle came riding to our gates. We would all die rather than to submit to their indignity.

"They now have the dream to defeat us, and they now have the means as well. We could slaughter all of them, and yet the Wanderers, whom we can never catch, will carry the word, will carry the knowledge as well, as they already do with those who stopped the pox sickness. It is impossible to stop now."

Tamuka stood up and walked down to the bank of the river and looked across to the city. A flash of light lit the sky. From farther up the river a trail of fire rose into the heavens, cutting an arc across the midnight sky. It seemed to hover for a moment and then ever so slowly dropped downward, moving ever faster, and then disappeared. There was a flash of light, and long seconds later a dull thunder rolled back across the river.

"We must learn all there is to be learned from them," Tamuka said forcefully, looking back into the shadows where Hulagar still sat. "We must learn to fashion with our own hands the weapons they have, and not just trick cattle into forging these things for us."

"The world we have known for countless circlings will be no more then," Hulagar replied.

"Then it will be no more."

"My Qar Qarth plans to use these cattle weapons against the Bantag."

"Foolishness."

"Why?"

"It is they who are the enemy," Tamuka said, pointing to the city. "All of us are threatened by what they are. Let the cattle slaughter cattle, but why must Merki slay Bantag?"

"For it is how we have always shown that we are warriors, it is the reason we ride, the reason we live. That is what war is for, to drive our enemies, to feel our ka exalt at their lamentations."

"The cattle have discovered war as well, Hulagar shield-bearer. But for them it is to destroy us. Glory is meaningless. All must be made to see that truth, that the very reason for war has changed forever until we cleanse this strange thinking from our world."

"I have noticed something, though," Hulagar replied. "Where do the machines that kill, that ride upon water without wind, that we have heard even move without horses across dry land—where do these things come from?"

"The buildings they call factories," Tamuka responded. "Why?"

"Buildings do not move. If we wish to make these things, we must make these buildings and the machines that make machines and labor ourselves within them."

The reasoning of Hulagar stunned him; with a heart full of bitterness he looked back at the city.

Is that our doom? he thought with loathing. To live we must become like that, no longer ride with the wind in the face, but labor before the hot fires the cattle have created. To fashion with one's hands rather than to draw the bow with one's strength.

"And think upon this as well.

"I saw the first cannon that the Yankees created, the one they traded to the Carthas for their metal to make more such things. It was small—the barrel could almost be lifted by one warrior. Now they make new ones, ones that it would take the strength of fifty to lift, that can strike down walls, can slay like the one that just shot so far away one cannot even see his foe.

"These cattle are cunning. The one Keane makes a weapon, then Cromwell makes one even stronger.

"I suspect, even," he added, "that when this Keane returns he will have weapons even more powerful. I have seen the sacred bows of the Qar Qarth hidden within the holy yurt, bows held by sires a hundred circlings ago. They are all the same. It is not so with the Yankee weapon makers. They will continue to change things even as we change."

"I told you of the new thing that I saw in the Cartha city," Tamuka said hopefully. "It contains even a device of our most ancient ancestors in it."

"Perhaps for the moment it will help us," Hulagar said, "but the Yankees will forge something in reply."

Tamuka felt his senses reeling with all that he was now contemplating. If they were using something taken from the barrow of an ancient found upon the endless steppe, what might they not find upon the roof of the world, the sacred place where the ancestors had dwelled for countless generations? What might they find there to save themselves? he wondered.

All that would have to be done if they were to survive. And he realized as well that he was a shield-bearer, trained to such thinking. How would the Qarths of the clans receive such things? How would the warriors who thought only with their ka react if told to think such things? How would the Zan Qarth, who would lead his people to such new things, react as well?

That, after all, he realized, would be his greatest task. The responsibility of all that he was tasked to do was now clear.

"I understand why you have made me consider this," Tamuka said, looking back at Hulagar with admiration.

"The Qar Qarth is the noblest of Qarths," Hulagar replied. "He has led since Orki, he has held back the strength of the Bantag with his cunning. The ka of the shield-bearer could never do such a thing—that is why he is the Qar Qarth and such as we are not. Yet I fear he will not truly understand all that needs to be done for our people.

"Though Jubadi did not see all these other reasons, nor, I think, could he ever understand them, I believe Mantu will. There is, it seems, a touch of our thinking in him. His ka was never as strong, but we need one now who beyond having the cunning of a true warrior must have the ability to heed our words as well."

Hulagar stood up and walked down to join Tamuka.

"Vuka could never be the one."

"The injunctions still must be obeyed," Tamuka sighed. "Mantu has been chosen. It is a shame about Kan—he could have served as well. I must ensure that Vuka's spirit will ride in peace. The ancestors would surely turn away from us if his spirit went to them in disgrace."

"Let us hope you can choose the time soon."

Tamuka nodded, his spirit burdened by what he must do, and by the understanding now of all that it meant. He sensed that the crisis would soon be upon them, that somehow the one called Keane would return. Perhaps it would be there, perhaps it would be when the long-awaited umen arrived at last to secure this place. He would know when it was time.

"At least I hope to again see the Barkth," Hulagar sighed, "and then I shall be content. Perhaps it is as I fear, and I will have ridden upon the last circling. Then it will be your concern, my friend, for we will need your guidance of the Qar Qarth if we are ever to ride again.

"We should go back to the ship," he said.

Hulagar walked over to the small boat and climbed in. Tamuka walked up to the craft, jumped in, and grabbed hold of the oars. Pushing against the bottom, he edged the boat out into the river and started to paddle.

"We were not made for water." He laughed softly as the boat spun around and on a ragged zigzag course started back to the *Ogunquit*.

"I think it's time that we left," Jim Hinsen said quietly, looking around at the weary Cartha soldiers and Jamie's pirates gathered on the deck of the galley.

"We've still got several hundred men spread out on the plains, and some of them are my lads," Jamie objected. "And you want to leave them behind?"

"I think what we've got here is far more important," Hinsen snapped.

He motioned to the midsection of the ship. Tied down and firmly secured rested the locomotive that had broken down near the Kennebec bridge and was left behind. The ship had a decidedly uneasy feel to it with so much weight riding above the waterline. It was going to be tricky bringing her home, but he could well imagine the reaction of the Merki when he presented them with such a thing to take apart and use. After thirty days of playing cat and mouse with Kindred, he knew the game was up. They had laid a secured line all the way to the bridge and even now were forcing track out on the other side. The last raid to try to delay them had been a disaster; Kindred had outsmarted him and had ambushes set up several miles out from the line. He had lost nearly fifty men in that one, and he'd be damned if he was going to be shot at and killed in the middle of some godforsaken tract of wasteland.

Yet he could come back the hero nevertheless, for after all, it would be he who reported all that they had done against the ten thousand Yankees arrayed against him.

"They've tricked us," Hinsen said, using his most persuasive tone. "They're coming by sea—you heard the messenger. If we stay here, they'll bottle us up in the river and wipe us out."

Jamie fell silent, looking at Hinsen warily.

"I have good friends back out there," someone from the back of the group snarled.

"Then if you want, go back out there and join them."

Leaning back against the cabin door, he watched them closely, gauging their reactions.

"We can be home to Cartha in seven days," Hinsen said. "Back with your families, the first soldiers to return as heroes."

"And the others?"

"I promise you, they'll be rescued. If we don't leave now, none of us will get out. Keane will surely stop here and come up the river to find us. Then our friends will truly be trapped."

"Back to Cartha?" Jamie said craftily. "Why not to Suzdal?"

"Would you rather go to Suzdal or home?" Hinsen asked softly.

The men looked at each other, and he saw the hopeful smiles on some of their faces.

"We leave within the hour," Hinsen announced, and without waiting for a response he stepped into the small cabin at the stern of the ship and closed the door, and as he did so he finally let a smile cross his features.

Reaching under his bunk, he pulled out a bottle of Cartha wine. He uncorked it and drained off a long drink. If Keane really was coming by sea, there could only be one of two results.

If Cromwell wins, I will still merely be in his shadow, he thought. But if he should lose . . . Lifting the bottle, he took another long swallow, then lay back, looked at the ceiling, and smiled.

"Battery, fire salute!"

The carronade below deck kicked off with a hollow thump, and a wreath of smoke punched out from the turret below his feet.

Andrew shook his head. It was a rather pathetic salute for Marcus, but every ounce of powder was precious and it was all he was going to get.

From atop the mainmast of Marcus's flagship the purple

standard bearing the eagle dropped down in reply and then was hoisted back up. The galley swept past. With its experienced crew it seemed virtually to fly across the water, the men digging their oars in and lifting them in unison.

"It looks good, real good," Emil said.

"You know, Emil, when I first read Polybius's accounts of the rise of the Roman Empire, the wars with Carthage always held me the most," Andrew replied. "I always rooted for the Carthaginians, though."

"How come? They were a terrible people," Emil replied.

"Oh, I don't know. Perhaps because they were the underdogs, perhaps because of what the Romans finally did to them in the Third Punic War. How could I ever have imagined I'd be caught in the same type of conflict?"

"There is one difference, though," Emil said. "We have the Merki, they didn't."

"Here come our boys," John said, pointing to the first galley clearing the bar.

Andrew watched appraisingly. The ship definitely did not have the trim or agility of the *Roum*, Marcus's flagship. It tended to drift to port ever so slightly on each stroke, but Andrew could sense the enthusiasm of the crew as they came racing past, the men cheering the group assembled on the *Suzdal*. Andrew snapped off a sharp salute and then took off his hat and waved.

It seemed that a virtual explosion of galleys was pouring out of the roadstead in front of Ostia. The water foamed with the passage of the ships.

"It's gonna be hell sorting all of them out once they clear the harbor," Andrew said, shaking his head. The galleys had been divided up into units of ten, a Roum ship captain commanding each of them.

"We'll have five days to do it in," Bullfinch replied. "The voyage over there will be a good shakedown cruise for all of us."

"Let's just hope the damn things float," Emil replied.

"Ah, always the pessimist, aren't we, doctor," Mina retorted.

"In my business you learn to be. Good God, I'll most likely be treating twenty thousand sets of blisters come nightfall. It's too bad that wind doesn't shift around to one side or the other so we could at least use the sails."

As the last of the galleys passed, a puff of smoke appeared behind the bar, and inching its way out, the ironclad *Republic of Rus* came into view, commanded by Dimitri, whose only former experience on water had been piloting a small trading vessel up and down the Neiper. The ship had a strange dark menace to it, the largest of all the ironclads at nearly six hundred tons. Its blockhouse was a third again as big as the *Suzdal*'s and contained two of the precious carronades. the twin stacks billowed a spark-studded shower of smoke. The built-up armor protection around the paddle wheels gave the vessel the appearance of some strange hump-backed creature gliding across the water. A raft piled high with firewood bobbed behind the ship, containing the extra hundred cords of fuel necessary to see them through to Suzdal.

From atop its pilothouse, the burned, shot-torn standard of the 5th Suzdal fluttered in the breeze.

"The old 5th," Andrew said softly as the ship chugged past, Dimitri standing atop the pilothouse and saluting smartly.

"That regiment will rival the 35th if someone ever writes a history of all we've done," Ferguson whispered.

Surprised at Ferguson's sudden turn to history, Andrew looked over at him and smiled.

Behind the *Republic of Rus* the rest of the ironclads started to emerge, the propeller-driven ships moving somewhat slower than the paddle wheelers.

Andrew counted the vessels off, and after the sixteenth emerged the water was empty. The last vessel in line swung in close, her captain standing on the pilothouse.

"The *Novrod* busted a propeller driveshaft," the captain shouted. "She's still up at Ostia."

"Goddamm it," Andrew snapped, looking over at Ferguson, who shook his head.

"Sir, we're lucky we've got seventeen going. We'll be lucky if ten of them make it to Suzdal. Each ship has a spare shaft, but it'll take them three or four days to put it in."

Andrew could sense the defensiveness in his voice.

"It's all right, Chuck, you've done just fine. It's just we're leaving three behind already, and I hate to lose another before we even clear the harbor."

"Remember, it can still stand here as harbor defense," Mina interjected. "We've left that city damn near naked. The one other ship with the misaligned engine won't be ready for several days as well."

Andrew weighed the odds for a moment and finally nodded in agreement.

"Tell him they're staying behind. That'll leave two ships afloat at least. By the time they catch up the battle will most likely be over anyhow."

"So that's about it, gentlemen," Andrew said, looking back out to sea, where the fleet of over a hundred ships moved slowly over the waves. "Anything else?"

His staff shook their heads, and he could see in their eyes they were anxious to begin.

Forcing a smile, he looked over at Bullfinch.

"Admiral Bullfinch, tell the dispatch boat to cast off and carry the message back to *Novrod*. Sir, I am in your hands now. Let's get moving."

"Yes sir, admiral," Bullfinch said, and shouting out orders, he scrambled up to the pilothouse.

The crew of former Union infantrymen scrambled to their tasks, the deck crew running forward to hoist the anchor, which was nothing more than a heavy block of granite held to the ship by an arm-thick length of rope. Even as the men labored at the wooden windlass set low in the bow, the twin stacks behind the gunhouse started to blow smoke. The *Suzdal* inched forward. A shudder ran though the vessel as the engines picked up their tempo, and a white wake began to spread out behind the ship as Bullfinch swung it around on a westerly heading.

Andrew could feel the deck slowly begin to rise and fall beneath his feet.

With a weak smile he looked over at Emil, and taking the single chair that had been brought on board for his convenience, he settled down to endure the ordeal.

"It is simply incredible," Tobias said. "It would be like Keane to pull something like this off."

"You presented him with the impossible," Hulagar replied. "In our circlings we have crossed many stretches of land that cannot support us. They are difficult treks. Your Keane was trapped, and he had to find another way."

Tamuka sat quietly in the corner, watching the Yankee captain with disdain. He had created something that caught his opponent by surprise, but then had expected him to follow the path he had wished him to. His gaze shifted for a brief moment to Vuka, who sat in silence. His behavior had been most curious. Where before he had swaggered and boasted, now he spoke barely a word, dwelling on some inner thoughts. Not a dozen words had they exchanged since his return, yet another sign that Vuka knew the reason he had been sent back. At least in that he had shown some decency, not abasing himself by trying to win back through his shield-bearer what he had lost. Turning his gaze away from Vuka, he focused his attention back on Tobias to see what the cattle would now do.

"It took you nearly a year to build the ships you have," Hulagar asked. "How could they do such a thing in merely thirty days?"

"I had nothing when I came to Cartha," Tobias said defensively. "It was worse than medieval. We had to build a foundry, a mill, and lathes. That took time."

"Roum was the same way," Mantu said quietly.

Tobias could feel the anger building within. How could these bastards ever understand what he had done for them, what odds he had faced? So they were judging him now as well.

"They had a foundry and the beginnings of a mill already in the city."

"And you did not destroy it."

"I had planned to," Tobias said slyly. "That is, until the people rioted and we were driven back."

As he spoke he looked over coldly at Vuka with an accusing glare.

Vuka said nothing, his gaze fixed straight ahead.

"That is in the past," Hulagar said quickly. "I desire to understand the present and what you see as the future."

Tobias leaned back in his chair, and the cabin became silent.

"They must have used the locomotive engines," he began cautiously. "Moved them down from Hispania, along with rail iron for armor."

"Would these ships be strong?" Hulagar asked.

"Perhaps. We won't know till we meet them. But I can guarantee this. It would be impossible to cast heavy guns like the one aboard our ships. There's nearly five tons of metal in our fifty-pounders, nearly ten tons in the hundred. Reaming out the bores would take some damn heavy machinery."

"So you believe we are stronger."

Tobias nodded confidently.

"How many ships would he have?"

"The messenger saw only one. But he did report plumes of smoke along the river. I would guess maybe five or ten. Keane would be mad to attempt this with anything less. Those galleys will be to transport his men, nothing more. He's most likely going to try to run up the coast and drop his army off."

"And if they do?"

"He'll have an advantage on land. His troops are better —we knew that before we even started this."

"Then what is your plan?"

Tobias forced a smile. The nightmare memory of the *Merrimac* steaming down upon his stranded and defenseless ship came back to him with a cold chill. But this would be different. This time he would own the *Merrimac* and Andrew's pitiful effort would be fodder for his guns.

"I'm pulling the fleet out," Tobias said evenly. "I'm also taking the galleys with me. They can maneuver a lot faster. They should be able to run down his wooden ships while I handle what he has left. I'll leave five thousand men behind to hold the city."

"But why?" Mikhail protested, coming to his feet. "We hold the city, but they are still dug in at the factories. If I only have five thousand they might break back in."

"If I stay here in the river, I'll have no room," Tobias snapped. "I want to catch them out in the open and sink them before they can land their army here."

"If you leave," Mikhail shouted, "they might attack me here."

"You are not to worry about that," Hulagar replied sharply, and the two men looked over at him. "I want Keane and his army dead. Everything else is not of importance at the moment."

Mikhail looked over suspiciously at Hulagar but said nothing.

"It is almost dawn," Tobias said quietly. "If we pull the men off the siege lines during daylight, they will notice. When night comes we'll abandon the lines around the factory. The two mortar boats will keep up an all-night barrage to cover this. The following morning we'll move the fleet and start to run up the coast."

"And myself?" Mikhail said grimly.

"If he's moving as the spy reported, we'll be back in three

days," Tobias said coldly. "When those fools see Andrew's body, they'll know there's no hope left."

Hulagar stood up, bending over in the low cabin.

"I am looking forward to seeing ships fight ships, Cromwell," he said evenly, and he turned and went out the door, the other Merki following him.

"He still does not know that the Vushka are coming," Tamuka said in Merki as they stepped out onto the main deck of the ship.

"Why should he?" Hulagar replied. "If he did, they would all know that we will occupy this city and betray him. Let him find out when it is done and not before."

"The Vushka coming here?" Vuka said sharply, coming up to stand before the two.

Tamuka groaned inwardly at his indiscretion and looked over at Hulagar.

"Yes, the Vushka," Hulagar replied slowly.

"And my father, does he ride with them?"

"That was his intention," Hulagar said.

A thin smile crossed Vuka's features, and he turned and walked away.

"You might have to do it even without honor," Hulagar whispered.

"I cannot take that responsibility," Tamuka replied. "Remember that the Qar Qarth said that if he redeems himself he may still live."

"Redeemed or not, can one believe his actions? He knows his father will be here to judge him. He suspects as well that he is considered judged, and therefore what he does will be done with that thought in mind. Remember what we talked about. For the sake of our survival you must act soon."

Tamuka looked back at Vuka and saw him talking with Mantu. The two of them laughed softly. Vuka put a friendly arm around his brother's shoulder, and the two walked off into the shadows.

"He has always hated Mantu," Tamuka whispered, and his voice was cold with suspicion.

# Chapter Sixteen

"How old would you say the message is?" Kal asked, looking over at Hans, who sat on the edge of the table looking down at the rough map spread out before them.

"The first line of fortifications is a hundred miles southwest of here. We have two lines of pickets beyond that—the first fifty miles out, the second another fifty. Half a day for the semaphore to get it back to the fortified lines. Our telegraph station at the railhead at Wilderness Station is thirty miles down, and the messenger said it took him over a day to get up here, cross the river, and swing into our lines above Novrod."

"Two days," O'Donald whispered. "Those bastards move fifty miles a day on the march."

"Remember, they're going through the gaps in the Shenandoah Hills—it'll slow them a bit. I'd guess they've moved maybe seventy-five miles since then. They should hit the defensive line tomorrow."

"You think the line will slow them down?"

"What line?" O'Donald replied. "Less than three thousand troops and a couple of thousand laborers covering a stretch nearly a hundred miles across? There are still holes out there big enough to ride a whole umen through mounted stirrup to stirrup. The best bet for those boys is simply to get out of the way and hole up in the blockhouses. Besides, the Merki aren't interested in our fortifications, they're after Suzdal."

"But only one umen," Pat said. "Our reports say the Merki have over forty. How come so few?"

"Maybe pressure from that other horde to the south,"

Kal replied. "Maybe they think it's already in the bag and they don't need any more for right now. After all, their servants already have Suzdal."

"Perhaps I should have fought for it after all," Kal said, his voice full of self-recrimination.

"You made the right move," Hans replied sharply. "We never could have held both the factories and Suzdal once they got into the town. If they'd taken the factories, everything we've worked for would have been lost."

"But if the Merki are in Suzdal," Kal said, "it'll only strengthen Mikhail's hand. They'll hold the largest city of the republic. With the additional strength of those ten thousand, along with what Cromwell can bring to bear, we'll be run out of here in a matter of days."

"Their only way across is up at the ford," Pat said. "That'll add at least an extra day to the march. Perhaps we could slow them there."

"With the *Ogunquit* on their side?" Hans replied. "If we tried to move any troops up from Novrod and then down through the hills, they'd still have to march for twenty miles along the river road with the *Ogunquit* shelling them every inch of the way. Like it or not, during the Tugar war that ship played hell with their advance. As it is, all they need to do is use some galleys as ferries and they could bring some of them beasts across right here in front of the city, or land them anywhere behind our forces on the road."

"So it's all going to depend on Andrew," Kal said nervously. "And he's only got three days, four at most, to eliminate Cromwell and block the river."

"There's still Mikhail inside the city," Hans stated. "We still have to contend with him as well."

"Are there any other suggestions?" Kal asked.

Hans shook his head dejectedly.

"If we should attack the city, we'll be back where we were earlier, covering too much territory. We've got the factory area armed to the teeth, so at least we can hold here a bit longer. But I'd suggest, Father Casmar, that you think up one hell of a prayer."

The priest smiled sadly and nodded.

"I'll get working on it, General Hans."

"All right, then, gentlemen, I think it's time we all got a little sleep. It's damn near dawn," Kal said, barely suppressing a yawn as he came to his feet.

As he stepped out into the chilled morning air, Kal stretched and looked about the foundry compound.

A scattering of low clouds drifted past, catching the first red glow of dawn.

"Weather's changing," Kal said. "It feels like the first touch of late summer in the air."

"Like late August out on the prairie back in America," Hans said quietly. "My favorite time of year—the high heat of summer starting to drift away. You'd wake up one morning and there'd be the first scattering of frost on your blanket. It might be a hundred that afternoon, but at least you knew the season was changing."

"Harvest time soon," Kal said quietly, "and here we're in the middle of a war."

"General Hans!" The voice floated down from above.

Looking up, Kal saw the lookout atop one of the foundry chimneys waving excitedly.

"They're gone! The ships are gone!"

"What in hell do you mean, they're gone?" Hans shouted.

Hans, with O'Donald behind him, raced over to the side of the chimney and started up the open ladder.

"Damn it all, general," Kal shouted, "snipers!"

"They couldn't hit the broad side of a barn at this range," O'Donald laughed.

A puff of shattered brick exploded alongside of him, and with a curse he urged Hans to move faster. The two climbed up to the fifty-foot height, pushing their way into the small lookout post secured to the top of the chimney. Grabbing the lookout's telescope, Hans swept the western horizon.

"Can't see the river," he whispered, "but there's no smoke, and that ironclad anchored off the mouth of the Vina is gone."

"Give me that," O'Donald snapped, and reaching over he grabbed the telescope out of Hans's grasp.

"You know you need glasses," O'Donald quipped. For a long minute he swept the city, barely visible from the top of the chimney, and then shifted his gaze to the Cartha lines dug in to the north and south.

"It looks awful quiet," O'Donald finally said. "They've got their campfires going and the tents are still there, but I don't see much of anything else."

"Mortar fire," Hans announced quietly.

"Mortar round coming in," the lookout shouted, leaning over the side of the box.

The cry was picked up across the complex of factory buildings, and everyone out in the open looked up and to the west.

O'Donald leaned back in the box, watching the round arc up higher and higher. The distant boom of the discharging gun washed across the morning sky. The round seemed to hover nearly overhead and a little in front.

"It's going to be close," the lookout whispered fearfully.

A faint whistle was suddenly audible, growing louder by the second. Unable to move aside, O'Donald sat in awed silence and watched as the round came tumbling down, fuse sparkling against the dark blue sky.

"Close, real close," Hans announced. Standing up, he leaned over the side of the box.

"Kal, the rest of you, get the hell out of there!"

The round shrieked in, crashing through the roof of the foundry directly below the chimney. Hans and O'Donald looked at each other, waiting, counting off the seconds.

"A dud," O'Donald hissed, letting his breath out.

The two looked at each other and started to laugh.

"I think if I'd had a chew in my mouth I would have swallowed it," Hans said softly.

Leaning back, he looked out over the enemy lines.

"They're pulling out," O'Donald said sharply.

Hans nodded, and standing up, he leaned back over the box. "Father Casmar."

From out of a bomb-proof shelter built next to the factory, the black-clad prelate appeared.

"Father, you sure know how to make one hell of a prayer."

"What do you mean, son?"

"They're pulling the fleet out and some of their forces. Andrew's on his way back!"

An exuberant shout went up from the group below.

"Let's get back down," Hans said. "We've got some planning to do."

Smiling, O'Donald slipped through the bottom of the hatch, pausing to gaze back up at the lookout.

"Son, you can keep this job," O'Donald said with a rueful shake of his head.

The silence was a blessing. Looking aft, only a light plume of smoke was rising against the early-evening sky from the smokestacks.

The narrow bay was aswarm with ships, the galleys lined up along hundreds of yards of beach, bobbing gently in the light swell entering the bay from the south. Along the shoreline, men by the thousands were stretched out, or washing themselves, their laughter rolling across the water like the cry of distant birds. It was the first break he had allowed since leaving Roum three and a half days before. The crews had been rowing half on, half resting since then, and even Marcus, eager for battle, had agreed that an overnight rest was needed ashore, now that they were approaching the last leg of their journey. There had been no sign of Tobias so far, but the mouth of the Kennebec had been empty, with recent signs of an encampment. It could only mean that their approach was now known. Maybe as early as tomorrow they would make contact.

Looking back south, he saw the *Antietam* rounding the edge of the bay, moving slowly. Directly behind it the *Republic of Rus* wallowed at the end of its tow line.

"That's seven since we left," Andrew said quietly, looking over at Bullfinch.

"You expected it, sir," Bullfinch replied, trying to force a cheerful tone.

"I reckon I did, but still I'd have liked to go in with everything we had."

"When you're fighting ships," Bullfinch said, trying to sound like an old hand, "you lose more of them from breakdowns, the weather, and just plain old accidents than you ever lose in a fight.

"Still, it's a wastage that hurts," Andrew replied softly.

He fell silent, leaning against the pilothouse, grateful for the silence, and the lack of motion beneath his feet. The wind from the south had died down and the ocean had turned as flat as a woodland pond. For the first time since leaving Roum he felt that his stomach was finally settling down. Emil had even managed to force some meat broth into him at noon, and it had stayed in place.

"Do you suggest any changes in the plan?" Andrew asked, finding it surprising that he was looking to a twenty-two-year-old boy for guidance.

"The old Nelson and Perry tradition," Bullfinch replied with a smile. "Close in fast and fight it out. Cromwell has all the advantages. His guns will have the range, and I would guess that he's built ships that will have the speed as well.

Our only hope is to run in sharp and hard, with the ships in line abreast, the galleys protected to the rear. We'll try to ram him, but ramming is a hell of a lot harder than you think. If you don't hit him at an almost perfect right angle the boats will tend to simply slide off each other. At close range we should have the advantage of quicker reloading, and we'll just try to pump a shot through a gun port. Believe me, sir, if a seventy-five-pound ball gets inside an armored gun deck there isn't much left to tell about afterward."

"Have you ever been in action against another ship?" Andrew asked, realizing that he had never asked the boy before.

Bullfinch suddenly looked sheepish.

"Ah, no, sir," he said quietly.

Andrew smiled and patted him on the shoulder.

"Afraid?"

"Of course not, sir."

"I was petrified," Andrew said quietly as if sharing a dark secret. "The only thing that saved me from making a complete fool of myself was old Hans Schuder. My company captain got killed right in front of me, ten minutes into my first fight as a new lieutenant, and I was damn near set to run when suddenly Hans was beside me, whispering advice. Funny, a lot of people said I behaved like a hero, but I'll tell you, when it comes to Antietam I can't remember a damn thing other than Hans and the captain lying there dead.

"And I'll tell you something else—I'm still scared to death every time I go in. I'll be counting on you, son, when the shooting starts. This will be my first sea battle as well."

"Don't worry, sir," Bullfinch said, his voice slightly shaky. "You'll do all right."

Andrew smiled.

"Thanks for the encouragement."

Andrew climbed up into the open hatch to the pilothouse and stepped down into the narrow box. Squatting down, he peered through the narrow slit as the *Gettysburg*, commanded by John Mina and armed with one of the captured fifty-pounders, slowly steamed past, fifty yards off the bow. In the gathering twilight it had a dark, sinister look. The range was equal to close rifle fire or double canister with land artillery, yet this was the distance they would most likely fight it out at, like two lumbering knights of old, smashing at each other with maces.

Looking down through the open hatch into the gun deck, he grabbed a ladder rung, and lowered himself into the open space below. It felt a mite ludicrous being this tall in such a cramped ship. Even with his feet on the deck his head was still up in the hatchway.

Nodding a greeting to the gun crew, Andrew climbed into the hatch leading down into the powder room and ever so slowly lowered himself down. At least when the ship was still he had mastered getting up and down between the decks.

The dimly lit powder room was empty, the boy topside with the gun crew. Working the sliding latches, he slipped through the double doors into the engine room.

"So, Emil you're up and around," Andrew said, walking between the piles of firewood to where the two engines rested in silence, the only sound the faint hissing of steam and the dull clanging of a fireman stoking the blaze in one of the engines to keep a head of steam up in case of an emergency.

"Good place to make a hot cup of tea," Emil replied. "Care for one?"

Andrew hesitated.

"It's a good herbal mix, my own concoction. It'll do you good."

Without waiting for an answer, he nodded to the fireman, who pulled out a mug, stuck it under a water discharge line, and drew off a near-boiling cup of water. Emil pulled out a small pouch, opened it, sprinkled in some leaves, and swirled the cup around.

"Go on, Andrew."

Andrew raised the cup to his lips and took a sip.

"Like peppermint."

"Seems the same. I never saw a plant like it on earth, but I guess it serves the same purpose."

Andrew took another sip and smiled as the warmth hit his almost empty stomach.

"Captain touring the ship the night before battle?"

"You know I always do that," Andrew replied. "Even when I was still a company commander, I'd stay up with the men."

"I think there's some sort of naval superstition that a captain, or admiral, whatever the hell it is you are, would do that only if he thought they were going into a desperate fight with little hope of winning."

"This one has too many unknowns to it," Andrew replied. "With the Tugars we knew what our weapons could do, and what they could do. We won't know a damn thing until after we start fighting this one."

"Well, there's only one way to find out," Emil said evenly, "and we should have that answer soon enough."

"So you're telling me to stop worrying."

"I'm always telling you that. It's bad for the stomach and the heart. Your nerves are going to kill you someday."

"Death by that's the least of my worries, good doctor," Andrew replied, shaking his head and laughing softly.

"Maybe you should try to get some sleep, son."

"In a little while, Emil," Andrew replied. "By the way this is good tea. My stomach is feeling better already. I'll just take a last walk around."

Putting down the cup, Andrew went over to the aft ladder and ever so slowly climbed back up to the main deck. A dinghy was pulling up alongside the *Suzdal* from out of the shadows. Ferguson climbed out, and the boat turned back into the night and rowed away.

"How's the *Republic*?"

Ferguson looked around with a start, vaguely saluted aft, and then, seeing Andrew, saluted again and came up to join him.

"Am I supposed to ask permission to come aboard and to salute the colors at night?" Ferguson asked.

"Oh, it's just Bullfinch and his naval traditions," Andrew said. "It beats me. Let's just call this an army ship for now and forget about it. Now tell me about the ship."

"A bent driveshaft on the left engine."

"Damn, that's the second one."

"I know," Ferguson replied glumly.

"Can she still move?"

"It won't be much use in a fight. Maybe three miles an hour with the helm all the way over and the one engine going at full speed."

"So that's another one out of the fight."

"Well, I do have an idea, sir," Ferguson said, his oil-covered face lighting up into a smile. "I remember reading about it in *Harper's Weekly* back when we were all in Virginia. The rebs had gained a bit of an upper hand on the Mississippi river, and some fellows made a Quaker boat that really put the fear of God in the Johnnies."

Andrew smiled.

"A Quaker boat, you say."

"I've got the stuff at hand to make one out of the *Republic*. Who knows, it might just work. We could have it ready by morning."

"Well, give it a try."

"I already am. I have some people working on it right now," Ferguson replied with a delighted grin. "Hell, maybe we should put General Hawthorne in command."

Andrew knew Ferguson meant no disrespect, but the comment still bothered him.

"You're doing fine, Ferguson. Now get some rest."

Drawing away, Andrew walked forward to the bow of the ship and looked out across the waters into the Inland Sea.

Most likely tomorrow, the day after at the latest, it would be decided. Though I know so damn little, still it will be in my hands, he thought.

A cool breeze whipped across the water, and the *Suzdal* ever so slowly started to shift around on its anchor line, turning to meet the wind cutting down from the northwest.

The water on the bay started to cross-cut into a light chop, the gentle waves from the south now countered by the wind coming in nearly the opposite direction.

Damn, it would have to do this to me now, he thought, and he wondered if somehow it was an omen.

Jubadi Qar Qarth reined in his mount before the flame-scorched remnants of the blockhouse and dismounted. Behind him the vast array of the Vushka continued to thunder past, line after line, a hundred across, breaking the silence of the night with their thunder. Jubadi looked back, his heart swelling with pride. He knew he should be back at Cartha, but this campaign would be short, only thirty days, and if something occurred, the courier line that stretched across a thousand miles would let him know before three days had passed. Though he dreaded to consider it, the great monster that even now was being carried along the coast by ship could return him in but a day if need be.

Beneath the light of the Great Wheel he saw Suvatai emerge from the blockhouse. The commander of the Vushka barked out a greeting and, bowing low, beckoned for his Qarth to enter the building.

"It wasn't even a real fight," Suvatai said, the glow of a

torch reflected in his wolflike grin. "Our advance scouts were able to ride right through the position."

Suvatai beckoned toward the dozen flame-scorched bodies, which like all bodies that had been burned were curled up into tight balls, their contorted faces locked in the grimace of death.

"How many total?"

"Not more than fifty, my Qarth. We lost nearly a hundred, though."

"If that is the start, Suvatai, it had better be the end of it. I will not tolerate such casualties against cattle."

"Somehow their guns are different from the ones Cromwell made. They shoot twice, nearly three times as far. We advanced as we had been trained, spread out, so their cannon could not cut down more than one or two. We stopped an arrow's flight distance and dismounted. Suddenly our men began to drop one after the other. We charged—that's all we could do."

Suvatai nodded back out through the door where the barrow had already been raised.

"They shoot farther? How can that be? The guns look the same."

Suvatai handed over a captured musket. Curious, Jubadi examined the weapon closely but could see no difference.

"The bullets are different, though," Suvatai said. "Here, this was dug out of one of our wounded."

He handed over the shot, and Jubadi held it up to the torchlight.

"It is bent from hitting our warrior, but see, it is not round, it is pointed at one end, and flat at the other and hollowed out. Somehow that must make the bullet fly farther and hit harder as well. Some of the wounds are ghastly— big enough to put one's fist into."

They keep changing things too fast, Jubadi thought darkly. Now all they had trained for in fighting the Yankees would have to be changed again, all because of this misshapen piece of lead.

He stuck the bullet into his kit pouch.

"How far ahead are our scouts?"

"Maybe three hours' ride."

"And any sign of resistance behind here?"

"None, my Qarth. They had at best five thousand here, spread along this line they were building."

"How long is it?"

"It stretches from the sea to the high hills within the forest, well over a day and a half's swift ride. In sections it is quite formidable, great earthen forts, deep trenches with holes and stakes before the trenches to break our charge. But it is only partially done. Of course, I chose a weak spot here where they had yet to dig to come through."

"Give them a year and this could be a problem," Jubadi said quietly.

"They won't have a year, my Qarth," Suvatai replied.

Jubadi nodded absently. But another two or three umens and he would feel far more secure in this move. Damn the Bantag, they were stretching him far too thin as it was, forcing him to cover all the passes, to keep strength with the horde itself, which only now was crossing into Cartha territory, and to occupy the city as well. But it could not be helped.

"Less than three days and it will be over with," Suvatai said confidently.

"Let us hope you are right," Jubadi replied.

"Are you hungry, my Qarth?"

"Starving."

"A couple of the bodies in there aren't too charred. I've tried them, and actually they're rather good, if you peel the skin off."

"It sounds wonderful," Jubadi said with a smile.

He found it impossible to sleep. Rising from his sweat-soaked bunk, Tobias pulled on his trousers and threw his uniform jacket over his shoulders, then stepped out onto the gun deck.

All was silent, the boat rocking ever so slightly at anchor. Climbing up the ladder, he stepped out onto the top deck. A sentry standing watch saluted, and with a nod, Tobias motioned for him to go forward.

Alone, he walked over to the stern and with a quiet sigh leaned against the signal mast.

All the old features were gone from her, he thought with a wistful smile. He had joined the navy when billowing canvas was entering its last great days of glory; when there was no hissing rattle below deck, no grimy smoke sweeping down the ship. Only the snap of the heavy canvas in the breeze, the creaking of wood, and the exhilaration of running before the wind.

How long ago was that? he wondered. We've been here over three years, and I joined in '38 as a midshipman on the old *Constellation*. Over thirty years. The thought filled him with sadness. No family in all that time other than the family of the sea. But then, how could he ever have a family? And he pushed the thought away, for there was something dark and fearful in it.

All those years alone, walking the night watch, lying in the cramped cabin of a junior lieutenant while others rose above him, to live in the great cabin astern. All of that was finally to be vindicated here.

He looked back out at the long dark menace of what he had made out of the *Ogunquit*. They would never have given such as this to me back home, he thought coldly, but even better, I have made one for myself. All the rest of his ships rode at anchorage around him. The eighteen gunboats, like low dark beetles, circled the *Ogunquit* like evil night creatures surrounding their brood mother. Beyond, anchored off the beach, were the galleys, the crews sleeping at the oars.

This is the place where I will wait, this is the place that will be my victory.

"The night before battle is always a time for thoughts."

Startled, Tobias looked up.

The damn creatures still struck him with a dread chill.

"You could not sleep?"

"Just considering tomorrow," Tobias said, looking closely to see who he was talking to.

"I am Tamuka. It is easier for me to see you—you humans cannot gaze in the night as we can."

He barked a soft laugh, and Tobias felt he had been insulted, but the tone was almost considerate.

"When there is battle in the wind, the spirits stir," Tamuka said evenly. "The ancestors gather in the everlasting sky to gaze down, to watch, to call out their encouragement, and most of all to judge those who will be fit to ride with them.

"The spirits stir even now. There will be battle tomorrow."

"Why would your spirits care what we do?" Tobias replied. "After all, we are only cattle."

Tamuka looked over at Cromwell, sensing the sarcasm in his voice. This one knew he was safe, though how safe he truly was he would not know until it was too late.

"It is a war that concerns us as well," Tamuka replied.

"And there are Merki here, who will be aboard your ship, who might die as well."

The old Zan Qarth for one, Tamuka thought, and the new one as well.

"Your plan—is it all in order?"

Tobias nodded in reply.

"The galleys will put out from this bay at dawn with two of the gunboats. They'll move very slowly eastward in screen, saving their strength. When Keane appears, if he appears, he'll be running close to the coast—his people don't have the skill to navigate over open water. The galleys will retreat back across the mouth of the bay, and then the *Ogunquit* and the rest of my ships will sally out. The galleys will then come about and charge back in."

It is almost like the maneuver of the horns, Tamuka thought, the favorite entrapment maneuver of the hordes, to lure an enemy into a chase and then strike in with your main strength from the flanks while the center turns.

"But you have no force out to sea to close the net."

"Our ships are far more seaworthy than his. We spent a year building them; he only spent a month. And besides, if I run a couple of ironclads out there, he'll see the smoke on his flank from twenty miles away. This bay is perfect. The hills to the east of it are high, which should mask our smoke, and Hamilcar will leave some men on shore to tend smoky fires, as if it were an encampment area. That should further cover our own smoke. Coming up from the sea, he won't know there's a bay here till he's almost on top of it. There's a chance he might have some Rus sailors with him who know this coast and warn him, but even so, I'll still have the element of surprise."

"Let us hope so for your sake."

"For our sake," Tobias snapped in reply. "Remember, you're on this ship as well."

"But of course," Tamuka said quietly.

This cattle was indeed curious. Somehow the man was not a true warrior. There was always a nervous look to his eyes, not the steady gaze of one like Hamilcar, who even when addressing one of the Chosen Race still would not lower his gaze. This one put on the bluster of a warrior, but Tamuka could sense that inside there was a terrible dread.

It was a heart that would not be worth eating, he thought coldly.

"Then to our victory," Tamuka whispered, and he turned and walked away.

Tobias watched as the Merki disappeared into the night. There was something going on between those bastards. He had seen the tension between them ever since their damn princeling had ruined any chance of holding Roum.

Somehow it might affect him, but he had yet to fathom how or why.

The cool breeze from the northwest continued to pick up, and Tobias pulled his cloak in tight around his shoulders.

Is this the moment I am supposed to feel heroic? he wondered, looking up at the sky. The paintings he had so admired, showing Nelson on the deck of *Victory*, or John Paul Jones shouting out his defiant reply, had always held him. When the war started he had dreamed that someday in the center spread of *Harper's Weekly* there would be an engraving of him upon the quarterdeck, bearing down on a rebel ram.

The truth fluttered through him for a moment, the memory of falling over the side of the *Cumberland* when the shell exploded. They had always suspected him of jumping but could not prove it. All because of that.

But am I supposed to feel heroic now, the admiral looking over his fleet the night before battle? He wondered what Keane was doing now. Was he on the deck of his ship, filled with his damnable confidence, his circle of admirers gathered around him?

"Damn him," Tobias whispered, as a gust swept past, sending a shiver running down his spine.

# Chapter Seventeen

"Red rocket forward!"

Stirred from his misery, Andrew stood up, banging his head on the low ceiling of the gunhouse. Rubbing his brow, he looked over at O'Malley.

"Going up," he said weakly.

The artilleryman came over, and grabbing hold of Andrew, he helped him up through the pilothouse hatch. Bullfinch, reaching down from above, pulled Andrew into a sitting position inside the cramped turret. Standing up on trembling legs, Andrew came up through the outside hatch and half crawled, half climbed out onto the top deck.

"The forward galley," Bullfinch said, returning to his telescope. "She's definitely coming about. It can only mean one thing."

Shortly after they had pulled out of their anchorage, a lone Cartha ship had been seen on the horizon directly ahead, and throughout the morning it had kept out of reach, half a dozen miles ahead. His own picket ships, six of Marcus's fastest vessels, had tried to close the gap. The rocket could only mean one thing.

"We've hit them," Andrew said sharply.

Bullfinch looked over and nodded.

"We'd better signal the fleet to go to quarters!"

Andrew, feeling somewhat out of place, sick as he was, nodded in reply.

"Signalman! Send up the pennant—enemy in sight!"

The lone occupant on the top of the turret beside

366

Bullfinch and Andrew went over to the wooden mast affixed to the pilothouse. Pulling open a box strapped to the side of the pole, he drew out a large red pennant and ran it aloft to fly directly beneath the regimental standard of the 35th and the old national colors flying one above the other on the same pole.

Looking over at the *Gettysburg*, rising up over a low-cresting wave, Andrew saw Mina waving in response, the same red flag going up beneath the standard of Rus.

Across the whitecap-studded ocean, from every ship the red pennant appeared, distant cheers rising up from the galleys riding astern of the ten ironclads.

"Their spirits are up," Bullfinch said. "It's about time we got into this."

"There, I can see them," Bullfinch cried.

Andrew, raising his own field glasses, braced his arm against the pilothouse and looked forward. The ocean kept bobbing up and down. After several sweeps he stood up, his legs wide apart.

For a brief moment he held the western horizon steady. Numerous dark shapes rode upon the water. There was a flash of light, and then a series of them.

"What's the light?"

"Reflection from the oars. They're almost like mirrors if the angle's right."

"So it's just galleys."

"I think I see a couple of traces of smoke. Wait a minute."

Andrew lowered the glasses. They had done him in. He was so used to the ritual now he didn't even care who saw him or where it happened. Going down on his knees, he leaned over the side of the gunhouse, being careful, at least, not to hit the open gun ports. Gasping, he came back up to his feet.

Bullfinch looked over at him sadly.

"Maybe once things get started it'll go away, sir."

Maybe I'll just get killed and end it, he thought. Never in his life had he felt so miserable. At least when he was hanging halfway between living and dying after Gettysburg, the pain had been in his arm and head, not in his stomach.

"You know, if there's a torture in hell for me," Andrew groaned, "the devil will put me on a boat."

"How we doing?"

Emil stuck his head up through the hatch and looked over at Andrew.

"The usual."

Emil held up a large mug.

"Don't say no. It's broth—drink it."

"It'll come back up."

"Dammit, drink it and try to keep it in. You're going to need it in a couple of minutes."

Trembling, Andrew took the cup and forced the contents down. He had learned that after the nausea won, it would leave him alone for at least a brief span before starting the torture again. The warmth of the drink was soothing, and he gulped it down.

"At least it will give me something to bring back up," Andrew gasped, passing the cup back to Emil.

"I see two gunboats for certain, sir, running behind the galleys, nothing else. The enemy fleet is pulling back."

"Where's the rest of the fleet?"

"Could he have left them back at Suzdal?" Bullfinch asked.

"I doubt it. If he knew we were coming, he'd run everything out here to smash us up."

"Maybe they don't know our size," Emil ventured. "Now that they do, they're pulling out."

"Get Vasili up here, Emil."

The doctor disappeared down the hatch. Moments later the Rus sailor came up topside with Emil behind him.

"What's up ahead, Vasili?" Andrew asked, pointing forward.

The young sailor looked along the coast, shading his eyes.

"The point of St. Gregory, sir, about four versts ahead. We call it that since the rock looks like the blessed saint's head. It is a day's sail down from Rus, twenty versts beyond the beach where you first appeared. See, their ships are already disappearing around it."

Andrew looked forward, but all he could see was bobbing dots.

"On the other side of the point."

"Ah, a wonderful place for fish. Even the great whales can be found there. A deep anchorage, though, with steep hills on three sides."

"A bay."

"Yes, a bay."

"He's waiting there for us," Andrew said evenly. "The bastard's pulling us straight in and then he'll knife out."

Andrew looked forward again, shading his eyes. A light mist of spray and sweat clouded his glasses, and with a curse he took them off and handed them over to Emil. It was yet another thing he had never quite mastered with only one hand, the art of cleaning his own glasses. The last several days had been far too humbling, revealing to him too many weaknesses he wished he did not have to admit to others or to himself.

Emil patiently wiped the lenses clean and handed the glasses back up to Andrew. The pause gave him an excuse to think.

So, we're walking straight into the trap he wants, he thought. Always before, Andrew had strived to lead the enemies onto his own ground, tricking them into action on his own terms.

He turned to look out over his fleet. Six ironclads were to landward, fifty yards separating each, with the closest one in less than a hundred yards out from the beach, while the other three were arrayed to his left farther out to sea. Several hundred yards behind, the galleys were arrayed in ragged groups of ten. Far astern he could barely see a smudge of smoke, Dimitri and his ironclad now converted to a Quaker boat, struggling to catch up. Now that he thought about it, it was absurd, and he dismissed it, looking back forward.

"What are your orders, sir?" Bullfinch asked.

"Signal the fleet to prepare for battle."

"You're going straight in?" Emil asked, incredulous.

Andrew watched as the second red pennant went up.

"That's what we built this fleet for," Andrew replied. "To seek him out and destroy him. These men aren't sailors, they're soldiers, so it's going to be a frontal assault."

Bullfinch looked over at Andrew and smiled in agreement.

"Besides, there are going to be a hell of a lot of men in the water in another hour or so. I'd rather see it happen close in to shore than three or four miles out. It might make the difference for quite a few thousand lives before this day is out."

Now that action was coming, it all seemed so terribly slow and stately in its progress. He was used to the terrible waiting before going in, as on the day at Fredericksburg when they had stood for hours in the freezing cold, watching wave after wave go up Mayre's Heights to be slaughtered, knowing that the moment would finally come when the order came to go forward. But when the order did come it was almost a release, a rushing forward into the charge.

This was so strangely different. He could now see the enemy galleys. No longer were they dots here and there; a ship would turn for a moment, revealing its long, slender form. But there was nothing, just the slow tension of the closing.

He looked back astern to the galleys. Already they were starting to spread out from their formations. All of them were riding dangerously low. The ones closest in to shore, where the water was calmest, were almost up on the iron-clads, while those over a half mile out were wallowing in the three-to-four-foot seas, each wave breaking up over their greenwood sides. From more than one boat he saw the crews bailing furiously.

The row of half a dozen picket ships were still far ahead, spread out across a front of a mile.

"They're sending out a line!" Bullfinch announced.

Raising his glasses again, Andrew saw a dozen enemy galleys charge forward.

"They're driving back our picket line," Andrew announced. "That's it—he's definitely on the other side of that point. How far is it now? I'm not good at judging distance out here."

"About three miles, sir."

Forty-five minutes to go. Dammit, it felt like an eternity.

"We've just got some reliable reports in from a fisherman down by the coast," Kal announced, as O'Donald and Hans came into the room and nodded to a white-bearded man standing in the corner, hat off and obviously rather frightened.

"Go on, grandfather, tell him," Kal said gently.

"I was down on the beach," the old man said nervously. "I hid my boat in the rushes when they came and went into the forest. Well, I had to eat, my Helena's not been well, you see, and I promised her a nice baked fish for dinner."

"About the boats," O'Donald said impatiently.

"Yes, yes," the old man said, and he reached into his tunic and pulled out two sticks.

"This is them."

O'Donald took the sticks and looked over at the man as if he was mad.

"Counting sticks," Kal said quickly. "Feyodor, isn't it?"

"Yes, your excellency."

"We all used them before your people made parchment so cheaply. He notched a stick for each galley that passed."

"And the smaller stick for the devil ships of smoke," Feyodor interjected quickly.

Nodding, O'Donald took the two sticks and started to run his thumb down the line of notches.

"Eighty-two galleys," he announced and then took the other stick up. "Eighteen ironclads."

"And then there is this," Feyodor announced, pulling out a small block of carved wood, deftly shaped like the *Ogunquit* complete to its stack and gun ports.

Breaking into a broad grin, O'Donald clapped the man on the back.

"I watched as all of them sailed away to the east until they finally disappeared."

"We thank you, Feyodor," Kal said, coming around from behind his makeshift desk.

The old man started to bow low, but Kal grabbed him by the shoulders, pulling him back up.

"You say your wife is ill?"

Feyodor nodded sadly.

"Then leave here at once, and tell the guard outside you're to go to my wife and tell her everything. We'll send one of our nurses with you by horse."

"The blessing of Perm upon you," Feyodor whispered. "My only son died in the war against the devils. She is all I have left."

"We will help to make her well again, my friend. Now go." Kal guided the old man out the door, then closed it and looked back at the two officers.

"So they're definitely going to meet Andrew," Hans said.

"That leaves just the two mortar boats and twenty galleys for the city. Four thousand men, along with whatever people in the city sided with Mikhail."

"We could try to hit them at one point at night. Once we break in, it's ours."

"Four thousand men," Hans said, shaking his head, "and they're behind the finest fortifications in the world. We'd be slaughtered charging it even at night. We could muster up twenty thousand militia, but we've got only one good brigade of men. The militia on a night assault would be more hindrance than help. It'd be like Cold Harbor again—we'd be piled up dead in front of the trenches."

"If only we had some people on the inside the same way Mikhail betrayed us. If we could force a single gate and pour the militia in, at least in those streets spears against muskets will stand a better chance."

"We've got two days at best before the first of the Merki appear."

The three sat in dejected silence. O'Donald finally stirred and stood up.

"Well, if you gents don't mind, I've got something to attend to. I'll be back in a couple of minutes."

Hans looked over at O'Donald, and a grin of delight crossed his features.

"Good old Emil! His pet project's the answer."

"I've heard the doctor called a lot of things," O'Donald snapped, "but never 'good old Emil.' I wish the bastard was here right now to give me a little blue mass. I sure as hell need it."

"That's just it—it's our way into the city."

O'Donald looked over at Hans as if he were mad, and then ever so slowly a smile lit his face.

"Of course, my good general. You'll be the one to lead them in."

"Not this time," Hans said with a grin, "I'll be running the militia on the outside. You're the only one I could trust with this, and besides, O'Donald, I've just made it an order."

O'Donald looked at Hans with disgust.

"I'll be back in a minute," he said sharply. He opened the door, then looked back.

"Shit," he said, and he slammed the door behind him.

Tobias looked up at the flagman standing atop the high rock, which he suddenly realized bore a slight resemblance to a human face with a long beard. The flagman held up two red pennants, waved them in circles, and then let them drop. On the decks of the other ironclads he saw the ships' captains acknowledge the signal and then disappear into their pilothouses.

Tobias slipped back down the ladder, pulling the hatch shut behind him, and nodded to the pilot.

"All engines ahead full."

\* \* \*

"Range to the galleys is eight hundred yards, sir. You'd better get below," Bullfinch announced.

Andrew hesitated. Once inside the gun deck he'd be sealed off from the rest of the world. He spared one final look at his fleet. The ironclads were still holding a ragged line, the ships farthest out to sea lagging a little behind. The galleys were now a good quarter mile behind, the double line of boats moving forward like a line of calvary cantering forward, waiting for the call to charge.

"The gunboats just fired!"

Andrew looked forward. Two puffs of powder smoke snapped away from the ships, curling out to sea.

Two geysers of water shot up a couple of hundred yards forward.

"They're skipping them!" Bullfinch cried.

Andrew could see the shot bounding up out of the water like a flat rock skipping across the surface of a pond. The shot screamed past, the first one slapping the water off the port side of the *Antietam*, skipping back up, tumbling end over end, then slamming into the water behind the first row of galleys.

Almost lazily the second ball arced over the *Suzdal*, and he turned to watch it pass.

"Merciful God," he gasped.

The shot slammed into the bow of a galley almost directly behind him, and a shower of broken wood sprayed into the air. The boat slid out of line, heeling over on its side and wallowing in the choppy water. Ever so slowly it started to settle at the bow.

Men staggered up over the railing, jumping into the water, and he could hear the high distant cries of the wounded.

"They're coming out!" Bullfinch shouted.

Andrew looked forward, and from behind the high rock marking the point he saw plumes of smoke climbing into the air.

"Get below!" Bullfinch shouted.

"In a minute," Andrew replied calmly, raising his field glasses for a better view.

The air around the high rock was swirling with smoke, and then he saw it, a black smokestack moving out, disappearing behind a fold in the rock, and then all at once the great mass of the *Ogunquit* slid into view. Another ship slid out beside it, and then two more.

"Enemy galleys are coming about, swinging in behind

him," Bullfinch cried, his voice edged high with excitement. "Signalman, run up ahead full."

Leaning over the outside speaking tube, he shouted out a command, then looked back up at Andrew.

"I'm buttoning this ship up, sir. Now goddammit, get inside!"

Five snaps of light winked from the *Ogunquit*'s broadside battery. Andrew stepped over to the pilothouse and started to lower himself inside. Geysers of water shot up ahead of and behind the line of ironclads.

"Coming down!"

Without waiting for O'Malley, he dropped his legs through the hatchway into the gun deck and let go, falling through the hole. Bending down, he stepped away from the hatch and looked back up as the signalman jumped through behind him and went to his station, where through a narrow hole in the ceiling he could continue to run up flags. Bullfinch looked down at Andrew from above, saluted, and then slammed the hatch shut, sealing himself off inside the tiny cubicle.

The deck beneath Andrew's feet shuddered, a pulsing vibration running through the vessel as Ferguson pushed the engines to full ahead.

"It's like fighting inside a coffin!" Emil shouted, coming up to Andrew's side.

"A hell of a statement at a time like this, doctor," Andrew shouted. "And what the hell are you doing up here? Get below where you belong."

"I've got a confession to make, Andrew. I can't swim. I'll be damned if I'll be stuck below if this thing goes down."

"Well, I haven't tried swimming since I lost the arm," Andrew replied, shaking his head. "We'll make a damn fine pair in the water."

Andrew went over to a narrow viewing slit alongside the gun position and looked forward.

Water was breaking up over the bow of the ship, sending up a fine spray that was whipped to windward. The *Ogunquit* had slowed, its broadside exposed, while the ironclads and the enemy galleys were approaching at an oblique to cut into the left flank of his advancing fleet. He debated changing the orders but knew it was useless. Battle would be joined in another couple of minutes, and to change plans now would simply cause his ill-trained sailors to become completely confused.

"We'll fire at a hundred yards!" Andrew shouted, and he felt his pulse starting to race.

"Jesus," O'Malley shouted, motioning to the still-open gun port on the starboard side, "can you hear it?"

Andrew went over to the opening.

"The madmen, he thought, and his pulse quickened. Across the waters he heard the high clarion cry of a bugle sounding charge, its notes picked up by yet other bugles, the regimental drummers countering in with the long roll. It sent a shiver down his spine.

O'Malley looked over at Andrew with a wild grin, even as he reached over and slammed down the gun port, sealing them into a near-funereal darkness, lit only by the thin shafts of light streaming through the viewing ports.

Going forward, Andrew looked through the view slit.

A whistle shrieked next to him, and he unplugged the speaking tube.

"Two hundred yards," Bullfinch shouted. "Run 'em out at a hundred. I'll try to ram the bastard. If not, we'll go under her stern, come about, and try to fire on her from our right side."

"Prepare to open gun port," O'Malley shouted.

"She's opening her gun ports!" Andrew yelled.

"Open port and run it out!"

A gust of cold air raced through the gun deck as two of the crew pulled down on the cables attached to the armored port and raised the barrier.

The gun crew, straining at the cables, ran the carronade forward, the muzzle protruding out of the port.

O'Malley stood behind the gun, crouching down, sighting over the barrel.

"To the left, to the left!"

Straining, the gun crew heaved on the lines, inching the gun over.

"She's firing!"

It felt as if a giant had slammed the ship with a hammer. One moment he had been leaning against the heavy crossties, looking through the firing slit; an instant later he was on his back, his head ringing. A cloud of dust hung in the air.

Dazed, he looked about. Some of the men were on the deck; others were already rising back up. Kneeling, he saw O'Malley, still crouched behind the gun, suddenly leap back, grabbing the linstock.

"Stand clear!"

The carronade leaped back, smoke geysering into the room. For an instant Andrew saw a shower of sparks snap up from the side of the *Ogunquit*, as it started to pick up speed, sliding across the gun port.

"Where were we hit?" Emil shouted.

Still shaky, Andrew looked around.

"Reload, dammit!" O'Malley roared, even as the crew slammed the gun port shut. Andrew went back up to the viewing slit. The *Ogunquit* was moving to their left, and swinging out from behind her a gunboat was turning to run straight at them. The *Suzdal* continued to run straight ahead, passing wide under the stern of the enemy ship.

"What the hell is Bullfinch doing?"

"Andrew!"

He turned and saw Emil standing at the aft end of the gun deck looking up.

Andrew came over to join him.

Something wet splashed his glasses as he looked up at the closed hatch.

"It's blood," Emil whispered.

Standing under the hatch, Andrew pushed up. The doorway edged up a notch and a spray of blood came down.

"It's jammed."

"Somebody open the aft gun port!"

"Andrew?"

"Shut up, Emil!"

Two riflemen came over and hoisted the cables. Before Emil could say another word, Andrew crawled out, rolling onto the open deck.

He felt as if he were in the middle of a hurricane of sound. Heavy shot screamed through the air, and a musket ball hissed past, striking the gunhouse by his side. Looking up, he saw the stern of the *Ogunquit* fifty yards away, the rear hatch open. An explosion kicked off and a spray of metal hissed past, one of the *Suzdal*'s smokestacks flipping end over end into the water behind him. The other gunboats of the fleet were already starting to turn, even as the *Suzdal* steamed straight ahead. *Antietam*, cutting across the stern of *Suzdal*, continued its swing. Its gun fired, the shot striking the side of the *Ogunquit*. A section of iron plate buckled in, boltheads rebounding out like bullets.

Andrew scrambled up the outside ladder, landing atop

the pilothouse. Shards of rail iron were lifted up over the side. An enemy gunboat was still bearing down less than fifty yards ahead, gun port open, smoke pouring out of its stack.

Desperately he started to yank the hatch open.

The gunboat fired. The shot screamed past, striking the side of the *Antietam* aft on the waterline. An instant later a scalding plume of steam shot up the *Antietam*'s stacks and an explosion ripped out the side of the ship. The ship started to slide around, its stern dropping below the water.

A ventilation hatch shot straight into the air, fire blowing up from below.

"Get out!" Andrew screamed. "For God's sake, get out!"

The enemy ironclad steamed straight past him, not fifty feet away. Wild with impotent rage, he pulled out his revolver and fired at the enemy ship, realizing at the same time how insanely stupid he must look.

The *Antietam* continued to settle, lying over on its starboard side, the bow rising into the air. Relentlessly the enemy ship bore down on its crippled foe. Above the roar of battle the sound of iron striking iron reverberated across the water as the ship slammed into the *Antietam* amidships.

Realizing that he was fast going out of the fight, Andrew leaped back up on the pilothouse, pulled the hatch open, and crawled inside.

Bullfinch was sprawled against the back end of the pilothouse, blood pouring from what was left of his face. His mouth moved spasmodically. Beside him the signal officer lay over the hatch. Horrified, Andrew looked at the decapitated body, and in the cramped quarters realized that he was leaning against a wall which was covered with blood, brains, and fragments of bone. The viewport forward was crushed in, the entire side of the pilothouse buckled.

Andrew uncorked the speaking tube.

"Engine room!"

"What the hell's going on up there? Is that you, colonel?" it was Ferguson.

"Helm hard over!"

"Which way?"

"Left!"

He pushed the pilot's body away from the hatch and yanked it open.

"I need help!"

O'Malley looked up through the hatchway.

Andrew grabbed hold of Bullfinch's legs and pushed them through the opening.

"I can't see," the boy gasped. "My eyes!"

"You'll be all right," Andrew cried, trying to brace him up as O'Malley grabbed his legs and then pulled him down.

"Another one," Andrew shouted as the hatchway was cleared. He pushed the dead signalman's body forward through the hatch, wishing he could lower him feet first, but there wasn't the room to turn him around.

Cries of shock came up from below as the body tumbled through the hatchway and hit the deck below.

The ship was still turning, he realized. He looked forward, and realized again it was impossible to see that way. He stood straight up, sticking his head and shoulders through the upper hatch, and then leaned back into the pilothouse.

"Straighten out the helm!"

It was going to be awkward, ducking in and out to issue commands.

The *Suzdal* had cut a wide arc through open water. Several hundred yards ahead, a terrible melee was underway, the Cartha ironclads circling around his own ships, trading shots. The *Ogunquit* was several hundred yards away, turning eastward, cutting into the galleys, the Cartha galleys ranging out alongside the heavy ship.

The bow of the *Antietam* seemed to hover in the air, the ship over on its side, the water pouring into the gunhouse, men scrambling out through the hatches, its killer backing away.

"Ferguson, give us everything you've got! Inch the helm a little to the left."

Just stay there one more minute, damn you! he thought.

"We're going to be rammed!"

Vincent looked up, and through the swirling confusion of ships he saw the enemy vessel come through the pack, oars digging in, water curling over its bow, heading straight for the center of their ship.

"Helm over!" Marcus roared. A geyser of water snapped up alongside the ship, and splintered oars tumbled through the air. Stunned, he turned to see an enemy ironclad churning the water on his right. Cutting through the line, the galley alongside of him tried desperately to turn, but was hemmed in on either side. The ironclad smashed straight into it, slicing clean through the bow, lifting the stern end of the ship into the air. The vessel rolled over, the ironclad pushing relentlessly forward.

"Keep turning!" Marcus shouted. "Left rowers stop rowing!" Most of the men lifted their oars out of the water, but some, caught in the confusion, continued to labor on, even as the vessel heeled over, the right-side rowers spinning the galley around.

The enemy galley slid past. Musket shots rang out, spears arced over the water.

"Stern corvus, cut it now!" Marcus screamed.

The heavy plank slammed down, smashing into the midsection of the Cartha ship. There was an explosion of wood as the iron spike snagged into the deck, the heavy board twisting as the two ships, now caught, spun around. The bolts securing the corvus snapped. The board sliced across the deck and then went over the side, dragging in the water alongside the Cartha ship as it continued past, now turning about from the drag of the corvus hanging off its side. The heavy pole holding the corvus snapped and went over, dragging its cables with it.

"Musketmen on the left, pour it in! Right-side rowers, keep rowing!"

A ragged volley slashed out from the side of the *Roum*. The volley slammed into the enemy ship, and Cartha rowers collapsed at their oars. The *Roum* started to slide over toward the enemy ship, bow closing in on stern.

"Forward corvus!"

The heavy board dropped down, this time securely anchoring the two ships together.

"Board!"

Roum sailors leaped up and started to race toward the corvus, while along the side of the ship the Rus infantrymen continued to pour in a deadly hail of bullets.

"Come on!" Marcus shouted, drawing his sword and pushing his way forward through the confusion. Caught up in the lust of battle, Vincent pulled out his revolver and followed. A rain of spears continued to pour out from the Cartha ship. The first wave was already over the corvus, men pitching into the water between the two ships.

Another volley slashed into the enemy ship, the range so close that bullets which did not strike flesh and bone slammed through both sides of the vessel.

Gaining the edge of the swaying board, Marcus jumped up, joining the press, Vincent by his side. At the far end of the plank a vicious battle of cut and slash was being fought out. The man before him tumbled over, a spear in his side. Crouching low, Vincent pressed in. Suddenly there was a Cartha before him, coming in high with sword already arcing down.

Laughing, Vincent fired into his face, and the man pitched over.

"Come on, goddammit!" Vincent shrieked, leaping on the deck of the enemy ship.

"Now, O'Malley, fire!"

The deck rocked beneath his feet.

"A hit!"

The aft end of the enemy ship blew inward in a spray of metal.

"We can punch through them!" Andrew yelled. "We can do it!

"Helm, more right!"

The stern of the enemy ship slowly continued to swing around. He wanted it edge on. His own bow started to swing, tracking on the enemy turn, and then ever so slowly the opposing vessel started to lurch forward.

Grabbing hold of the side of the pilothouse, he braced himself.

The bow slammed in, catching the enemy ship with a glancing blow. The bow skidded off, tearing up a sheet of iron from the side, and they started to slide down the length of the ship.

Smoke was pouring out of their gunhouse, and a side port was open, a wounded man crawling out.

For a brief instant he saw the hole they had punched in, twisted metal torn away from the wood backing. Horrible screams echoed from inside the ship, and then they were past, the wounded vessel turning across the stern of the *Suzdal.*

Andrew uncorked the speaking tubes to the gun deck and engine room.

"You've knocked one out! Good shooting!"

Ramming, as Bullfinch had said, was a hell of a lot harder than one would think. At least from his side it was most likely going to be gunfire that decided it.

Drawing a deep breath, he looked out over the ocean.

Directly ahead, his own galleys were cutting through, coming in around him. The main action was now farther out, nearly a mile from shore, where the Cartha galleys had sliced in and were cutting into the left flank. Explosions echoed across the water as gunboats seemed to have paired off, circling each other, trading shots. Even as he steamed back eastward the battle was drifting down toward him.

Several dozen galleys were bobbing in the water around him, their captains turning them about.

"Get a bugler up here!" Andrew shouted. "Engine half speed!"

A moment later the hatch popped open and a young Suzdalian boy wearing the blue uniform of the 35th climbed up beside Andrew, looking fearfully at the blood-splattered interior of the pilothouse.

"Get out on top!" Andrew shouted, ducking away from the hatch.

The boy started to say something, his features gone white.

"Get up there, boy, I need you!"

The boy looked up at the open sky above and then scrambled up the ladder and out onto the deck. Andrew stuck his head up beside him.

"Now blow recall, and make it loud!"

"Cut through their galleys!" Tobias shouted, looking over at the pilot. "Run down anything in your path!"

"What about their ironclads?" Hulagar shouted, trying to be heard above the yelling crew struggling to run their guns back out.

"My own gunboats have them occupied. These fifty-pounders loaded with grape will slaughter them. We've got his whole army out on the water now—let's finish the job."

"Sir, we've got another gunboat coming up out of the east."

Tobias stepped up to a viewing port and looked out.

"It's just another ship—we'll finish him later."

Turning to look back forward, he saw the ocean covered with ships circling each other, smoke drifting across the water, boats going down.

"Let's get in there!"

"They're surrendering," Marcus cried.

Revolver long empty, Vincent continued to push forward

with spear lowered, driving the enemy back. Cartha sailors
were leaping into the water, pouring over the sides.

"Finish them!" Vincent screamed.

Suddenly he was at the end of the ship, the enemy crew
on their knees, arms outstretched. Terrified of what he was,
yet losing himself in it, he started to raise his spear up.

A heavy hand knocked him aside.

"It's enough!" Marcus roared, looking into his eyes.

Struggling for control, Vincent looked back at the terrified men in the stern. With a gesture of contempt, he threw
the spear down.

"Someone who speaks Cartha, tell those bastards to get
the hell off this ship and swim for it," Marcus shouted.
"Twenty men as a prize crew, row her into shore and beach
her. The rest of you back with me."

The deck of the ship was a charnel house. The devastating
effect of rifle fire had simply shattered the sides of the
enemy vessel. Below his feet, in the slowly rising water,
Vincent barely noticed the dozens of dead and wounded,
the water in the bilge pink with blood.

Joining in the push, Vincent went back over the corvus
and aboard the *Roum*. The battle was now forward and
several hundred yards away. Around him was nothing but
wreckage, sinking vessels, and those struggling to get back
into the fight. An ironclad was steaming back around, and
with a sigh of relief he saw it was the *Gettysburg*, its gunhouse
scarred from a glancing hit.

"Are we winning?" Vincent shouted.

Marcus looked around and then back at his friend.

"Who knows? But I don't have much hope with that thing
out there," and he pointed to the *Ogunquit*, which was
bearing straight down in their direction from half a mile
away.

"Hoist the corvus!"

The prize crew, armed with axes, spear points, and iron
bars, slashed around the edge of the plank. With a groaning
shudder it broke free.

"All oars, battle speed!"

"Engines all ahead full. Bugler sound charge!"

With nearly thirty galleys spread out around it and two
ironclads falling in with the advance, the *Suzdal* surged
forward, pressing straight into the middle of the melee, the

calls of the bugles sounding across the water as the attack group swarmed into the fight.

Half a dozen enemy galleys came out of a bank of smoke, angling to strike the group on the right. Four-pounders snapped off, spraying the water with shot, striking one of the enemy ships. Still they pressed in. Several of Andrew's group turned off to meet them, and the farthest enemy out was slammed into amidships. A corvus rang down, catching the Cartha ship before it could withdraw, while another galley swung up alongside, the crew dropping oars and raising their muskets to rake the enemy ship.

Three Cartha ironclads started to cut in front of the group, gun ports opening, revealing their weapons shifted amidships.

One after another the guns let off. The deck beneath his feet jumped, a spray of iron rising up in front. The bugler dived down by Andrew's side.

"Gun deck!"

"Couple of men wounded, bolts getting driven clean through, one man dead, but we're still working!"

"Hold your fire till we're on top of him!"

O'Malley fired at the nearest enemy ship, less than a hundred yards away, the shot disappearing into the smoke.

The enemy gunboat turned its stern to the *Suzdal*, the water foaming beneath its bow, leading them straight into the melee.

Onward they pushed, oared ships shooting past. A galley in flames slowly rolled over, men leaping into the water. Horrified, Andrew watched as one of his ships, riding low in the water, banked hard into a turn. Water lapped up over the gunnels, and the ship kept going right on over, turning turtle in the water. A shot came skipping out of the fight, splashing into a cluster of men holding a plank, lifting bodies into the air. His galleys now slightly ahead seemed to slash straight into a wall of ships. Corvuses slammed down. Clusters of vessels, some up to half a dozen in number, were locked together, men fighting, musket shots ringing out. The sound of wood smashing into wood and iron against iron thundered across the water. Through the confusion he saw the *Ogunquit* cutting through the heart of the fight.

"Engine room, helm to the left!"

As if bent on suicide, a Cartha galley shot in front of the *Suzdal* as it turned. The iron prow slammed into the boat, and a shudder ran through it as it sliced the enemy vessel in half, scattering wreckage across the water.

Pushing in to the heart of the melee, Andrew aimed straight at Tobias's ship.

"Fire one off and clear that gun, O'Malley."

A second later the deck rocked again. The shot screamed over the struggling galleys, slamming into the side of the *Ogunquit* and shattering.

"I want an extra pound of powder in that bore, and load one of the wrought-iron bolts!"

"Colonel, she hasn't been proofed for that kind of load!" O'Malley shouted back.

"Do it now!"

"Look out for the gunboat!" Vincent shouted, pointing straight forward.

"What the hell do you think I'm doing? We're going to board her!"

The enemy ironclad continued its turn, coming about to face the line advancing back in from the east.

"Pull harder!" Marcus screamed.

The galley seemed to leap forward, gaining on the ship.

"Corvus now!"

The board slammed down, striking into the stern of the ship. The iron spike skidded across the enemy deck and then snagged on a torn-up section of metal.

"Let's go, riflemen, everyone!" Marcus roared, leaping onto the plank and running forward.

Vincent leaped up to follow him. The men struggled across the swirling gap of water.

Leaping off the corvus, he skidded on the deck of the ship, struggling to stay afoot.

"The damn thing's covered with grease!" Vincent roared.

Stunned, Marcus looked about, trying to gain a foot and pushing forward.

More men climbed aboard.

"Look out!"

From across the bow of the ironclad a Cartha galley cut in hard, slamming straight into the side of Marcus's ship, pushing the galley around in a pivot on the corvus. From the far side of the enemy ironclad a line of galleys bore down, and suddenly it seemed as if the sea was aswarm with ships, musket fire rattling, light field guns booming off, men screaming. A Roum ship smashed into the side of the Cartha galley that had destroyed Marcus's ship, driving it up against the side of the ironclad, which was still steaming forward.

Another Roum ship swung up on the opposite side of the ironclad, dropping both corvuses. In an instant, men swarmed down, hitting the deck, slipping and sliding, even as the corvus skidded across the iron-backed surface of the ship.

"Now what the hell do we do?" Vincent shouted.

"The engine-room hatch!"

Marcus slid over to the door, grabbed hold of the iron ring, and pulled.

"They've bolted it shut."

"Well, of course they would, goddammit!" Vincent roared, feeling foolish standing on the deck of the ship with no way to get in.

The aft gun port of the ironclad suddenly swung open.

"Vincent!"

Sliding across the deck, Marcus pushed him into the water, even as the gun exploded.

"Fire when she bears," Andrew shouted, "then run the gun over to the right side. I'm swinging in parallel to her."

"I hope this works," O'Malley shouted.

The gun kicked off with a thunderclap boom. A hundred yards away he saw the shot slam into the side of the *Ogunquit*, and an iron plate spun up and away from the side of the vessel.

"Engine room, bring us around to a heading of due north!"

Five gun ports opened and the long barrels were run out.

Remembering the bugler who was kneeling up on the deck, Andrew reached up, grabbed him by the collar, and ducked down into the pilothouse, dragging the boy in head first.

A crash snapped through the *Suzdal*, echoed by a high piercing scream below.

Pulling open the hatch, he stuck his head in to look. The room was filled with smoke and dust.

To the right of the forward gun port the side of the ship was buckled in, the railroad crossties fractured, fresh wood showing where splinters had been ripped away. A man lay on the deck writhing in agony, a jagged hunk of wood sticking out of his arm.

Andrew slammed the hatch shut and stuck his head back out.

"Helm steady! We're running alongside!"

The *Ogunquit* looked like a monster riding low in the water, not thirty yards away. Behind him the *Constitution*, its forward deck furrowed from one end to the other by a shot, was keeping formation. The *General Schuder* was cutting in ahead, trying to cross in front of the *Ogunquit*.

Andrew spared another look around. They were in the middle of the galley fight. Most of the ships were locked together, corvuses linked to Cartha galleys. He suddenly felt a surge of hope. Out of all the maddening confusion he saw that wherever ships were hooked together, the musket fire of his Rus troops was overwhelming the Carthas, who had gone in expecting maneuver and ramming to be the key. Even when they had successfully rammed, a corvus was still dropped, hooking the two together in a death grip. Once ships were hooked together, rifle fire was reducing the enemy ships to splintered hulks filled with bodies. They had been totally unprepared for the corvus, the same way their ancestors had been caught, he realized, over two thousand years before.

Their only hope was to outmaneuver him, but in the square mile of ocean in which the battle was now spread out, there was precious little room. The fight had degenerated into an uncontrollable brawl without any semblance of formation, each ship a miniature battlefield unto itself.

"Gun ready!" O'Malley cried, and without waiting for Andrew's reply, the deck below snapped out another round. At such close range there was no way to miss. The wrought-iron bolt slammed in, slicing through the iron plate with a sound like a hundred great bells striking at once, punching a hole clean into the side of the ship.

The *Constitution* fired off, striking the vessel astern, slicing off a section of armor near the top of the gun deck, sending a spray of fragments heavenward.

Andrew looked forward. They were going to have to turn—the shoreline was racing up less than a quarter mile away. Right under the bow of the *Ogunquit* the *General Schuder* opened its gun port.

There was a thunderclap explosion. For a second he thought the gun inside the *Schuder* had burst. The gun deck seemed almost to lift off its foundation as a section of wall several feet across was crushed in like a rotten shell. Lengths of rail iron went spinning into the air, and the entire ship seemed to slide sideways from the impact.

"My God, what does he have forward?" Andrew gasped.

Horrified, Tobias looked back down the length of his gun deck. The first shots that had struck had slammed in hard, cracking some timbers but nothing more. But the last three had hit with devastating effect. A dozen men were down, blood streaming from their splinter-torn bodies. A section of wall had buckled clean in, and a heavy timber snapped off and slammed against the other side of the deck.

Yet what he had done forward had somehow recovered him. The hundred-pound shot had punched right through the side of their ship.

He still had the edge.

"The battle with the galleys is going against us. They're using planks to hook the ships together," Hulagar shouted, trying to be heard above the screams of the wounded and the shouts of the port and starboard gun crews, who were running their weapons back out.

"When we finish the ironclads off, we can turn on the remaining galleys!" Tobias snapped.

"Helm hard to the right!" Andrew shouted. "O'Malley, run your gun over to the left side!"

Even as they started to turn, the *Ogunquit*'s gun ports swung open again. He continued in on the turn, coming straight in toward the stern of the enemy ship.

A tower of flame shot up across the water. A Cartha ironclad seemed to lift straight out of the water, rising into the sky, splitting in half.

The guns on the *Ogunquit* snapped off, and a geyser of water sprang up off his left side, drenching him and the side of the ship.

The *Ogunquit*, continuing forward, started to turn as well, its stern shifting around.

Andrew looked straight over at the aft gun port, which now swung open.

"Jesus, that's no fifty-pounder!"

The gun cut loose, the round screaming past him, slamming into the stern of the *Constitution*, slicing through the armor protecting her paddle wheels. A confetti of wood shot out the back of the ship, and instantly it slowed.

Andrew looked around for support. In less than a couple of minutes the *Ogunquit* had smashed two of his precious ships.

A quarter mile away he saw half a dozen ironclads slugging it out, their decks nearly touching. One of them, whose he couldn't tell, was pushing a large wave before it, its deck under the water, the stern already lifting into the air.

The *Ogunquit* continued its turn to the east, cutting straight through the galley battle.

"Helm steady, continue running east!" Andrew shouted.

He shot through a tangle of ships that seemed anchored together like a floating island. In the middle of the fight were two of his own, hooked to each other by corvuses, the men ringing the sides of the floating fortress pouring out volleys of fire into the Cartha vessels around them. A Cartha vessel lay low in the water, its side holed by a four-pounder shot.

"Bring us a couple of degrees to the left."

The *Suzdal* edged over, slamming into the stern of the Cartha galley and snapping it in half. The crew threw down their oars and leaped into the water.

The ocean was carpeted with struggling forms, hanging on to wreckage, swimming toward shore. On the beach he saw hundreds of exhausted men, wearing the white of Rus and the varied clothing of Roum and Cartha. They were already grouping together, but the fight seemed out of them as they stood along the shoreline, sometimes within feet of each other, watching the struggle still going on out at sea. It appeared that there was almost a truce on land, as if the shipwrecked men, having survived the madness out in the ocean, saw no further sense in trying to kill each other.

At least the frenzy hadn't gone that deep yet, Andrew thought, knowing that if it was humans and the horde fighting like this there would be no quarter, on sea or on land.

The starboard gun ports of the *Ogunquit* swung open. He suddenly felt naked—there was only one ship running alongside of her. For a brief instant he looked around as if hoping to find another ironclad to somehow hide behind and to take the horrible punishment for him.

He ducked down into the pilothouse.

A crack snapped through the ship, followed an instant later by two more hammer blows. The second one knocked him across the pilothouse and into the bugler, who shrieked with pain.

His head ringing, Andrew scrambled back. The boy looked up at him white-faced, holding his side.

"Get below, son!" Andrew shouted, even as he stuck his head back up out of the hatch.

A twisted section of rail stuck straight up in the air beside him. From below he could hear more screams.

An instant later the deck rocked beneath him and a wrought-iron bolt snapped out, slamming into the side of the *Ogunquit*, tearing off another section of armor.

A high whistle sounded, followed seconds later by the second one from the engine room.

"Engine room, colonel. We're taking water," Ferguson shouted.

"How bad?"

"Coming in pretty quick. It's hard to tell—everything's smoke down here. Our draft on one of the engines was knocked out when they hit the smokestack."

"Get the pump running."

"Gun room, colonel. They cracked it clean in, six more men down, you can see daylight on one side!"

"Keep at it, O'Malley!"

Desperately, Andrew looked back out. It was his ship and the *Ogunquit*—the rest of the battle was now drifting astern.

The *Ogunquit* started to swing over hard.

"Engine room, reverse! O'Malley, run your gun forward! She's going to run in front of us."

A grinding shudder ran through the ship, and he felt it surge forward for a moment.

The *Ogunquit* continued its turn, and the gun port forward started to come into view. Onward the ship came, its bow slowly turning like an unstoppable force, water peeling up in front, splashing over the side.

The *Suzdal* slowed, and then ever so slowly started to back up. Looking straight in at the enemy ship, Andrew could see the forward gun crew frantically working to inch their weapon over, trying to bring it to bear. The bow of the vessel sliced past, the wake slapping up over the front of the *Suzdal*.

"Come on, O'Malley!" Andrew shouted, pounding his fist on the side of the pilothouse.

The first gun port shot past, and then the second and third. He could see the shattering damage of his last hit, shards of splintered wood sticking out of the shot hole.

The fifth gunport went past, and then the deck beneath his feet snapped.

A geyser of water shot up from the side of the *Ogunquit* even as the stern went past.

"Waterline hit!" Andrew roared.

And then from the corner of his eye he saw the stern gun port swing open. In the excitement of the encounter he had momentarily forgotten the stinger in the enemy's tail. The gun kicked off.

Hands reached over the side, pulling him up out of the water.

Coughing and sputtering, Vincent lay back on a rowing bench.

"Marcus?"

"We got him too, sir."

Vincent looked up into the powder-smeared face of a Suzdalian rifleman.

"A hell of a fight! We've got them on the run!"

Coming to his feet, Vincent saw the vast array of ships locked together in a crazy-quilt maze of twisted wood.

Vessels in the middle, both Cartha and Roum, were smashed in, their gunnels under the water but still floating. An artillery piece snapped off next to him, slamming into a Cartha galley recklessly charging in. The men standing in the bow of the ship were swept over the side by the spray of canister.

The ram bore in, slamming into the ship, knocking Vincent off his feet.

More than a hundred men, hiding down below the gunnel, stood up as one, lowered muskets, and at point-blank range slammed a volley into the vessel. Rifle balls punched through the wooden siding. Dozens of Carthas were swept down.

A corvus dropped down from the bow, locking onto the Cartha vessel. A flag-bearer leaped up, holding his standard high, and raced across the planking, the riflemen pouring across behind him.

"If they sink us, we just take their ship and wait for the next one!" his rescuer shouted, and turning, he raced off to join his comrades.

"I never thought we'd fight it this way," Marcus cried, his eyes bright, coming up to stand by Vincent. "By the gods, I think we're winning!"

"We've still got the *Ogunquit* to worry about," Vincent said, pointing to where the ironclad was swinging back out to sea, a quarter mile away to the east. A lone gunboat was swinging in behind the vessel, and Vincent saw a shower of water rise up from the enemy's side.

"Got him!" Marcus shouted.

A tongue of flame shot out from the aft end of the enemy ship, and it seemed as if the gunhouse of the solitary gunboat exploded in a shower of flashing metal.

"No," Vincent said quietly, "it's the other way around."

His heart trembling, Vuka peered through the smoke, trying to make some sense out of the madness around him. This was not fighting, this was waiting to be smashed apart without ever a chance of crossing swords with one's foe and besting him by strength and cunning.

The fat cattle ran up to his side, not even deigning to notice him.

"Pilot, bring her around."

"Why?" Hulagar shouted. "You smashed its gun in. There are other targets!"

"It's Keane's ship. The colors of the 35th are flying above it. I'm going to smash her down and finish him."

"We're taking water below deck. We might have to pull out soon."

"Finish Andrew, then we can lay into the galleys and end this fight."

"Captain, there's another ironclad coming up out of the east, the same one as before," the pilot shouted.

"The hell with him," Tobias cried.

Dazed, Andrew crept through the shattered deck. Not a man was standing. Looking to the starboard side, just aft of the gun port, he saw the entry hole, big enough to crawl through. Crossties had been ripped out of their mounts and laid in a crazy tumble on the opposite side of the room. An entire section of rail iron had been driven clean into the ship, impaling a man on the opposite bulkhead. Sickened, Andrew looked away.

Miraculously the carronade was still in place, pointing through the forward gunport.

"Emil? Goddamm it, Emil?"

"Over here."

Over in the starboard corner, up by the carronade, he saw the doctor sitting against the bulkhead.

"You all right?"

Absently the doctor nodded.

"I swear the damn thing bounced around in here," he said, his voice distant. "I was working on the bugler."

He looked down at the body, its lower half torn away. Beside him was Bullfinch, bandages around his face, crying softly.

"Have you seen my glasses?" Emil asked.

Andrew turned away.

O'Malley, blood pouring out of his nose and ears, staggered up, several men behind him.

"Come on!" Andrew roared. "We can still fight her!"

O'Malley looked at him uncomprehendingly.

"Goddammit, man, we can still fight!"

Andrew went up to the speaking tube set by the forward gunport and blew through it.

"Engine room. Chuck, send some of the boys up here. I need extra hands."

"Water's coming in faster, colonel. That last shot tore some more loose down here."

"Five minutes—that's all I want."

"Maybe, sir."

"Bring our helm over to the right—head us south."

"Get the gun port open," Andrew shouted.

From up out of the magazine hatch the wood crew came scrambling up, joined by the riflemen who had been waiting below deck until they were needed.

Andrew looked back out at the now open gun port, while the makeshift crew labored beside him to load the carronade.

The *Ogunquit* was coming about hard, smoke pouring out of its shot-torn stacks, water foaming up from its twin screws.

"We'll have one last shot. Make it good!"

Andrew crouched down behind the gun while the rammer pushed the elongated wrought-iron bolt home.

"Raise the barrel a notch."

Several men levered the breech up, and Andrew slid the triangular block of wood back one click.

"Drop her down!"

Sighting down the barrel of the gun, he felt at first that it was too high—they'd shoot right over the enemy ship. But as it continued to bear down, the top of the enemy vessel rose into view.

He noticed his speed suddenly start to drop away, and he reached over and grabbed the speaking tube. "What's happened?"

"Water's hitting the boilers—we're filling with steam, and the power's going."

"Chuck, get the hell out now!"

"Gun port's opening, sir!"

Andrew leaned over and looked out.

The heavy forward gun was staring straight at them. The *Ogunquit* was less than a hundred yards away. He ran back behind the carronade. They were still too high.

O'Malley stepped past him, momentarily blocking his view as he stuck in a long pin to pierce the powder bag inside the barrel. He pulled the pin out, uncorked a powder horn, and filled the breechhole. Stepping back, he took up the broken linstock, swung it around to get the burning taper glowing, and then looked over to Andrew, waiting for his command.

"He's coming right over us!" a gunner screamed.

"Wait, wait!"

The *Ogunquit* fired. A tower of water slammed up in front of the *Suzdal* and the vessel bucked up high.

"Wait!"

The ship surged back down and then slowly started to rise up again.

"Fire!"

Andrew leaped aside as the carronade shot back.

An instant later the two ships hit, the *Ogunquit* slamming into the port bow of the *Suzdal*, tearing along the side of the vessel, peeling up rails and hunks of lumber in a shower of sparks.

Andrew felt the ship lurch under his feet, rolling hard to the right as if they were going to roll completely over.

"Everyone out!"

The massive bulk of the *Ogunquit* thundered past. For a brief instant he saw the old national colors, which Cromwell still defiantly flew, snapping from the stern, and then the ship was gone.

Water was pouring in through the shattered hole in the starboard side.

"Out! Get out!" Andrew screamed.

In the confusion he saw Emil struggling to pull Bullfinch up.

"Emil!"

"I'm not leaving him!"

Andrew reached over, grabbing the boy by the shoulder. The carronade came sliding down where he had just been, the weapon dangling at the end of its cables.

A geyser of water shot up through the shot hole, spraying into the gunhouse with blinding force.

The carronade crashed away from the open gun port and disappeared into the water.

He saw O'Malley go through the port and disappear.

"Emil!"

The doctor floundered up beside him, still clinging to Bullfinch.

Andrew cursed the useless stump of his arm as he waved it back and forth, trying to somehow move in the swirling torrent.

The ship lurched again, hanging on its side, dropping down.

Men were screaming, struggling past him, clawing for the open gun port.

The open hatch into the pilothouse swung down beside him.

Andrew pushed Bullfinch toward it.

"Climb, boy, up through the pilothouse, or we're all dead!" Andrew screamed.

Bullfinch disappeared up the hatchway.

"Emil, move it!"

Water started to pour back down the opening.

"Go, Andrew!"

Screaming hysterically, Andrew pushed the doctor into the hatch, and losing his balance, he fell away into the water.

Tobias looked up at the gun.

Its trunnion snapped, the long barrel of the hundred-pound piece rose up at a drunken angle. Casualties were down all around him, men shrieking in pain. He lifted his hand from the deck. It was sticky and warm.

Looking over, he saw the body lying next to him, sightless eyes gazing back into his.

Terrified, he came up to his feet and looked around.

The ship was still going forward, heading straight for the beach.

He had to do something. He had to act.

He knew they were looking at him, gazing at him with mocking eyes, seeing his terror at the blood that covered his arms, the deck, the walls around him.

"Bring us around," Tobias cried, his voice cracking.

"Port or starboard?" the helmsman shouted, looking down from the pilothouse above him.

"Port, port, dammit."

Shaking, he stepped away and turned.

Hulagar was looking straight at him. Damn him, why hadn't the shot struck him and his dogs arrayed behind him?

"We finished him," Tobias said, trying to control the shaking in his voice.

"And we're losing the rest of the battle," Hulagar shouted, "while you were busy finishing off an already wrecked ship."

"Captain, that other ironclad is still bearing down on us," the lookout shouted, sticking his head back down from the pilot house.

"What other ironclad?"

"The one to the east."

Turning away from Hulagar, Tobias went over to the ladder, climbed up into the turret, and looked out through the viewing slit.

"Merciful God," Tobias whispered.

Reaching back up, he blindly grabbed hold of the hatch and hung on. The flood of water continued to pour in, threatening to tear him lose from his fingerhold on life.

Gasping, Andrew drew in a last lungful of air as the water washed up over his head.

Everything suddenly went dark. He could feel the current pulling at him.

I can let go, I can let go of it all, a voice whispered to him. All the years of struggle, the ceaseless killing that was destroying his very soul. All the torment of inner doubt, which haunted his every waking moment, could be gone now. He suddenly felt a strange detachment from all of it. The thousands of faces that he had looked down at through the years, all the boys he had helped to kill, who still whispered to him out of the night, seemed to be gathering around him. The nightmare of Johnnie, his brother, dead at Gettysburg, seemed to drift away. The anguish of Mary, his first innocent love, the fiancée who had so brutally betrayed him, a betrayal he knew in his heart he would never quite get over, tugged at him to forget.

And then there was Kathleen, and the unborn child. Would she ever understand this?

"Kathleen!"

There was a light, he felt he was reaching up to it. Its brilliance burst around him, spreading out. He felt he was rising upward.

With a shriek he hit the surface, gasping in the precious air.

"Andrew!"

He was going back under, and terror seized him as he desperately thrashed on the surface, his heavy wool uniform tugging him back down.

"Hang on, sir."

Ferguson came up alongside of him, pushing out a broken oar for him to take.

Desperately he grabbed hold, pulling the stump of his left arm up over the oar, locking it in tight against his chest.

"Emil?"

"Behind you."

Andrew turned to see the doctor sitting atop a section of wooden grating. Bullfinch was lying by his side.

Ferguson, still holding on to the oar, pulled Andrew over and helped push him up out of the water.

Water streaming down his glasses, he looked over at the *Suzdal*. The ship was still going down, turning back upright as it hit the bottom. As the ship settled, the flagstaff reappeared, the banners of the 35th and the national colors hanging limply in the breeze.

"What happened to you?" Emil gasped. "The last thing I remember was going up the pilothouse, the water pouring in, and you weren't behind me."

"I don't know," Andrew whispered. "Anyhow, I thought you couldn't swim."

"I'm a quick learner." Emil said weakly.

"You were down there a couple of minutes," Emil said, and Andrew could see the tears of relief in the doctor's eyes.

"I just don't know," Andrew said.

"The *Ogunquit*?"

Ferguson pointed, and Andrew looked up.

The ironclad was heading off to the west, cutting back through the galley battle.

"He's still in it and we can't stop him," Andrew said, and he lay back on the raft.

A shot boomed off from the east, the sound followed by the splash of a round striking water, but he didn't bother to stir.

"I think he's heading out of the fight!" Emil said.

Andrew sat back up.

Squinting to see through the distortion of his dripping glasses, he saw the *Oqunquit* continuing to steam a path straight westward.

From the other side of the galley fight a Cartha ironclad broke away, turning its bow to swing in behind Tobias's ship.

"What the hell is wrong with him?" Andrew shouted. "He can smash up the galleys and turn the tide."

"I've lost the forward gun!" Tobias roared. "We're taking water almost as fast as we can pump it out."

"You're leaving your galleys behind!" Hulagar snarled.

"Most of them are sunk already!" Tobias shouted.

"With the *Ogunquit* you can smash the enemy at your will," Hulagar replied, his voice choked with anger.

"And fight that? Goddam you, look at that ship!"

Hulagar crouched down and peered through the slit.

"It's as big as we are," Hulagar said, looking back over at Tobias.

"It's bigger! I've lost my most powerful gun forward. If I face him, we'll be smashed apart."

"It's impossible," Hulagar said. "It took you a year just to change this ship. It's impossible that he could have made such a thing."

"Impossible? It's out there. You've got eyes, damn you, you see the same thing I do."

Enraged at the tone Tobias was using, Hulagar looked at him coldly.

Tobias stepped away from him.

"You're terrified," Hulagar whispered.

"I'm not frightened," Tobias snapped, his voice breaking. "You saw the gun fire from the ship from over a mile away. It means he has heavy weapons aboard, perhaps as big as our hundred-pounder. I tell you, that Keane is a demon if he could have made such a thing."

"So fight him here. Keane is dead—we destroyed him.
You might be throwing away a victory which you can still
win."

"That ship has three guns forward. You can see them
sticking out," Tobias said, trying to gain control of his
voice. "We have none. We pull back to Cartha, and we
repair our heavy gun and fix the damage below deck. Then
we can come back and take care of him. Have you ever
fought a sea battle before?" he snarled.

Hulagar shook his head.

"I have—I know what I am talking about. We can still get
out of here with most of our galleys and ironclads. We refit
and in two weeks we come back here and finish him off."

Tobias broke away for a moment and nervously looked
back out through the viewport. Raising his telescope, he
watched the ship for a brief moment and then looked back
at Hulagar.

"Three guns forward, double smokestacks. He must have
another ten or fifteen guns on her sides. She'll smash everything we have."

"Why was Keane, their commander, not on that great
ship?"

"It was a trick, this whole thing. They wanted to lure us
in, to damage us, then bring that monster up to finish us.
Keane's back there."

Hulagar paused for a moment.

"We go back to Suzdal."

"Why there?"

"Have you forgotten you left Hamilcar and four thousand
of your men there?"

Tobias hesitated.

"We can't refit there."

"That ship is slow. We can gain a day on her going back.
Repair your ship."

Without waiting for a response, Hulagar turned away with
a snort of disgust and walked away, head lowered to clear
the cramped deck.

"He is panicking," Tamuka whispered in Merki, coming
up beside his comrade.

"The ship is big."

"We are throwing away a victory here. At such a moment
we should charge in, ram it as he rammed the other ship."

"He knows this fighting at sea better than we," Hulagar said coldly. "We must trust his judgment."

"He is a coward."

"The Vushka will be in Suzdal, and what is left of the Yankees will be outside. We can take his factories by land. All we need is for this vessel to guard the river for three or four days and the issue will be decided."

"I hope you are right in this," Tamuka whispered.

Hulagar looked over at the shield-bearer, and from the corner of his eye saw Vuka gazing at him warily. He had wanted to put Vuka on one of the galleys for this fight, but Tamuka had argued that the heat of action would be with the *Ogunquit*. That had been a tragic mistake. From the looks of the battle at least one of the problems facing the horde could have been solved right here. If Tamuka did not decide this thing soon, honor or not, he would finish it for the good of the horde.

"He's running from a goddam Quaker ship," Andrew gasped.

From across the open water, the sound of battle was dropping away to be replaced by wild cheers. Behind the *Ogunquit*, five ironclads and a small knot of galleys were breaking away and heading westward.

Exhausted, Andrew lay back on the grating and looked over at Bullfinch.

"How is he?"

"He'll live," Emil whispered.

Andrew pointed to his eyes.

"I don't know."

"I'll be all right, sir," Bullfinch gasped.

"Sure you will, son."

"You'd damn well better," Emil said. "You almost killed both of us getting out of that ship."

"The *Suzdal*'s gone?"

"Went down fighting," Andrew said. "When we launch the new one, you're the admiral."

"Thank you, sir," he whispered and then lay back.

The ocean was awash with wreckage. Wounded ships dragged past, riding low in the water, cutting in for shore before they sank. Cries filled the air, men screaming for help, floundering in the water.

Along the shore there seemed to be thousands of men, many of them in the water, helping to pull in others.

"I still don't know if we've really won or not," Andrew sighed. "It's going to be hell sorting this out, and Tobias still holds Suzdal. We're going to have to salvage what we can and press on in."

He looked over at the Quaker ship, which was now slowly bearing down.

"I did a pretty damn good job of it, didn't I?" Ferguson announced.

The vessel looked huge, more than two hundred feet in length. Across the bow there was a massive blockhouse, with two logs sticking out. In the middle of the contraption the *Republic of Rus* chugged painfully along, its one gun port marking the center of the vessel.

"Some rafts we were using for hauling firewood strapped alongside, a lot of canvas, logs for guns, a couple of barrels of tar for paint, and there it is," Ferguson laughed.

"We fooled him once with it, but I doubt if it'll work again," Andrew said quietly. "That's going to be the problem. We've still got to get the *Ogunquit*. If not he can still hold Suzdal for ransom."

"Let's find out what we have left first," Emil said.

"It doesn't look like much," Andrew whispered, feeling dejected.

"I do know one thing," Emil said. "You certainly got cured of your seasickness awful damn quick."

Surprised, Andrew looked over at the doctor.

"Terror, doctor," Andrew whispered. "Pure stark terror."

# Chapter Eighteen

The burning ironclad cast a lurid light across the now calm waters of the Inland Sea. Its gun deck burst asunder, and a mushroom cloud of fire and smoke shot up into the evening sky. The deep throaty growl of the exploding magazine rolled across the ocean, striking against the shore, causing the thousands of men on the beach to look up, pointing at the closing chapter of the battle, as the ship settled back down and with a hissing of smoke finally settled beneath the wreckage strewn waters.

In the dying light Andrew looked down the length of the beach.

Soldiers of the Republic, Roum sailors, and Cartha warriors were all intermingled, numbed by all that they had done to each other through that terrible morning and afternoon.

Andrew looked over his shoulder and saw a line of Carthas, digging with boards, shards of metal, and some with their bare hands, scooping out a long trench. Those they meant to bury seemed to stretch out across the beach forever. Already there was that faint lingering smell in the air, which he felt was somehow part and parcel of his life, the sickly-sweet cloying stench of a battlefield.

Two Roum sailors came up out of the water, dragging a body, its features blue, hands upstretched as if somehow in his last seconds the man had desperately tried to reach out, to claw his soul back into his drowning body.

"Any figures yet?" Andrew said, looking over at Mina. Somehow his chief of logistics had come through the fight aboard the ironclad *Gettysburg* without a scratch, even though the ship had been holed twice when it had lain alongside a Cartha ship and traded broadsides at pistol-shot range, knocking its opponent out of the fight.

"There are still hundreds of men out in the water," John replied, pointing to where half a dozen captured Cartha ships were slowly cruising back and forth, looking for survivors. "We've got over six hundred dead on the beach, and five hundred or so wounded. The 3rd Novrod took it really bad—two of their galleys got raked by canister from a gunboat, and they went down a couple of miles out. The 35th and our gunners aboard the ironclads got hit hard as well. We lost over thirty of the old boys from the regiment, along with at least six of the men from the 44th serving as gun commanders."

"God, more of them gone," Andrew whispered. He dreaded the moment when he'd have to run down the list and check yet more names off the regimental roster. It would mean that half of the men who had come through with him were dead in just three years.

"A couple of hours back I'd have thought half the army was drowned," Andrew said, letting a slight note of optimism creep into his voice.

"You know, the son of a bitch had the battle won," John said. "Those two heavy weapons were smashing us to pieces, and then he ran away."

"There's something terrible locked inside that man," Vincent interjected. "When I talked to him I could sense it. He has a remarkable cunning, but inside him his fears are eating him alive. I guess they got him this time too."

His fears, Andrew thought. Were battles like this simply a matter of perception? Was victory at times merely a matter of one side becoming convinced it would win, and the other not? After a galley had fished him and the other survivors of the *Suzdal* on board he had stood upon the deck of the ship looking out upon the insane confusion of over two hundred ships locked together in battle. It was impossible to decipher what had occurred. In some ways the fight had been like the Wilderness, when the Army of the Potomac had smashed into Lee's forces in a mad tangle of forest all ablazing and slugged it out for two days. It had seemed like a defeat then, and yet Grant had simply refused to call it such and kept on going.

"Still, the galley fight went our way," Marcus said, grimacing as he adjusted his arm, which was bound tight with a blood-soaked bandage. "Between the corvuses and our gunfire we tore them apart. I never dreamed I'd see the day that we'd drive the damn Carthas from the waves."

Marcus looked over at Andrew, and he sensed that in this fight the Roum consul and his people were now firmly bound to the Rus. At least the battle had done that. Looking back across the beach, he saw that the Rus soldiers and the former slaves of Roum, who throughout the long month of building and training had kept apart, were now sharing whatever they had, working side by side, the barrier of language no longer a problem.

"If we still stand any chance of ever saving our city," Andrew replied, "it's because of your help."

Smiling, Marcus patted Andrew on the shoulder.

"What next then?"

"What did he get away with?" Andrew asked, looking back over at John.

"It's hard to get a clear picture. We know for certain that the *Ogunquit* made off at good steam. Five of his gunboats withdrew with him as well, though one was definitely in serious trouble, lagging far behind. The estimate runs that fifteen, maybe upward of thirty galleys got out as well. We've got six thousand, maybe up to ten thousand, Cartha prisoners along this beach."

Andrew paused and looked over at several Cartha wounded lying not thirty feet away, one of their comrades sitting beside them, gently trying to feed a man who was horribly burned.

"Any problems with the prisoners?"

"I've heard of a couple of incidents. The fight seems out of them, though. Some are just wandering off into the hills. The rest are just staying put for now."

"Do we have a regiment that's fairly well intact?"

"The 2nd Kevan barely took a scratch and are beached a couple of hundred yards away."

"Detail them off as guards."

"Vincent, did you find any of their commanders and someone who can speak Rus?"

Vincent nodded to four men who stood off to one side, a

single sentry behind them. Andrew could sense the coldness in Vincent. Something had definitely gone wrong with him. Marcus had even taken a moment to tell him how the boy seemed to go berserk in battle and nearly had to be restrained from killing some men who had already given up.

"Have you talked to them?" Andrew asked.

"Only as you ordered me to, sir," Vincent said coldly.

"Well, come over with me."

Andrew and his staff went over to the four prisoners. The men looked exhausted, defeated, yet he could still sense a cold pride in them as they stared at him with dark eyes, their black beards giving them a bearlike look.

"Which among you speaks Rus?" Andrew asked.

One of the men stepped forward.

"Your name?"

"Baca, commander of ten galleys."

"You fought well, Baca. I salute you for your courage."

Baca looked at Andrew suspiciously.

"Yet still we lost," he finally replied.

"There is no shame in that. It was your commander if anyone who lost, not men such as you who fought with bravery."

Baca stared at Andrew as if tempted to say something and then shook his head.

"Are you Keane?"

"I am Colonel Andrew Keane."

"Why do you wish to speak to us?"

"I want you to translate what I say to your comrades, and they can then speak to the rest of your people.

Baca nodded.

"First, is your high commander among this group?"

Baca shook his head.

"Hamilcar is not here. Draxus, who commanded our galleys, is said to have killed himself rather than be taken."

"I am sorry that he did that," Andrew said. "I would have treated with him as I now do you."

"And how will that be?"

"For now we will keep you and your comrades here on the beach. I will be posting guards over you. Tell your people it would be foolishness to try to fight again. I don't want to see another Cartha killed, let alone my own people. Tell your men as well that if they want to escape into the hills they are free to try. But there is little food up there.

There are some scattered Rus villages, but those people will be armed and would fight if your men attempt to harm them or take their food. I can assure you things will go poorly for anyone who tries."

Baca nodded in reply.

"What do you plan then to do with us?"

"For right now, we will try to feed you and help your wounded. I'm leaving my best surgeon behind. He's already been ordered to help your people and mine together, the most seriously injured to be looked at first regardless of where they come from. If you could detail off any of your people who have experience treating wounded to help him, I'd certainly appreciate it."

"Sir?"

"What is it, John?" Andrew asked quietly.

"Sir, we've lost most of our food in the fight. I left some stockpiled back at our last anchorage, enough for six days, but the rest was aboard the ships. We've barely got enough to see us through the next ten days."

"Then we'll all go a little bit hungry," Andrew replied with an even smile, "but I'll be damned if I'm going to starve helpless prisoners."

"Are you toying with us? Is this some trick?" Baca asked coldly.

"You can believe that if you want," Andrew replied, letting a slight tone of being hurt creep into his voice, "but the proof will be that in spite of what my master of provisions says, I'm not going to let your people starve out here. Now translate that."

Baca spoke hurriedly to his comrades. Andrew quietly looked over at a Rus sailor who had stood to one side of the group as if casually watching the actions of his commanders. The sailor nodded almost imperceptibly.

Baca was not altering what had been said.

The other three looked over at Andrew with obvious surprise, and one of them spoke sharply to Baca.

"What will you do with us later?"

"As long as this war is on, I regret to tell you that you will be prisoners. You will be treated honorably. I will allow those of you who are noble to keep your swords or whatever badges of office you hold. If the war should continue for a long time, we will move you inland. I will ask that your men help us with the harvest—I think that is only fair, since we are feeding you. We'll find some villages for you to settle in. As long as you obey our laws, no one will be locked up.

"Once the war is over, all of you will be free to go wherever you want. You may return to your homes, or if you want you may stay here."

He paused for a moment as if to add emphasis.

"Or, if you wish, you may even return home, get your families and friends, and come back here, where we will give you land and you will be safe from the slaughter pits of the Merki."

"Are you speaking the truth?" Baca asked in open surprise.

"There is no way to prove it to you now—that will only happen over time—but I swear to you, upon my honor, that what I have just said will be honored, may your gods and mine strike me down if I ever break that word. Now tell your friends what I have said."

Baca spoke hurriedly, and Andrew looked back over at Marcus, who had been listening to Vincent's translation of the conversation.

"After what they did to my city," Marcus growled, "I still think the lot of them should be sent back to Roum to repair the damage and then kept in slavery forever."

"I thought you banned slavery," Andrew said in Latin.

Marcus grumbled, shaking his head.

"Then prisoners of war."

"Marcus, we've got a chance here. These Carthas are innocent of what has happened," and as he spoke he looked over sharply at Vincent. "They were trapped into this fight by the Merki and Cromwell, who gave them the weapons. Maybe they would have done the same thing even if they were on their own, maybe not. But where I come from, when the battle's finished you treat your opponent with some form of Christian charity. Ask any of the men from the 35th and they'll tell you."

Andrew looked back at Vincent, who lowered his eyes in obvious shame.

Whatever had happened inside that boy, he had to somehow pull him back from it. But he knew the hard part would be the sense of inner loathing for having abandoned the standards that he had been raised with, and that had formed him into a man who dwelled on such moral questions, which all too many never even bothered with.

"We have but one question," Baca said, interrupting Andrew's thoughts.

Andrew looked back at the barrel-chested Cartha, whose black beard set in thick curls swept down nearly to his waist.

"You are wondering why?" Andrew replied.

"If the battle had turned the other way, we would have taken you into slavery."

"To bring us back to the Merki, whom you are forced to serve."

Baca lowered his head and said nothing.

"We are not your enemies," Andrew said heatedly. "We fought and you were defeated, and as far as I am concerned that is the end of it. But take a look back out over that ocean," and he pointed out to sea.

"Who got killed out there today? Human beings slaughtering each other. You also smashed much of the wealth and machines we have labored so hard to build.

"It is the hordes that are the real enemy, not you, and not I or Marcus and his Roum.

"Do you know that we smashed the Tugars, set our people free from them, and ended the slaughter pits?"

Baca nodded. "But that was different. You surprised your Tugars. From that the Merki knew what to do. We thought of doing the same ourselves, but before we could even begin to act, half an umen of the horde was in our city. Then that Cromwell came and the machines began to be built. The Merki promised us exemption from the pits in exchange for a victory against you."

Baca paused for a moment.

"That is why I still pray to Baalk for Cromwell to win," and his voice was defiant. "For if we lose, the Merki will turn their fury against our people."

"And better that the Rus and Roum feed the pits than Carthas," Andrew said coldly.

"If it were we who had defeated the Tugars and you were trapped thus, would you not consider the same?"

Andrew was ready to make a quick reply, but inside he knew he was not sure. What if they held Kathleen, and all those he knew—could he honestly say that he would personally refuse to help see others slaughtered rather than himself?

"I honestly can't tell you what I would do," Andrew replied quietly.

A sad smile crossed Baca's features.

"Perhaps now you understand why we fought."

"And of course we will fight to save what is ours," Andrew said softly, "as you would do as well. Both you and I are trapped in this battle, which if the world were different would not have happened. Yet my offer still stands. If we win, I think your people are going to need a place to escape to."

"And after all of this I still have to ask why."

"Because, by God, it is the way I am. I'll not sit back and watch people get slaughtered by those animals. We can use you as well. We'll need people who know ships, who helped in the rebuilding of the *Ogunquit*, who once they escape the Merki pits will be willing to fight to save their families from such a degrading death.

"And besides," he added quietly, "if we do win, do you honestly think you can ever go home again anyhow? The Merki will slaughter all of you the moment they get their hands on you. For that matter, even if you win they will slaughter you anyhow. All of you are living in a dream if you think that after this war is done and if we are destroyed, the Merki will suffer you to live with the knowledge and weapons you have gained. I can guarantee you that if we are defeated, there will be three smoking ruins—Rus, Roum, and Cartha for good measure."

Andrew tried to control his voice, but his cold anger at what these people had managed to accomplish, even though they were forced into it, left him with a sense of bitterness. Cromwell was still afloat, most of the railroad to Roum was wrecked, either back on land or with the endless miles of twisted rail and flooded locomotive engines now on the bottom, and long rows of bodies lay on the beach.

"I have other things to attend to now," Andrew said, the lines on his face tightly drawn.

Baca looked at him, and then to Andrew's surprise he stepped forward and extended his hand.

Andrew hesitated and then reached out, the Cartha grabbing him by the forearm.

"I believe you to be a warrior with honor," Baca said, and then drew back.

Andrew nodded a reply and started to turn away.

"Keane."

Andrew looked back.

"We captured your city of Suzdal over twenty days ago."

Stunned, Andrew looked at his staff, who stood around him as if struck.

"You did not know, then?"

"No."

"Some of your people let us in."

"Mikhail, that damned bastard," John hissed.

"Yes, that was the one. We held half the city, your people the other half. When your leader refused to surrender, Cromwell threatened to burn the rest of the city down. Then suddenly your army slipped away, falling back to the place with many brick buildings."

"Why have you told me this?"

Baca shrugged.

"I have a home too. If it fell into the hands of the enemy I would want to know."

"It already is in the hands of an enemy," Andrew said quietly.

Baca nodded.

"I know. I am sorry for both of us."

Andrew hesitated, and then turned and walked away.

"You might have the beginnings of an alliance," John said.

"I wish the hell they'd thought of that two years ago," Vincent replied.

"We let them know what we were doing back at the very beginning, the summer before the Tugars came," Andrew replied. "Perhaps we missed our chance then, to offer what we could to help them."

"We were too damn busy trying to stay alive ourselves," John interjected.

Andrew realized that John's argument was valid, but inwardly he berated himself. If he had only planned better, perhaps all of this could have been avoided.

"They're still damn Carthas," Marcus said, shaking his head, "and it was a pleasure destroying them today. So don't even suggest I take those illborn bastards in after this war is over."

"My dear Marcus," Andrew said, shaking his head, "I daresay they wouldn't want to have anything to do with you."

Marcus looked over at Andrew, who broke into a grin.

"John, get over here, I want the rest of the news. What do we have left?"

"In good condition?"

"Anything that will fight."

"There are two ironclads, the *Gettysburg* and the *President Kalencka*, that came through fairly well intact. Four more are in various states of destruction. The *Maine* will never fight again—she's ready for the junk heap. The other three have gun decks shot apart, and one of those is shipping water and has a cracked boiler.

"There's also our Quaker boat. Dimitri had them push the second engine at top speed to get up here, and it's damn near shaken the whole thing apart. That boat's out of the fight as well."

"He still saved our hides," Andrew said, shaking his head and looking over at their savior. Though he had not said anything to Baca, he could well imagine the disgust and rage the Carthas must have felt when they realized that Cromwell had abandoned them and thrown away the battle to run from an illusion.

"The other six boats that went into the battle are out there," John said quietly, nodding out toward the sea.

"We captured two Cartha boats, both with flooding engines and gun decks in ribbons. Eight are on the bottom, and the other two are burned-out wrecks on the beach. I was inside one of them, Andrew—our shot tore those things apart from one end to the other. Cromwell built the *Ogunquit* damn solid, but I guess he never figured on the gunboats facing seventy-five-pound shot."

"What about galleys?"

John shook his head.

"Maybe thirty out of our entire fleet are still in shape to sail. Another fifteen or so were beached and we might be able to fix them up. The good news is that we captured thirty Cartha galleys fairly well intact. There are a hell of a lot of boats still wallowing around out there—the damn things don't really sink. I'm trying to organize some salvage crews to go out and pull them in."

"What can we put under oars by tomorrow morning?"

"Tomorrow morning, colonel? Hell, it'll take a couple of days to sort this out. Sir, we lost damn near half our rifles out on that water today, and half our field artillery as well.

As for the rest, most of the rifle and small-caliber artillery powder we've got left is soaked."

"I'm pushing off before first light tomorrow. That will put us off the Neiper by dusk."

"To do what, sir?" John said coldly. "He's still got the *Ogunquit* and maybe four or five gunboats. Hit those two boats with those heavy guns of his and you'll have nothing. It's going to take me a day to bring up the supplies from our last anchorage just to make sure we have enough food for everybody, including those Carthas you want to feed.

"Give me three or four days," John said, his voice almost pleading. "We can strip the rail off a couple of the ruined ships, we can build up the sides of the two we've got left and then try it."

"I don't have the time!" Andrew shouted, turning on John. "He'll have a whole day ahead of us back off of Suzdal. Give that bastard three or four days and he can repair his damage as well. He could build a battery on shore, he could do damn near anything. Goddammit, I'm keeping the pressure on!"

"With what?"

"With what I've got, with what you're going to give me by dawn."

"And just what the hell are you going to do when you get there?"

"I don't know," Andrew shouted, regretting his words even as he roared them out.

Shaking, he turned away from the group, raging at his loss of control, but struggle as he could he found he simply could not get his composure back.

He felt as if he were in a desperate struggle to keep from dissolving into tears. The pressure of this insane struggle had simply not let up from the moment the telegram had arrived, shattering all his hopes, no, his fantasies, that somehow they could prepare and in the end the threats of the outside world would pass away from him.

He looked out at the ocean of wreckage floating before him. In the gathering shadows he saw a group of Rus soldiers wading in, towing a raft stacked with yet more bodies. Men gathered around the group and pulled the bodies off, taking them up off the beach and dropping them down in the long line waiting for burial.

Just what the hell am I going to do now? What's happening in Suzdal?

He knew they were looking at him, waiting for answers.

All he could hope for was to protect the galleys, run them up close to the Neiper and get the men the hell off, and then fight it out with the *Ogunquit*.

And checkmate, an inner voice told him. He couldn't think beyond that; the word kept screaming at him. Cromwell, in spite of all that was wrong within him, in spite of all the wrong that he had created, would win, and he would die a useless sacrifice.

He could feel himself starting to shake. Would they see it, he wondered, or would the darkness hide this final humiliation? Yet inside he knew what was happening. He was starting to break apart at last. Part of him screamed to let go, to start laughing, crying, to turn and run away. The other part was barely hanging on, as if he were sliding down the side of a piece of glass into the darkness, struggling to maintain control just a bit longer.

"Sir, do you have any orders?" John said, as if pressing in.

Damn him, he knew what it was like, he had seen John being used up by his own orders. Couldn't the man see he was being used up as well?

Andrew turned to look back, fighting to somehow speak. "The orders stand."

"You mean we move out before dawn?"

Andrew nodded his head.

John looked as if he were about to speak, and then with a muffled curse he turned and stalked away.

The rest of the group stood silent, waiting for the encouraging comment, the smile, the burst of confidence upon which they would always draw as if taking a bit of his life away to fuel theirs.

"That's all, gentlemen," Andrew said softly, and the men turned and started to walk away.

Vincent hesitated and then came over to Andrew.

"What is it, sir?" Vincent said quietly.

Andrew tried to force a smile.

"Nothing, son, nothing at all."

"Like hell, sir," Vincent replied.

Startled, Andrew looked into Vincent's eyes.

"You're played out, sir, I can see that."

Andrew turned away and started to walk down to the water's edge.

Vincent came around to walk beside him.

"Mr. Hawthorne, you have other business to attend to. Go help Marcus with getting his ships and people organized."

"He can do it himself," Vincent replied softly. "And don't order me away, sir, because I'll refuse."

"So you've picked up insubordination along with your other habits," Andrew snapped.

Instantly he regretted his words. He could see the pained expression in the boy's eyes, as if he had taken a child and whipped it.

"I'm sorry, son," Andrew gasped. "I didn't mean it," and he put his hand on Vincent's shoulder.

"It's all right sir," Vincent whispered. "I deserved it."

"What's happened to you?" Andrew said softly.

"It's not me I'm worried about, sir," Vincent replied. "It's you."

"So we're each worried about the other."

Vincent shook his head, forcing a sad laugh.

"I've admired you, wanted to be like you, since the day I joined the 35th," Vincent said softly.

Andrew felt himself drawing back and away.

"And you don't need to hear that childish hero worship now, Colonel Keane," Vincent said hurriedly. "It's just I wanted you to know I think I understand what's happening inside you."

Andrew looked away. He felt as if he should now force the usual smile, shake his head, and say that everything was just fine and for Vincent to run along.

"After what I've seen," and he paused, "and what I've done, I know it's like a cancer inside me, slowly consuming me. I think of the men who've died because I said do this, or go this way. I think of the men, and yes, even the Tugars, I've killed, and God help me, the hatred I've learned.

"It's just, sir, I wanted you to know you've done all right."

Andrew smiled sadly and looked over at Vincent.

"Tell that to the people out there," he sighed, nodding toward the sea. "Tell that to whatever we've got left back in Suzdal, and tell that to the men who are going to die tomorrow evening because frankly I've been beaten."

"I could tell you that you've done your best," Vincent

replied, "and I know no matter how often I told you, you still wouldn't believe me. When something goes wrong, you always blame yourself first. I think we're alike in that way, sir. We look at the mistakes in our lives, the real ones and the imagined ones, and we torture ourselves, wishing somehow we could go back, to relive them, to somehow make it all right again."

"And we can't," Andrew whispered.

"We never do anything completely right, sir," Vincent said. "No one, not even my hero Andrew Lawrence Keane, does it all right," and he chuckled softly.

"I think, sir, you are even regretting letting this small weakness show in front of a very junior officer. You're thinking the proper commander is alone, always acting confident, hiding his fears."

Andrew looked back at Vincent.

"Just this once it's different, sir. It doesn't change how I feel about you. I'll never speak of this to anyone. When this moment passes it will be as if it never happened. And sir, it does not affect the confidence I'll always have in you whether we win or lose."

"It's just there's no room for mistakes," Andrew said, struggling to stay silent even as he blurted out the words. "Tomorrow night I'll go in with a gunboat to face him again," and he fell silent.

After what had happened aboard the *Suzdal*, the mere thought of going back aboard another boat like that sent a shiver of fear through him. How was he ever to face that again?

"We'll see what we can do, then," Vincent said softly.

Andrew found the slightest of smiles crossing his features. The boy was looking up at him, and yet he had to keep remembering that Vincent Hawthorne was no longer a boy. He had helped to turn him into a man, if learning to become a remorseless killer was what a man should learn.

Somehow he had hoped for better for Vincent, as if he were a replacement for his brother Johnnie.

"Yourself, Vincent," Andrew asked gently. "What has happened to you?"

"I'd rather not talk about it now, sir," Vincent said evenly.

"They finally got to you, didn't they? One too many killings and suddenly that's all you could do in return."

"I almost felt pity for Cromwell," Vincent said. "There's

a terrible hidden anguish in that man. And then I saw all that had come out of that, the men of my regiment lying dead in the palace, the taunt about your wife and mine, and then finally that Merki hanging on the cross like some sick caricature of a barbarian Christ.

"Yet where was my God? That Merki looked down upon me for pity, yet he would have torn my family apart in front of me with no more remorse than I would have for a venomous insect under my boot. Where was my God, sir, the God who since we came here I believed kept whispering to me, holding the sinfulness of killing before me, calling to me to find some better way?

"I remember reading the transcendentalists, Emerson, Longfellow, who talked about all of us being part of a greater soul. And there was that Merki looking down, the mob howling at his torment, and the strength of his dying arms was nourished out of our own blood and flesh.

"If there is a God, how could He have ever created a place like this? How could He make a place where to survive we must murder or be murdered in turn?"

"The world is madness, sir," Vincent whispered.

"And we're both lost in it," Andrew replied, putting his hand on Vincent's shoulder.

Vincent looked up at him.

"Maybe somehow we'll both find a way out of it," Andrew sighed. "Come on, son, you'd better find Marcus, and I've got to help get things moving."

The two turned and started back up away from the beach.

"Thank you, Vincent," Andrew said quietly.

"Thank you, sir," and drawing back, he saluted.

Andrew nodded in understanding, and returned the gesture. Vincent hesitated for a moment and then stepped off into the shadows.

"Colonel Keane, sir?"

Andrew looked about and saw Ferguson standing nearby.

"What is it, Chuck?"

"I didn't want to disturb you, sir," Ferguson said, "but something just hit me and I could damn well kick myself for it. I feel like a complete ass for not thinking of it before."

"Go on, Chuck, what is it this time?"

"Can I see your revolver, sir?"

Andrew reached down to his holster and pulled the weapon out. The weapon was still wet, and he could imagine

O'Donald, who was such a perfectionist about weapons, shivering at the sight of one of the few precious revolvers in all of Valennia being treated in such a manner.

Ferguson took the weapon and held it up.

"See that you fired a couple of rounds, sir."

"At a passing ironclad," Andrew replied, chuckling at the memory.

"So what is this all about, Chuck?"

"This, sir," and he slipped a percussion cap off the nipple of an undischarged chamber and held it up, his eyes aglow with enthusiasm.

"This, sir, is the answer to all our problems."

# Chapter Nineteen

"The Merki will be on the other shore by early evening," O'Donald shouted. "I don't give a good damn if Cromwell is here or not, I'm leading that attack in."

Kal, feeling as if he were being torn apart, sat in his chair. The day had been one of hopes crashed, rising up again, and then crashed yet again.

During the previous evening they had swept out of their lines, driving the light screen of Cartha pickets back into the city, regaining all the outer countryside held over the last month. Novrod militia had swelled their ranks, and a sense of triumph was in the air.

And then in the morning word had come that the *Ogunquit* and four of the gunboats were back at the mouth of the Neiper. For four agonizing hours he had felt that it was truly over, that Cromwell had defeated Andrew and had returned to secure his prize. Compounding that were the reports of the advance of the Merki. Wilderness Station had been abandoned that morning, and one scout had braved a mad swim across the Neiper, under the eyes of a patrolling galley, to report that their outriders were closing in.

And then but an hour ago, yet another report had arrived that a fleet was seen far down the coast, coming up with two gunboats in the lead.

"We'll be splitting our forces if we do," Hans said, his voice full of despair. "Cromwell's got the *Ogunquit* and four gunboats. If the report is right, we only have two. At best

Andrew will be able to land whatever he has left down on the coast and then bring them up here. If we attack, we'll be pouring men into the city, and Cromwell can shell the town into oblivion. And remember, we're going to lose a hell of a lot of men in the process. By tomorrow we might have thousands of our best-trained troops, fully armed, to support us."

"By morning they'll be ferrying Merki across," Pat replied. "They'll have a foothold on this side, they'll have our capital and Mikhail with them. For God's sake, that bastard might be able to turn some of the outlying cities against us. Remember these people, Hans—the city is the symbol to them, even more than the factories. We abandoned it to spare it, figuring Andrew would come back and we'd somehow take it back. With Mikhail backed by the Merki, it's finished.

"At the very least give me the chance to kill the son of a bitch and put up a fight for Suzdal. It just might rattle Cromwell if this springs up at the same time Andrew's closing in."

Hans stood up, paced to the far end of the room, and looked out the window.

"It'll be dark in another couple of hours," he said quietly and then looked back at Kal.

"Your opinion, General Schuder," Kal said evenly.

Hans walked over to where O'Donald sat, and leaning over he reached into the artilleryman's jacket and fished out a cigar.

"My last one," O'Donald protested.

"We'll split it," Hans said, breaking it in half, holding the two ends up, and then tossing the smaller portion back. He bit off a sizable chew and looked at the small group of government officers and regimental commanders that flanked the table around Kal and Casmar.

"I've always believed in two rules of war," Hans said. "First is get your strength together and punch the bastards with everything you have. The second is hit him first and keep on pushing him off balance.

"If we wait, we'll obey that first rule. If we go in tonight, it'll be the second, because once those Merki start pouring into the city, we'll never get it back."

Chewing vigorously, he looked down at the floor and then

with a shrug let out a jet of dirty brown juice into a corner of the room.

"Attack tonight. That damn redheaded mick is right. I know Andrew—he isn't going to wait, he's going to come crashing straight in, because damn him I taught him damn near everything he knows about the fine art of killing. If we attack, maybe we'll take some pressure off his side of things."

O'Donald pounded the table with his fist and looked over at Kal.

"Then do it, and may Kesus look down upon all of us," Kal said evenly.

"I wish to speak with you."

Nervously, Tobias looked up at Hulagar.

"I want to make sure this gun is mounted correctly. Then we'll talk," Tobias said sharply, pointing to the huge bulk of the hundred-pounder that had laboriously been moved up from the stern to replace the damaged gun, which had been sent back down to the aft end of the ship.

"That can wait," Hulagar said.

Tobias could not help but notice the distinct difference in tone Hulagar had adopted since the retreat of yesterday. He wanted to shout back at him to wait, but somehow he sensed that the ability to do that had been lost.

Beckoning for Tobias to follow, Hulagar pulled open the hatch to the lower deck, bent over, and inched down the ladder, Tobias following. Gaining the lower deck, Hulagar walked doubled over, his long arms dragging along the floor, and stepped into the confined quarters where he and the other Merki were berthed. Nervously Tobias stepped into the room, trying to suppress a gag.

The creatures had a strong musky smell, which was near to overpowering in the confined quarters. In the dim lamplight they looked at him coldly.

"When will Keane's fleet arrive here?"

"Sometime after sundown."

"And your plans?"

"I'm going out tonight," Cromwell said quietly.

"No. For tonight you are to stay here in the river."

Tobias felt as if his heart were about to stop. Just what the hell were they doing? When he had finally realized the full extent of his losses, he had known it was over. Once the damage was repaired and the firewood replenished, his plan was finally clear. He'd pull the ship out, and then at the right moment kill all of the Merki bastards. Once freely out to sea, he'd use the Cartha crew the same way he had used the Suzdalians who had followed him before. Hell, with the *Ogunquit* intact the Bantag would surely make him an offer.

"Why is it so important to stay here tonight? By tomorrow they might have us bottled in."

"With what, two smashed-up ironclads? You know there's no great ship—you heard what the prisoners said."

Tobias cringed inwardly. The humiliation of that revelation had seared into him. He could see it in the eyes of his crew, in the eyes of Hulagar.

"They are lying," Tobias said quickly.

"I have broken many human bones," Hulagar said darkly. "I know when their screams are truth and when they are lies."

Tobias fell silent. Again it was the same, the table before him, the taunting stares from the other side.

"Even I was fooled by the ship," Tamuka said evenly. "Such things often happen in battle. Victory can come from deceit as easily as from force of arms."

Tobias looked over at the Merki, wondering why he offered such an excuse.

"Perhaps we should kill him now and simply take the ship," Tamuka said softly in Merki, looking back over at Hulagar. "He must suspect something."

"There are three hundred Carthas on this ship and but twenty of us," Hulagar replied forcefully. "None of them know the Vushka are here. If we should kill Cromwell, they might grow suspicious, they might turn, they might even go to the other side. Play out the false promise this one last night. Let him think he will rule this place, though the fool must realize that with his army lost all hope is gone. We must not allow a single enemy ship to gain the river. He knows how to fight this ship. Let us not create a deceit within ourselves to think we can do it.

"Could any of you have understood yesterday's fight and commanded it?"

He deliberately looked at Vuka, who said nothing.

"We still need him, though he does not understand why. Tomorrow when the Vushka are in the city we will see. He will be brought ashore and our warriors will secure the ship.

If he reacts well, he will live. We can still use him to make yet more such ships."

"Just hold the river open—that is all we ask for now," Hulagar said, looking back to Tobias and speaking in Cartha.

Tobias nodded slowly, unable to reply.

"We have twenty-two galleys left, do we not?"

"Yes."

"It would be foolish to waste them in battle," Hulagar said absently. "They should stay safely in the city."

"I still need something to patrol forward," Tobias insisted. "They're a lot faster in the short run than one of my gunboats."

"Vuka," Hulagar said quietly.

He looked up with a start.

"I want you to command a galley. You are to patrol in front of the *Ogunquit* tonight. We need someone with the night eyes that these humans do not have."

Vuka nodded slowly, and said nothing.

"We must offer Tobias some logical hope," Tamuka said in Merki, as if Hulagar's orders were but a minor detail.

Hulagar nodded in agreement.

"It is not as grim as you believe," Hulagar said, looking back to Tobias. "Our Qar Qarth has created something that will soon be here to help you."

"What?" Tobias asked suspiciously.

"A device that you first told us of and how to make," and as Hulagar continued to talk a growing smile crossed Tobias's features.

As the galley swung in toward the beach, Andrew felt the nervousness would cause him to explode. The first wave of five ships had landed ten minutes ago; the line of skirmishes had disembarked and gone up over the edge of the beach into the high grass. A light splatter of musketry was starting to ring out.

It was damn near the same spot where they had first arrived here over three years before. The low mound of their temporary earthworks was now overgrown, returning back into the earth.

The bottom of the galley scraped into the sand. Andrew grabbed the side railing to keep his balance as the ship came to a stop a dozen yards from shore.

The survivors of the 35th, who had been at the oars,

started to come forward, leaping over the sides, rifles and cartridge boxes held high. Andrew hesitated for a second, then, sitting up on the side railing, he slid over into the warm water and advanced with his men. The blue wave of men rose up out of the water, going into the shadows, following their shot-torn standards retrieved from the wreck of the *Suzdal*.

He found it all to be slightly ironic. Over three years before, they had sailed on the *Ogunquit* to do precisely this, make an amphibious assault on a Confederate fort. Well, they were finally doing it, but it was to fight against the commander of the ship which had brought them here.

Another galley slid in, and then an entire wave of twenty ships hit the beach one after the other.

"We've got a messenger, sir!"

Several of the men from the scout ship came running back to the beach, half-dragging a man from the 44th New York between them.

The artilleryman, seeing Andrew, found the strength in his legs to come forward and snap to attention.

"Sergeant Ciencin reporting, sir, and damn glad to see you alive."

Andrew returned the salute, then stepped forward and shook the sergeant's hand.

"I'm damn glad to be back, Ciencin. Now report."

"Sir, Sergeant, I mean General, Schuder sent out a half-dozen of us men from the 44th along with guides to try to find you. It's been a hell of a day getting through."

"Sir, Mikhail turned traitor, and he's got the city."

"I know that."

"Well, sir, O'Donald is leading an assault into the city tonight to try to take it back."

Andrew looked over as Marcus, with Vincent beside him, came running up the beach to join him.

"What the hell for?" John asked, "We'll be up there by tomorrow with nearly all our troops."

"The Merki are closing in, sir."

"What?"

"Just that, sir. The Merki hit our defense line to the southwest three days ago and cut right through it. I was sent out this morning to reach you. I guess by now they're most likely on the other side of the river."

"What's the road like up to the city?" Even as he spoke, the light rain of musket fire ahead was increasing in volume.

"Damn near impossible, sir. I had to go way the hell around the reservoir and ride cross-country. They've got raiding parties out in a wide net. Sneaking down here I lost my Rus guide and both our horses. I'd say near old Fort Lincoln they must have near a thousand men that they landed there yesterday. Though I didn't see it myself, I stopped up with the fellas that were holding the mines and they claim they saw two gunboats anchored to cover the road."

"A damn good delaying force," Andrew said sharply.

"That explains why Cromwell didn't come out," Vincent said. "The Merki want him to cover the river while they cross over."

"Where the hell is Ferguson?"

"Over here, sir!" The engineer came up out of the water to join the group.

"We're going to do it now, tonight!"

"All right, sir," Ferguson said wearily. "I had a gut feeling you'd want to rush into this.

"I'm going to have to rig them up in the dark. It'll be a bit touchy once I set the triggers on them, so I'd strongly advise everyone to clear this section of beach."

"How many were you able to make?"

"Only six, sir. There's precious little powder and not enough time."

"Get to work then."

Andrew looked back at the rest of his staff.

"Darkness or not, we're going to drive toward the city tonight. The 35th will lead the advance in a line of skirmishers. They're to be supported by the first brigade of the second. I want a brigade to swing out wide to our right flank. Find some men in your units who live around here to act as guides. They might have a surprise up in the hills, but I doubt it—I think what they've got left will either be in the city or deployed as a blocking force. The rest of the army will follow the advance of the 35th.

"Any questions?"

"A night march is awful risky, sir," Vincent said.

"It'll be just as risky for them. I want to keep the pressure on. When O'Donald hits, I don't want them to be able to shift support. Besides, it'll give us cover if we've got to run the boats or flank past Fort Lincoln."

Andrew paused for a moment.

"Ciencin? Kal, Hans, all the others," and he hesitated for a brief second, "and my wife—are they all right?"

"They're fine."

And he breathed a sigh of relief.

"My wife?" Vincent asked nervously.

"She couldn't be better. Sir, it was yourself we thought was dead—they sent your sword in to us. They said all of you were gone, but I knew better than that. The good Lord wouldn't want any of you, and the devil would lock his gates at the sight of you, so here's the only place we figured you could be."

Andrew smiled and then looked over at John.

"Colonel Mina, you will assume the command of the 35th. General Hawthorne, you will act as his second."

"What are you talking about, sir? You're in command of the 35th," John replied suspiciously.

"I'm going in with the boats."

"Now wait a minute, Keane," Marcus snapped.

"No arguments," Andrew said quietly. "Marcus, you're staying here on the beach. I'm giving you an order."

"Me an order?" Marcus roared.

Andrew smiled sadly.

"Maybe this idea of Ferguson's won't work, maybe it will. By tomorrow morning the Merki might be in Suzdal, and the *Ogunquit* will come booming back down that river, with two beaten-up ironclads to fight her. If that's the case, Marcus Licinius Graca, as a representative of the Republic of Rus I am releasing you from the bonds of your alliance. You're to take the galleys and get the hell out of here as fast as you can. Get back to Roum, try to carry on the fight from there. There are enough tools there for you to rearm. I'd like to think that at least Roum in the end will defy the Merki and survive."

"That's one hell of an alliance," Marcus snapped. "As consul I gave my word to this bond, and I will not abandon you now."

"And what the hell good can you do here if we lose?" Andrew snapped angrily. "Stand on the beach, your men armed with spears and swords, and tomorrow the Merki come thundering out of Rus, while the *Ogunquit* smashes everything you have on the beach? You've got nine thousand men, Marcus. Take them back and use them where they can do the most good."

Marcus shook his head.

"In the morning you might see better," Andrew said quietly, "so don't let your pride stop you from what is right for you and your people."

"Andrew, you're not going in with the boats," Vincent said sharply.

Andrew looked over at Vincent, surprised that he had addressed him by his first name.

"That's Colonel Keane," Andrew replied, his voice almost gentle. "And yes, I am going in with the boats, and by God you are staying on shore as ordered.

"Gentlemen, I'm getting started over here, so would you all kindly clear this section of beach," Ferguson shouted.

Andrew looked over his shoulder and saw Ferguson standing in the water in front of one of the smaller fifty-man Roum galleys, with a crew of Rus soldiers around him dragging a long slender pole.

"The discussion here is finished," Andrew said sharply. "Now, gentlemen, get to your posts, and God willing we'll see each other in Suzdal come morning."

Andrew turned away and started to walk down to join Ferguson.

"Why?"

Andrew looked over his shoulder and saw Vincent following him.

"I think you if anyone should understand," Andrew replied.

Vincent hesitated, and then a sad smile crossed his features as he stopped and wearily saluted.

"I'll see you in the morning, sir."

"So that is the city of the accursed Yankees," Jubadi said coldly, dropping the reins on his horse as it lowered its head to drink from the Neiper River.

"It will make a wonderful fire when the time comes," Suvatai replied.

"My Qar Qarth."

Jubadi shifted in his saddle and from out of the darkness Hulagar emerged. Coming up to stand before Jubadi, he bowed low, pressing his forehead against Jubadi's foot before rising again.

"Is all in order?"

"There have been problems, my lord."

"Then tell me."

When Hulagar had finished recounting the events of the campaign, Jubadi sat in silence for long minutes.

"I should have slit his throat as soon as the boat was finished and manned it with our own."

"It might still have turned out the same in the end, my Qar Qarth," Hulagar replied. "We lost nearly fifteen thousand Carthas in the fight. That would have been an umen and a half of our finest warriors. Better their blood spilled to weaken the Yankees than ours. That is how it was planned from the beginning."

"I want our people going into the city tonight," Jubadi said sharply. "This Keane has proved himself far too resourceful already, far beyond what we had ever dreamed possible. If he is still alive, let him return tomorrow and see our warriors manning his walls."

Jubadi laughed at the thought of it. The legendary fortress of Suzdal turned upside down to keep out the very cattle who had built it.

"The boats are waiting, my lord, just up the river."

"Return to your ship, Hulagar. We will get started here."


"Shit!"

"Goddamm it," O'Donald whispered, "of course it's shit. Now shut the hell up."

He looked back up over the edge of the pipe. The walls of the northwest bastion were less than fifty yards away. He knew there would be people up there, but the weather was still playing to him, the clouds concealing the light from the Great Wheel and the twin moons, which would be rising soon.

Standing waist-deep in the Neiper, he ducked down and went into the drainpipe. He felt as if he were going to lose his last meal on the spot. Crouching low, he scurried in, moving quickly, the man behind him following.

He thanked God the shortage of bronze had prevented Emil from having the last section cast, which would have hooked in at the end of the brick section and taken the sewer straight out into the Neiper. The whole scheme would have been impossible then.

He finally let go of his breath and inhaled.

That was it, damm it, and he doubled over. Cursing, he spit the vomit out of his mouth, nodding grimly as he listened to the man behind him gagging as well.

Pausing, he pulled out a match and held his breath. One of Emil's assistants had said something about gases that could explode, but the hell with them—he'd be damned if he'd crawl up a quarter mile of sewer blind. He struck the head and it flared into life. Lifting up the lantern, he lit the wick and then continued on.

With lantern held forward, he took off at a slow run, doubled over in the narrow passage. A hole appeared straight overhead, under the bastion. He prayed his men would stay quiet, and prayed as well no one directly above was using it. If I ever get out of this, he thought darkly, I'll never joke about falling into an outhouse again.

Reaching a turn in the pipe, he looked back. The long line of men were behind him, mumbling curses. Another lantern flared up. A hundred in so far, and they still hadn't been spotted.

He pressed on, counting off the paces.

A small pipe went off to the right. They were inside the city.

As he continued on, more pipes kept branching off into the new sections of the city. He hit eight hundred paces and stopped.

It was impossible to tell if the men were still coming up. He had hoped to get a thousand into the city this way, but if they only got five hundred they'd be lucky.

He looked up.

Could I have missed the damn thing?

Going slower, he pushed on. A square brick line went off to his left, half the size of the one they were in. This had to be it.

Grimacing, he went down on his hands and knees and scurried in, sliding in the damp muck.

Overhead he saw the square opening going up.

He put the lantern down, stood up, and hit the wooden barrier. Bracing his feet, he shoved hard, and the barrier broke upward. Grabbing hold of the side, he pulled himself up through the privy hole into the bathroom of the 35th's barracks.

Leaning half out of the hole, he pulled his revolver out and found that he was laughing at the absurdity of it all.

The room was empty and dark.

By Jesus, if I'd been sitting here, he thought, I'd have died of apoplexy.

He came up out of the hole and turned to pull the next man up after him.

"You and the next man, give a hand up to the others."

With revolver still out, he slipped out of the bathroom and into the barracks hall. Pausing, he pulled off his filth-covered jacket and threw it aside.

The building was ghostlike, empty. The cots were in their long orderly row, beds made as if the regiment had simply stepped out for an evening drill and would be returning shortly.

Going down to the end of the corridor, he peeked out the door.

The town square was like a ghost village. Nothing stirred; all the buildings were dark.

Turning, he ran back down the corridor and into the bathroom, which was filling with men.

"Get the first party formed up in the barracks hall, and uncork your muskets. Grab some sheets, wipe your locks clean, and load 'em up. Now move it!"

He felt it was going far too slow; it seemed an eternity between each man coming out of the hole.

"The signal rockets, sir," a man gasped, coming up out of the hole pushing a tar-covered canvas bag ahead of him.

O'Donald took the bag and tore it open. He pulled out the three rockets, carried them into the next room, and laid them out on a bunk.

Nervously he paced back and forth as the room gradually filled. He knew the stench must be unbearable, but since they all smelled equally bad, it was becoming hardly noticeable.

"Someone's coming."

O'Donald crouched low, moved up to one of the windows, and cautiously peeked out.

"Jesus, they're Merki!"

Four of the towering creatures were moving up across the town square. In the dim shadows he could see them looking about, moving casually, their deep guttural conversation punctuated by sharp barking laughs.

Suddenly one of them paused. His head turned, looking straight at the barracks.

O'Donald froze, not daring to move.

The single Merki broke away from the group and started to come toward the building.

"I'll kill any man who shoots," O'Donald whispered. "Use your bayonets!"

He shifted his gaze to the men crouched on the floor beside him.

The one Merki continued to advance toward the barracks and reached the stairs. The others called to him, and for long seconds O'Donald listened as they spoke hurriedly to each other. He drew his head back, slowly standing up against the wall beside the window. Suddenly the rest of the group started to come forward, stepping up onto the long veranda. O'Donald slipped his sword out of its scabbard.

The Merki filled the window, leaning over and pressing forward to look in.

O'Donald swung around and slammed his sword forward, driving it straight through the window and into the Merki's face.

"Bayonets!" O'Donald shouted, crashing through the window in a shower of glass. Still hanging on to his sword, he staggered forward. The Merki fell back, a howl of startled pain escaping his lips.

The rest of the Merki stood transfixed. Crashing through the double doors and through the windows, the men swarmed out, bayonets lowered. Another Merki went down under a swarm of bayonets. O'Donald leaped over the porch railing even as one of the Merki turned and started to run with a long-legged gait. Angling in low, O'Donald dived for him, and saw the flash of steel as his enemy pulled his scimitar free. The two tumbled over, O'Donald rolling away as the blade slashed down. A shadow swept past him, and a loud shriek tore across the square as a Suzdalian stood above the creature, leaning in with his bayonet, driving it deep into the Merki's chest.

The Merki continued to shriek even as O'Donald leaned up and slashed its throat.

O'Donald came back to his feet. There was a moment of silence which seemed almost haunting, and then came a distant cry in Merki.

"We can't wait!" O'Donald hissed. "Grab the rockets.

Tell Johnson he's in command here. Any more men coming through should hold in reserve to cover our path. All you men, follow me!"

At a run, O'Donald turned and raced across the side of the barracks and down the street.

"All of you gather round," Ferguson said, and Andrew looked up to see the six ship captains, all of them Roum, come forward to stand in a tight circle around the engineer.

"Before we get started on this," Andrew said, "I want to ask everyone a last time. I know you men volunteered for this job, and all your crew are volunteers as well. You can still change your minds, and by God I won't think the less of you for it."

He looked around at the group, and they shook their heads.

"I'm after my vengeance for what he did to us," one of the men growled, and the others nodded.

Andrew looked over at Marcus.

"You didn't order any of these men, did you?"

"Damn near every one of the captains volunteered. I simply chose the best."

Andrew shook his head at what was being offered to him by the Roum.

"All right, Ferguson, you talk, I'll translate."

Ferguson nodded.

"Gentlemen, this thing is called a spar torpedo. I've taken the poles we used to hold up the forward corvuses and mounted them to the six light galleys behind me. Attached to each of the poles is a twenty-five-foot boom, now raised up. When it's lowered, it will fall through a slot I've cut in the front of each of your vessels.

"Attached to the end of each boom is a barrel," and he paused to point at the ship directly behind him to illustrate his point. "When that boom is dropped, the barrel on the end will be under five feet of water.

"Now inside each of those barrels is a hundred and fifty pounds of gunpowder and one of these."

He held up a Springfield rifle, the barrel sawed off just above the lock.

"The working end of this gun is full of powder and stuck into the main charge. The back end is sealed off inside a small chamber so the hammer can strike down cleanly.

There is a rope attached to the trigger, which is already cocked. That rope will go through a piece of cork pushed into the barrel and then to the outside and straight back to your hand.

"All you have to do is row up to your target."

The men chuckled grimly, and Ferguson smiled.

"The key thing to remember is that you've got to slow down just before you get there and then lower the boom. Don't drop it hard—it might set the charge off on the surface. The barrel is weighted down with lead, so it will sink. Come up to your target and slow up even more. Hit him too hard, you might bust the barrel, and that's it. So slow down when you feel the barrel hit the side. Then yank the rope hard.

Ferguson walked back away from the men and pointed the sawed-off gun at the shore and pulled the trigger.

A tongue of flame shot out.

He looked back at the group.

"That's all there is to it," he said quietly. "It'll blow a hole right through the bastard. Hitting him with a hundred and fifty pounds underwater will be like hitting him with half a ton of powder on top. He'll go down like a rock."

"What going to happen to us?" one of the captains said.

Chances are you'll be blown out of the water as well," Ferguson said softly. "As far as I know, it's only been done by a surface boat once before, by a Lieutenant Cushing, back in our old war. He sank a reb ironclad doing the same thing.

"And he lived," Ferguson said softly, "along with most of his crew.

"That's it sir," Ferguson said.

"How much powder do we have left for the guns?"

"I left three rounds per gun, sir. Everything else is with your ships."

Andrew looked back at the group around him.

"The two ironclads will go in first. With luck, they'll draw the fire, and also they'll scout the river. The rest of us will follow in single file. The *Ogunquit* is the main target. If we get that, then anything left will be used against Cromwell's other ironclads. The river's fairly wide by the old fort we had there, and I would guess that's where he'll be.

"Now let's move!"

The captains turned and went back to their ships.

Andrew paused for a brief second and looked over at Marcus.

"Remember, what your people are doing here is more than enough. If we fail, get the hell out!"

Marcus smiled sadly and then turned away.

Andrew went down to his ship, where the crew was already waiting, the captain grabbing hold of the railing and climbing up ahead of him. Smiling, the men reached over the side and pulled Andrew aboard.

Ferguson came up alongside and started to climb in as well.

"Like hell, Chuck!" Andrew shouted.

"Thought I'd come along for the ride."

"What, and lose my best damn engineer? Now get back on that beach."

Ferguson looked up at him angrily.

"Goddammit, sir, sometimes I wish I had a little less brains."

Andrew laughed.

"That's just about what it takes to do something like this!" Andrew said. "Now step aside!"

The Roum captain shouted a command, and the hundreds of men who had been standing along the shore rushed down into the water, pushing on the sides of the ship.

With a creaking groan the vessel was backed out into the sea.

Nervously, Andrew looked up at the long pole, which creaked and swayed, the barrel on top hanging above him with a dark menace. The oarsmen started to pull, and the vessel slipped out into deeper water.

The six ships formed up and started forward, and from farther out the two ironclads came in, cutting in front of the line. A light breeze fluttered across the water, and looking up, Andrew saw the line of clouds moving across the sky, the stars appearing behind them as if a curtain were being rolled back.

The ocean started to brighten, and then as if the stage lights had been struck, the first of the two moons appeared, flooding the ocean with a ruddy glow.

"Move it, goddamm it!" O'Donald shouted.

The men spread out to either side, racing up the steps of the inner city gate. The first musket went off, the bullet smacking the pavement by his feet.

Pat stood before the arched gate, watching as his men hit the top of the battlement. A body tumbled over, crashing to the hard stone pavement. A flurry of shots rang out. A deep-throated horn sounded.

"They know, damm it! Send up the signal!"

The gate before him swung open.

"Let's go!"

O'Donald charged through the opening, his men following.

A musket shot rang out, and the man next to him tumbled over. With sword raised, O'Donald ran forward, crossing through the empty rail yard, rushing toward the drawbridge for the main track.

A volley of shots snapped from the bastion to either side, and more went down.

A rocket slashed behind him into the night sky, bursting red.

"That's the signal! They've lost the surprise!" Kal shouted.

"Stay on the track, by column charge!" Hans screamed.

Leaping to the front of the formation, he started up, racing through the darkness, cursing the fact that crossties never seemed to be laid so one could conveniently run from one to the next.

Staggering his pace, he pressed on, running full out, his hat flying off, the color-bearer keeping pace beside him.

Musket fire rattled out along the wall. There was a sharp flash, and a slash of canister screamed overhead, slamming into the men behind him.

"Don't stop!"

He heard the hollow sound of wood under his feet. They were crossing the moat, and he noticed that it was getting brighter out.

Damn, the sky was clearing. He cursed inwardly. And directly ahead, the drawbridge was up, the heavy wooden barrier closed, the last half of the moat gaping before him.

The men behind him kept pressing in.

There was nothing else to do, so he leaped forward, landing between two sharpened stakes.

Screams were echoing around him. In the ghostly light he saw one of his men writhing, a stake in the bottom of the moat driven clear through his body.

"Come on!" he screamed. "Hit the wall!"

Another shot rang out, and a man standing above him on

the bridge seemed to disappear over the side. Scrambling forward, he started up the side of the moat. The top of the bastion seemed an eternity away. He could see musketmen lining the crest, leaning over, pointing their weapons straight down.

Flashes of light rippled along the wall. Men beside him desperately tried to crawl up, were hit, and tumbled back down. A flag-bearer charged past, screaming hysterically, colors held high, and made it halfway up the slope. He pitched forward, driving the Rus flag into the earthen wall.

Hans looked back to the long column stretched out on the bridge. It was breaking up, canister slashing through them. A terrible knot of men continued to spill over the edge of the bridge, falling, leaping into the moat, pushing past their impaled comrades. Others were spreading out from the far end, sliding down the sides of the moat. A flurry of rockets soared up from the battlements, illuminating the vast field. Looking back, he saw the column going back for hundreds of yards into the darkness, the men bunched up, still pushing forward.

"It's a disaster!" someone screamed.

Hans looked around, trying to gauge his chances. All surprise had been lost. The attack had gone forward like an arrow striking at one point. But the way in was closed. They were being slaughtered.

Sick at heart, he started to slide back down the bastion slope, oblivious to the bullets snapping past. The city was lost now forever. There was no sense in slaughtering what was left of his army before the fortification which he had helped to make impregnable.

"Bugler, bugler to me!"

Hans staggered through the mad confusion trying to find a way to signal the retreat and get his men out before they were all murdered.

"Bugler to me!"

"Over there!" someone shouted, rushing past Hans and pointing back to the base of the bridge.

Pushing back through the men, he found the bugler, lying spread-eagled on the ground, face buried in the mud.

"Get out of here!" Hans roared. "Retreat!"

Men looked at him, and released from the madness, they turned and started to run back out of the moat, sliding up the steep sides, the Cartha musketmen hitting them, sending them pitching back into the gully.

There was a loud rattling behind him. Turning, he looked back in dumbfounded amazement. The drawbridge was crashing down!

The bridge slammed across the moat, the impact buckling it in the middle.

"Charge!"

As if a dam had suddenly burst open, the men charged forward, screaming with battle rage. Bodies continued to rain down from the trestle. Hans ran back across the moat, scrambling up the side and shouldered his way into the flood. They crossed through the cut in the earthen walls, the Cartha above raining shot straight down, and then suddenly he was on the inside.

"Twenty-second Suzdal, the next gate!" Hans shouted.

The men, already drilled, continued straight forward, unmindful of the losses on their flanks. The standard of the 1st Kevan burst through the cut, the men behind the flag-bearer swinging out to either flank, broadening the breach.

"Keep moving!" Hans roared, standing by the opening, pointing his carbine forward.

"Sorry we were late."

Hans turned to see O'Donald leaning against the side of the bastion, looking over at him with a wan smile.

He drew closer and wrinkled his nose.

"You smell ghastly," Hans shouted.

O'Donald nodded slowly.

"The Merki are already in the city. I've left a blocking force up by the barracks, with orders to hold the road open into the center of town."

"Let's get going, then," Hans snapped.

"Just a second, you damned Dutchman," O'Donald said softly.

Hans drew closer.

"What the hell is wrong?" He felt his voice shaking.

O'Donald looked up at him and drew his hand away from his stomach.

"I guess I stopped one."

"No, no." He grabbed hold of O'Donald as he started to slide down to the ground.

A sharp grimace crossed O'Donald's features.

"Feels like I spilled hot soup on myself," he gasped.

"Lost nearly everybody getting to the gate, had to keep going, had to cut the line."

"Rest easy, Pat. Don't talk."

Hans tore O'Donald's shirt back and saw the ugly pucker of a bullet hole in his stomach.

"It's not that bad," Hans whispered, as if by some magic of words he could somehow change it.

"Too much of an old soldier to believe that," O'Donald grunted. "Belly wound and you're in the grave. Do me a favor."

"Anything."

"Shoot me."

"Like hell."

"Damn you," O'Donald cried. "You know what's going to happen to me." He smiled weakly. "Goodbye, Hans. Now get it done."

Hans knelt beside his friend, unable to speak. It would take four or five days for him to go. He'd start to swell up, his insides rotting out, puffing up with the stink of death. There'd be the horrible delirium, the screams of anguish. In the end the face would already look like a skull.

He looked over at his carbine lying on the ground beside him. This way it'd be over in seconds. He looked back at Pat. His eyes were closed, his lips moving.

"Hail Mary full of Grace . . ."

For the first time since he had seen Andrew wounded at Gettysburg, Hans felt tears come to his eyes.

He reached over for his carbine, stood up, and saw the survivors of his staff standing around him waiting for orders, the battle still raging to either side not fifty yards away.

"Detail four men, make a stretcher, and get him the hell back to the hospital area."

"God damn you, Schuder," O'Donald cried. "You know I'm a dead man. Now finish it!"

How could he explain? He had done it once before, out on the prairie, when one of his troopers had stopped a Cheyenne arrow in the gut. They couldn't leave him behind, and the boy, a Catholic, said he couldn't do it by his own hand. So he had volunteered. Nearly twenty years ago, and it still haunted him. The boy had whispered the same prayer, crossing himself and then smiling sadly at him before he closed his eyes and turned his head away.

"Pat, I can't," Hans whispered, leaning over and almost

tenderly brushing the hair back out of the wounded man's eyes.

"God damn you," O'Donald gasped.

Hans stood up and looked back again at his men.

"All of you know," he snarled, "I want Mikhail alive. Make sure that's obeyed. Now let's take this goddam place back."

Hans started forward. He paused for a brief second to look back at his friend, and in the swirling confusion of men O'Donald disappeared from view.

Wide-eyed, Vuka saw the billowing clouds of spark-laden smoke turn the bend of the river before him. They were coming. He looked over at the Cartha ship captain.

"It's going to get hot out here," the captain said, looking up at the Merki beside him.

"It is madness for us to stay in the middle. Get us out of here—take us in close to shore."

Startled, the captain quickly nodded his head and turned the tiller over, the galley swinging about to head upstream. Hulagar had ordered them to stay in front of the ships, and he fully knew the reason why.

Hulagar be damned. He'd find the proper excuse later. For now he would simply watch.

Rounding the bend in the river, Andrew felt his stomach tighten. Beneath the double shadows of the moons, Tobias seemed to be waiting for him. The *Ogunquit*, brightly silhouetted in the middle of the Neiper, was anchored stern-first, her heavy gun pointing straight downstream. A hundred yards forward were the other four ironclads.

It would be a half-mile run straight up against the current. The only sound was the creaking of the oars as they turned in their locks, and the splashing of the paddle wheels of the two ironclads steaming fifty yards ahead and now spread out to run side by side.

A bell started to rattle in alarm, counterpointed by the harsh screech of a steam whistle.

So much for surprise, he thought coldly.

He picked up a speaking trumpet.

"First three boats make straight for the *Ogunquit*. Number four and five stand back and prepare to take out the nearest ironclads. As soon as the *Ogunquit*'s hit, if any of you haven't struck yet, take out the nearest target, and for God's sake don't hit one of our own!"

He hated to hold back, but this time he knew the reserve might be all-important.

A snap of light ignited on the water, and seconds later a tower of hissing water rose up between his two ironclads. The galley rode up over the waves and continued on. The commanders of the other ships called for battle speed, and the vessels seemed to leap forward.

Too soon, dammit, but he knew it was useless to call them back now that their blood was up.

A shower of sparks rose up out of the *Ogunquit*'s stacks.

The range was closing painfully slowly, and he paced back and forth in the narrow confines of the bow.

They were down to six hundred yards, and ever so slowly the first enemy gunboat started to slip out into the middle of the river, blocking the path in to the *Ogunquit*, followed seconds later by a second boat.

There was another snap of fire, and a shower of sparks soared up from the *Gettysburg*, the metallic clang of the hit booming across the water. The ship pressed on, clawing its way up the river to get into carronade range.

Andrew felt as if time had dropped to a crawl as they crossed through five hundred and then down to four hundred yards.

The first two enemy ships were now making steam, coming straight down the river. His two ships seemed to fire simultaneously, their shot screaming up the river, one striking the lead ship, the other skipping across the water into the darkness.

The four ironclads seemed to be on a collision course. The three galleys forward continued to press straight in, the other two swinging out wide to either flank.

In the narrow confines of the river he felt that there wasn't an inch of space left for maneuver.

The range closed down to a hundred.

The enemy ships fired. A shot slammed into the gun deck of the *President Kalencka*, and a shower of metal and wood fragments sprayed across the water. The one ironclad started to turn, running straight into the middle of the channel, heading at the three galleys.

"Get out of the way!" Andrew screamed.

He saw the pole of one of them drop.

"No, goddammit, the *Ogunquit*!"

The galley swerved in toward the first ironclad, and another galley followed suit, turning to run in front of its supporting gunboat, racing straight toward the other ship.

"Goddammit!" Andrew roared.

He felt the concussion through the water. There was a dull flash, and then with a thunderclap roar a column of water seemed to leap straight for the heavens. The massive bulk of the enemy ship seemed to lift straight up on its side. His galley swerved over, the captain aiming it away from the tremendous explosion ahead. He could hear the shouts of excitement and fear from his crew. Now they really knew what they had volunteered for.

The second galley slammed into its target and another explosion soared upward, followed a brief second later by a detonation from within the ironclad that tore it into an expanding cloud of deadly debris.

The mushroomlike explosion slammed across the water. Andrew felt the deck jump beneath his feet. The boat started to slide off back into the middle of the channel, and he looked aft.

A section of railing had been torn away and half a dozen men were down, screaming in anguish.

A wave of water, laden with steam and stinking explosives, washed over them. The boat plunged through the smoke. The water was foaming around him, and in the dank stygian mist he saw the shadow of the first ironclad rolling over on its back, horrified shrieks echoing from within the doomed ship. Like a curtain pulling back before him, they shot out the other side. Ahead his two ironclads were still pushing in. Behind them he could see two of his galleys.

The third had simply disappeared in the cataclysm.

Andrew picked up his speaking trumpet.

"The *Ogunquit*! The hell with the rest—get the *Ogunquit*!"

The ship continued forward, and he looked back at the crew, their backs to him as they labored at the oars.

They must know their chances now, and yet still they were hanging on. Everything he and his men had suffered for Roum he felt was already paid back in full.

He looked forward.

The *Ogunquit* was less than three hundred yards away. Another couple of minutes was all they needed.

A brilliant snap of light burst from the front of the ship.

An instant later an explosion of wood burst out the aft end of *Gettysburg*'s paddle-wheel armor. A tearing shriek of wood grinding itself up issued from the ship as it instantly slowed. Within seconds, Andrew shot past the vessel as it lost way and started to drift back down the river.

He looked forward, and it seemed as if the *Ogunquit* was not any closer. In the moonlight he could see water starting to foam underneath the ship's stern as the vessel slowly started to back up.

"More speed!" Andrew screamed. "We need more speed!"

Terrified, Tobias looked back at Tamuka through the curtain of gunsmoke filling the deck.

"They're torpedoes! You saw what they did!"

"Torpedoes? Can these things get us?"

Tobias felt an inner twinge of pleasure at the note of confusion in Hulagar's voice.

"I'm backing her up. We've got to get the hell back. We're reloading the gun with canister."

"Can they sink us!"

"Goddammit, yes, they can sink us!" Tobias shrieked.

"Then you should have thought of this before," Tamuka said darkly.

Again, damn them all, yet again they had tricked him, and yet again he would be judged. How could he ever have planned for this? Roum was supposed to have fallen, Andrew was supposed to have come back by land. No one was ever to have thought of making torpedoes against his ship.

"If need be we can run back to the city."

"You can't," Tamuka snapped.

Tobias turned and looked at the Merki. There was something in his voice—he was hiding something.

"Why?"

Tamuka was silent.

"Why, damn you, why?"

"Fight your ship here," Tamuka replied.

"Not until I know!" Tobias roared back.

"Because the Vushka are crossing the river even now."

Stunned, Tobias backed away from Tamuka, whose hand now rested upon the hilt of his blade.

"So you lied to me all along," Tobias hissed. "You promised me Rus to rule as my own. You cheated me, you bastard."

"You can still rule," Tamuka shouted. "But without us, you are nothing! Now fight this ship."

Tamuka stood over him, his features dark. Tobias, his hand resting on the butt of his pistol, was tempted to draw the weapon but saw the look of warning in the Merki's eyes.

He tried to hold his gaze, but the eyes burned into him, taunting him darkly, with all the dredged-up fears.

Shaking, he turned away.

"Aback slow!"

"What the hell was that?" someone shouted, pointing off toward the south. Seconds later he saw it, a flash of light soaring up into the night sky.

"They must be fighting along the river. Now keep moving!"

The column ahead continued the charge straight up the main boulevard, and suddenly the Great Square was before him. Turning, Hans saw the endless stream of men pouring into the city behind him, the flashes of gunfire along the wall marking the rout of the Carthas, the breach into the city widening with every passing second.

"If that bastard's hiding anywhere, it's in the capitol!" Hans shouted. "Form line by company, skirmishers forward!"

Men started to sprint across the open area, while the regiment behind him raced across the front of the cathedral, showing a skill under fire born out of countless hours of drill. Hans felt a trembling in his heart at the sight of his old veterans falling into place.

The battle flags came up into the center. A flash of light snapped across the square, and a spray of canister swept into the ranks.

Hans held his carbine up.

"For Rus!"

The line broke, leaping forward.

Screaming with rage, he fell in with the advance. Half a dozen cannon snapped lose their deadly loads of canister. It seemed as if hundreds of men went down, but the charge did not falter. The men raced in, bayonets forward. The Cartha gunners worked feverishly to reload while the charge closed in. A man broke away, turning to run back up the steps, and instantly the entire battery broke, men throwing down equipment, bolting in every direction, throwing up their hands shrieking for mercy.

The charge went up and over them, and with Hans in the lead stormed up the steps.

An arrow slammed past him, dropping the flag-bearer. He looked up to see a line of Merki archers, and at the sight of them the wild screams of the charging regiment changed into a near-primal roar of hatred.

Onward they came, oblivious to losses. The Merki before him threw aside his bow and swept out his long scimitar.

Hans, laughing coldly, aimed his Sharps straight into the warrior's face and fired.

Crouching low, he broke open the breech and slammed in another round. A Merki charged up to him, sword cutting the air. Hans rolled back, raising his gun to fire. A Suzdalian came in from the side, slamming his bayonet into the Merki's back. He pulled the blade out, clubbed his musket, and swung it back around, smashing it into the creature's face, shattering the stock.

Hans came up, looking over at the wide-eyed soldier.

"Come on!"

They burst into the building. A vicious hand-to-hand battle had erupted in the hallway, and dozens of Merki filled the corridor. Musket shots rang out, and screams of rage, human and nonhuman.

Regardless of losses, the Suzdalians continued to pour into the building, climbing over the fallen, throwing themselves bodily on the Merki, slashing with their last ounce of strength to take one of the hated enemy with them.

The melee pushed up the hallway, the floor slippery with blood.

Reaching the double doors to the presidential chambers, Hans burst the doors open. An arrow snapped past, striking the man next to him. He raised his carbine and fired, knocking the lone Merki off his feet. Men poured in around him. Leaping over the furniture of the front office, he quickly reloaded, then kicked in the doorway into Kal's office.

The doorframe next to him exploded, and the room filled with smoke.

And beyond his wildest hope, Mikhail stood before him, a smoking single-shot pistol in his right hand, a still-loaded weapon in his left.

Mikhail started to back up.

"Drop the gun, Mikhail," Hans said softly.

"I'll take you with me."

"Not the way your hand is shaking," Hans growled. "Now drop the pistol. I'll promise you a fair trial."

Mikhail looked at him, his eyes wide with terror, and then his gaze slowly started to shift to one of cunning.

"The law prevents capital punishment, Mikhail. At worst you'll go to prison. Maybe we'll trade you for some prisoners."

Mikhail lowered his weapon and let it drop to the floor. He started to laugh softly.

"Then take me away, Yankee, and remember, I know my rights as a senator. Your laws protect me now."

A thin smile creased Han's features.

"Not before you get this."

The crack of the carbine filled the room. Mikhail staggered backward, slamming into the wall.

Stunned, he looked down at the red smear already spreading out from his stomach.

"You promised," he gasped.

"And I've just given you your trial, you bastard," Hans snapped.

"You lying peasant scum!" Mikhail whined.

Bill Webster, who had joined the attack against orders, stepped forward, and shouldering his musket, he slammed another shot into Mikhail's stomach.

*"Sic semper tyrannis,"* Webster snarled, and he stalked out of the room, Hans following him.

There was another shot, and then another, Mikhail's shrieks echoing into the corridor.

An angry cry welled up from the Suzdalians as they poured into the room, explosion following explosion.

Fighting raged farther down the corridor as yet more Suzdalians stormed past.

The shooting in the room continued unabated, men re-emerging, their faces grim. Reloading, they swept on into the fight.

Hans turned away from the fight and walked back down the blood-soaked corridor and out into the night. Thousands of troops were pouring across the square, spreading out in every direction. Going over to the edge of the steps, he leaned against a pillar and looked over at Webster, who had followed him. Reaching into his tunic pocket, he pulled out the stub of the cigar O'Donald had given him that morning, bit it in half, and offered the rest to Webster, who took it.

"I should have killed that bastard years ago," Hans said, his voice distant. "Maybe, just maybe, all of this would never have happened."

A flash of light lit the sky to the south, and he turned to look out toward the river. Long seconds later a distant boom echoed up the river.

"If they still have the *Ogunquit*, we'll be back where we started," he whispered, as if to himself.

"We need more speed!"

One of the enemy ironclads swept directly in front of him, its gun exploding. A storm of shot boiled the water to one side, whipping it into a milky foam.

To his left the *President Kalencka* continued on. Its carronade fired, and the gunboat before him seemed to explode in a shower of debris. The galley beneath his feet swung over, avoiding the fight, and Andrew cursed wildly.

Every yard was precious in this mad race between the limits of human strength and the unrelenting power of the *Ogunquit*'s engines.

The other two galleys were ahead, one of them racing straight in toward the *Ogunquit*'s bow. The pole forward dropped, the barrel disappearing into the water. An instant later the forward gun fired.

It seemed as if the galley simply disappeared, in a swirling torrent of iron hail, shattered wood, and broken bodies.

The other galley, running up parallel to the *Ogunquit*, suddenly turned in, spar dropping. Andrew held his breath. The galley raced in, slamming into the side of the ship. The moment seemed to stretch into an eternity. The galley spun away, and the *Ogunquit* continued its retreat.

"Goddammit!" Andrew screamed. "More speed! We've got to catch him!"

He knew he was drawing the last strength out of the fifty rowers behind him. He could hear their fevered groans with each stroke, the men cursing, the boat leaping ahead.

The other galley drifted past.

"The trigger rope broke!" the captain screamed, and then they were behind him.

A geyser of water shot up beside him, and looking back, he saw that one of the enemy ironclads, passed several minutes ago, had come around and was already racing up past the *President* and closing in from astern.

The Roum captain shouted, the men looking up at the death trying to close down upon them from astern, and it seemed as if the sight of the ship wrung the last ounce of strength from the rowers.

The bow of the *Ogunquit* was off their side, not twenty yards away.

"A couple of seconds more!" Andrew shouted. "Just a bit more!"

They drew abreast the first gun port.

"Lower the spar! Take us in!"

The two men standing beside him released the ropes, letting them play out, and the barrel splashed into the water. The galley started to swerve over and he picked up the lanyard, and then he felt as if his heart would freeze. He was looking straight into the barrel of an enemy cannon.

Tobias looked down the length of the heavy gun. Shouldering the gunner aside, he took hold of the lanyard to the flintlock trigger. The galley started to swing straight in, and he saw Keane looking up.

Keane seemed to be staring straight at him. All of it was coming together at last, the dream of all the years, the final vindication. He stepped back from the gun, holding the trigger line taut. From the corner of his eye he saw Tamuka, his mouth open, screaming at him to fire, staring at him as Keane was.

Tobias turned his head and looked straight at the Merki who had betrayed him, as everyone had betrayed him. A tragic smile lit his exhausted features, and he let the lanyard slip out of his hand and drop to the deck.

"Back oars!" Andrew screamed. He felt the boat surge beneath his feet and waited one last second.

"Jump, all of you, jump!"

There was a jarring bump.

Even as he heaved on the trigger line he threw himself backward.

For a split second he felt a heartbreaking sickness. It was not working. In the next instant he felt himself tumbling backward through the air. The world seemed to be nothing but water, all the universe, sky and river, jumbled into one.

Strangely there seemed to be no sound, only a drumming pressure that made his senses reel.

He tried to breathe, but some instinct prevented him. Something slammed into his head, and he was floundering on the surface of the river, a column of fire and water seemingly suspended above him.

Debris was raining down. It was hard to see, and he realized that this time he had lost his glasses. The shadow of the *Ogunquit* was still sliding away, and for an instant he thought that somehow they had not hurt her. But around him a ragged cheer was going up. There was another thunderclap, a shot of flame burst out of one of the gun ports, and the giant ship started to turn, heeling over, its bulk seeming to block out the sky.

"She's going down!" someone screamed excitedly.

Andrew felt himself going down as well. Floundering in the water, he felt someone grab his side.

"I've got you, sir."

To his amazement it was the Roum captain.

"We got her, we got her!" the captain kept chanting.

In the wavering light, Andrew saw the bow of the ship already slipping beneath the water. He could hear the cries of the Carthas, and see dim forms pouring out of the hatches.

An ironclad shot past him to his right. He felt a moment of terror, but the ship didn't slow. Swinging wide around the *Ogunquit*, it kept on up the river, the *President* following in pursuit.

"We'd better get away from here!" the captain shouted, and pointed out into the water.

"I can't see too well."

"Looks like a Cartha galley. Hang on to me," and the captain started to swim straight back down the channel.

Cresting up over a wave, Vuka hung on as the galley slapped back down.

All around him the water was aswarm with cattle.

"Bring us around to the ship!" Vuka cried.

He knew that he should feel rage at this moment, but there was a cold inner triumph. So they had sent him out to die, and now the tables had been turned at last. The great ship was settling quickly, lying nearly on its side, water pouring into the gun ports. There was another flash from within, and a tongue of fire burst out. Horrified shrieks echoed across the water as from within came the crashing of guns, snapping free from their moorings and sweeping across the deck, crushing their crews, smashing into the opposite bulkhead and adding their weight to the death roll.

A rumbling blast of steam shot up through the collapsing stack, scalding cattle who were already in the water, and Vuka listened to their cries without concern. Carefully he scanned the water, looking, peering into the darkness.

And then he saw him.

He leaped into the water, and coming to the surface he grabbed hold of a plank, gasping and coughing. Kicking his legs, he pushed through the current and saw him, bobbing up and down, feebly hanging on to a piece of wood.

He came up alongside him.

"My brother, I'm hurt," Mantu groaned. "I'm burned."

"Let me help you," Vuka said, and he grabbed hold of him, pulling him away from the board. Mantu looked into his eyes and he understood, even as the blade cut into his throat.

"My brother," Mantu gasped as the water around him turned scarlet.

Vuka pushed him away, yet he continued to struggle feebly, hands grasping the air, and then he disappeared at last beneath the water.

Vuka struggled through the wreckage, grabbing hold of another board, and he started to kick toward shore.

He paused for a second, bringing a hand up. The dagger —he still held the dagger. He let it drop. There was a brief flash of silver and then it fluttered down into the darkness below.

The water felt cold, terribly cold. He crawled up higher on the board and then looked up.

A snap of light crossed the midnight sky, the arrow of an ancestor coming down from the heavens, and he started to shiver.

"Over here!"

There was a splashing of oars, and Andrew looked up to see a boat bearing down toward them.

"A Cartha ship," the Roum captain whispered.

The boat drew closer.

"Over here!"

"Damn me, it's Marcus," Andrew gasped.

Oars were raised and eager hands reached out, pulling him up out of the water.

Crawling up on the deck, Andrew squinted as Marcus came up and clapped him on the shoulder.

"I thought I told you to get the hell out of here," Andrew sighed.

"And leave my men to drown up here? Not likely."

Andrew shook his head wearily and leaned back against the ship's railing.

"I'm damn glad to see you," Marcus said softly. A sailor came forward and threw a blanket over Andrew's shoulders while another man passed over a sack of wine, which he eagerly took.

The river was dark, and for the first time he realized just how quiet it was.

"Have you found any?" he asked sadly.

"You'd be surprised. I've got a dozen boats up here, and we're pulling them out by the hundred."

"Thank God," Andrew whispered.

"That was one of the dumbest things I've ever seen," Marcus said gruffly, and Andrew looked up.

"Your going in like that."

"I had to," Andrew replied. "I felt as if I had failed in everything. I couldn't ask your people to make a sacrifice like that unless I went with them."

"It won't be forgotten by me," Marcus said. "But you've given me a hell of a problem."

"What's that?"

"When these men get back home, they'll be insufferable with arrogance. They'll be almost as bad as you Yankees."

For the first time since it had all started, Andrew found that he was laughing.

"Why, my dear Marcus, we'll make good republicans out of all of them by the time we're finished."

Cold with rage, Jubadi stalked along the bank of the river. In front of him the city which he had so confidently believed was in his grasp looked as it did before, except for one detail—the walls were now lined with white-clad soldiers. From down the road, he saw the blue column moving quickly, approaching the south gate of the city, the cheers of the cattle echoing across the waters.

In the middle of the river a single ironclad was afloat, a

ship of the enemy blocking any hope of attacking even if he had wanted to.

"We go back," Jubadi snarled, looking over at Hulagar.

"We lost but five hundred of the Vushka," Hulagar replied softly. "Our strength here is intact."

"If I had ten times their number, perhaps. But I will not waste my elite in an uneven battle in which they hold the strength. They have beaten us for now."

"If we do not destroy them here, every day they will grow stronger."

"I have the Bantag on my other flank!" Jubadi roared. "If I sweep north, they will follow. They smell our blood. I am still caught between two fires, and I will not be backed into this one with the Bantag behind me."

"My Qar Qarth," Hulagar said quietly, "I have fought these cattle now, I have seen their weapons, I have seen the terrible power of the ones we had and lost. If you should delay, I fear what they could create by the time we settle accounts to the south."

"Then I will make new weapons as well," Jubadi growled. "We will keep the Carthas who can make weapons, and grant them exemptions. The rest we will feed upon this winter, since the Rus will not serve our needs. I will keep the pressure on the Rus, and when the time is right I will finish them."

Jubadi turned away from the river and started back up the bank. Then he saw the other shield-bearer.

"You are hurt, Tamuka," Jubadi said, his voice showing concern.

"Only some burns, my Qar Qarth."

"And you have news."

Tamuka nodded.

"Then out with it," Jubadi whispered, his voice suddenly nervous.

"We have not found Mantu. I know he was injured. I pushed him through the hatchway and then lost him."

"Then he is dead."

"He is not on our side of the river, my Qar Qarth. Either he is a prisoner or he is dead."

"He is dead," Jubadi sighed. "For his ka would not allow him to live the ignominy of capture at the hands of cattle."

Jubadi turned and looked at Vuka and nodded slowly.

"Come, my son," he said quietly. "We must plan what to do next."

He looked back at Tamuka.

"As the Qar Qarth, I ask that you again be shield-bearer to the Zan Qarth."

"Which I desire as well," Vuka said softly.

Stunned, Tamuka nodded his head in reply.

Jubadi paused and looked back at the city. Unsheathing his sword, he held it up and brought it along his forearm. There was a splattering of scarlet. Holding the blade on high, he looked to the heavens and let out a long cry of pain and rage, and then drew back and hurled the sword into the river.

"Mark this spot well," Jubadi snarled, "for I will take that blade up yet again." and motioning for Vuka to follow, he leaped up onto his mount and galloped off.

Tamuka looked over at Hulagar.

"He is the only heir now, and cannot be touched," Hulagar whispered.

"Only as long as he is the heir," Tamuka replied. "But when he is Qar Qarth, then I will be shield-bearer."

"Watch your back," Hulagar said softly.

"Perhaps Mantu should have watched his," Tamuka replied.

"Come, let us leave this accursed place," Hulagar said, and he went over to his horse and climbed into the saddle.

Tamuka paused and looked at the naked cattle bound and flanked by two guards.

"Look one last time at what was your home, what still could have been yours, traitor," Tamuka snarled.

Tobias tried to look straight ahead, to ignore the horror of what was gazing at him.

"You are afraid to look in my eyes, aren't you, cattle?" Tamuka roared. "Tonight is the moon feast, cattle. Do you know what that is?"

Tobias was silent, still looking off as if his tormentor were not even there.

"We will strap you to a table. With my own hand I will slice the skull from your head while you are still alive. Traitor, I will gaze into your eyes as I reach into your skull and pull your brains out, and devour them. The last thing you will ever see is my hate-filled eyes, your brains being ground between my teeth."

Tobias felt as if he were floating inside a vast dark tunnel at the end of which all he could see was the taunting gaze, and yet he felt that somehow in the end he had won after all.

He spit in Tamuka's face.

With a scream of rage, Tamuka struck him across the face, shattering his jaw.

Going to the horse, he swung into the saddle and looked over at Hulagar.

Hulagar reached out and touched him on the shoulder.

"After you are done with him, will you join me? There is much to speak of, now that you are shield-bearer to the Zan Qarth again."

Tamuka nodded.

"A position I hope I do not hold for long."

Hulagar looked at him inquiringly.

"Don't worry, my friend," Tamuka sighed. "But if you are to see your prayers fulfilled, if we are to see the Barkth Num ever again, we will have to act more forcefully."

Without a backward glance at the city, the two shield-bearers rode off.

Tobias did not feel the pain of the blow, nor the roughness of the horse's back as they strapped him naked behind the saddle. He raised his head, and all he could see was the city, and the blue column of men marching in to faint distant cheers.

Were they cheering for Keane? Of course they were cheering for Keane, for all the others, all the countless others. And he felt somehow that he wanted to laugh even as his tears dropped away to the ground. In a way, he felt, they were cheering for him as well.

# Chapter Twenty

The room fell to a nervous hush as Emil walked in and sat down.

"How is he?" Andrew asked anxiously.

"That mick's got the constitution of a horse," Emil said. "The fever broke, and he woke up an hour ago and asked for a drink of whiskey."

"Glory hallelujah," Vincent shouted, slapping the table.

Andrew was stunned to see Hans pull out a handkerchief and blow his nose noisily.

"Just a cold," Hans whispered, and Andrew shook his head.

"You're a miracle worker," Andrew said, leaning over to pat Emil on the back.

"Just lucky this time as well," Emil replied. "A lot of things helped. He pulled that shit-covered jacket off before he got hit—I think that would have finished him. He hadn't eaten in nearly a day and had thrown up the rest in the sewer, so the stomach was empty. The bullet was lodged in the stomach and nothing had spilled out, so all I had to do was clean the wound and sew it up."

Emil held his hands up. "I think I'm on to something with that carbolic acid to kill infection, but it's hell on my hands. I should find something to cover them in the future."

"It's the first time I ever heard of a man surviving a gut shot," John said admiringly.

"Same for me," Emil said softly. "We never thought it

was even worth the bother of operating before. But damned if I'd let him die."

"How we doing with the rest of the men?" Andrew asked.

"Bullfinch is going to look like a regular pirate with that patch, and he's going to have a hell of a scarred face to mar those pretty looks, but he'll pull through, and at least we saved one eye. The burns and the scalds are giving me a problem, but for the type of campaign we fought, Andrew, the bill could have been a lot worse."

"Nearly twenty-five hundred dead and three thousand wounded was still too much," Kal replied.

There was a mumbled chorus of agreements.

Kal paused and looked over his shoulder at the dozens of bullet holes that pockmarked the bloodstained wall.

"At least he paid the price,"

"All right, let's wrap this up," Andrew said. "I've barely had time for Kathleen since I got back here. John, what's our status?"

John smiled, looked at his notes, and then pushed them aside.

"We can salvage the *Ogunquit*, and maybe all the boats that went down. If so, that'll give us a fair-sized fleet. We should strip the rails off all our ships, and the engines as well. They're more valuable to us that way. Within a couple of weeks I'll be able to load those supplies up and ship them by sea back to Roum. With Marcus's help we might have the railroad up and running again inside of three months, with a full link between here and Roum. We'll bring back some boxcars and engine chassis by sea, and that way we'll have some service going out of Suzdal inside of twenty days or so.

"The big loss in equipment was over eight thousand rifles and damn near all our powder reserves. The factory's up and running now, turning out half a ton a day."

"When the weapons start coming out," Andrew said, "make good on our losses first, then we split the production between our army and Roum."

Marcus smiled openly in agreement.

"Arm them and you'll have to give them the right to vote," Vincent said quietly, and there was a chorus of chuckles.

"Hans, latest scouting report."

"They tore up some of the blockhouses and pulled back

to the hills a hundred miles south of our defensive line. Beyond that, Andrew, we know nothing. That's the big question now. We know they'll be back, the question is when. If they show up before we've rearmed, it'll be difficult. Getting the *Ogunquit* up will at least give us a barrier, and with the Cartha boats that surrendered or were captured, we can put a solid curtain out on this side of the river."

"The Cartha?" Andrew looked over at Vincent. He had deliberately assigned the task to him. He knew the hatred was still there, and he could only pray that this exposure might somehow soften it.

"We've got nearly fourteen thousand prisoners, sir, including their commander, Hamilcar. I've given them the same offer you made back on the beach, and they're damned surprised, most of them. Hamilcar, however, has asked for some galleys."

"Tell him to go to hell," Marcus snapped.

"Why?" Kal asked softly.

"This Hamilcar says they know they can't go back home, the Merki will kill them. He says some of them want to try to rescue their families."

"Give them the ships," Kal said.

"After what they did?" Marcus snapped.

"We agreed earlier, Marcus, that the captured galleys were yours. I'll buy six of them back—name your price. But by Perm and Kesus I want to give them a chance. We'll let the six go. If they come back as promised, I'll give them more. We can use these people, and even if we couldn't, I'll help anyone trying to fight or escape from the horde."

Andrew looked over at Marcus, who shook his head.

"You're nothing but a lot of damned idealists," Marcus growled, and Vincent laughed softly as he translated.

"All right, then."

"Anything else?" Kal asked.

"Declare tomorrow a day of rest and thanksgiving," Casmar said evenly. "We all deserve it."

"Agreed!" Kal announced. "Now let's end this. I want to get up to the hospital and see that O'Donald."

The group got up and left the room. Kal fell behind, and Andrew paused in the hallway and watched as Kal walked through the doorway into the Senate chamber.

The rest of the men proceeded up the hall, and he motioned them on. Turning, he went in to join his old friend.

Kal stood alone in the middle of the room. As Andrew entered, Kal looked back at him self-consciously.

"For a time there I didn't think we could survive it," Kal whispered. "I thought all you had told us might have been stories after all, that your dream could never survive the harsh realities of a world such as this."

"As long as there are people of strength such as yourself, to stand against men such as Mikhail who would make a mockery of our dream," Andrew said evenly, "it will endure."

Kal nodded absently, and taking up his crumpled stovepipe hat, he put it on and walked out of the room, Andrew by his side.

"Andrew, you'd better get out here!"

Hans was standing in the doorway. There was an urgency to his voice that sent a shock into him. Andrew ran down the corridor and out onto the steps of the capitol.

"Over there!" Hans shouted, pointing off to the south. Andrew looked up and felt his heart tighten with fear.

"What in the name of the devil?"

"It's a balloon," Vincent shouted.

"Hell, it looks like a cigar!" Hans growled.

A faint buzzing filled the air, and Andrew noticed that everyone in the square had fallen silent. The dark ship drew closer, the sound even louder.

"A thousand feet up at least!" Vincent said. "Damn, who owns it?"

"Field glasses, someone get some glasses!"

"In my office," Kal shouted. "Behind the desk."

Andrew walked down the steps of the capitol, still looking up. The sound was getting louder. An orderly came running back out of the capitol and handed the glasses over to Andrew.

"Merki," Andrew whispered in awe. "Two of them sitting in a cage underneath it. There's something blurry behind it. It must be a propeller of some sort. But there's no steam, nothing."

The ship passed directly overhead, its thunder washing over the city, and then turned eastward.

"My God, the factories!"

The ship started to angle downward and then seemed to disappear.

The airship reappeared, climbing rapidly into the sky, and behind it a column of fire and smoke leaped up to the heavens.

"The powder factory's gone."

An explosion washed over the town, the few surviving windowpanes shattering across the square, glass tinkling into the street.

The airship continued eastward and disappeared from view.

In consternation, the men looked at each other.

"The war is still on, gentlemen," Andrew sighed.

He looked at their crestfallen faces.

"And dammit, we will endure, no matter what they send against us."

"Colonel Keane."

Andrew looked away and saw Tanya running across the square, Ludmilla desperately trying to keep up behind her.

"Tanya, what is it?" Kal snapped peevishly.

She stopped before the group and looked over at Andrew with a sly grin.

"It's Kathleen, Andrew."

"What's wrong?"

"On, nothing. It's just that you'd better get on home—you're about to become a father."

Stunned, Andrew looked at her and then forced his gaze away to look back at the still-spreading column of smoke.

"As president of Rus," Kal said quietly, "I'm ordering you to go home. We'll talk about this later. John, Hans, you go down to the factory. Emil, go with them. Vincent, go find that Petracci fellow. He built the last balloon—well, he's back in business."

Kal looked over at Andrew again and forced a smile.

"Just like what you would do," he said quietly.

Andrew still felt torn.

"Andrew, we'll endure, and even as we do, we'll continue to live. Now go home to your family."

Andrew looked at the other men, who gazed at him with open affection.

"Go on, son," Emil snapped. "I'll be up later."

He felt an inner release. At least for one moment he could somehow escape all that had happened to him, that would happen. No matter what they did to him, he would still have his family. Clumsily, Andrew Lawrence Keane saluted his president, and following Tanya, he turned and ran back across the square.

The men looked after him.

"At least let's give him this small moment of peace," Kal sighed. "The rest of us had better get back to work."

The soldiers saluted, and calling for their mounts, they started out across the square.

Kal and Marcus stood alone.

Kal looked over at the consul, and with a smile he put a friendly hand on his shoulder. The two started to walk back up the steps of the capitol.

"So are you going to run for president?" Kal asked.

"President?"

"First off, you've got to get the right uniform, like mine," he said, and together the two walked up the steps and disappeared from view.

## ABOUT THE AUTHOR

**William Forstchen**, born in 1950, was raised in New Jersey but has spent most of his life in Maine. Having worked for more than a decade as a history teacher, an education consultant on creative writing, and a Living History reenactor of the Civil War period, Bill is now a graduate student in military history at Purdue University in Indiana. *Rally Cry*, the first volume in The Lost Regiment series, was published by ROC Books in 1990.

When not writing or studying, Bill devotes his time to the promotion of the peaceful exploration of space or to one of his numerous hobbies, which include iceboating (a challenge in Indiana), scuba diving (an even greater challenge in Indiana), and pinball machines.